ARCHIMIMUS

(Ark-ee-my-mus)

The Life and Times of Lukitt Bachmann

Clio Gray

urbanepublications.com

First published in Great Britain in 2019 by Urbane Publications Ltd
Unit E3 The Premier Centre Abbey Park Romsey SO51 9DG

A CIP catalogue record for this book is available from the British Library.

ISBN 978-1-912666-52-2
MOBI 978-1-912666-53-9

Design and Typeset by Michelle Morgan

Cover by The Design Studio

Printed and bound by 4edge UK

URBANE
urbanepublications.com

PREFACE

I'm sitting atop the Lanterne des Mortes in some Alsatian hole but here, in Sansonnet-St-Genès, lives my only friend. I'm crouched below the casement window, knees to chest, hands beneath armpits; the fire in the old upturned bell is burning, but still there's frost on the walls, breath billowing like early morning mist. It's high up here, thirty feet above the cemetery; the tower cylindrical and hollow, spiral staircase of stones protruding from its inner wall. It's All Souls Eve, hence the bowl-fire, a *Lux Perpetua* leading the villagers from their mean houses as they hum the hymn of the *Dies Irae*, packets of bread clutched beneath their jackets, along with small flasks of oil and wine. They reach the cemetery surrounding the Lanterne des Mortes, begin tidying plots and graves, scrubbing down crosses and angels, pruning corpse-shrubs, straightening portraits hanging from rusting chains, poking mildew and lichen from roughly sculpted names and dates. They leave their gifts of bread, oil and wine; stick candles to the stones with warm-dripped wax: teetering will - o'- wisps in the darkness.

The priest arrives and intones the rite of Mass, everyone kneeling in the frost: old hips creaking, bunions aching, fingers clutched about each other turning white. Mass soon done – two more to perform the following day - everyone back home soon as they can decently go.

Only a few more hours now.

Only a few more hours.

Lukitt Habakkuk Bachmann in his tower, waiting for his friend.

How did you end up here, Lukitt? How did it all lead to this?

1

From Farm to Herrnhuter to Seiden See

Lukitt Habakkuk Bachmann.

A complicated name.

A complicated life.

A complicated beginning.

Father: Nethanel, migrant worker, member of the Herrnhuter Brethren who were a little too protestant for the Protestants, exiled from their origins in Saxony; some migrating as far as Greenland and the West Indies; others, like Nethanel's clan, settling closer to home by the Voralberg Mountains in Austria.

Mother: Trudl, farmer's daughter, same farm on which Nethanel turned up one summer: fruit-picker, weed-hoer, vegetable-cutter, tattie-hoiker, hay-scyther.

Neither noticing each other - unpretty peasants working side by side with Trudl's brothers and Nethanel's Brethren - until Trudl faints in the milling barn from the heat, from the dust that has clogged up nostrils and throat, when Nethanel puts his lips to hers and breathes her back to life.

Stolen moments then, bodies uncomfortably aware of each other, sunny autumn evenings twining themselves together in the laundry pool, on its dappled green banks.

Unforeseen pregnancy, hasty marriage.

Trudl's father throwing them both out on their ears.

Herrnhuter Elders more forgiving, until Trudl's swollen belly could not be hidden and sums were made, behaviours condemned. Elder Zebediah calling Nethanel a fool and his new wife a whore, causing them to leave the Herrnhuter.

Lukitt Bachmann born on a by-road in winter darkness, afterbirth spooling away into a ditch to be eaten by rats; Lukitt lucky not to go the same way. Lukitt taken up by his father, strapped to his chest; Trudl staggering along beside him, bleeding down the inside of her thighs.

The thrown-away family arriving at the only place they know to go: to Trudl's Great Aunt and Uncle's farm below the Voralberg mountains in the valley of Gargellan. Hermistus and Hermione, brother and sister: gaunt and angry people. Folk who'd never married, never managed out of each other's care. Folk who took in Nethanel and Trudl grudgingly, and only because they were old and the farm was falling down decrepit about their ears, needing the help they could not otherwise afford.

Drudgery for the Bachmann family then, for all three – when Lukitt was old enough: put to work in the fields, to look after the sheep, the goats, the cattle, the dairy, the crops, and the bees Hermistus cares for more about than he does them.

Lukitt ten when mother and father engineer his escape, get him down the valley, having previously fixed him employment skivvying for the pastor in the small village surrounding the Seiden See in return for bed and board, a place in the school.

The journey from the farm in Gargellan to Seiden See the beginnings of Lukitt's awakening, for oh, he'd never seen anything more perfect than he was seeing now as mother and father bundled him onto their cart and hied him away down the track at dawn, Lukitt spying the black-blown skins of puffballs, wondering at small pillow-fights of feathers left by swoops of harriers and buzzards, sees countless dew strung spider-webs shivering in the breeze as the cart's wheels roll by. And then the real reveal: turning a corner, seeing blue-green hills rolling down from every side, the lake at their base as round as a coin, still and serene, hand-mirror of the clouds, not a breath nor ripple of wind to disturb its surface. Scatter of houses hemming its western arc, green roofs shimmering in the sun, walls washed blue by the water's reflections, small jetties leading out into the lake. Beyond them the church, on a small mound of green, its manse tacked on like a forgotten pocket.

Père Ulbert waiting for them, expecting them, hand held up against his brow as he saw them come.

No long heart-felt goodbyes, no hearty welcomes.

'Be good,' Trudl whispers, hugging her boy to him, Lukitt squirming for release.

'Try to make something of yourself,' Nethanel begs, 'for us if not yourself. Come back and look after us when we're old.'

Père Ulbert impatient, shifting from foot to foot, grabbing Lukitt's shoulder as soon as he was down from his cart, not a word of thanks to his parents, merely outlining Lukitt's duties as he led him away up the path towards the manse.

'You'll do breakfast and dinner. You'll clean and tidy. You'll make the beds. You'll help me with my sermons. At school you'll work hard. I'll not have you embarrassing me by being a slacker.'

No looking back for Lukitt at Trudl and Nethanel, head pushed forward by Père Ulbert's hefty hand, Lukitt fighting against it, trying to turn but unable. Trudl beginning to cry, and not just for this parting, but for the whole of her life that had gone so wrong. Wishing to God she'd had another child, but that first birth in the mountains had ripped her up inside, and no more had come. Nethanel strong beside her like a bole of oak.

'It's the best thing for him,' Nethanel stated, 'and for us.'

Hoping to God he was right, that he hadn't delivered his son from one slave-driver to another.

2

Manna and Thanking God

Lukitt fearing the same, at first a drudge as before, but Ulbert impressed by the lad's adaptability, his lack of tears after his parents left, his evident focus not on what he'd left but on what he might gain because of it. Hermistus a known curmudgeon and hard task-master, Hermione even worse. Sticks old before their time, sticks that got harder with every year, Ulbert never having much truck with them: old farmers in the wilds who rarely, if ever, bothered to come into town.

He'd assumed Lukitt would be of the same ilk: a bone-headed bigot, illiterate and lazy, an indigent who would probably move on as soon as he could. No idea of the Herrnhuter inheritance, that Nethanel had schooled and taught him well with the one book he had to hand, which was a bible with commentaries attached. Ulbert quietly impressed by Lukitt, by the evident joy on his face every morning to glimpse from the windows the lake as he made their breakfast. Ulbert intrigued to discover him - a few weeks after he'd settled - ferreting stealthily through Ulbert's library by candlelight when he'd assumed Ulbert was asleep; Ulbert watching through a crack in the door as Lukitt fell on those books like he was coming out of a desert and discovering running water for the first time in his life. Ulbert asking slyly, a few mornings later, if Lukitt was sleeping well.

'Oh yes, thank you, father. Don't think I've ever slept so well as here.'

Lukitt not lying; dreams no longer filled with aching fingers clawing at black walls for escape; dreams here rich, woven through with the stories pilfered from the several hours he spent each night in Ulbert's library.

Ulbert hiding a smile as Lukitt hid a yawn, but no complaint from Lukitt. Lukitt going about his duties with the same diligence as before. And a quicker learner Ulbert had never met: Lukitt mastering a few simple meals from the receipt book scratched out by one of Ulbert's previous maids – a girl who'd upped and left with a peddlar passing through and ended Lord knew where. Probably dead in a ditch, the girl never bright and that peddlar about as wrong as any peddlar can be. Lukitt's fish stew better the first time he'd served it up than the girl had managed in three years.

Ulbert coming to the realisation that Lukitt was uncommon, and not so unlike Ulbert himself; Ulbert a man who, in his youth, had taken himself off to Paris, walked there on his own two feet, joined a seminary, become a priest, survived the aftermath of the French Revolution, escaped the guillotine by the skin of his teeth. Had gone from Paris to the Holy Land like a Muslim on Hadj. Had even met with Muslims, talked with them, argued theory and theology, learned from them as he hoped they'd learned from him. And, when he returned, brought back with him several vials of sand gathered from the deserts of Negev and Sinai; soil from the Via Dolorosa, from Bethlehem and Nazareth; pebbles from Golgotha and the Mount of Olives; small replicas of the huge wooden key-and-lock fittings employed in Sidon designed by Solomon himself; dried locusts, frogs, flies, pomegranates and any number of other examples of wildlife from the places where Jesus had lived, worked and preached. All these treasures artfully mounted in glass cases in Ulbert's home and church. A reminder to him of what he'd been, of what he might have become, had not the church seen fit to send to him to this backwater of a shite-hole in Austria, every petition for removal or transfer ignored, every plea for advancement politely declined. Ulbert not applauded – as he'd hoped - for his sojourns to France and then the Holy Land but tainted by them, a man no longer to be trusted; a man who might have soaked up revolutionary ideas in France, and ungodly ones in the Holy Land by associating with members of that other abhorred religion.

Ulbert rejected by his church and embittered because of it.

Ulbert starting to wonder if Lukitt might be able to tread where he could not.

'Time for you to properly see my church,' Ulbert announced, one morning; Lukitt so far never having been invited in, except for the usual services Ulbert insisted he attend. This time different; this time only Ulbert and Lukitt. Lukitt hardly through the door before Ulbert thrust into his hand a ram's horn.

'Blow into it,' Ulbert commanded, and Lukitt complied. Produced an eerie wail as of loons on distant water.

'And look at this,' Ulbert went on, pointing to a tiny casket Lukitt hadn't noticed on his previous visits that had been born of duty, in and out, no tarrying. 'Some actual exemplars of manna,' Ulbert explained, 'that could be either honeydew from an acacia or maybe tree resin, or wafers of lichen, or the dried sap of the ash. All the same to the Israelites in their exile.'

Lukitt heart-struck; Lukitt placing his fingers against the glass, Lukitt wanting to take them out and examine each more closely, decide which of the options Ulbert had presented was reality; Lukitt leaning down to take his look - really looking – for his answer. Ulbert's eyes brightening in the twilight of his church. No one ever appreciating his treasures as Lukitt was doing now. Ulbert fascinated as Lukitt traced his fingers over the glass.

'All those places you've been,' murmured the boy. 'All those footsteps you've trodden in. Maybe one day I'll be able to do the same.'

Ulbert closing his eyes, thanking God this Lukitt had been brought to his door.

First time he'd thanked his God in a long, long while.

3

Poured Out Like Water

Ulbert sits expectantly as he calls Lukitt forward.

All summer, children have been working on their projects.

So far nothing more exciting than one boy bringing in a stinking fish and explaining how to gut it – which everyone knew how to do; another having a piece of hide, and oh yes we do this to it and that, which again everybody was familiar with.

And now Lukitt Bachmann comes forward obediently, placing a covered glass box on Ulbert's desk before turning to his audience to pitch his wares. Everyone sighing, already bored. Lukitt a small child, delicately featured, his face at rest exuding an earnest expression that seemed to belong to someone far older. Lukitt a lecturer, for which he was despised and disliked. Unlike him, they'd grown up together, knew their limitations and expectations; school merely filling the gap until they could take an apprenticeship, help their fathers' businesses, get married, have children, carry on as everyone here had always done. Lukitt a boy apart, brought into their midst with no frame of reference, no set function, outstripping them in every aspect of education, and would probably move on soon enough to places they hadn't the imagination to conjure up.

'My project has been on something rather obscure,' Lukitt stated. 'I've several objects here I'd like you to come and see.'

His classmates suppressed their sighs but stood up dutifully.

'Take a look,' Lukitt said, whipping off the cloth from his exhibit, revealing a pair of gloves, a fine stocking, an ornately carved box, a stick covered with some kind of goo, a piece of indigo cloth, a lump of red sealing wax. Fellow inmates filing by, some vaguely interested, leaning their heads in for a quick gawp, most walking on without a glance.

'Take a guess at what made them?' Lukitt challenged, once the children had returned to their desks.

'Your aunt up at Gallapfel?' one responded, to a few sniggers, Hermione to them – and indeed to Lukitt – a crone with a heart of stone who might even be a witch.

'All to… do with… insects?' asked another boy, another relative newcomer, hesitation in every syllable, not having the faintest idea what any of Lukitt's exhibits were, but knowing of Lukitt's keen interest in bugs and beasties.

'You're almost right, Pregel,' Lukitt quick to reply, to encourage. 'They're all products of insects and arachnids. The gloves and stockings were made from spider silk by a French scientist on the express orders of Napoleon, wanting to revive the silk industry there so as not to be dependent on imports from China.'

'So they're made out of spiders?' one girl asked, bemused, not quite getting the gist.

'Not out of spiders,' Lukitt explained, 'but from their silk, which is what they make their webs of. There's seven different kinds people know of so far. Some spiders use it as a line to fish for prey, some sail for miles in the wind like a kite; others spin silk balloons around a bubble of air and live in it underwater, and in the great forests of Asia there's spiders make webs so strong people use them to net fish and birds.'

This statement met with laughter and incredulity until Lukitt brought out a book – gleaned from Ulbert's library – and held it up, its illustrations clear for all to see, though he still had his doubters. Ulbert smiling from his perch, Ulbert having given Lukitt the freedom of his library and his collection over the summer months. Ulbert aware that what Lukitt had brought to the class was so above their usual calibre it had sailed high above their heads. Had made Ulbert proud of his library, his collection and Lukitt too.

'That was really brilliant!' Pregel said, coming up to Lukitt after the rest of the class had been dismissed. 'How'd'you know all that stuff?'

'I read it,' Lukitt said, carefully covering his box, pleased for the compliment.

'It's just amazing!' Pregel went on. 'Who knew spiders could do all that?'

'Who knows what anyone can do?' Lukitt replied easily, something Pregel thought on for a long time, coming back to Lukitt several days later with his answer.

'You think anyone can do anything?' he asked, approaching Lukitt just before lessons started.

'No harm trying,' Lukitt said, a little surprised, for no one in class had really talked to him before, not that he'd minded. He'd recognised they were already established in their circles, had clumped together in groups and friendships that would probably survive their whole life through. He'd seen Pregel at their periphery, jumping from one set to another, only attendant here two years and having dropped down a year because of it, and yet obviously – now that Lukitt thought about it - an outsider like himself.

'Even me?' Pregel asked.

Lukitt's serious face broke into a smile.

'Especially you,' he agreed. 'There's a lot more to life than just sticking around here. All of us can go anywhere we please and find anything we want, if only we bother looking.'

'That's what I want to do!' Pregel said, delighted. 'I like this place, but I feel all sort of wrong here. My folks have slotted in fine, but not me, and maybe not you. So maybe we can be friends? Would you mind?'

Lukitt didn't mind in the slightest, and it didn't take long before Pregel adopted the desk next to Lukitt's, the two of them going on through the rest of their school years together, their own little knot of friendship, everyone else in the class glad for it, no longer having to pretend a care for either, abandoning the oddballs to their own company and hoorah for that.

Ulbert too approved the match. He'd worried about Pregel, who had never found his place. An odd combination: Lukitt so intelligent, Pregel hardly having the wit of a hay bale, but it worked out better than all right, and it was Lukitt who discovered Pregel's real talent a few years down the line. By then Ulbert was comfortable with Lukitt; Lukitt cooking their evening meal, the two then setting down about the fire to discuss one book or another Ulbert pulled randomly from his shelves. Lukitt a revelation, bringing back to Ulbert what learning was all about: discussion, explication, logic. Like he was back in Paris, or Jerusalem. Snatches of the past, intellectual stimulation, revelled in then as now.

'He can really sing, Ulbert,' Lukitt confided, Lukitt learning of it by accident, over-hearing Pregel warbling in a field where they were picking wild strawberries. 'Learned it at his last school he said, and honestly you have to hear him. He's really good.'

Ulbert having Lukitt bring the boy to church one evening after vespers, Pregel nervous and hesitant, unwilling to push himself forward until Lukitt did the pushing for him.

'Go on, Pregel,' Lukitt prompted. 'Do that psalm you did for me.'

Pregel shifting from one foot to the next, looking at Lukitt, seeing the encouragement on his friend's face, the belief. And so he opened his mouth and sang, and my God, what a pure voice. Ulbert had rarely heard the like.

I am poured out like water...

Pregel started, getting stronger and clearer with every word – not that he understood them - until he was going with the certainty of a robin at the top of a tree of an autumn evening.

I am poured out like water,

My bones are out of kilter,

My heart like wax that has melted within my breast,

My strength dry as a potsherd,

My tongue cleaved and joined to my palate because you haven't heard me,

Because you have laid me unto dust.

'From Psalm 22,' Lukitt supplied when Pregel came to a stop, Ulbert rapturous, patting Pregel on the back.

'But that was wonderful, Pregel!' Ulbert said, and meant it. 'I don't understand why your parents have never mentioned this to me before.'

Pregel looked down at his clogs, embarrassed.

'They're not really in favour of singing,' he explained, Ulbert nodding, understanding. Like the Herrnhuter he'd since learned Lukitt had sprung from, Pregel's family were strict; Moravians, for whom such frivolities as singing not top of their list. That didn't stop Ulbert, who went the very next day to Pregel's home to ask that Pregel be allowed to join Ulbert's choir.

'He's not much for schooling,' he told the parents, which was an understatement as they well knew, 'but we'll count this as a music scholarship, meaning he'll matriculate with the best of his class.'

Enough for Pregel's parents who jumped at the chance to have their boy top of something for a change; Pregel happier still, dancing with joy at being good at something instead of middling to downright bad.

More surprises to come when Ulbert drew both Pregel and Lukitt aside after class a few months later.

'I didn't want to say anything earlier, boys,' he began, 'not until I'd cleared it with your families, but come Advent we're going on a little trip. Just the three of us. I'm going to take you to the monastery up the valley, assuming the snow is not too bad, give you a chance to show what you're made of.'

Lukitt and Pregel exchanging glances, uncertain what this meant but knowing it had to be good, a start on the road the two of them had already made a pact to travel together: off to find new places, discover the wonders of the world far away from the perfect blue bounds of the Seiden See.

4

Fairs and Wonders

Lukitt and Pregel were fizzing with anticipation as the day of their departure to the monastery drew near. A hellish cold winter was yet to come but, early December, it was mild yet, leaves still clinging to the birch-scrub - glorious golden scrunched-up things - snow having fallen sporadically since the end of October but not enough to impede their going, the track still passable.

The morning they're due to leave, a travelling carnival arrives completely unexpectedly into town, setting up their signs announcing jugglers, acrobats and theatre. The *Kunterbunt Trudelndschau* - the Higgledy-Piggledy Travelling Show – consisting of a single family who immediately began drumming up trade, a crowd gathering the moment they'd been sighted on their way into town. Herr Pfiffmakler, the patriarch of the Kunterbunt, bowing deeply and announcing that the show was about to begin.

Herr Pfiffmakler holding up a finger, whipping the tar-cloth off a box he'd beforetimes been sitting on, deftly releasing hidden hinges and clasps as he flicked it up into a puppet booth. Already enthralled, the small crowd clapped their hands as old Mother Pfiffmakler appeared, liver-spotted hands banging on a drum, bracelets of bells jingling on her prune-skin wrists, and in came her daughter-in-laws from stage left, whirling in the meagre snow, pluffing out their skirts, clashing cymbals with great streams of ribbons writhing off around them and old Mother ululating so loudly everyone grimaced in astonishment, open-mouthed children standing in awe. Another family member began handing out sugared crab-apples and twirling sweetmeats into pieces of brightly coloured tissue paper - conjured from thin air - slipping them into a pocket here, a small hand there.

Hardly had this largesse been appreciated by more clapping than in came two young boys tumbling into the arena, flipping themselves hands over heels, their sequinned suits creating sparkling wheels that rolled at random across the thin layer of snow. They stopped abruptly by Herr Pfiffmakler's booth and ornately bowed, arms spread wide, indicating that the real show was about to begin. With a great bang and a flash of purple smoke the curtain was drawn back from the stage, accompanied by the sound of a single lute-string being continuously plucked, filling the air with an eerie lament, before the lutist cracked the spell and went into a merry jig as two bulbous heads burst into sight, their garish paintwork ferocious in the late morning light, motley rags spinning around them as they chased each other up and down the length of the small stage, vying over possession of a large sausage, each cackling loudly:

'Kaspar, Kaspar! You must give me the liverwurst! You know I'm cooking for the mayor tonight!'

'Devil hang the mayor for the pig that he is, Marika, you know we owe him two months' rent.'

'All the more reason to be polite to him…ouch! Ouch!'

Poor Marika yells as Kaspar beats his wife over the head with the sausage.

'Ach, Kaspar! Kaspar!' Marika gasps as she is beaten below the level of the stage. 'How … else …. should …. we … pay … the … mayor?'

Marika bouncing back up again.

'If it's liverwurst he wants, it's liverwurst he'll get!' shouts Kaspar, thwacking his puppet wife off the stage completely, turning to his audience, shrieking with laughter, his audience returning the compliment, beginning to shout:

'Behind you! Behind you!'

Kaspar feigns ignorance and flaps his arms up and down.

'What's it all about then?' says he, unaware of a figure recognisably the mayor, weighed down as he is by the enormous gold chain about his neck, approaching Kaspar with raised sword. By now the younger children, along with Pregel, are jumping up and down, pointing and worrying.

'Look out! He's behind you!'

Kaspar's in the middle of repeating 'What's it all about?' when the sword whooshes down and slices off the end of Kaspar's sausage,

Kaspar letting out a ferocious skirl as he turns, lowers his head and butts the mayor in the stomach, the mayor flying to the side of the stage before rebounding back, almost skewering Kaspar against the other side; Kaspar groaning dramatically, thinking he's done for, before realising the sword has missed and he goes straight back at the mayor with his sausage truncheon.

'Take *that* for your fat belly! Take *that* for your stinking taxes! Take *that* for your taxing stink!'

The mayor responds with swipes of his sword, diminishing Kaspar's sausage truncheon slash by slash, pieces flying off in every direction, until Kaspar takes a large needle from his pocket and jams it into the mayor's fat belly when there's the sound of a punctured balloon and, with a great green puff of smoke, the mayor's fat belly is gone, Kaspar shoving the last of his truncheon down upon the mayor's head and pushing him below the stage.

Everyone claps, the allegory of peasant versus greedy officialdom not lost on them, and there's a general gasp as a crowd of thin policemen (one per finger) suddenly appear and grapple Kaspar to the ground, tying a rope about his neck as they drag him to the suddenly appeared gallows. Kaspar swazzles a tuneless lament of good bye to friends and family before giving an almighty flick of his body that scatters the policemen far and wide, freeing himself from the noose, and is left alone upon the stage.

'Devil take you all!' he shouts in triumph, and the audience clap and hoot and then, and then, a ghastly silence falls as green smoke billows from behind Kaspar and the awful apparition of the mayor arises slowly into the air, somersaults and turns into the devil himself: great horns curling from his head, nasty snarl on painted lips, dragging the limp figure of Marika by the hair, accompanied by the sound of crackling flames and a welling up of smoke.

'Kaspar Larriscarri,' the devil booms, 'you have called me out once too often and defied my friend the mayor and have not paid him his dues, and for that you will lose everything you hold dear.'

Mercilessly he shakes Marika's sagging body, her red boots swinging from side to side.

'I have set your pathetic hovel to the flame, and all your children in it.'

Behind him a horrid scene appears from the clearing smoke: a house engulfed in the lurid lick of flames, small blackened figures tumbling from its windows, Kaspar's youngest roasted in their cribs.

Kaspar and the audience stand aghast until, with a horrifying screech, Kaspar lunges for the puppet devil and hooks the noose about his neck, hauls him high from the gallows, Marika sinking below the stage only to reappear a second later joining in a dance with Kaspar as the music fires up to full pitch and the audience, breathless with relief, start clapping and shouting, only Pregel crying freely for the little burned babies disappearing into darkness; Kaspar and Marika caring not a whit and leaping like lunatics from one side of the stage to the other, their legs going everywhere, their voices as one:

Ha, ha for the stupid mayor and his stupid devil,
Time now for song and revel,
For it's his own pretty mansion his men have set alight,
His own wife and children he's put to plight.
We switched the names on our houses
And there's nothing to douse it.
His children are many and fat
So the fire will go on all night!
Hurrah! Hurrah! Kaspar and his own are all right!

Marika's arms suddenly filled with white-swaddled babies as the lute fires up and the two boys start tumbling, and out dance their cousins - bottle girls par excellence - whirling and twirling through the audience, holding out small tubs, winding in and out of one another so it's impossible to tell which is which, their orange skirts aglow against the snow, making it pink with their shadows, making everyone smile and laugh as they sing for their supper.

A penny for Kaspar, to help pay his debts,
A penny for the punch-man, and all his pretty pets!

The folk of Seiden See entertained, enchanted, pennies coming out aplenty.

Most astonishing for Lukitt and Pregel was Père Ulbert telling them the show was not here by chance, that the Pfiffmaklers were to put on a few edifying theatre shows at the monastery to celebrate the start of Advent.

'And we're to be their guides there,' Ulbert announced breezily, Pregel leaping into the air as if an apprentice Pfiffmakler himself.

5

The Triungulin Mosaic

They set off up the valley the moment the Pfiffmaklers were all packed up and on their several carts, Ulbert striding into the lead, Lukitt and Pregel taking the rear, both entranced by the two young daughters of the troupe, Ludmilla and Longhella, who bounced along on their trap, turning every now and then to look at their followers, dark eyes glinting in the boys' direction. They weren't twins, but near enough alike to seem identical at a casual glance, an image cultivated by them wearing the same red aprons over orange petticoats, weaving their long chestnut hair into identical loops and plaits that bobbed and swung in unison down their slender backs.

It took the rest of the day to reach their goal, the carts being heavy and unwieldy on the narrow track, most of the Pfiffmakler family disembarking to make the going easier, Ludmilla and Longhella falling into step with Lukitt and Pregel who were dumbstruck as the girls chattered easily in their mixed languages that seemed designed to obfuscate and intrigue. Lukitt, though, soon picking from the threads of their conversation words he recognised, filling in the gaps, giving meaning to their sentences, gathering this was their first time in the Voralberg, that they usually spent their time in lowland Austria, Germany and Hungary, going from one Fair to the next to make their living. He was impressed by how far and wide had been their wanderings and all they'd seen, something in this landscape reminding them of when they'd watched the salt miners of Salzburg perform their ancient sword-dances; jumping immediately onto another topic, giggling about the strange salt-licking oath they'd witnessed the peasants of Pongau perform.

Lukitt didn't know what these odd rituals of sword-dancing and salt-licking signified or entailed, but one thing was certain: he meant to travel to those places and find out for himself.

Sundown was almost upon them when they came in view of the monastery, the retinue met by a muddle of monks eager to get them on, excitement hanging in the air like baubles from a tree, fragile, contained, but unmistakably there. The monks moving quickly, with controlled but definite haste, eyes hurriedly averted from the womenfolk - Ludmilla and Longhella in particular, young though they were, for not the sort to hide themselves away, faces and dresses shining over the snow, casting orange reflections as they caught the dying light of the sun.

The Abbot himself came out to greet them, effusive and a little breathless.

'Oh, it's such a pleasure to have you here with us,' Abbot Ettershank began, 'and on such an auspicious occasion. Come in, come in! You must all be hungry and tired after your journey.'

He wasn't wrong there, everyone eager to settle themselves in the refectory and get at the meal the monks had waiting; everyone except Lukitt, who had more important things on his mind. He tugged at Ulbert's sleeve repeatedly until Ulbert had to stop, irritated, but understanding.

'Excuse me, Abbot,' Ulbert said. 'But I fear I must leave you briefly, having made the rather rash promise to Lukitt that I take him first to see your famous stained glass window. I rather talked it up, I'm afraid, but I did promise it would be the first thing he saw once here, and sunset will be a grand time to witness it at its best.'

The Abbot paused, bid his monks lead the rest away and turned back to Ulbert.

'But of course,' he acquiesced, proud of his window, prouder still that someone – even a lad as evidently young as the boy with Ulbert – would prefer to take his look before partaking of food after a long day's travelling. 'We'll need to make it quick. There's a storm coming in,' he looked over to the mountains, at the heavy clouds gathered above them yellow and grey, swollen with unspilled snow. 'Indeed, I wasn't sure it would hold off long enough for you to get here,' the Abbot went on, 'so you can understand how happy I am that you've made it at all. But…Lukitt, is it?'

Lukitt nodded.

'Well, Lukitt,' said the Abbot, impressed by the eagerness on the lad's face, 'then of course you must see it. It's a wondrous thing, and in a light such as this. You head along, Ulbert. I'll take the boy myself. It's the pride of our monastery, famous throughout the whole of Austria...'

Ulbert watched them go, smiling briefly, the boy so dogged and serious, the Abbot so eager to impress as they stepped toward the chapel that loomed against the white-topped hills, its high-up steeple-bell, glinting in the bronze rays of the sun, beginning to sway with the wind that swept with sudden ferocity down the valley. Ulbert shivered and turned towards the refectory, stepping into the warmth, glad they'd got here before the storm that was undoubtedly on its way.

They reached the chapel, a strong gust of wind grabbing the door from the Abbot's hand as he pushed it open, slamming it several times against the wall behind before he got it fixed.

'On you go,' he said, pushing Lukitt before him.

Lukitt doing as bid, Lukitt holding aside the heavy curtain that shielded the chapel's interior from outside drafts. He took a step inside then stopped abruptly, lifting his head, looking through the dark shadows of the chapel, transfixed by the vast expanse of the mosaic window filling the wall beyond the altar edge to edge, huge and circular, like a harvest moon hanging above the hills and so much more. The air a-glimmer with the colours streaming from it onto floor, walls, onto Lukitt. He could feel their warmth on his face as he dropped the curtain and came in a few more yards, held out his arms, saw the colours shifting slowly over them as the sun began to drop; heard the sighing of the wind moving about the exterior of the chapel, like a lime tree in early summer when its canopy is a-buzz with bees and flies suckling at the pollen, everything alive and promising more to come. The window more marvellous than he'd imagined possible: at its centre the cross of Christ, the Saviour pale and wan, skin tinged blue with shadows, brow a sickly green where the thorny crown had slipped and bruised him; his pallor extreme, feet struck through with a wooden stake, shards of bone splintering from the wound, blood spurting in a torrential river below him that carried away the souls of the damned to hell.

The details of these last were many, the divisions of lead-work enhancing their suffering, rending them away from their lost Saviour up above, their wretched souls bumping and twisting in the red flood: torn, broken, or impaled on the needle-sharp rocks of their own sinfulness, splashing their faces with Christ's blood from which grew a vine that soared into a magnificent tree blossoming with the snow-white souls of the saved being born upward to heaven.

The symbolism extreme and unsubtle, but Lukitt looked beyond, saw colour and light and the perfect mingling of both as the sun began to pass its final degrees down into darkness and, just before it did, Lukitt saw the second crucifixion scene set into a small tableau behind the main item, showing the two robbers crucified with Christ, hauled over their own patibulum with ropes, shoulders coming out of their sockets, grimaces terrible to behold. On one side the penitent thief Dysmas, casting his eyes up to the Gates of Paradise, remorse and pity his salvation; next to him his companion Gestas, unrepentant, unbelieving, and only one way he was going and that was down.

Lukitt frowning, the flaw in the fable only just occurring to him: Jesus specifically telling the Good Thief Dysmas: *This day will you be with me in Paradise,* directly contradictory to the scriptures that had Jesus spending the following three days after his death – before his resurrection - harrowing Hell, and the next few after that wandering about his old stomping grounds, showing himself off to his disciples. There was a lot Lukitt didn't get about religion of either Ulbert's or his father's kind, finding the first too Catholic and cluttered, the other too sparse and uncompromising, both lacking the logic he desired - and here was a prime example: a lying Jesus at the centre of both.

Stopped in his thinking by the sun descending below its hill, setting the colours of the window racing up the walls and into the ceiling space as if they feared their own extinction; a single shaft of orange shimmering in the air for a few seconds before being snuffed out, leaving Lukitt staring into darkness, the solemnity broken by the Abbot laying a gentle hand upon his shoulder.

'Time to go, young Lukitt. There's food for the soul and food due the belly. You've had one. Let's go get the other.'

They'd not been gone long, but already the refectory was humming like a hive, newcomers mixing with monks, each swapping names and stories, trading tales of places they had in common, discussing the politics of the day: how Metternich was upholding the liberal principles of governance, espoused by the contradictory uses of a regimented police force and a strict code of censorship. It was all news to Lukitt, the folk of Seiden See not really going in for this kind of talk, too wrapped up in their own lives, preferring to concentrate on trade and survival, paying as few taxes as they could get away with. He listened as he ate, gathering from his chatty neighbours the intricacies of the Pfiffmakler clan, and how Grandmother Pfiffmakler had enough religion for the lot of them put together.

'Do you remember when I met you back in Prague?' one of the monks was saying loudly. 'I was at the seminary, called in to help with a crib show, the jestle, as we called it there.'

'But of course!' Matthys Pfiffmakler replied, slapping the brother on the back, their talk aided by the alcohol the Abbot had approved, given the season. 'We were at that grand house…I can't remember its name…'

'Just outside Terezin,' the monk supplied helpfully. 'You had me rigging up your tableau between two chairs and us hiding ourselves beneath blankets…'

'So we could move our little figures through the slots in the table,' Matthys went on, laughing, 'You were absolutely hopeless!'

The monk held up his hands.

'I was training to be a priest, not a puppeteer,' he said in his defence.

'Point taken,' Matthys admitted. 'And it was certainly memorable. I laughed about it for days when you sent the whole thing crashing to the ground, it being the Tower of Babel, so quite apt.'

'The children enjoyed it,' said his partner in crime.

'So they did, so they did! No sermonising for them that night,' Matthys finished, wiping his eyes with his napkin.

'You should be ashamed of yourselves,' croaked old Frau Pfiffmakler, who took her profession seriously, her family in earshot rolling their eyes, knowing what would come. 'It's a sacred task, showing these cribs at Christmas,' she creaked on, 'telling the story of the birth of our Lord.'

Lukitt stopped eating and looked at the old woman a couple of tables over, wondering if this might be a good time to mention his revelation in the chapel about the Lying Christ.

'*Mütterchen*, don't distress…' someone began, but the old woman was having none of it.

'Think on where we are and why,' she said, nailing the Abbot with a steely eye he wasn't that keen on, him enjoying the evening so far and not wanting to get bogged down in ecclesiastical essentials. 'We show the truths the mortal eye cannot normally see,' she was remorseless, 'recreating the stories and parables of the Good Book for those who can't read it for themselves…'

She tailed off, breathless with her outburst, began a cackling cough that had the entire room silenced, everyone hoping she wasn't about to croak on the spot; revived by a glass of water she spluttered down, after which she was silent, to general relief.

'To Christmas!' shouted Matthys loudly, standing up, apparently not sharing his mother's religious sentiments, bidding everyone top up their glasses for the toast, which they eagerly did.

'To Christmas!' everyone shouted back, the Abbot included, enjoying the wine, for his Lord and Saviour had never denied them that. Lukitt shouting too, taking Pregel's hand, though Pregel didn't respond, his eyes having taken on a luminosity Lukitt hadn't seen before, like pebbles washed over with water: suddenly become brighter, more defined. Lukitt watching his friend closely, seeing a stillness to him that was unusual and unsettling.

'I want to stay here forever,' Pregel whispered, a sentiment so unexpected Lukitt dropped his hand.

'Can't you feel it?' Pregel asked urgently. 'It's like we've stepped into a whole new world.'

'Well of course it's a bit different,' Lukitt countered. 'We're in a monastery, for heaven's sake. But what do you mean? Feel what exactly?'

Pregel shook his head, astonished that Lukitt – always the quickest of their crew of two – could be so slow.

'It's like I talked over with Père Ulbert,' Pregel explained, 'to become an… oblate…'

Stumbling over the unfamiliar word, the back of Lukitt's neck prickling as he understood, and that he'd been excluded from a conversation of such import not only by Pregel but Ulbert too; feeling a jibe rising in his throat, Pregel hurrying on.

'He said I should wait until I got here, that I might feel differently. But I don't. I really don't. It's like I've come to the place I was always meant to be, and I can sing here all day long.'

He let out a long sigh, every muscle in his body relaxing now he'd got the words out; and Lukitt saw the deed was done, that Pregel would stay, that Lukitt would lose his first and only friend.

He cast a glance over at Ulbert, saw him talking closely with Abbot Ettershank, saw them both looking over towards Pregel, the betrayal sudden, visceral and venomous.

He couldn't bear it.

He stood up without a word, stood up and marched towards the door, heaved it open and went out into the night.

6

The Flicker Threshold

Lukitt sat outside the chapel on a rough-hewn stone seat, staring into the snow that was coming at him in vicious flurries; not that he cared, blinking spasmodically to rid himself of tears, especially once he heard Pregel's voice, strong and clear, rising into the night from the refectory: the words of the *Anima Christi* prayer Pregel had been practising the whole week before they'd come here, he and Ulbert knowing all the while why and what might come of it, but never telling Lukitt.

Anima Christi, sanctifica me;
Corpus Christi, salva me.
Sanguis Christi, inebria me,
Aqua lateris Christi, lava me.
Passio Christi, conforta me,
O bone Jesu, exaudi me....

The words clear and beautiful, Lukitt rubbing his eyes with his knuckles, sucking in freezing air through gritted teeth, his mind chasing itself through the darkness – Ulbert and Pregel having secret conversations; Ulbert and Pregel making plans and never counting him in; Ulbert and Pregel conspiring to do the exact opposite; Pregel's voice ringing out like a beam of light that served only to keep Lukitt in darkness. Years he'd been with Ulbert, rocky at first, but then serene, joyful, feeling for Ulbert like he'd never felt for his own father: that they were akin, shared the same intense lust for learning.

The injury felt was absolute and unforgiving; and there was jealousy too, souring the mix: jealousy of Pregel's newly acquired singularity, the narrow sense of purpose that had nothing whatsoever to do with Lukitt; the loss of loyalty and friendship; Pregel using him to get to Ulbert, who in turn could get him into the monastery.

He knew this last was monstrously unjust, that Pregel was without guile and could never have thought up such a devious plan, let alone carry it through. But Ulbert: that was something else entirely, and Lukitt wasn't sure he could ever look the man in the eye again. There'd been trust before, companionship, intellectual understanding; all squandered, trampled underfoot as surely as a load of wild boar stamp away the new grass growing beneath the canopy of a forest.

From this day forth he was done with the two of them.

His face was numb, tears frozen halfway down his face, feet numb too, fingers stuck to the bench's base where they gripped hard in his anger.

He would sit here and freeze, was his decision.

He would sit here and freeze himself to death, make Pregel and Ulbert spend the rest of their unhappy lives in guilty penance. And so he might have done, had not a shadow dropped over him, a man appearing out of nowhere, his white habit virtually indistinguishable from the backdrop of snow.

'I'm not sure you should be sat there much longer, boy, not if you want to wake up with a full set of digits.'

Lukitt jumping at the interruption, or would have done had not he not by then been completely stuck, trousers and fingers welded to the stone as if he really might have to carry out his ultimatum.

'So do you want to stay here all night, or shall I set you free?' asked the interrupter, no hint of irony or humour, waiting for Lukitt to answer as if Lukitt's previous course of action had been legitimate.

'S…s…set…m…m…me…fr…freee…' Lukitt managed to get out between chattering teeth, suddenly aware how cold he was, how ridiculous his planned revenge.

The man coming forward, gently holding a warming bottle against one of Lukitt's hands and then the other before lifting him up.

'A little heat is all you need,' says he, carrying Lukitt easily in his arms, taking him along one side of the chapel and down a flight of steps towards the crypts, pushing open a door at its base with his shoulder and bringing them in. Lukitt seeing warm winks of wood glowing in a pot-bellied stove, everything else in darkness. Lukitt deposited at its base while his rescuer opened the stove door, shoved in a spill, got a couple of lamps lit.

'A little light,' he said. 'That's better. Never could stand the dark. I'll warm us up some wine and we'll be hot as toast in a few minutes.'

He pulled up a battered stool, plonked Lukitt onto it, grabbed a sheepskin rug from the floor and threw it over Lukitt's chest. The stranger was right; ten minutes of this treatment and Lukitt was warm enough to hold the cup he was given, sipping its contents – hot wine spiked with cinnamon, oranges and something vaguely medicinal – Lukitt taking in his surroundings: a small room, evidently somewhere below ground level, wall-space taken up by shelves piled with heaps of tattered books, papers and mysterious pieces of equipment. Lukitt recognised a microscope, but could make no sense at all of the various mirrors and pieces of coloured glass hanging high above his head, all different shapes; unnerved to see a giant knee embedded in the ceiling, until he realised that parts of his body were being caught and magnified by the glass, distorted reflections that tilted and expanded, shrank and revolved, depending on how he held himself.

He noted too the small tables shoved against the walls, each smothered with papers, pens, scatters of glass, a glittering cone that shone in the lamplight catching flickers from the fire, throwing tiny pinpoints of light skittering across the walls, the roof, the floor. A miniature of the mosaic that must be somewhere up above him in the chapel.

Lukitt's rescuer dragged over an armchair patched together from a couple of crates and worm-eaten sheepskins, putting it to his liking by the fire, tossing an ancient quilt over Lukitt in case he wasn't quite warm enough; got himself comfortable, took off his boots, rested his feet before the stove. He took up a short-legged pipe and got it filled, got it lit, an aroma settling over the room of warm liquorice and mint, a hint of aniseed.

'Still cold?' says the monk. 'If so I've some chestnuts. Can get them roasted in a trice.'

He put his arm behind him and produced a string bag that had been hanging from the back of his chair, took a handful of nuts and threw them on top of the stove. Almost immediately they began to jump and hiss, the sweat on their skins soon bubbling into steam. Outside the wind was rising, the snow making strange sweeping sounds as it was dragged over the glass skylights, the door whumping arhythmically within its frame. The monk snuggled into his chair, smoking contentedly, watching the chestnuts smoulder in their blackening cases, listening to the wood settling in the stove and groaning spasmodically as the wind whipped down the flue.

'I damn near froze to death myself once,' the monk started without preamble, letting out a long curlicue of blue smoke. 'Long time ago now but, by Peter's teeth, I mind it like it was yesterweek. We'd a young brother got sick, and by the time we'd got him through a couple of months of fevers and shivers he was skin and bone, lost all his teeth and hair, including eyebrows and lashes. He didn't complain a whit, but it didn't seem right, him being so young and not yet twenty. And then we got wind of a tinker down in Seiden See selling all sorts of medicines and accoutrements, including wigs and proper bone dentures. So off we set, me and Jerome – for that was the lad's name. It wasn't the best of weathers, coming on early winter, but it wasn't too bad. He'd still not got all his weight back on so he's on the pony and I'm walking the way beside him, a sled tacked on the back with a few bolts of cloth tied for trading. Shouldn't have taken us more than a half a day, as you must be aware having just come that way yourself, especially with us going downhill. But you know what mountains are, and from the bluest of skies came the darkest of clouds and we're not in sight of a farm to rest up in. Well, that wind whipped up strong enough to rattle our bones inside our skins, and down came the snow - and not the soft kind like outside just now. Not at all, more like flattened hail, and enough of it so we could neither see two yards ahead nor two behind, and within ten minutes we couldn't even see the track.'

A few of the chestnuts jumped and crackled, the monk stopping his tale long enough to scoop a few into a bowl and placing it into Lukitt's cupped hands, hot as a warming brick from the fire.

'So what to do?' the monk went on, sucking once more at his pipe, leaning forward every now and then to pick off cooked chestnuts to add to Lukitt's stash. 'Jerome was bundled up in fur like a dormouse but still was suffering, as was the pony. Nothing for it but to stop, lie everyone down, pony included; huddle up behind the trap that I'd tipped on its side for a bit of shelter along with the sled. Couple of hours it went on and the wind was the worst; never known one that could tear the whiskers from your beard but if ever there was one, that was it. When it finally blew itself out there was hardly any light left, and Jerome stiff and curled as a wrought-iron door knocker. Seeing him like that punched all the nerves out of me and got me going. I hitched up the pony, tossed Jerome onto the sled, slapped the pony an almighty whack on its rump to get it going and just had time to chuck myself onto the trap and rolled in the blankets before we were off.'

Lukitt cracked the chestnuts one by one, peeling them, putting them slowly into his mouth, mind filled with the old monk's talking so he saw himself out there in the storm: the judder of the sled going over the snow, fingers tingling to remember the cold out there on the bench and how much colder it must have been for the old man gripping the sides of his trap so he didn't tip out at every corner; found himself staring at the old man's fingers cradled about his pipe stem and how short they were, the last joint and tip of them lost, the veracity of the tale and its implications dawning on him.

'Did you lose all your toes too?' he asked quietly, the monk turning his head slowly, staring at the boy bundled in furs just as Jerome had been.

'Well now, young man, what a thing to ask…'

Lukitt lowered his head, hadn't meant to offend, but the man didn't sound angry and instead barked out a short laugh.

'Ulbert told me you were quick,' he said, with a hint of admiration, 'assuming you are Lukitt?'

Lukitt nodded, surprised Ulbert had spoken of him to this man.

'And I'm Brother Ommaweise, or Opapa Augen as you'll find the others call me,' he said, 'and you're quite right, Lukitt. Frostbite in all toes and fingers by the time we got to Seiden See. Had to get the barber to snip them off one by one and sew them up into pretty stumps. Never got the feeling back into their ends.'

He raised his free hand, wiggled it for Lukitt's inspection, Lukitt looking on with interest.

'Worst were the big toes,' Ommaweise confided. 'Took quite a while to get my balance back with them gone. But that's adversity for you. No point complaining. What's done is done, and at least Jerome got a serviceable set of teeth, though never took to the wig.'

'And it never grew back? His hair, I mean?' Lukitt asked, curious what sort of illness could so completely denude a man.

'No more'n my toes nor fingers did,' Ommaweise confirmed, 'least not that I knows of. Left us a few years back. Became secretary to some burgher in Freiberg. Speaking of which, let me show you something he sent me only a couple of weeks ago. A specialty of Freiberg, so he says.'

Brother Ommaweise stood up and went to a table, returning with a small box and a hammer, both of which he handed to Lukitt.

'Open it up. Tell me what you see.'

Lukitt opened the box, revealing a silvery-yellow lump of stone speckled with black. It didn't look impressive, but Lukitt was well tutored in the truism that things are not always as they first appear.

'Some kind of mineral?' he guessed.

'Not bad,' said Brother Ommaweise, 'but now strike it smartly with that hammer...'

Lukitt did so, a few sparks flying up, which was pretty, but the sparks were not the lesson at all; what was odd was the faint but unmistakable smell of garlic that drifted up from his hitting. Lukitt made to pick the object up, inspect it further but Ommaweise shot out a hand and caught Lukitt's wrist.

'Don't touch it, Lukitt. That's Mispickel, or Arsenopyrite as it's more properly known. Very unusual to find any mineral that possesses a smell, so I understand your urge to pick it up and examine it, just as I would've done if I'd not been forewarned. Mispickel unusual in more ways than one. Poisonous to the touch. Can make you very ill indeed.'

Ommaweise leaned over and shut the box, took the hammer from Lukitt with blunt-ended fingers.

'A shame really,' he continued, 'as it's such an enjoyable experiment and such good fun. Garlic from a stone, indeed. Nature can be truly miraculous.'

'Some ant nests smell of gorse flowers,' Lukitt put in. 'Ghost ants, they're called. Comes from the dead bodies of the workers.'

Ommaweise raised his eyebrows.

'Well, well, and have you experienced this yourself?'

Lukitt shook his head.

'You don't get them here. But I've read about them,' he said eagerly, 'and they're really odd looking. Dark heads, transparent abdomens, and very small.'

'So you like your books?' Ommaweise asked mildly, already knowing the answer.

'Oh yes!' Lukitt said with enthusiasm, moving his body forward, the quilt slipping to the floor. 'And I'll travel the world one day, like Ulbert did. See all these things for myself.'

And thinking on Ulbert, some of his earlier anger returned, though not for long. Let him and Pregel keep their secrets; he had his own, just as he'd spilled out to this Brother Ommaweise.

'Well, my young friend,' said Ommaweise, standing up and going to the door, turning the handle, pushing at it gently with his shoulder. 'You'll not be doing any travelling just now, I'm afraid. We're stuck for the night. That snow has a habit of coming down fast and the wind blowing it full down the steps, like now.'

Lukitt didn't look alarmed and Ommaweise smiled.

'They'll dig us out in the morning,' he went on, 'and meanwhile we can carry on talking. It's quite a pleasure to meet another inquiring mind.'

He settled back in his chair, but not before taking another bottle of wine from a cupboard and a couple of plates that he filled with sweet rusks and a side helping of wild strawberry jam.

'Why do they call you Opapa Augen?' Lukitt asked, once he'd broken up one of the hard biscuits, dipped it in the strawberries and swallowed it down.

'Well now,' Ommaweise started, 'essentially we're a Benedictine order, encouraging learning and education, true scholarship and good art for the service of our community and our God. Our Triungulin Mosaic is a prime example. It took a year to design, another two to have the glass and lead made and one more to piece it altogether and get it erected. And we also copy manuscripts and illuminations. All this work requires good eyesight, and that is not something comes easy, not to the older monks who, by definition, are the most experienced at their work.'

Ommaweise got up, called Lukitt to follow him which Lukitt did.

'Look at this,' he said, pointing to a rhomboid of some transparent material sat on his desk. 'This is a piece of Icelandic Spar, what we call Doppelspat, that has the strange property of double refraction. See?'

He rolled a cone of paper and brought over a lamp, placed the cone of paper in front of it to produce a point of light on the Spar.

'When you shine a light on it,' he went on, 'look what we get.'

'Two points of light coming out the other side?' Lukitt asked, seeing that it was so.

'Exactly!' Ommaweise went on happily. 'And look again. If we put a black spot on a piece of paper and place the crystal over it…'

'Two spots!' Lukitt exclaimed, a great smile on his face, this first introduction to experimental optics fascinating him. Reading books was one thing, Opapa Augen demonstrating those theories quite another.

'And now we can do this,' Ommaweise continued, enjoying his little lecture, this time rotating the crystal over the black spot, Lukitt amazed to see that the original spot remained where it was but that the second dot was moving in an exact circle around it.

'We can put this to practical use,' Ommaweise explained 'We can grind this crystal and smooth it down, reform it, make it focus its light in a very particular way. It can act as a microscope, a magnifier. I've made spectacles from it for all the brothers doing close-up work; hence my name of Opapa Augen.'

'That's amazing,' Lukitt whispered.

'Not as much as this will be!' Opapa couldn't stop himself. Never had anyone been as interested in the mechanics of his work as this young blow-in from the Seiden See. 'You're in luck, Lukitt. I've a specimen laid out on the microscope slide, fixed and ready. Come look at this.'

Lukitt there in a second, putting his eye to the instrument, adjusting the focus, the slight smudge of light suddenly splitting into myriad luminous points.

'You're looking through the eye of a glow-worm,' Opapa said quietly. 'Right through its very eye. Excised by me and placed on that slide. You're seeing the world as a glow-worm sees it: a mosaic, like our window. A single image made up of lots of tiny pieces. The world split into shards, taken apart and put back together. So what do you think of that?'

Lukitt had no words for what he was seeing or thinking, only that his world had shifted at least as much in this last hour as Pregel's must have done by his coming here, realising that reading and doing were two different things. And just when he thought he could learn no more Opapa Augen went and did it again, him climbing onto a chair leaning against the far wall and sliding away a scrap of velvet to reveal a tubular hole in the wall. He scribbled a message onto a piece of paper, rolled it up into a metal cylinder, picked up a pair of sturdy bellows and, with a couple of strong blows of air, sent it on its way.

A few minutes later the cylinder returned, plinking onto the floor, Opapa opening it and unrolling the message held within.

'Message understood,' he read out loud. 'Digging will commence before Prime. Tomorrow's shows: The Creation of the World and the Deluge. Pregel taking Quid Petis at evening service. Blessings, Hanson.'

Lukitt yawned and rubbed his eyes.

'Time for sleep,' Opapa announced, rearranging the sheepskins and quilts about the fire, laying himself down; Lukitt taking the other side and, although tired, found it hard to sleep. Kept thinking about all he'd seen in this small undercroft, the lamps soon self-extinguished, air thick with darkness and the burning smoke from the chestnuts Opapa had neglected to remove before he subsided into quiet breaths and gentle snores.

Quid Petis - what do you seek?

Lukitt thought about that long and hard during his night spent in Opapa Augen's snowed-in study; Lukitt making plans, devising exit strategies; realising for the first time that Père Ulbert was not the beginning and end of his education; that there were better places to learn, better places to be and by Christ, Lukitt meant to find them.

7

Victus Theatrum

They witnessed the creation of the world!

The Pfiffmaklers knew how to put on a show.

The Brothers - Lukitt, Pregel and Ulbert with them - watched the canopy of heaven lift itself from the earth in a green explosion of Bengal Fire, felt the spray of water as the oceans parted from the land and saw fishes leap and flash as thunder and lightning crashed over the rivers that ran through Eden.

They saw Eve deceived by a red-haired man who turned into a serpent and wound his way up a tree, flicking down upon her an apricot with a rattle of his tail. They cried out for her to throw it away fast as she could, but Adam decided it was too good to part with and both ate, all the while the audience shouting at them to stop.

Too late, and now came the din of cymbals crashing and drums rolling as God's voice came down upon the garden, great spluttering cascades of stars bursting from the candle footlights as handfuls of silver dust were thrown there by Ludmilla and Longhella, God's anger darkening the skies, cursing his children for their disobedience, flinging them some scraps of fur to hide their shameful nakedness as Adam and Eve wailed and were sent out of Eden.

'The covenant is broken,' God sternly announced. 'Your only lot in life now is toil and sweat, blood and tears, sin and death.'

Lukitt riveted, not so much by the tale as the theatrics. He knew it was being engineered by the Pfiffmaklers: a combination of puppets manipulated from above and the smaller members of the troupe dressing in black so they could move about the stage, practically unseen, performing the more deft operations, making the puppets move in ways the wires couldn't do on their own. But it was so realistic it was like watching the real thing.

Another roll of thunder making him jump in his seat, eyes wide and glistening as he waited for what would come next, which was the brutal slaying of Abel by Cain, a great splash of red going up behind the two, framing them in Abel's blood. And out boomed the voice of God again as Abel died and Cain returned to his family, giving voiceless mime to his ignorance, his distress, his denial, but no mention of the fact that God had indiscriminately accepted Abel's offerings but not Cain's.

'And so my world,' God mourned, 'created in light, becomes dark again; mankind's line tainted from the second generation with jealousy and treachery, murder and death. The first martyrdom of the good at the hands of the wicked.'

'Am I my brother's keeper?' Cain asks of God and his parents as the latter weep beside Abel's prostrate body, fratricide the first fruit of their seed of sin. Cain's denials not accepted, God having none of it; His judgement heralded by an overwhelming crash of cymbals and the constant beating of drums that has everyone's hearts going a little faster.

'Your brother's blood cries up to me,' God announces from His Heaven, 'cursing you from the ground that opened up its mouth to drink your brother's blood.'

The audience rapt, Pregel gripping hard at Lukitt's hand and Lukitt squeezing back, because it had occurred to him during the night in Opapa Augen's undercroft that perhaps Pregel's secrecy had not been all it seemed. He'd asked Opapa about it in the morning, before they'd been dug out, in the quiet time when the snow muffled every sound, keeping them cocooned.

'What does an oblate do?' Lukitt had asked, Opapa busy tidying up: filling his lamps, sweeping away the remnants of burnt chestnuts from the stove's top, tutting as he scrubbed with wire wool at the wobbly circles of charcoal they'd left behind to mark their passing.

'It's like a lay brother,' he told Lukitt. 'Someone assigned to the monastery for a certain duty but who doesn't take our vows, or not necessarily. Oblates are usually young, like Pregel, which I assume is why you're asking.'

Lukitt nodded.

'It's just he never told me about it,' Lukitt said, admitting his perceived betrayal out loud. 'And Pregel always tells me everything.'

Opapa stopped his scrubbing, looked over at Lukitt.

'If there's one thing in life you need to learn, my boy, then it's this: no one will ever tell you everything. People are like ropes made of myriad strands all wound together from various times and places, sometimes at their own bidding, sometimes at someone else's. And in the case of oblates, at least one as young as Pregel, they cannot take this course without their family's express approval or command.'

Lukitt quiet, taking it in.

'So you're telling me it was Pregel's family sent him here? That they told Pregel not to say anything, at least not to me?'

Opapa shrugged.

'You must realise I can't say yea or nay to that, Lukitt. Oblates come and oblates go. Some can stick it and some can't. What I'm saying is that every apparently unreasonable act will always have an underlying logic of its own, even if that logic is wrong. And an enquiring mind like yours must seek that logic out, whatever the outcome.'

Lukitt doing that right now, squeezing Pregel's hand the harder because of it, as the music changed timbre, moved from loud to solemn, gossamer-thin curtains falling over the stage like wisps of mist, Abel's body lost to sight as was his murdering brother's. And when those shroud-like curtains lifted, an entirely different scene was before them, everyone leaning forward in their chairs into utter darkness; no sounds but those of the audience readying themselves, the creaking of their chairs.

Another skinny curtain descending, rippled gently by mechanical bellows, the effect being that of black sky and silver rain falling down upon the stage, the illusion aided by the plinking of dried peas being moved about a large sieve. From the back of the stage a boat-like contraption hoved into view, lit by a single lamp that shivered and wobbled as it came centre stage; just enough light to make out that there were four men stranded out there on a lonely sea in the falling rain - presumably the deluge Opapa's tubular message had predicted - but not so straightforward as it might have been.

'The end of humanity,' came a voice, sudden and shocking from the silence. 'A flood sent by God to sweep away the righteous and wicked alike, the savour of the salt of His creation tainted and gone. So who is to save us from the enormity of Original Sin?'

Lukitt and Pregel frowned in puzzlement but apparently were alone, the religious brethren three steps ahead of them, raising their heads, eager to see how the argument would pan out.

'Here,' came the voice of the omnipotent narrator, 'are the men who will argue humanity's corner.'

And they were men, Lukitt could see that. No puppetry this time, just four young monks eager to take part in the Pfiffmaklers' show, briefed by Abbot Ettershank, sitting in their rocking boat as they tried to navigate the stormy seas of hundreds of years of differential theology. A swift arpeggio on the violin jerking everyone to attention as the first man got up to introduce himself.

'I am Augustinius,' he announced, 'and I stand by the theory of Original Sin and that every man is destined to err on its side unless by the intercession of God.'

He sat down as the second man stood up to the rumble of a bass chord, twisting the great white beard that fell right down to his waist.

'And I am Pelagius,' he declared, 'and I cannot believe that mankind has an inherently sinful nature for, if that were the case, he could not help but sin and if he cannot help sinning because it is his nature to do so, how can he be commanded not to sin, or be condemned for it or held responsible?'

'What're they on about?' Pregel whispered to Lukitt, his attention lost now the theatrics had come and gone; not so the rest of the audience who were looking on in expectation, as was Lukitt.

'Shush a minute,' Lukitt whispered back, letting go Pregel's hand, listening intently, ignoring Pregel's soft sigh as Pregel leant back in his chair; the third man rising from the edge of the rocking boat.

'My name is Kolb Calvin,' a perceptible rustling as the Gargellan monks drew back to express their disapproval of the views they knew he would hold. 'And I say that if God is omnipotent and all-knowing then it stands to reason that whatever happens can only happen by His express desire, including the sinful nature of man, His own creation.'

Lukitt was impressed, for it seemed to him this theory had legs, because if God truly was all-knowing and all-powerful over His creation then how could it be otherwise? Apparently no one else felt the same, because there were a few hisses coming from the crowd about him, arrested only because the fourth man in the boat stood up beside Kolb Calvin, shoulder to shoulder.

'And my name is Doctor Thomas Angelicus,' he smiles, to small claps of approval all around as Angelicus puts his hand on Calvin's shoulder and pushes him down, an action accompanied by a sweet melody from Heraldo Pfiffmakler's lute.

'It seems a paradox,' the saintly Angelicus went on, 'but it is not. God created many creatures, Man amongst them, but only Man was blessed to be in His image, only Man who was told not to eat of the tree of good and evil, only Man who was given the gift of being able to choose to be within God's Will or without it. And that was our Original Sin, our collective giving back of that gift, our choosing to step outside His Will. But God's love for His creation is such that He gave us a second chance, the choice of each individual to reclaim that gift if he so chooses, to walk within the way of God and our Saviour Jesus Christ.'

More gentle lute playing, and then more rain, and then a soft roll of thunder as Augustinius stands up suddenly again.

'But surely that means that Man, by his very nature, is predestined to sin unless God chooses otherwise, and therefore He has already chosen who will be in His fold and who will not…'

The audience begin to hiss their disapproval, until the sounds of the lute rein them back as Angelicus turns to face his interlocutor.

'So you hold for the predestination of saints?' he asks gently.

'Another paradox,' Augustinius says sadly, shaking his head. 'For why should a man be required to bear the misery of guilt for sins he cannot by his nature prevent himself from committing?'

'I agree!' Kolb Calvin gets up again, the boat rocking wildly, his voice loud and vociferous. 'For it surely follows, if you take the theory of God's omnipotence to its logical end, that what any man does he does by the Will of God, and that therefore Adam and Eve were only carrying out the Will of God when they succumbed to temptation by the Devil! We can go further and state that therefore God Himself intended the Fall of Man and Nature with him, and that He also created the angels - of whom Lucifer was one - knowing that Lucifer would become Beelzebub himself and bring evil into His creation!'

A huge crash of thunder now, and the rain is apparently getting heavier, the wind stronger, the boat heaving from side to side, its inmates vying for standing room, pushing each other to make sure they have enough space to make their say. The Abbot is getting anxious, having no idea where this is going or why his four actor-monks aren't sticking to the party-line, which is to demonstrate their Order's beliefs, quash the rest without remark. This extended debate and its attendance to theological detail not at all what he'd had in mind. Behind him, Lukitt jitters in his seat, thrilled with the excitement of a real live debate going on in front of him. It occurred to him that his father might have enjoyed this too-ing and fro-ing, this exercise of argument, of logic over blind belief; might have made more sense of his conflicted views of the Herrnhuter who'd brought him up, looked after him and then booted him out, views he'd expressed every now and then back at the farm. The thought of the farm and his parents sending a small tremor of guilt running through Lukitt for, once at Seiden See and in Ulbert's care, he'd not returned home once, too focussed on his own goals, his pursuit of knowledge and new things. He lifted his head briefly, wondering if the snow would permit a small excursion on the morrow to visit his parents who were not so far away, thoughts interrupted by a sudden shout from the wings.

'We need help! We have need of a man who knows each side of the square that is stumping us!'

The boat stops its rocking as each of its inhabitants stand still, like men before the dock.

'We must find a devil's advocate before we can adjudicate, so who will it be?' the voice asks as someone scampers through the audience with a small light, stopping briefly by Abbot Ettershank who shakes his head, unable to rise to the call, fearing some trick, that these people he's employed to entertain and educate his flock have brought some sinister influence to bear upon their actors that has so swerved them off script. The light moves on from brother to brother, but everyone is unnerved by their Abbot's refusal, unwilling to risk having their beliefs challenged right down to the core.

Lukitt looks at Ulbert a few seats down, for surely no better man to do the deed. Ulbert stays where he is, although Lukitt detects a small shift to his shoulders, a slight turning of his head in Lukitt's direction as if he already knows that Lukitt has listened, has learned, that Lukitt will not let this pass.

'I'll do it,' Lukitt says quietly and gets to his feet. 'I'll be your devil's advocate,' he says a little louder. Pregel is dragging at Lukitt's sleeve, trying to bring him down.

'What are you doing?' Pregel whispers urgently, but Lukitt has made up his mind and brushes Pregel off, takes the several yards between self and stage in a few seconds, clambers up, takes his place by the boat, feels a great surge of strength to see his audience spread out before him, the ranks of upturned faces pale in the shadows. He catches the eye of Heraldo, one of the Pfiffmaklers boys, in the wings who winks and tips his head in encouragement, a wide smile upon his handsome face. Lukitt blinks, stands tall and is not nervous, feels as he did when setting out his insect project at school, blessing Ulbert for the opportunities that have prepared him so well.

'I've listened to all four arguments,' Lukitt says loudly, 'and have to say, I find all four wanting.'

A huge intake of breath from everyone in the audience, Pregel's mouth agape in admiration, hands making silent claps as he watches his friend; Ulbert sitting straight-backed in his seat, shoulders squared, small smile upon his face.

'And what is it you find wanting?' the unknown narrator asks from the wings. 'Feel free to interrogate the witnesses,' he adds, 'for everyone here is as keen to learn the truth of it as you.'

Lukitt takes a breath, begins to speak in the formal way Ulbert has taught him when they have their own debates in Ulbert's home, Ulbert asking him what he's learned that week, getting Lukitt to sum it up precisely, the arguments for and against.

'It seems to me,' Lukitt began, his mind riffling in a flash through Ulbert's books on philosophy and religion, the commentaries at the back of his father's bible.

'It seems to me,' Lukitt repeated, 'that this entire debate might be based upon a fallacy, namely that the gaining of knowledge is a bad thing. Surely there's an argument for the opposite. That the greatest achievements of mankind have come from the gaining of knowledge, curiosity about the world we all live in.'

He looks about him, seeks out Ulbert's face in the audience and sees him smiling serenely, sees Abbot Ettershank a couple of seats along frowning deeply, several of the brothers rubbing their foreheads with their fingers.

'For isn't it the case,' Lukitt goes on, 'that had Adam and Eve never eaten of the tree of knowledge they would have gone on living in the Garden of Eden, the two of them naked, taking everything for granted. Just like all the other animals God had created...'

'That's blasphemy!' someone shouts into the darkness, a call taken up by one or two more, Lukitt swallowing hard, wondering if he's gone too far, but his mind is already leaping ahead and wasn't about to stop. He spread out his arms and took a step towards the boat where the four men representing the theological positions on original sin were standing mutely, now realising the Pfiffmaklers might have misled them into overstepping their instructions, unsure how to respond.

'Wait!' Lukitt says loudly to the dissenting monks, 'just wait! Doesn't it strike any of you as odd that God would keep the best of His creation hampered by a lack of free will, of wanting to make themselves better than they already are? Someone spoke about the predestination of saints...'

'That was me,' the monk playing Augustinius waving a hesitant hand from the now very stationary boat.

'Right!' Lukitt said, turning to the man briefly and smiling. 'But how could there possibly have been any saints in the first place if there was nothing to be saintly about?'

Loud boos from the audience at this pronouncement, but Lukitt is in his stride. Logic was logic, as Opapa Augen had so recently affirmed, and had to be put to the fore.

'But don't you see?' Lukitt argues his corner. 'If we hadn't stepped out of the Garden of Eden then we wouldn't have developed the tools to assess and weigh arguments, as we're doing now. We'd have been kept in a state of innocence, never knowing right from wrong, good from evil, never battling against the odds. There'd be no writing, no books, no education, no inventions, no progress, no understanding of mathematics or nature or astronomy, and no monasteries, no matter their denominations. In short, we would be stuck. We'd have no notion at all of God's greater creation. We'd be children in a playpen, and no chance of ever climbing out.'

Lukitt stopped, sweat beading down his back. He glanced at Heraldo, saw the bright astonishment on his face, felt the immobility of the actor-monks in their boat behind him, suddenly aware he'd taken centre stage.

'So what you're saying,' the false Kolb Calvin stood up on shaking legs, Lukitt turning towards him with anticipation, 'is that if it weren't for Lucifer and his temptation in Eden then we would still be in darkness?'

'Lucifer does mean the Light Giver,' player-Pelagius quietly pointed out, hunching his shoulders, lowering his head, unable to meet the eyes of his neighbours.

'And he is playing devil's advocate,' put in the ersatz Angelicus, putting up a hand immediately to his mouth to stop the nervous giggling that was threatening to spill from him.

'Enough!' Abbot Ettershank commanded, standing up, turning his stern face on the company. 'I think it's time we took a short intermission. I assume, Herr Pfiffmakler, we'll be moving on hereafterwards to the Tower of Babel, as previously agreed?'

'We will, sir,' came the elder Pfiffmakler's voice, booming far louder than he'd intended, having neglected to remove the God/Narrator amplification trumpet from his lips, a little anxious at the way things had gone, hoping he'd not displeased anyone enough to stop due payment.

'Very well then,' Abbot Ettershank went on, his voice tight and clipped. 'Let's be heading to the refectory for refreshments. We'll recommence in an hour.'

'Best keep the boy away from Babel,' someone towards the back of the room piped up, 'for Lord knows what he'll make of that!'

Ettershank looked around sharply to locate the malefactor, but he was lost in the general tide of scraping chairs and the murmurings of monks as they exited swiftly towards the door. He caught hold of Ulbert as Ulbert went to pass him by.

'I hope you're pleased with yourself,' Ettershank muttered, Ulbert smiling nonchalantly.

'Certainly not, Abbot,' Ulbert replied easily, 'but I'm pleased with the boy and so should you be, for what use is faith if it isn't challenged every now and then?'

'Don't you start,' Ettershank retorted, but clapped an amiable hand upon Ulbert's shoulder, giving a sigh. 'And yes, you're right. Such challenge is entirely healthy. My young actor monks may have pushed the…ahem…boat out a little far in their enthusiasm…' he smiled at his small joke as he fell into step with Ulbert. 'But tell me, what else have you been teaching the lad? That the moon is as square as the earth is round?'

Ulbert laughed.

'You mayn't believe it, Abbot, but what Lukitt was saying? Well, that was entirely new to me and a completely unexpected deduction from what was being proposed. But he does have a point.'

'A point that would have had severed him through the heart a couple of hundred years ago,' Ettershank pointed out, 'if not burned at the stake.'

'Ah, but that was then,' Ulbert stated, holding up a finger. 'Everyone has to move with the times, and even you have to agree these times are moving fast. Only a few months ago I heard about an English mathematician, Charles Babbage, who's created a machine that performs basic mathematical calculations far more accurately than most men can do, and in far less time.'

'The devil's work,' Ettershank said, but he too was smiling now. 'Lucifer the Light Giver, indeed! I'll need to have words with that young monk, and with all four of them, come to that.'

'Don't go too hard on them,' Ulbert advised. 'They were only doing what you asked. And I'd no idea anyone would be tasked with playing devil's advocate, nor that Lukitt would spring on it with such alacrity.'

'Speaking of which,' Ettershank said, looking up at the stage, seeing Lukitt there, stranded for the moment, Caleb – one of the older, most conservative monks, getting ready to harangue him, Caleb not seeing the humour in the situation as Ettershank did. 'Don't you think you should go lend him some support?'

Ulbert shrugged.

'Not I,' he said. 'Lukitt has made his bed. Got to learn to lie in it.'

8

Worlds Upon Worlds

'You think that was funny, boy?' Caleb said, rounding on Lukitt, holding a fist a few inches from Lukitt's face, knuckles hardened and strengthened by his forty one years spent in these hills doing manual labour of every kind.

'Leave him be,' said one of the younger monks, leaping from the boat and coming to Lukitt's aid.

'It was our fault,' said another, though stayed behind the confines of the wooden prop, not liking the look of that fist nor the face of old Caleb who was wielding it.

'We got a bit carried away,' added the third young monk, stepping between Lukitt and another of Caleb's posse who was creaking a slow way across the stage with the help of a wicked looking stick.

'We just wanted to shake things up a little,' said the last, removed from the façade of the wooden boat as the Pfiffmaklers hauled it on its wheels away into the wings.

Caleb glared at Lukitt and his defenders, and began to grumble incoherent words of protest but didn't stop to pursue his cause, turned from them and swept away, dragging with him his stick-using friend, almost toppling the man down the steps from the stage in his haste.

'Well done! Well done!' the young monks crowded around Lukitt.

'That was really something!' added the first. 'My name's Alameth, and these here are Micah, Andrew and Joseph. We're all novices, due to take our vows on the seventeenth of December, on the feast day of St Sturm.'

'If they'll still have us,' one of his friends commented gloomily.

'Oh don't be so melodramatic, Andrew,' Alameth dismissed his concerns. 'Of course they'll take us.'

'But what if Caleb objects?' the almost-giggler Joseph said, winding his fingers together, his nerves not having entirely subsided.

'So what if he does?' Alameth said with unconcern 'Everyone

knows backwaters like these are in decline and will take anyone they can get. And this young lad here has perfectly illustrated why. What's your name, by the way?'

'Lukitt,' Lukitt said, feeling adrift, despite the lack of ocean and boat, looking around for a Pfiffmakler to rescue him, though none were to be seen.

'Well then, Lukitt,' Alameth said. 'Good on you. We all know that religion is moribund, that places like these can't last the century out, not with all that's going on in the outside world.'

'So why are you here?' Lukitt asked quietly, taking his first proper look at this Alameth: short blond hair, face slightly on the swerve, an effect that made him more handsome than he would otherwise have been.

'Because he wants to conquer the world,' the novice Andrew said, the bite of contempt in his voice unmistakable.

Interrupted by Heraldo Pfiffmakler marching over to join them, lute swung up between his shoulder-blades like Lucifer's unfolded wings.

'That was some show!' Heraldo declared, clapping the nearest two on the back. 'Don't know how Alameth recruited young Lukitt here, but it was genius. Genius!'

Alameth smiled.

'I didn't,' Alameth admitted, 'all his own work. But you're right. Genius is what it was. Don't think I've ever heard anyone boo at a Christmas pageant before.'

'Nor me,' Heraldo agreed, 'at least not this kind. Sometimes get it with the Kaspar Larriscarri sketches, but that's only to be expected. But a load of monks? Never!'

He shook his head in wonderment.

'Shouldn't we get off to the refectory?' Andrew asked quietly.

'Pffft!' Alameth waved a hand. 'Go if you want to, but I for one don't choose to be anywhere near the rest when they've wooden spoons at the ready.'

He laughed and winked at Lukitt, who was bemused but pleased to have people like Heraldo and Alameth take his side.

'Come on through the back,' Heraldo offered. 'We've always a few plates of this and that out so we can grab some food when we've time. It's a long business, this Christmas pageantry lark. Kind of takes the wind out of you after the first couple of hours.'

'How long does it go on?' Lukitt asked, incredulous the Pfiffmaklers could carry on their wonders for so long and still come up fresh.

'All bloody day,' Alameth said, 'excuse my language. But honestly, they do sometimes drag.'

'Not with us about, they don't,' Heraldo put in, slipping into easy patter. 'We've lots more to amaze and astound; wonders to be witnessed, plays to...'

Cut off by Alameth, interrupting with a broad grin.

'All right, friend, we get the picture. But where's this food you were on about?'

Heraldo took the hint without rancour.

'This way. Hey, you two!' he called at Andrew and Joseph's retreating backs as they snuck off down the stairs from the stage.

'Ach, just leave them,' Alameth said. 'And what about you, Micah?' he asked the last of the actor-monks, who was twiddling his thumbs, looking uncertain.

'Um, they told us not to consort with the Fairs' folk after we'd done our bit...'

Heraldo opened his mouth and held up his hands in mock surprise

'Surely not,' he said, 'with us being so completely heaven-bound and religious.'

Alameth less contemptuous with his advice, understanding Micah's conflict, if not feeling it himself.

'You go on with the others,' he said. 'Don't worry about me. I'm in my own good and rightful company, and don't forget to tell Caleb and the others that what we did in the boat was all my idea.'

Micah blushed but did not demur and scurried off, soon lost from view.

'No backbone,' Alameth sighed.

'No backbone at all,' Heraldo agreed, the two of them a double act that had Lukitt creasing his brows, wondering if this could possibly be the first time they'd met.

'I'll come with,' he said hesitantly, fearing they'd forgotten he was there. They had not, as Heraldo and Alameth made immediately clear.

'But of course you will!' Alameth exclaimed.

'The hero of the hour!' Heraldo put in, an arm about Lukitt's shoulders pulling him on. 'Wouldn't think of leaving you behind.'

And they did not, and back behind the stage they went, Lukitt asking all sorts of questions about the pulleys, mechanisms and puppets; how they'd made the grumbling sounds of thunder, storm and rain, engineered the explosions and light shows, made the off-scene narrator's voice so loud.

All explained by Heraldo as they tucked into various sausages, gnocchi and noodles, Lukitt's eyes round and bright, taking in everything, wanting to make notes, wanting to remember it all, wanting to perform his own pageants the moment he got back to Seiden See, astound his fellows; thinking that perhaps Pregel's calling to be an oblate was not such a mad idea after all, not if it meant meeting the likes of Heraldo and Alameth who were opening up worlds upon worlds with every word they spoke.

Heraldo right about the Christmas pageant which lasted not one day but two: Lukitt watching closely, putting Heraldo's explanations to good use, trying to figure out how everything was being done.

His brief notoriety being devil's advocate eclipsed by the rest of the entertainments.

The Tower of Babel came and went, followed by the Exodus, the Trials of Job, the experiences of Ezekiel in the Valley of Bones that culminated in the most magnificent ascending into heaven of his chariot of fire anyone had ever seen.

The spectacles ending late afternoon of the second day with a moving rendition of the Nativity of the Christ Child, with singing shepherds and disparate Eastern Kings proffering gifts prefiguring the coming life and death of the Saviour.

After all was done, the monks went off to the chapel for mass, their Advent Sunday almost complete, all of them exhausted, fulfilled, brimming with the spirit of the season; able, ready and willing to subject themselves to the next few weeks of meditation, asceticism and prayer leading up to the forty eight hour fast that would only be broken on Christmas Eve, when the feasting – meagre as it might be – would begin. A regimen that hadn't changed in hundreds of years, the only difference now being the astounding spectacles put on for them by the Pfiffmaklers who'd exceeded every expectation; so far removed from the usual, dry-as-dust sermonising Mummers' Plays that were their normal Advent fare.

Two days not forgotten by any and, at the end of it, all looking forward to what the Pfiffmaklers would bring them the following year, assuming Abbot Ettershank could persuade them back.

'So,' Ulbert asked Lukitt, as they settled themselves into their allotted guestroom. 'What did you make of it? Did you enjoy yourself?'

'Enjoy it!' Lukitt beamed. 'I loved it! I've never seen anything like it! Heraldo explained some of the mechanisms and, if you'll allow it, I'd really like to experiment with their methods when we get back home.'

Ulbert raised his eyebrows.

'So you've forgiven me?' he asked, looking at Lukitt who was struggling with the knots his boot-laces had become.

Lukitt stopped his endeavours and frowned.

'I mean for not telling you about Pregel,' Ulbert explained. 'Your anger didn't pass me by.'

Lukitt coloured.

'It wasn't exactly anger,' he said, bending down once more to his task, unwilling to meet Ulbert's eye, though his fingers were still.

'That's exactly what it was,' Ulbert said. 'And I don't blame you. But you need to understand certain things pass between a priest and a member of his congregation that have to remain hidden. And Pregel's new vocation was one of them.'

'Was it his father who asked you to keep it secret?' Lukitt asked, daring to look at Ulbert, remembering what Opapa had said.

Ulbert tipped his head.

'Well, yes and no to that,' he said, sighing as he began to take off his own boots and socks, wiggling his toes in the cold confines of the room. 'We talked about it, his parents and I,' he went on. 'We all know how open and generous Pregel can be, and also that he's not the sharpest knife in the box. But when you had him sing for me, well, I saw a way out for him; a life more fulfilling than spending his next twenty or thirty years gutting fish on the side of the Seiden See. You see that, don't you?'

Lukitt saw, and nodded.

'But we'd no idea if he'd go for it,' Ulbert added. 'We'd no idea if he'd take to the life, if he could fit into its ways. It's no easy path to follow, being a monk – if that's what he ultimately chooses. It demands certain…strictures, certain abnegations of worldly desires. I only told Pregel about our suggested plans on the way up here because I knew, Lukitt, he could never keep such a secret from you.'

Lukitt closed his eyes, rubbed them with his fingers.

'I thought you'd both betrayed me,' he whispered. 'I thought you'd both gone behind my back. He's my only friend, the only one I've ever had.'

Ulbert went down on his knees in front of Lukitt, who was sitting on the corner of his bed, took Lukitt's hands in his own.

'I know,' he spoke gently. 'But there was no other way for it to go. Pregel's parents and I both agreed that if he liked it here, if he felt comfortable, if he thought that spending his days here singing and fitting in with all the other tasks…well. It could be a good life for him, a great life. Better than any he would otherwise have. But your life, Lukitt, yours is going to be something entirely different.'

Lukitt snorted, flinging away Ulbert's hands.

'But what is that to be?' he asked loudly. 'You've mapped out Pregel's life for him, but what about mine? I can't tell! Only that I don't want to be confined to Seiden See and this valley for the rest of my life, go back to the farm, God forbid.'

Ulbert shocked, not so much at Lukitt's outburst as at his entirely valid questions, for in truth neither Ulbert nor Lukitt's parents had thought so far ahead. They all knew Lukitt was as unusual in his own way as Pregel was in his, that he gleaned facts as a goose downs corn, but where to take it after Ulbert's schooling finished had never been discussed. University was never going to be an option, given Lukitt's family circumstances, not having the money to support such an option. But to educate a boy, give him hopes and then crush them would be unforgivable. So where to go next? Ulbert had no idea.

'There's scholarships,' he said weakly.

'Scholarships!' Lukitt spat. He knew all about them. 'They never go to people like me.'

Ulbert winced, for Lukitt was right. Scholarships went to well-connected people who knew well-connected people, and neither he nor Lukitt were of the sort. He tried to take Lukitt's hands again but Lukitt was having none of it.

'Maybe I should stay here too,' Lukitt said, quieter now. 'Maybe I should take my teaching from Opapa Augen. Maybe I should learn what I can and then let that learning go right down the pan.'

Lukitt sniffed back self-pitying tears. He knew he was being ridiculously self-important, but couldn't stop himself. He knew, just knew, he was better than this, better than the situation his birth had dropped him into; that all he needed was the chance he was never going to get, unless it was of his own making, and that it was never going to come from Ulbert, nor from his parents. Thinking instead on Heraldo and Alameth, a plan forming in his head, an escape strategy that might have actual legs if only he could put it to purpose, get it engineered, much as the Pfiffmaklers had brought on storm and ravage, light and dark, their sudden revealing of what no one had expected that had everyone gasping in its wake.

9

The Chapel Bells Ring Out, as Does Lukitt

Lukitt and Ulbert spent an uncomfortable night in the guestroom lying on their cots in darkness, in mutual silence, staring at a ceiling they couldn't see, both puzzling about possible future paths, before falling to uneasy sleep.

Lukitt woke first, rolled onto his side as he opened his eyes, seeing Ulbert on the opposite cot, grey-stubbled face closed and troubled as if Lukitt's harsh words of the night before still ran his sleeping through. Lukitt ashamed of his ingratitude, yet didn't regret voicing his doubts about where he was to go next. He blinked, sat up quickly, heart quickening as the memory of the mad plan he'd stumbled over in the night came to the fore, all the different pieces of it having shuffled through his dreams into definition.

He moved quiet and slow, unwilling to wake Ulbert; put on trousers, socks, boots and jacket and tiptoed across the floor, opened the door. Once outside, he saw the vast spectacle of the Gargellan valley opened up before him: the snow on the peaks of the dark mountains glimmering with the light of a sun not yet risen from behind their ranks. He regarded them with familiar awe, the longing to be a part of them strong, and yet the longing to leave them even stronger: so much more to see in the world, both Ulbert and the Pfiffmaklers proof of that.

He was startled by a small scraping sound coming from the direction of the chapel and turned his head, boots squeaking in the newly fallen snow as he changed direction, heart lurching as he made out a monstrous shape in the pre-dawn gloom.

'S'only me,' came the familiar voice of Pregel, as Lukitt made a hesitant approach.

'Pregel!' Lukitt said, letting out a long breath, hand over his heart. 'What on earth are you doing?'

'Chapel bell's stopped up with ice,' Pregel explained, tripping over the ladder he'd been attempting to manoeuvre against the chapel walls that had made the awful shadow Lukitt had just seen. 'Got to get it loosened. The Abbot wants me to sing at Lauds, but we can't do anything if the bell doesn't bring in the monks.'

'So you're what? Going to climb up and loosen it?' Lukitt asked, incredulous.

'That's the plan!' Pregel answered lightly.

'Like hell you are,' Lukitt butted in. 'Who's big idea was this anyway?'

'Not sure,' Pregel said and bit his lip. 'Old monk woke me up a bit ago and said it needed doing and no one nimbler.'

'Does he know you?' Lukitt asked, immediately wishing the words back, seeing the hurt on Pregel's face. 'Wait on,' Lukitt added quickly, striding up, taking the ladder from his friend and getting it stable, heaping a load of snow around its legs so it couldn't move.

'Get to the refectory,' Lukitt said. 'There's sure to be someone about. Get them to put hot water in a bucket, and fetch a broom, bring them both back.'

'So we'll do it together?' Pregel asked, Lukitt smiling broadly. Far better for him to do the hard part than Pregel. He'd bet money the old monk had been Caleb - or one of his cohorts - eager to put a dampener on things by setting Pregel an impossible task.

'Always together,' Lukitt said as Pregel scampered happily off, Lukitt starting up the ladder one rung at a time. It looked a daunting task from down below, but in fact the small cupola that housed the bell was not that much higher than the lowest part of the chapel's roof, separated from the top of the ladder only by a yard or two of snow-covered tiles. Lukitt most of the way up when Pregel got back with his bucket of hot water in one hand, broom in the other; the sounds of Lukitt's ascent, the scraping of his ladder against the guttering, and Pregel's return, bringing out a further spectator: Opapa Augen emerging from his crypt.

'My Lord!' Ommaweise declared loudly. 'What on earth are you doing? Is that Lukitt up there?'

'It's me, Opapa,' Lukitt shouted down. 'Bell's iced up, needs thawing. Pregel's got the doings.'

'Go careful, lad,' Opapa advised, not that Lukitt was doing otherwise.

'Lift me up the broom,' Lukitt commanded, Pregel sending it up head first so Lukitt could grasp it easily, get it manoeuvred into place, tail end lodged in the gutter ready for action.

'And now the bucket,' he called down, Pregel this time having to climb the rungs of the ladder with the bucket's handle crooked in his arm, slopping out a good deal of the contents, stopping as he got to the rung below the one holding Lukitt's boots.

'Good!' Lukitt called. 'Down one rung, Pregel, so I can get the broom in…'

Pregel obeyed, and Lukitt got the brush dipped and soaked in the hot water, moved its handle up and held the brush to the bell, going at the top axles that were just within reach, the hot water doing its job, melting the ice, so that after a few more applications the bell was swinging free.

'I'll go check!' Opapa said with enthusiasm, ducking back down the steps to his crypt and out a door the other side that led directly into the chapel, going to the small hidey hole that hid the bell-pull and tugging on it hard. The bell ringing out clear and loud, so loud Lukitt juddered on his ladder with the shock of it, and then began his descent, bumping into Pregel on his way down.

'Job well done,' Lukitt said as he and Pregel hit the snow, Pregel dropping the pail of hot water on his descent, a circle of melt-water opening about his feet.

'Job well done!' Pregel repeated, laughing loudly, jumping in and out of the newly created circle, plainly delighted; Lukitt looking on, wondering what his life was going to be like without Pregel by his side. Interrupted by Opapa going hard at the bell, bringing every monk from every cell, along with any willing guests from their guestrooms. The only folk not present being the Pfiffmaklers, who had their own tents and carts and kept their own hours.

But this was Pregel's moment, and soon enough the monks crowded into the chapel, if a little sleepily, and right on time.

Lukitt didn't follow.

He was waiting for one monk in particular or, more precisely, one novice. Not overly surprised when Alameth appeared later than everyone else, rubbing the sleep from his eyes, yawning and stretching, one boot undone so the laces kept catching on the other, tripping him from side to side. By then Pregel's voice was coming clear and pure from the chapel, Alameth making for the door, arrested by Lukitt grabbing at his arm.

'What the…Lukitt?' Alameth muttered. 'Is that you? What the hell are you doing? No need for guests to be out…'

'I just wanted to ask you something,' Lukitt said, keeping his voice low.

'About what?' Alameth asked blearily, wishing he was back in his bed, wishing he was anywhere but here in the snow, shivering with the cold.

'What if you could get away?' Lukitt asked. 'What if you could go and explore the world, like you've always wanted?'

Alameth blinked, let out a breath.

'Can't do nothing about that,' he said. 'Too many brothers and sisters. No way to provide all of us a trade or a good marriage. Parents have me here, and no going back.'

'But what if you didn't have to stay here and you didn't have to go back?' Lukitt persisted, a little breathlessly. 'And what if I don't either? What if we two took off into the world on our own?'

Alameth stopped halfway through a yawn and looked closely at Lukitt.

'And how're we to do that?' he asked, scrunching up his eyes a couple of times to wake himself up, better understand the proposal being put to him.

Lukitt let out a long breath, watched it curl into vapour and disappear.

'I'm just thinking,' he said, very quietly, 'that perhaps the two of us have reached the end of where we're going: you here, me down the valley.'

Alameth leaned back.

'But I thought you had it fine,' he said. 'From what I've been told you've been plucked from your little farm and stuffed into a school with all the learning you could want.'

Lukitt grimaced.

'But that's just it!' he exclaimed. 'That's exactly it! Yes I have, and I've learned and learned and I want to learn more. But how am I going to do that? Once I've reached the end of next year's schooling and grade out with all the rest that will be the end of it. And I can't bear it, Alameth. I can't bear to think that everything I've done will go to waste, that I'll never be able to take it further.'

Alameth shook his head, sympathising.

'It's a money thing, Lukitt,' he stated baldly. 'It's trapped me here and it'll trap you there. I don't see how there's a way out of it.'

'There's always a way out,' Lukitt announced after a short silence, 'and two together will get on better than one.'

'Are you suggesting we run away with the circus? Or with the Pfiffmaklers, to be more precise?' Alameth smiling despite the cold, for the idea had occurred to him in his wilder moments, particularly after meeting Heraldo. Not that he'd really considered the option viable, for what on earth could he possibly offer the Pfiffmaklers that they didn't already have?

He stomped his feet to get his circulation going.

'I've really got to be off,' he said. 'Folks'll be missing me, and that means more black marks and more duties on the latrines…'

Alameth made to move away but was halted by Lukitt gripping once more at his arm.

'I've a plan,' Lukitt confided. 'Just listen for one minute, just one minute…'

Alameth bided and Alameth listened, Alameth thinking Lukitt's plan might not be so half-arsed as he'd assumed it would be at the start.

'I'm not talking about running away with the Fair,' Lukitt explained. 'I'm talking about you and me leaving this valley, maybe in the spring. No point doing anything now, not with winter on us. But give it three or four months, Alameth. Give it until Easter. Give me time to check out opportunities, see where we lie, where we can go and how. Do you really want to spend the rest of your life here? Don't you think we both deserve better than that?'

'Still the devil's advocate,' Alameth commented slowly, Lukitt lowering his head, closing his eyes, sure Alameth had made up his mind. 'On the other hand,' Alameth added brightly, slapping a hand on Lukitt's shoulders, 'if anyone can plan our escape and put it into action then I believe it's you. And if you can come up with anything seriously doable, Lukitt, then come Easter I'll be with you all the way.'

Lukitt let out a breath, eyes shining with the first rays of the sun as its outer circle nudged above the snow-clad peaks of the hills.

'I'll not let you down,' Lukitt said quietly, grasping Alameth's hand and shaking it warmly.

'I really don't believe you will,' Alameth answered, 'and now…'

'Of course,' Lukitt said. 'Go…'

'Until Easter?'

'Until Easter.'

Alameth turned away, tripped once but not again as he strode towards the chapel, Pregel's voice swimming slow and clear as a mountain stream from the highest note of the Salzburg Psalm to the lowest, and with it the words that epitomised Advent:

He will give the childless woman a son and a joyous home.

Praise the Lord.

Praise the Lord indeed.

Alameth smiling, lifting his head to the rising sun, looking back when he'd got to the chapel's doors to see Lukitt taking the ladder away from the bell-tower's wall and laying it carefully in the snow, Lukitt suddenly jumping into the space between the first rung and the second, and then the second and the third, arms outstretched, eyes closed, as if his feet already knew where to go, as if they were already setting out on their unknown journey.

'If anyone can do it…' Alameth murmured, putting his hand to the chapel door.

The following morning Alameth went to the Abbot saying he was having doubts about his vocation, asking to defer the final taking of his vows.

'Until when, young man?' Ettershank demanded. 'This is most irregular, most irregular.'

'Only a few months, Abbot,' Alameth asked piteously, Ettershank understanding, knowing the stirring the Pfiffmaklers had caused within their ranks, the window they'd cast on an unseen world stretching out beyond the walls and mountains of their little monastery. But by end of day the Pfiffmaklers and their intoxicating tales would be gone.

'Very well, Alameth,' Ettershank decided. 'But I would have you remain in your cell the next few days to contemplate your decision. I'll send in Brother Caleb to keep you company at prayers, guide you towards the right path.'

Ettershank could have laughed out loud to see the immediate expression of dismay on Alameth's face at this pronouncement, well aware Caleb went at Alameth like bristles on a brush, the two going together worse than sugar with salt. But let the boy suffer just a little and, to give him his due, Alameth soon got his face under control and presented himself with due humility if not quite the words Ettershank had been expecting.

'As you say, Abbot,' Alameth managed to get out. 'If anything, anyone, can assist me in my decision then you've chosen rightly in Brother Caleb.'

Abbot Ettershank dismissed Alameth then, but there was no laughter now, internal or otherwise, for he understood that something else, someone else, other than the Pfiffmaklers, had got to young Alameth, and for the life of him he couldn't think who that might be, only that Alameth might truly be lost and only a few months to try to get him back.

10

Lenten Longings

Ulbert had a surprise for Lukitt when they arrived back in Seiden See. Both were tired and cold, but Lukitt soon had a couple of mugs of hot chocolate at the ready and Ulbert didn't want to wait any longer.

'Look what I've brought you,' he announced, humping in a crate and dumping it down in the middle of the floor, the effort making him flap his arms like a wet cormorant to rid himself of the sweat gathered in his armpits.

'What is it?' Lukitt asked, uninterested, his mind on other things, specifically what he'd talked about with Alameth. Ulbert looked embarrassed and turned away, poured himself a glass of much needed wine.

'I thought about what you said, and I spoke to Opapa Augen,' Ulbert explained, taking a couple of quick gulps, 'and he agreed to lend us some books so you can continue your learning in science such as I can't provide myself.'

Lukitt stood, astonished.

'You did that for me?' he asked quietly.

'Happy Christmas,' Ulbert said, handing Lukitt a crowbar to lever up the lid, and then the two of them began to laugh as they went down on their knees and cracked open the crate together, scattering the many volumes about them on floor and table as they moved from one discovery to the next like pebbles rolling on an incoming tide.

'Here's Jacques Cassini's book on electricity!' Lukitt said excitedly. 'Remember you mentioned it in your essay on using Leyden jars to stimulate nerves in frogs and fruit flies?'

'I do!' Ulbert was as enthusiastic, finding gaps in his own library he'd dearly like to fill. 'And I've a copy here of Berthollet's work with Lavoisier on their reinvention of chemical nomenclature...'

'Ooh...' Lukitt interrupted. 'Look at this,' Ulbert looking as Lukitt held up a copy of Robert Hooke's *Micrografia*. 'These illustrations of fleas are amazing…'

Lukitt silent for a few moments as he flipped the pages from fleas to bees to flies to caterpillars, before Ulbert broke in.

'And here's something by Christiaan Huygens describing his work on air pumps and telescopes! Maybe we could have a go at making them ourselves, if we can scavenge the parts.'

'And John Napier!' Lukitt interrupted. 'He was a genius. A real, proper genius…'

Lukitt gasping as he moved from one volume to the next, Ulbert's throat constricting with pride to see his young protégé hop-skipping through centuries of knowledge, no longer placing them at random but beginning to grade the books into piles: which he would read first, then second, then third, constantly changing his small stacks until he was finally satisfied, Lukitt rocking back on his heels and sighing with delighted content.

'Thank you, Ulbert,' Lukitt's voice was tight, his smile wavering, wanting to blurt out his plans but not wanting to blunt the moment. 'I thought that maybe after what I said at the monastery…well…'

Ulbert shook his head.

'You've no need to apologise. You were right. And this,' Ulbert waved his hand about him, 'this is Brother Ommaweise's doing, not mine.'

'I don't agree,' Lukitt demurred, as if he was up on that stage again amidst the Pfiffmaklers' lights and smoke, 'this is all you,' Lukitt insisted. 'I don't know what I'd have done…'

'You'd have done just fine,' Ulbert broke in, standing up, brushing his hands on his cassock to free them of book dust, Lukitt sneezing loudly several times.

'Shall I get the supper on?' Lukitt asked, once he'd finished pinching his nose shut several times, smiling up apologetically.

'I think you should,' Ulbert said mildly. 'It strikes me we've miles to go to get through this pile of learning, and miles to go means meals to see us through.'

The two of them settling back into their days, passing through Epiphany, Candlemas, Septuagesima and into Lent. Lukitt spending his days before and after school buried in his books. Every spare second not doing that used up by running down ginnels visiting shops and traders, doing odd jobs here and there for anyone who could provide them, amassing a sparse knowledge of what they did and how they did it, and a small stash of coins kept in a box beneath his bed. Ulbert's Christmas gift of Opapa's crate of books doing nothing to diminish his wanting to get on and out and do better for himself, instead exacerbating his expectations of what he might be capable of, if given the opportunity.

Lukitt's immersion in his studies - and his extracurricular activities about the town – not passing Ulbert by, neither their conversation at the monastery, and he too had not been idle. He'd written to every academy he knew of to ask about scholarships, called in every favour he could with people in positions of authority; had gone several times up the valley to speak to Nethanel about Lukitt's prospects. But despite all his efforts the answers remained the same: nothing doing for Lukitt Bachmann.

Once his schooling was over later that year in Seiden See Lukitt's only option would be to find employment, carry on his studies with the help of Ulbert and Opapa, no possibility of eliciting external financial support to put them to better use: too young to be employed as a tutor; too impoverished to enter any college, university or academy; too inexperienced to be employed by any publisher or bookbinder that might further a career in academia.

Nothing anyone could do about it, Ulbert thought dejectedly, except by Lukitt himself; and what Lukitt could do about it Ulbert had no idea, nor that Lukitt had already come up with a plan of his own.

'Can I talk to you a moment?' Lukitt asked Ulbert, a week or so before Easter, while Ulbert was busy scribbling out his notes on the various sermons that would be needed.

'Can't it wait?' Ulbert asked abstractedly, jotting down what specimens he was going to take up to the Gargellan monastery for his Annual Easter address.

The Pfiffmaklers had really put the pincers on, raising expectations.

'I really don't think it can,' Lukitt said, Ulbert looking up from his desk, seeing Lukitt standing there with his hands held over his stomach, fingers entwined but moving rhythmically, his face as serious as Ulbert had ever seen, felt a dark cloud gathering on his horizon and laid down his pen.

'Whatever is it?' Ulbert asked, heart churning hard within his chest.

'I know you've not forgotten all we talked about before, up at the monastery, and I know you got Opapa Augen to lend us his books and that you've written letters, talked to my parents, done all you can.'

'I have,' Ulbert managed to get out, all breath leaving his body, making it hard to speak. He'd thought the answers to those letters hadn't been seen, hadn't wanted to raise expectations only to dash them, but apparently that was not the case. Not that Ulbert had exactly hidden them, for they'd been filed away in his bureau and it was one of Lukitt's duties to keep his bureau in good order.

'I didn't forget either,' Lukitt forged on. 'And I made a plan then, one I've been working on all this while with the hope of seeing it through.'

Ulbert knitted his fingers together, knuckle clutching hard to knuckle. He should've known Lukitt would never let it go; should've known this day was coming; felt a hard knot in his stomach at what would come next.

'It's not that I'm ungrateful, Ulbert, you know that's not the case,' Lukitt went on, Ulbert nodding dumbly. 'It's just there's so much more I want to do, so much more world out there to explore.'

He looked over at Ulbert who'd taken off his glasses, very slowly folding down the temples and placing them on his pile of sermon papers, glasses Lukitt knew to have been hand-made by Opapa Augen, Lukitt sucking in a breath and rubbing one hand over the other.

'I know I'm young,' he said, 'but if I go, I won't be going alone.'

Ulbert looked up sharply.

'What do you mean, go? And with whom?' he asked, thinking immediately of Pregel, but surely Lukitt wouldn't drag him away from Gargellan. All reports from there stated quite clearly that Pregel was settling in better than expected, loving his new life, and certainly not wanting to leave; though he wouldn't put it past him if Lukitt begged.

'Alameth will come with me,' Lukitt added suddenly, Ulbert so relieved he laughed short and sharp.

'Alameth won't leave a feathered nest unless you give him better,' Ulbert said lightly, the words out before he'd thought them through, immediately regretting his flippancy on seeing the defiance flit across Lukitt's face.

'I'm sorry, lad,' Ulbert hurried on. 'But I've known Alameth as long as he's been up at Gargellan and he's always been talking about getting out, but it's always been talk, Lukitt. He won't go, not at the end of it.'

Lukitt curled his toes within his boots, cheeks flushing hotly.

'He said he would...' Lukitt began, Ulbert standing up and coming alongside him.

'People say a lot of things, but you can't believe them all. And anyway, what would happen to the farm if you went? Hermistus and Hermione can't last forever, and your parents are relying on you to take over their...'

'I'm not going back to the farm!' Lukitt shouted, brushing away the arm Ulbert had placed loosely about Lukitt's shoulders, Ulbert unnerved when Lukitt stamped his foot loudly on the wooden floor.

'Now wait a minute,' Ulbert growled, taking a step forwards, grasping Lukitt firmly, keeping his hot young body pinned into immobility, authority coming to the fore. 'We've all duties in this life, and I know you think you're better than staying here in Seiden See but you've other people to think on, most notably your parents.'

Lukitt pushed against his bounds, but Ulbert held him fast.

'We've done everything we can for you, and don't forget for a second they've made sacrifices by allowing you to stay here with me, take advantage of all the schooling not many have the privilege of. And Lord knows we've tried, Lukitt. We've tried to find you a way out, but sometimes you have to accept the situation you're in, make the best of what you've got. Opapa and I will carry on trying, and in time there's no reason you shouldn't become a teacher at the school. Widow Mengel will be retiring soon...'

'It's not enough!' Lukitt protested, wriggling free from Ulbert's grip. 'How can you show me all this and then snatch it away again? It's not enough!'

'It's a damn site more than most people your age and position get,' Ulbert shot back, his empty hands shaking with anger. It took a lot to rile him, but he was angered now. 'And right now, Lukitt, you need to weigh up your options, because I'll not tolerate this kind of ingratitude, nor hubris, come to that. It's Lent after all, time to admit our humility before God and realise what we have before wilfully throwing it all away.'

Lukitt subsided, sat down on the crate of books ready to be taken back to the monastery the following week, his mouth curled in an ugly scowl.

'It's not right,' Lukitt got out between clenched teeth.

'It may not be right, young man,' Ulbert relented, voice softening, for he should have seen the signs, forestalled this day before it came, known that it was inevitable, that building a path halfway through a forest would foster expectation of the wanderer getting out the other side. 'But that's the way it is. I'm sorry,' he added, 'but there's no reason you can't be content here. Look at me,' he tried to sound jovial, 'halfway around the world and yet it's this place I ended up in, and never regretted it for a moment.'

'Not for a moment? A single moment?' Lukitt asked, looking into Ulbert's eyes, hoping to see it was true, that Ulbert had been content in doing so, and that maybe Lukitt would be able to do the same.

'Not for a moment,' Ulbert replied, but was a beat too late and both knew it, and both turned from one other at the lie. 'Well, maybe for a moment,' Ulbert attempted to redeem himself, attempted a humour he didn't feel, thought on Trudl and Nethanel effectively indentured up at the farm, how they'd arrived there, how they could've bowed their heads to the Herrnhuter Elders and taken the easy way but instead had struck out into the unknown. Ultimate result being Lukitt here sitting abjectly on Opapa Augen's crate of books, a boy who could be broken here and now, or who could have his opportunities opened up before him like any of the books in that crate.

'So what's this plan of yours?' Ulbert asked softly, letting out a breath. 'Only tell me, Lukitt, and I'll back you to the hilt.'

11

Clear Blue Skies

Easter came early, back end of March when Lukitt and Ulbert returned to the monastery of Gargellan for the Easter service only two days away.

'Have you got it planned, then?' Alameth cornered Lukitt, soon as he was able.

'I have,' Lukitt smiled eagerly. 'You still up for it?' thinking on what Ulbert had said of Alameth, how he blew with the wind.

Alameth chewed his lip, and Lukitt held his breath.

'Think so. Depends on what's what,' Alameth said, without the absolute commitment Lukitt had hoped to hear. 'But I can't wait long,' Alameth added, 'it's either I go now or I stay.'

In truth, neither one of them had yet certainly decided they would go. Lukitt told Alameth of his small stash of coins and Ulbert's arrangements if they chose to take the path away, but it was a huge decision now they'd come down to it, and both were having doubts. Lukitt was fifteen, Alameth a year older, so to step out into the world on their own would be a formidable undertaking.

'Let's think on it,' Alameth advised. 'You said Ulbert could fix us to go on the boats? But I know absolutely nothing about boats.'

'Nor me,' Lukitt admitted, 'but Ulbert's on our side, has arranged us places with some old friend of his if we really want to go ahead with it. Few years on the Seiden See and then right out of Austria and into Italy.'

'Italy!' Alameth whispered. 'But that's like the ends of the earth!'

'Well, not quite,' Lukitt put his co-conspirator straight. 'It's actually not that far away. Just needs a bit of getting to.'

A bit of getting to was all they thought about whilst the Easter services went on, Lukitt wondering if he could really do it – leave Ulbert, leave his parents in the lurch, leave everything behind. Alameth less conflicted but less brave, more convinced than ever that he was unsuited to this life since the Abbot had sent Caleb so regularly to his cell in his confinement. If anyone had convinced him this life was not for him then it hadn't been Lukitt but Brother Caleb: so strictured, so stern, so absolutely implacable to any point of view other than his own. And yet still Alameth was not convinced that going was the right thing to do. He'd it peachy here, as Ulbert had predicted he would think; he'd a home, food, shelter, companionship and purpose, all on-going for the rest of his life, and that could not be dismissed.

Alameth and Lukitt, two lads who didn't know how to go, until they were brought out of their respective beds by the shouts and yells that told them something was terribly wrong.

'What's happening?' Alameth wondered sleepily, joining the other novices and lay brothers who were deserting their cells and running out into the early dawn.

'Pregel's up on the roof!' was the first Lukitt heard about it, dragged up from his bed by Ulbert, Lukitt confused, managing to shove his boots onto his feet and get himself upright, staggering out into the snow that had been there since the first week of March, snow that had melted briefly before hardening into an underlying slick of hardened ice below the rest that had fallen since.

'Got to free the bell!' Pregel shouted out merrily to those down below, Lukitt newly amongst them, a shiver running though his belly to see Pregel astride the coping tiles of the roof.

'How did he get up there?' someone asked of nobody.

'Ladder, I should think,' another replied. 'And for some reason he's a broom with him.'

'Oh my heavens!' Lukitt moaned, running forward, righting the ladder that had fallen sideways in the snow. 'Pregel! It's me, it's Lukitt. Don't move! Don't move an inch, d'you hear me? Don't move an inch!'

But Pregel, on hearing his friend's voice, moved not one inch but two, and not two inches but many, shifting his butt along the line of the coping tiles towards the bell.

'It's got stuck again,' Pregel announced, 'and I saw how you did it before…'

'No!' Lukitt shouted, voice hard and taut. 'No, Pregel. Stay where you are! I'll be up in a minute.'

But Pregel didn't wait, Pregel moved, Pregel had the broom within his hands and started shoving it at the bell, heart happy and glad that Lukitt was here, happier and gladder that this was the day he would take his vows, sing to the high heavens the miracle of Easter; happy and glad, until his backside slithered on the icy pinnacle, the broom throwing him off balance, no hands to steady him, letting go of the broom, the two of them slithering down the roof only to be stopped by the guttering, the broom teetering for a moment on the brink before tipping over the edge, Pregel gaping, laying his body flat against the roof, immensely relieved a moment later when Lukitt's head popped up.

'Hold still, Pregel,' Lukitt commanded, 'just hold still.'

And for once, Pregel did as told. Lukitt had slightly miscalculated, the ladder a little to Pregel's left, Lukitt leaning towards him, stretching out his arm, not quite reaching.

'Shift the ladder!' Lukitt shouted down, frustrated. 'Just pick it up and shift it with me on...No! Pregel, no!'

Pregel already moving, peeling himself off the snowy tiles, shuffling his boots along the guttering towards Lukitt, leaning too far over to get purchase, holding out his hand to his friend.

'Nearly got it...' Pregel murmured, making one last push, one last shuffle, overbalancing, tipping forward, flipping over, hands trying to grab at Lukitt, Lukitt trying to grab at him, Lukitt's face pale and contorted in his helplessness as Pregel's oddly serene face passed him by - brain too slow to catch up with what was happening – Pregel plummeting spread-eagled through the air, Pregel landing two seconds later, neck snapping clean through as he hit the compacted ice, bones breaking audibly, pink blush forming about his head in the snow.

People rushing forward.

Hands going to mouths.

'Oh Jesu, oh my Lord, my God, my God...'

Hands turning Pregel over.

Hands cradling Pregel's head.

Clear blue eyes staring sightless into the clear blue sky, dawn come so quickly no one noticed.

Death come so quickly no one could pass it by.

Pregel taking the quick way down, as he'd done from many a tree, but no getting up from it this time.

'Pregel!' Lukitt wailed, as he got down from his ladder, ran over to his friend.

'No, lad,' Caleb, of all people, snatching at Lukitt's arm and holding him back.

'Pregel…' Lukitt wept, Caleb's old arm about Lukitt's shoulder, Caleb's old chin coming to rest on Lukitt's head, Pregel locked away from Lukitt as others picked him up and bore his young broken body away.

And that was it.

Decision made.

Pregel's death too unnecessary and harsh to talk about.

Lukitt and Alameth choosing their own beyond because of it, no point havering when life might end at any moment; better to opt for unknown risks and rewards than never have the chance of either; Ulbert seeing the sense of it - no more talking, no more persuasion on either side - Lukitt and Alameth offered and taking the employment Ulbert had arranged for them on the fishing boats that plied the Seiden See, and with it the ability to save some earnings, attempt to get away from this dying no one could find any earthly reason for, nor a Godly one either.

Even Caleb was softened. Even Caleb blessed himself every night that he was still alive to see the snow going and the spring coming in, blessing himself when he noticed a new leaf on the pea shoots in the kitchen garden, a new flower on the bean plants.

Even Caleb – hardened, embittered and blinkered as he was - recognising some truth in what Lukitt had espoused at the Christmas pageant, and that God's Plan, admittedly unknown and unknowable, might have its faults.

12

Wooden Hooks, Bone Implements

New beginning for Lukitt and Alameth, Ulbert making the transition as easy as he could, both remaining in the manse under Ulbert's care while they learned their trade on the waters of the Seiden See. The two tasked, under tutelage of their skipper - Ulbert's friend, Grizzle Fischer – to run *Die Holzhaken*, The Wooden Hook, up one end of the lake, slowly covering their allotted span, then back to shore at end of day, all the while hand-hauling for trout, deep-trawling for char, sometimes lowering dead-baits into the reeds to pull in pike.

In eel-season they laid baskets at the mouths of the trip streams running into the lake and these were Lukitt's best days, when he was left to his own devices. Dropped at one part of the bank, picked up at another; laying the traps at dawn, emptying them at dusk; threading the eels onto sticks or into sacks, pushing them on a small hand-barrow, waving out to the *Holzhaken* when the load got too heavy and the barrow too full, Alameth jumping into the water that had warmed about the lake's edges, delighting in the shirt and trousers he now wore instead of his scratchy habit, the two of them hauling the catch out to the boat and returning to port.

Up then came the housewives, wanting this, wanting that, bargaining, pushing; Lukitt and Alameth sitting on the jetty's edge dressing the fish as needed: gutting, top and tailing, skinning for extra, filleting for more. The leftovers they took home to Ulbert: anything unsold that wasn't claimed by the smoker or taken up to the Castle, whose white parapets could be glimpsed above the dark forests at the farthest end of the Seiden See.

On the long lazy days of that summer on the boat Lukitt sits on deck, tweaking his lines every now and then, looking through his books in the interim; Alameth choosing to chatter with the skipper, who was as full of stories and advice as anyone Alameth had ever met. Lukitt watches the shadow of the mast upon the water, works out its length, calculates how many times it will fit into the shadow of the mountain on the other side of the boat, thereby figuring out the height of the mountain, how long it will take him and Alameth to cross it when they head for Italy, the real adventure the two young men crave.

He never wastes a moment, scoops up cups of water looking for *Daphnia, Hydra medusae* or other inverts he can later examine under Ulbert's microscope. He gets nipped by a backswimmer that is clinging upside-down underwater, Lukitt swearing, repaying the offender by imprisoning it in one of his many jars, snipping off its legs, dissecting its body, examining its fearsome beak, cutting out its poisoned fangs.

Monsters all, no matter how small.

Pregel not forgotten, nor the cruelty of his demise.

Come autumn, Lukitt looks up at the clouds, sees them piled in plates above the mountain tops, tracks the nimbostrati and tries to estimate how long before the boat will be deluged with rain; tries to rate wind speed by licking his thumb as Grizzle Fischer does, although whether the skipper is right or wrong when he makes his pronouncements is hard to say. Rain is rain and sleet is sleet, but whether the wind runs by at ten or fifteen miles an hour is anyone's guess. Old Grizzle says he feels it in his water, says his bladder gets tighter and tighter the colder the weather gets; proves it by peeing frequently over the side of the boat, spraying anyone foolish enough to stand beside him who doesn't possess his knowledge of which way blows the wind.

Eighteen months in, and there was a very arresting piece of news to mention, one that had Alameth leaping up and down.

'The annual Boar Hunt! And we're really going on it?'

Grizzle Fischer smiling deep within his enormous beard.

'Always been the way, boys; chosen apprentices from every trade getting a chance at it, drafted in to help the Graf's men,' remembering his first time out: the thrum of blood within his veins as he stalked those elusive beasts through the forest with his fellows, stench of the boars' rutting strong in the air; idea being to pick off the weaker ones, leave the strongest to carry on their mating with the sows.

'Bit of a competition,' Grizzle went on, 'between the trades, like. So make sure you lads do me proud.'

Alameth nodding vigorously, although Lukitt could see a problem.

'We're not supposed to actually…shoot them?' he asked tentatively, because if that were the case he and Alameth were going to let Grizzle down a bottomless pit, for he'd never handled a gun in his life, and he'd put money on it Alameth hadn't either. Grizzle looked at Lukitt, the slender boy so studious with his books, books that Grizzle had less familiarity with than Lukitt obviously had with guns, big smile forming beneath his beard, shaking his head, trying not to laugh.

'You're all right there, boy,' he assured, letting out a few chuckles despite himself. 'Guessing you don't know much about what goes on up at the castle?'

An easy guess, and a right one, Grizzle knowing Lukitt had spent his early years in the hills with Hermistus, a hard man who didn't give a cuss about the Graf, Hermistus being owner of his own land, unlike the folk around the Seiden See.

'It's like this,' he explained. 'Graf's the big man around these parts. Them Von Juskels've run this place forever, right from them forests you see over there,' he swept an arm to indicate the vast thickets that grew up from the western side of the lake, 'and the mountains that go up beyond.'

Lukitt looked. It seemed impossible one man, one family, could claim such huge tracts of lands as their own.

'Even when that Napoleon fella took Vienna,' Grizzle went on, 'gave away our Voralbergs to Bavaria,' a small sigh escaping him as he regarded the hills to the east, bitterness still burning thirty odd years later that some foreigner – and a Frenchie at that - had been allowed to step in uninvited and arbitrarily give away where he'd spent half his childhood.

'Anywise,' he went on, pulling at his beard, clearing his throat, shuffling off the memories, 'none of that mattered to the Von Juskels, and quite right too. Just went on like before. *Tradition is Tradition*, the old Graf said, and the son ain't no different. So thing is this,' he looked hard at Lukitt and Alameth, pointing his finger first at one and then the other. 'Here in Seiden See we've leatherworkers, we've wainwrights, bakers, weavers and fishermen. And we're the fishermen. You're the fishermen, an' every year during the hunt we send in our best, get them to do the tracking and beating, drive the boars towards the Graf's hunters. An' that's what you two are going to do.'

Alameth's earlier boldness deserted him.

'But how?' he asked. 'I've not the first notion how to go about it.'

Quick glance at Lukitt, who shook his head, for he'd no idea either.

'Good job you've me, then,' Grizzle smiled at them, clapping their two shoulders with each of his large hands, ''cos I done it years back, an' lots of times. Thing to remember is this: get keen in at the start; get yourselves noticed by your huntsman afore he gets out into the woods, let him know you're his beaters, let him know you're going to bring the boars out to east or west, north or south. Don't matter which, just make sure you're all going the same direction.'

Grizzle free with information, telling them everything he knew: what boar scat looked like, how to distinguish their trails from others made by deer or badgers, how to scent them, how to take a board with them to thrash at the undergrowth to drive them on.

'Working together's the thing,' was his last piece of advice. 'Figure out with your huntsman some whistles and signs. Work together, an' you'll not go far wrong.'

13

From Boar to Beetle

The night before the hunt, those who'd come from Seiden See congregated in the courtyard of the castle around a huge fire, a thick jostle of apprentices mingling with castle boys who were liberal with their drink to keep out the cold.

'Bit of a big one, this,' said the lad lodged beside Lukitt on one of the crude benches dragged out of a barn for the purpose.

'How so?' Lukitt asked, his companion drawing back his head in exaggerated surprise.

'Mean you don't know?' cocking his head to one side, wide smile revealing crooked teeth. 'Well guess not, you being one of them down below,' shaking his head like a wise old man.

'Guess not,' Lukitt commented mildly, which had the desired effect – namely that the boy couldn't spill the beans fast enough.

'It's for the wedding,' he informed Lukitt in quick hushed tones. 'Graf's oldest daughter. Twenty five, she is,' shaking his head, for twenty five was tantamount to being a crone when it came to marriage in these parts. 'Getting shoved off on some Italian bloke who couldn't hook one of his own. That `un there,' he added, nodding his head towards the huntsmen clustered at the top end of the courtyard who were inspecting their horses, making sure they were fed and ready. 'See the one in the yellow?'

Lukitt followed his informant's direction, distinguishing from the crowd a middle-aged man paunched over by an incongruous yellow jerkin; had a mild stab of regret for the unknown woman about to be handed into the care of a man who would choose to dress like that, which was like nothing he'd ever seen.

'And there's more,' his companion went on. 'First time out for the Graf's youngest, and he's only five, going on six Wants to give him a taste of thrill and kill, and the whippersnapper's right up for it. Got his own horse - if you can call a small pony a horse, as we're obliged to.'

Lukitt's fellow went quiet, took himself off shortly afterwards to bed down in his blanket, get some kip, Lukitt and Alameth doing the same; waking up five and a half hours later, jaws cracking with their yawning, eyes bloodshot and weeping with the cold air. But the enthusiasm was contagious and the two were soon pitching in with the rest as directed: rubbing leather pouches with neat's foot oil, greasing guns, slotting bullets into purses and bandoliers, introduced to the huntsman they'd be aiding: a man grandly uniformed, intimidating on his steed, stepping up in his stirrups as he looked down on his beaters, seeing two scraggly village boys who'd plainly never done this before, inwardly cursing the lot that had arbitrarily given such ingénues to his camp.

'Beat fast,' he ordered Lukitt and Alameth. 'Move through the trees, one to the left and one to the right on my command; keep about twenty yards between you. Move off the main paths quick as you're able…'

'Shouldn't we first establish a code of communication?' Lukitt interrupted, the Graf's huntsman looking down on the Fischer boy with a modicum of curiosity, assigned dunces so often he no longer bothered with finesse.

'You've suggestions?' he asked, Lukitt producing a piece of paper from his pocket and a whistle, thrusting both forward, the man having to lean down to take them from Lukitt's hand.

'One short blast,' the man read out loud, 'followed by two long if it's going straight ahead, two short blasts followed by one long if it's going to the left, one…'

He lowered himself in his saddle and looked at the boy who'd handed him this paper, this code, that could possibly win him the day. And winning the day meant winning his way up the Graf's ladder – possible top huntsman at the end of it, a prize worth the fight.

'How'd you get this?' the huntsman asked, suspicious, fearing betrayal, wondering why he'd never thought of such an obviously efficacious system before.

'Just made it last night,' Lukitt offered, 'not much time, but thought if we could head the boar off to top left of the forest...'

Looking over at Alameth, who was fingering his own copy of

Lukitt's codes, Lukitt looking back up at the huge man on his huge horse, wondering if he'd overstepped the mark, if he'd interpreted Grizzle's advice on the wrong side of the divide.

He hadn't. The huntsman was delighted.

'Right then,' he decided. 'That's how it will be done. Whistle loud enough and I'll hear and...' he was about to say obey, but obeying a boy was beneath him. 'I'll be about a hundred yards up from you, so you'll need to run fast and quick to keep yourselves up,' and off he went, horse and man champing to be gone.

'Gotta do it now, then,' Alameth whispered, never so confident as Lukitt had been in their plan. Lukitt nodding.

'We can do it,' Lukitt said, heart thumping with excitement, remembering Grizzle's words:

Them boar are cunning beasts, slippery as soap; think on that, think ahead o`them, and whatever you do don't get too close.

Remembering the outlay of the forest as Grizzle had detailed them: the Eberswald in shape broadly triangular, the point of it starting at the Kleine-Seiden, a small tarn of bulrush and reeds; to the right, a long-layered hedge of hazel inter-planted with blackthorn and briar and near impenetrable for anything save the smallest or most determined; the left edge dropping sheer away into a chasm through which flowed a rocky river - not wide, but deep - and with no bridges save several fallen trees into which some chiseller had carved out footholds so a strong headed person could cross with ease, but not a boar. The wood filled with oak and ash, some beech and lilac, holly, birch and several crabs – a democracy of species that tailed off into pine and spruce as it furthered itself away from the apex and up the mountains. Through the lower part went several wide thoroughfares, well demarcated, with numerous pathways winding and twisting off through low branch and undergrowth that ended back on the main walkways, or else sank into mire and morass, or terminated abruptly for no apparent reason, forcing you to retrace your steps.

Twenty odd huntsmen reining in their eager horses, forty odd boys behind them, two assigned to one, all waiting, eyes bright, hearts pumping, stamping their feet, rubbing their hands against the cold, other hands clutched about reins, about beating boards, everyone loading up: bags on backs, knapsacks around necks, guns on shoulders. Lukitt focussing briefly on an ash tree that was growing all on its own midway between the lochan and forest, wondering how it had come to be there all alone.

Then came the signal they'd all been waiting for: the *ooooo-eeeee whaooo-eeee* coming from the horn sounded from the very top of the Graf's tower, and they were off. Front of the pack were the Graf and his oldest son, done up like woodcock in brown leather and muted velvet; next came the Groom-to-be in his yellow vest that shone in the early morning sun, boots flashing; Graf's youngest son behind them, small and lithe, jumping up and down in his saddle: all heading towards the Eberswald, a sprinkle of frost creaking and crisp beneath their feet; breath of animals, huntsmen and beaters like a cloud fallen all about them; a few dogs whining in excitement as they strained against their leashes.

Everyone pouring from the castle down the trail that led to the lochan and from there into the Eberswald, each keeping to their own, everyone heading the same way: through the vast wood, from one end to the other, soon dissipating to their separate paths, calming as they went, as they concentrated: boar the main goal, but a few deer and birds not going amiss. Anything for the wedding feast, and the more the merrier.

Lukitt and Alameth following their instructions, veering off the main path to the lesser one their huntsman was taking, Lukitt going to the left, Alameth to the right, as planned. Two hours in and Alameth had lost his sense of direction, circling back unwittingly to the main path.

For Lukitt it went differently: strong smells in the morning of wet leaves and acorn mast beneath his feet, old foliage dropped, sweet scents of their rotting, fox musk catching in his throat; hearing the batter of beak on bark as woodpeckers fought to raise a final brood, clouds of gnats rising from the grass hovering in halos just above his head; intermittent scritlings and scratlings coming from the dark underbelly of the forest made by Lukitt knew not what. What he was aware of was the plan, and stuck to it rigidly, running head down along small paths between the trees, quick short whistle every five minutes to let his huntsman know where he was, getting the same in return. Nothing from Alameth, but Lukitt had to ignore that. This was all about the hunt and he battered his board with the best of them, running through the increasingly tangled undergrowth, eventually having to stop for a few minutes after crashing through a load of dying brambles that snagged him at every turn, needing to catch his breath, untangle himself.

He hears scattered pot shots reverberating through the woods, is reinvigorated by them, doesn't want to be the one left behind, doesn't want to let his huntsman down; crouches, takes a swig of water from the metal flask in his knapsack, brank-ursine high above his head with its large shiny leaves. Puts the canister back and then…stops. Hears a rustling to his left, strong musk in the air; he parts the leaves before his face: sees two great hairy boars, shoulders arched and strong, up-thrust tusks short and mean, bodies high at the head, low at the tail, each heavy, easily capable of stomping him into the mud, goring him through throat or belly where the skin is weakest, though both for now are focussed on each other, grunting, hooves pawing at the ground, hot breath going up in pluffs in the cold morning air, the fur along their spines horrent, small eyes black and vicious.

Lukitt keeps absolutely still.

Grizzle's voice whispering in his head.

They'll take you in a second, lads, if you're standing in their way.

Keep low if you're near them, and whatever you do don't run. If they scent you you're a gonner. Gotta take `em by surprise if they ain't taking off on their own…

Lukitt concentrates on the words, on breathing slow and even, afraid to drop his hands in case he rustles the leaves, alerts them to his presence.

They're moving, circling each other; snorting, stinking, clashing their teeth, angry with the rut and not about to leave; the blood withdrawing involuntarily from Lukitt's skin to the depths of him, to the safest places it can go, the sudden loss from his extremities causing his hands to shake, the leaves to shiver, the slightest shift in the boars' stance as they react to the changing circumstance and Lukitt knows it's now or never.

Stand quickly, shout and bawl, make all the noise you can...

Lukitt moves back apace, fingers fumbling at his knapsack – still open, thank God – and grabs the water canister, swoops up a stone from the ground, starts hammering it at the metal, starts yelling and prancing from side to side to make himself look bigger than he really is; keeps it up, voice hoarse with the shouting, a mad Pfiffmakler puppet leaping from foot to foot, arms above his head waving from side to side as he bangs stone against metal, dancing and prancing for his life. For one second, three, four, the two boars stay rooted to the spot, unwilling to turn away from each other in case of sudden attack; then a new distraction, a shouting coming from Lukitt's left.

'Lukitt! Is that you? Where are you?'

Alameth crashing his way towards his friend, eyes bleary with tears as he'd thought himself lost, finding himself unable to manage the whistle, filling it with spit so it hardly made a sound, never having learned such a simple boyhood trick, never having been in the company of those who could teach him the rudimentaries.

'Alameth!' Lukitt shouted. 'Alameth! Come towards me! Make as much noise as you can!'

The note of hysteria in Lukitt's voice caught at Alameth and he obeyed.

'Wooooeee! Hiyaaaa! Woooeee!'

He took up his beater board and began bashing it into the brambles, thwacking it against tree boles, running headlong to where he believed Lukitt to be, fearing what he'd find, finding him a few minutes later, Lukitt collapsed on the ground in a heap, breathing hard, tears running down his cheeks, incongruous smile breaking across his face as the boars thrashed off in the opposite direction to fight another day.

'What happened?' Alameth asked, going down on one knee, putting solicitous hands out to Lukitt and helping him up, Lukitt laughing and crying all at the same time, his body a fierce battleground of fear and astonishing relief.

'Boars,' Lukitt croaked. 'Two of `em. Just the other side of that thicket. Might've had me if you'd not come along.'

They sat for a few moments until their huntsman's whistle cut through the trees.

Two coming my way, that whistle said, and Lukitt knew why, scrambling up, dragging Alameth with him, following the direction the two boars had gone, more than eager to keep them going forward and not coming back, needing to keep them to the left side of the wood, not break back over the main path, Lukitt directing Alameth; Alameth finding it hard to keep up, but keeping up anyway, excitement in every sinew, Lukitt whistling as Alameth couldn't do, and they were close now: close to the top end of the wood, close to where the end would come. Several hours into the hunt and all soon to be decided, the two lads ripping through thorns and brambles, exhilarated, heading to the edge of the wood where the sunlight trickled through; hardened to the stinging of the nettles, oblivious to the prick of thistles and teasel growing at random in the sudden light; stumbling over roots, the hulks of fallen trunks, heading back into the thicket when they begin to hear more shouting, more shots, other people tripping and cursing, breathing hard, bags banging on chests, boards being dropped, bullet-bands tangling.

A terrier races furiously past, tongue hanging from pink gums, saliva frothing on white teeth, nose snarled as it tries to growl and draw breath and run at the same time, just as they're doing; everything, everyone converging on those two startled boars Lukitt and Alameth had hied up and set to running. The forest thins, a stream tumbles through the moss, a man stands in his stirrups panting hard – Lukitt's man – and out of the trees comes one of the boars – the smaller one, Lukitt thinks, as he and Alameth get there, hands to their sides to stop their running-stitches, the boar lathered at the snout, flesh quivering beneath its bristles, makes to run back but spots more enemies in Lukitt and Alameth, doesn't know which way to go, starts trotting in a circle, lets out a screeching that is terrible to hear as the Jagersman sets his gun against his shoulder and aims a shot, brings the animal down, great gouts of dark blood pouring from the back of his neck as he goes, cracking his knees, falling over slowly to one side, twitching as he hits the ground. Lukitt and Alameth coming up, catching their breath, hearts pumping, Jagersman slipping elegantly from his horse and finishing the boar off with a slice of his sharp knife deep into its throat.

'Well done, boys; couldn't have asked for better.'

Slapping at their shoulders, all watching as the last small bubbles of blood escape the animal's nostrils, last kick of its hind legs; about to find a stout branch on which to tie the boar and take back their prize when they're interrupted by another bout of shouting, and this time nothing to do with the boar.

'The Graf's boy! There's something wrong with the Graf's boy!'

Lukitt quickly up, blood on fire and nothing in his head but the next adventure, Alameth on his heels, huntsman staying behind to make sure his kill was his and his alone. Lukitt running towards whatever was new, stumbling into a glade where the fir trees thinned to ash, appalled by the high-pitched howling coming from a small boy lying on the ground, writhing like a snake struck through at its neck, stumpy legs kicking in a way that would be comical in any other situation, a couple of men standing nearby having no idea what to do. Lukitt catching a faint fluttering in the tree-canopy above him, seeing the odd glint of shiny green flittering through the air before landing here and there on the leaves, on the ground about the boy whose yelling was filtering into a wheeze as his throat begins to close, his face becoming blotched and red. Lukitt comprehending the situation in a rush, running forward, taking the boy by the shoulders and shaking him, hitting him hard on the back. Several other lads emerging from the trees to see Lukitt assaulting the Graf's youngest son, about to pile in and heave him off but Lukitt is shouting at them with dire intensity, arresting them to the spot.

'Who's got pickle? I need pickle! Pickled anything! Just get it me!'

One of them comes to life and flings away the brace of dead rabbits he's been holding by a string poked through their ears, unbuckles his knapsack, takes out a jar, hands it to Lukitt. Lukitt pulls away the cork stopper with his teeth and strains out the cubes of eel with his fingers.

'What's wrong with him?' the lad asks, but Lukitt has no time to answer, murmurs softly to the boy the words Trudl used to say to him when giving him bad tasting medicine: *In your gullet you've rats; time to drown them - down the hatch.*

And just like his mother used to do, Lukitt pinches the boy's nose closed and pours the vinegar juice straight down his throat, clamping his hand over the lad's mouth after it has gone.

'What the hell d'you think you're...' one of the standing men says, cut off by Lukitt.

'Just wait...we'll know in a few...'

The colour has drained from the Graf's son's face, Lukitt cocking his head forward, hearing a faint gurgling, seeing the boy's guts heaving with peristaltic tremors and immediately removes his hand from the lad's mouth, and out it all comes: vinegar and vomit, Lukitt not yet finished, picking the lad up by his heels and shaking him violently to get the last few dribbles out, before gently setting the boy back onto the grass and rubbing at his back as the boy's face returns to normal, crumples up as he starts to quietly cry, not understanding what has happened, only that it's over.

'Sorry I had to do that,' Lukitt says to the boy, then looks up at one of the standing men. 'You got brandy?'

The man's face is creased with perplexity but he nods, hands it over without a word, Lukitt putting the canister to the boy's lips.

'Almost done,' Lukitt cajoles. 'Just swish this around your mouth a few times and spit it out; it will help stop the burning.'

The boy snivels, grimaces, but does as told, Lukitt picking up a short stick and poking it through the boy's copious regurgitations.

'See these?' he says, to distract the boy from his discomfort. 'Beetles. *Lytta vesicatoria*. Guessing you put them in your mouth? Maybe thought they looked like pretty sweets?'

The boy nodded glumly, but fixed his eyes on Lukitt's stick as it prodded the black and green beetles stranded on their backs in his vomit, the blisters in his mouth numbed for the while by the brandy and the fascination of the investigation; said investigation halted by the arrival of the Graf's head Huntsman into the glade: an impressive man in his uniform, made all the more impressive by the swift athleticism with which he dismounts his horse.

'What the curse has been going on?' he demands, striding forward, sweeping his eyes around the gathered company, seeking out one man in particular. 'Where's Lukas? Why isn't he with the boy?'

'I'm here,' a man came panting into the circle. 'He got away from me. Was only gone a cupla…'

Lukas stopped by a leather gauntlet slapped hard against his face.

'Just one task,' breathed the head Huntsman, 'just one. This will not be forgotten.'

His reprimand cut short by the swift entrance of several other men on horseback, three with their guns raised in case the stramash was someone being gored and ripped apart by a rampant bore, another liveried like a lemon in his velvet, and behind them came the Graf himself.

'What's the hullaballoo?'

'Just about to find that out, sir,' Jansen Krommer, head Huntsman, answered, taking one yard with a single stride and in three was at the scene of the crime, looming over Lukitt and the Grafsohn sat next to him, Lukitt scrambling to his feet to explain.

'You've a swarm of Spanish Fly. Beetles, in the ash trees,' he swept his arm upwards to demonstrate the fact; Jansen Krommer looking, but not impressed.

'They like to eat the ash buds. And they're uncommon early this year,' Lukitt went on, 'and apparently this young lad here likes eating beetles.'

His humour was not reciprocated, Krommer tensing, gauntlet in hand, ready to strike.

'He swallowed a few,' Lukitt hurriedly completed the case file. 'Got one stuck in his throat. He'll have blisters in his mouth but we got them out of his stomach, so no …lasting …damage.'

Lukitt stuttered to a stop as Krommer's eyes narrowed, looked upon Lukitt as Lukitt had just been looking on the dead beetles chucked up from the boy's guts.

'We got rid of the rats!' piped the young offender to general surprise, only to be surprised all over again by the yellow flash of the Italian Cockerel barging his way onto the scene and picking up one of the beetles from the ground between gloved fingers.

'*Il Cantaride!*' Words breathed out between thin teeth that were blackened at their roots, his lilting Italianised German irritating all as he went on. 'Devil's Handmaids we call them. Very valuable,' he smiled, showing bad teeth to bad effect, irritating his host all the more, 'to certain men with certain …inadequacies …'

'Enough,' the Graf growled. 'Get my son back to the castle. Lukas!'

Lukas grovelled forward, the welts from the gauntlet visibly ridged and red upon his cheek.

'Get him back, and in one piece, and be sure I'll be speaking to you on my return. The rest of you – collect your sacks. If they're full, go on through the fields with Jansen; if not, get back through the woods and get them filled. Not one back empty. Understand?'

Everyone did, everyone glad to set to, all except Lukitt who stood stranded in the middle of the glade once Lukas had grabbed up the boy and taken him away, no one left but the Graf pulling at his horse and Lukitt, uncertain whether to go or stay, Alameth hovering in the trees some way to the left.

'I don't know precisely what has just occurred,' said the Graf to Lukitt, pulling at his reins, turning his horse in a tight circle, 'but you're obviously at the centre of it, so get you gone. But make sure you present yourself to Jansen once you're back at the castle because you, boy, are someone I want to speak to later on.'

'By all the Saints!' exclaimed Alameth, emerging from the trees once the Graf had taken off, Alameth grabbing at a low branch of the nearest tree, sending a dozen or so bright beetles falling before they flipped open their wing-cases and flew upwards to places they'd be undisturbed. 'What just happened?'

Lukitt shook his head.

'Don't really know,' Lukitt said, but Lukitt was lying, Lukitt was calculating, Lukitt was thinking this could be a way out for him and Alameth, if only he played it right.

Victus Theatrum, and all that. Thinking on Heraldo telling him he was the hero of the hour. An exaggeration then, but maybe not so now.

14

Out of One Wood, Into Another

Lukitt and Alameth threaded their way back through the Eberswald to fill their sacks as directed, joining a small retinue of men doing the same, the latter regarding Lukitt with equal measures of suspicion and awe. Separating yourself from the crowd under scrutiny of Jansen Krommer and the Graf could be good, could be bad, depending on how it went. But they weren't shy of making use of the two lads to pick up their shot game: three young deer, several pheasants and woodcock, a load of small songbirds çaught in the nets they'd earlier laid. Thereafter the guns were quieted, slung upon the men's backs as they trudged their return journey up to the castle, brought to life only to pick off a few last geese that had congregated in the meadows ready for the off, ready to head south for the winter, fat and plump - just as the castle cooks liked them. Evening fast approaching, and everything seeming right: seasonal and cyclical, just as the world ought to be, everything in its place.

Even the Grafsohn, deposited in his nursery, being decked out in clothes far too tight and clean for his liking, had such a feeling, and though his throat still smarted and his mouth still hurt, his gap-toothed smile had returned. He was a pretty lad, hair stiff and frizzy as spun wool, cheeks round and pink, only outcome from his adventure being that he's hungry.

Nothing like almost dying to bring on the most ferocious appetite.

His sister, Groleshka, not of so forgiving a nature, the freckles on her face legion, joining forces in her anger, giving a dull red glow to cheeks, forehead and chin. She stamped hard on the embroidery hoop she'd dropped, splinters skittering out over the hard boards of the floor.

'How could Lukas have let such a thing happen, today of all days?'

Beside her sits her father, the Graf, returned from the hunt, tired and in pain, teeth throbbing, joints swollen by arthritis made worse by all the riding; Heddel perched upon his knee, a reflection of his oldest daughter, though the two seemed to have got things swapped around: Groleshka's face too square and masculine, Heddel's too soft and round. But he'd no mind of that at the moment. He shuddered to think what might have happened if that village boy hadn't been there. He patted the frizzle-headed youth, administered another sweetie of syrup of cloves to calm the blisters, huffing into his beard, letting Groleshka shout out for them both, wondering – not for the first time since her engagement - if he will actually miss her when she's gone.

'What on earth were you thinking, taking Heddel with you at all?' Groleshka's outrage not yet spent. 'He's only a baby. What if he'd got truly lost? He can hardly find his way out of a pot of jam, let alone a wood filled with guns and rampaging beasts.'

The Graf's older son appearing at the door, knocking hesitantly as he hears Groleshka's loud karking. Konrad generally as domineering as was their father, but both conceding to Groleshka in any matter concerning Heddel, the Graf's sequential wives expiring on delivery of their respective children, Groleshka taking up each of their roles in succession.

'The Eberswald is small as woods go, Groleshka,' Konrad protested mildly, 'and the boar were hardly rampaging – we only got one of the blessed things in the end.'

Groleshka turned her viper's gaze upon her brother, hissing through clenched teeth.

'And that's your excuse? If so, it's a poor one.' She leaned forward and chucked Heddel fondly beneath the chin. 'What I don't understand is why you took him out at all, it being so dangerous.'

'It was for you, my dear,' the Graf spoke up, emboldened by Konrad's presence. 'We thought you'd be pleased to have Heddel involved in the preparations for your wedding day…'

Groleshka narrowed her eyes, voice going ominously quiet; an edge to it that might have been sharpened on a strop.

'I wasn't talking about the boar, you idiots,' she breathed out. 'A pig is a pig when you get to the bottom of it, and no reason to go stamping about the countryside blasting other people's heads full of iron shot.'

'Now wait a minute,' her father began, Konrad stepping heroically into the line of fire as he came across the room with a few angry strides. 'For God's sake, Groleshka. You're making too much of it. It wasn't like he...'

Groleshka sweeping suddenly towards Konrad, swishing her voluminous grey silk skirts, light rippling off them as she advanced, the great amber ring on her finger glinting menacingly in the last light of the dying afternoon.

'And you, Konrad, my little, little man,' Groleshka using her childhood name for him with dreadful effect, putting her bejewelled finger a hair's breadth from his face, Konrad taking a step backwards. 'You know what happens when you play fire for fire with me, and that I'll push you in soon as look at you if I think you're putting Heddel in danger. Little men who get shoved into the flames until their skin crackles and bursts and someone sprinkles them with salt thinking they've a fine piece of pork for dinner, and nothing for their mother to find but a pile of knuckle bones she pokes out of the ashes and puts in a pail to wash, plays dice with for the rest of her days, waiting for her little man to come home.'

Behind her, Groleshka's father let out a long breath and shook his head at Konrad, Konrad receiving the signal loud and clear but not happy about it, cheeks pink with protestation and the injustice of his sister's accusations. But he took the hint and retreated. She'd be gone soon enough from them, and she'd been a fair mother to Konrad in his dead mother's absence, never skelping him without proper cause, making him sleep in the stables only when – as she'd rightly pointed out at the time – he'd deserved to be horsewhipped. Tender and harsh by turn, teaching him how to treat his own children when he had them, when he would employ the very same methods: scaring them witless with nursery tales meant to enforce certain behaviours, discourage others; dragging them off to the very top of the round tower when they'd been especially bad - like she'd done to him, and Joderik when he was still alive - threatening to chuck them out into the wind that skirled around the tower like a cat howling in pain through the dark night, only light being a half-spent candle that dripped away its life,

Groleshka slamming the door on them, leaving them in darkness and abject terror, lesson learned.

The memory of Joderik softening Konrad, as it always did, for Groleshka's fears for Heddel were not without foundation: Joderik drowning in a pool whilst supposedly under Konrad's and his father's protection while they were teaching him how to fish. Only a few minutes of neglect, only a few minutes of Konrad and his father fiddling around with getting the knots about the hook tied just right. Only a few minutes of inattention and Joderik was in the water, hardly a splash – at least none they'd heard – no more noise than a carp coming up for a fly; Joderik face down and limp and no reviving him once they'd dragged him back up the bank.

Konrad held up his hands in submission.

'You're right,' he admitted, heels hitting the base of the door frame, gazing on Groleshka's face, at all those freckles that had practically coalesced into one in her rage, their concentration making certain Groleshka would never get a better marriage than the one she was committed to now; a marriage Konrad didn't envy, not so short-sighted he couldn't see how unsuited it was, nor that Groleshka might be dead within the year if the fate of their successive mothers was anything to go by.

Konrad leaving silence behind him, a log cracking in the hearth getting a hard stab for its trouble as Groleshka went at it with her poker, her brother's newly understood revelations no news to her.

'I'm sorry you're so unhappy,' attempted the Graf, 'that you're not keen on this marriage. But you know how it goes; that what has to be will be.'

Groleshka closed her eyes because yes, she knew too well how things must go. She should have been a precious ornament, passed from one family to the next; but she'd never been a bauble pretty enough for early barter when she might have had a choice; too old now to have any say in the matter, stranded the wrong side of twenty, being shoved off on anyone who would have her, time being of the essence and not much left of it, not if she was to retain any value supplying stock for the next generation. Worst of all being that she had to leave Heddel behind. Only a few days left to savour him, only a few days before she would be forced to leave the castle, be carted over the mountains to God knew where.

Bitter wasn't a wide enough word for what she felt, especially not when – right on cue – the Italian Cockerel burst himself through the open door Konrad had vacated, the man she was about to be shackled to for the rest of her life coming in without even a knock. Groleshka shuddering as he pranced into the room in his ridiculous yellow jerkin and the cocked hat he'd latterly embellished with a few pheasant feathers.

'Ah, my dears,' Conte Udolpho di Villanova announced in his annoying accent, frolicking across the boards and kissing Groleshka wetly on first her left cheek and then her right. 'A family gathering! How delightful! And how is the boy with the blistered belly? Why, it's a wonder you didn't burst, my boy. A lesser man would have and no mistake. But a brush with death, now that's a tale you must tell often down your advancing years. But why all so glum? Has the cellar run dry of brandy?'

Udolpho's wife-to-be clicked her nails in annoyance, Udolpho moving quickly forward, launching out a brown hand to cover her own, squeezing tightly, draining the blood from her fingers, a feather coming adrift from his hat and floating to the floor.

'Don't do that, my love,' he said, gripping so hard her fingers were arrested, tips sticking out from his like the blanched ends of new-born asparagus. 'You know how it upsets me. But where is that maid?' he carried on regardless, casual violence coming as easily to him as a mole shovels earth. 'I told her to bring brandy, or wine at the very least. By the way – and this will please you, my dear,' he gave Groleshka's hand another squeeze that had her bones grinding. 'I've taken it upon myself to get that boy back here, the one who knows so much about beetles. I know how fond you are of the little tick,' nodding towards Heddel. 'Thought it might be in order to give his saviour a little present for keeping your prize page boy alive long enough for our wedding.'

The Graf winced, held Heddel a little closer, aware the man had superseded his own orders concerning that saviour, no doubt deliberately. He'd no love at all for this Udolpho, but a marriage was a marriage when it came down to tacks and pins, and Groleshka had been on the market a long time and this man the only taker. He glanced at his only daughter, saw the blood drain from her face leaving the reckless freckles scattered over her skin like red rocks stranded on the pale sand of a beach.

'I'll go call for the maid again,' she croaked, rubbing her hands fiercely together as the Count released her.

'Come, come, Groleshka,' chided her Groom. 'You sound like you're the one who's had beetles in your throat. You'll have to chime out better than that tomorrow, ho hum! Wedding bells not dumb-bells is what we want, yes indeed.'

The hard sparkle of his voice leapt around the room and little Heddel suddenly tumbled himself off his father's knee and caught at the Cockerel's hand.

'Bells,' he trilled merrily, despite his blistered tongue. 'And I'm to have one all to myself?'

'That you are, my dear,' Groleshka raised a smile, clamping her thin upper lip with her teeth as the enormity of this marriage rolled over her like a wave, heading for the door to hide her face, saved by the arrival of the maid she'd been about to summon informing one and all that food and drink had been laid out in the lesser hall. Groleshka pleading a headache, holding a hand over her mouth as her father stood and departed with the Count, Heddel still clamped to the latter's hand; the weeping - that had never been far away the whole day - breaking over her as a swollen river over a weakened dam.

15

Dancing Monkeys, Drunken Men

Lukitt waited, as instructed, in the stable quarters until he was called for his audience with the Graf. He'd fidgeted at first, then pitched in with the stable lads to clean the tack, wash the horses, comb them down, polish the impressive brass-work that had hung around the Graf's steed's neck like a mighty necklace. Lukitt excited, polishing his pitch as much as the brass, figured he'd have maybe thirty seconds to advance his and Alameth's cause.

Jansen Krommer appeared as Lukitt was hanging up the brasses on their hooks, starting to rub their leather harnesses.

'Glad to see you've not been idle,' Jansen stood in the stable doorway, slapping his whip several times against his boots, his bulk dark against the weak light coming from the lanterns in the courtyard. 'Time to go. Someone needs a word.'

Lukitt nodded, stowed his cloths and bottles back onto their racks before following Jansen out across the courtyard, going beneath the great dark bow of the *Grafschwibbogen* - the main archway that led into the castle proper - coming to rest outside a vast wooden door.

From inside came the sound of voices, not many, but distinctly enlivened, very likely by drink. Jansen looking down at Lukitt who looked back as Jansen rapped sharply on the door with the silver handle of his whip.

'Come,' called a voice, and in Jansen went, Lukitt a soft footfall behind him, the room they were ushered into far darker than Lukitt had expected, lit only by the roaring fire in the grate tended by a small boy perched on an overturned log of wood, poker in hand, bored look on his face, and a single lamp on the table around which two men were sitting. A younger one wobbled over the piss-pot in the farthest corner of the hall, evidently a tad worse for wear. Strangely it was the table, rather than the men, that caught Lukitt's immediate attention, for it was large and overlaid with alternating squares of ebony and ivory – undoubtedly a chess table - with a scatter of oversized chessmen jumbled together in an open-topped casket that lay to one side.

'The boy, as asked for,' Jansen Krommer announced, stepping to one side, motioning Lukitt forward.

'Jansen!' the Graf greeted him heartily, eager for any company other than the Count. 'Come join us.'

Jansen twitched, equivocated, didn't want to be here.

'I'm not sure it's appropri…'

'It's entirely appropriate,' Jansen was cut off. 'My daughter's about to be married. Her last day…'

The Graf shook his head, the reality of Groleshka's leaving sinking in, but no choice now. Alliances with the Italians and all that. Times changing, everything changing, whether he liked it or no. He looked over at the man who, by the tail end of tomorrow, would be his son-in-law and liked him no more than when he'd arrived a few days previously. Pompous and vain had been his first thoughts of the man, and they'd not changed a whit, except that a certain level of cruelty had been added into the mix: not a trait he'd bargained for, nor one he wanted for Groleshka.

Too late now.

'So this is the lad who saved our young Heddel?' he asked, by way of distraction.

'It is,' Jansen replied, coming forward, the Graf pouring him a glass of wine, Jansen taking it but not putting it his lips, regarding Konrad with distaste as the boy emerged from the gloom buttoning up his trousers, legs a little shaky.

'My Honourable Older Brother,' Konrad slurred, slapping Udolpho on the shoulder as he slumped himself down in his seat. 'I believe that drinking game you got me into didn't go in my favour.'

He hiccupped loudly, Udolpho looking up at Jansen with a wink, a sly grin on his tawny face. Jansen cleared his throat. Like everyone else in the castle he regretted Groleshka's leaving. She'd been the fulcrum of all that went on here for years, a woman always fair in her dealings, a little high-handed perhaps, but on the side of the underlings all the same.

'This is Lukitt Bachman,' he announced, motioning Lukitt forward with a swirl of his whip, Lukitt stepping up obediently at his side.

'Is it, indeed?' Udolpho the first to react. 'Well come on, ragazzo. Let's get a proper look at you. Heave yourself up on the table and give us a twirl.'

Jansen frowned, as did the Graf, but Konrad was mighty amused at the suggestion, too far gone to recognise the humiliation this might imply.

'Oh but do!' he clapped his hands. 'Let him take the stage!'

As if Lukitt were the latest entertainment, not the person who'd saved Heddel from choking to death, Konrad more concerned that his sleeve was sopping wet from the arm-wrestling bouts he'd undergone with Udolpho – never winning – needing some diversion, shove his losing status onto someone else.

Lukitt was not put off. He'd prepared his speech, and standing on a massive chess table being scrutinized from every side was a small price to pay to get it said. He clambered up, disregarding Konrad's laughter as he did so, dismissing him, regarding rather the other men, wondering who of the two was more in charge and therefore most likely to vouchsafe his and Alameth's future.

'So Lukitt,' said the Graf. 'Not a name I've come across before. Where are you from exactly?'

Lukitt answered promptly.

'From the Herrnhuter and then Gargellan valley, but latterly I've resided in Seiden See with Père Ulbert. Spent the last eighteen months on the water learning the fishing trade.'

'Latterly,' Udolpho repeated slowly, evidently amused. 'That's quite a complicated word.'

'Père Ulbert taught me well,' Lukitt replied swiftly, catching the curious look the Graf cast up at him.

'Père Ulbert,' the Graf said softly, remembering. 'A great help to me when Joderik passed. Came all the way up here to offer his services and I've never forgotten his kindness. A great help,' he repeated, 'a great comfort during bad times.'

Udolpho crinkled his nose. Too much sentiment for him. Wanting to get on, set another game in motion.

'The point remains - Lukitt, was it?' he broke in, Lukitt nodding, Udolpho studying Lukitt as he spoke, weighing him up. 'It appears you saved the idiot child Heddel from killing himself today,' ignoring the grunt of protest from Heddel's father at this unkind description of his son. 'So how are we to reward you?'

Lukitt took his chance, put forward his carefully constructed plea.

'If any reward is due,' he began, speaking clearly, humbly, as rehearsed, amending his words to include the Italian, who seemed more or less in charge, if only by dint of being the most sober. 'It would be much appreciated if you or the Graf would consider myself and my friend for advancement. We're hard workers, quick learners, seeking only to better ourselves in life.'

Udolpho snorted, took a swig of his wine.

'Advancement, is it? To better yourselves? Oh my, that's a good one! Ever heard the expression *Egli s'avanzò, ma nel bosco*?'

Lukitt hadn't, but he understood.

'He advanced, but only into the woods,' he interpreted.

'Very good, my young sir,' Udolpho said, narrowing his eyes. 'Meaning a man should be careful what he wishes for.'

'He taught you well, your Père Ulbert,' the Graf interrupted, not liking the way Udolpho had hijacked the conversation, not a man to be readily usurped, drunk as he was. 'So why not take him back with you, Udolpho? Him and his friend? You've fishing boats going out from Liguria we both know, so perhaps the perfect place for two clever fisher lads wanting on with life.'

Udolpho strummed his fingers upon his neatly clipped beard, scratched his neck.

'Well, why not,' he agreed, smiling a bad smile. 'But I have conditions. My employees have to prove themselves. Earn their places. Go into the woods, where I might or might not abandon them. Are you ready for that, Lukitt Bachmann?'

'I am,' Lukitt stated, Konrad suddenly waking.

'Have I missed the monkey dancing?' he slurred, lifting his head, fuzzily aware he couldn't exactly remember the last hour, maybe two.

God, maybe the whole night. Udolpho laughing loudly, if not kindly.

'You've missed nothing, my young friend,' Udolpho replied easily, 'for the monkey,' he cast a quick glance at Lukitt as Lukitt got down from the table and retreated for the door, 'has yet to start his dance.'

16

Different Ways to Change Your Life

Ulbert gave the marinating hare another sprinkle of pepper. It had given him an idea for next Sunday's homily: the Hebrew legend of *Arnabet*, the biblical hare who'd had to change gender when his mate foolishly leapt from the Ark and drowned herself. He liked to try things out over dinner with Lukitt, and now Alameth too, before going full throttle into the pulpit, and missed not having them here the past couple of days, away as they were at the hunt. They were precious, those few hours after the boys came back from the lake tired and spent, but still willing to listen to him, still willing to learn what he could teach them – mostly Lukitt, if he was fair, for Alameth was usually so sleepy it was all he could do to keep himself from falling into his soup.

Given the Arnabet, should I do the moral of stupidity, or despair? Ulbert mused. *Or possibly the way we have to adapt to new circumstance.*

Interrupted by Lukitt and Alameth charging up the path – no mistaking those two, life and youth in every step – the lads coming into the manse, about to churn up Ulbert's carefully ordered life as surely as a hurried horse turns a neat path into mud and mire. Alameth rushing past Ulbert straight to the room he shared with Lukitt, starting to pack his meagre belongings; Lukitt coming to a stop before Ulbert, hesitant, but determined.

'We're leaving,' Lukitt stated baldly, unable to meet Ulbert's eye. 'Got an offer to take us over the mountains into Italy,' Lukitt persevering. 'Not long to get ready. Going with the Graf's new son-in-law once the wedding's done, bound for the Mediterranean. He's boats going out after the herring and he's given us a place…'

Ulbert stopped his stirring.

'It's a chance,' Lukitt said, stomach churning with regret and anticipation. 'You once told me that if chance came along I should grab it with both hands.'

Ulbert slowed, Ulbert stilled, for yes he'd said that once, though of

Pregel if he remembered rightly.

And look what had come of that.

The idea of Lukitt going was appalling, never mind he'd encouraged it, it never really occurring to him it would actually happen. He'd assumed that a couple of years on the boats would be enough, that Alameth would declare it too hard a life and return to the Abbey; that Lukitt would come back to Ulbert and be educated as a teacher, take over Ulbert's role when Ulbert got too old; divide his time between the school and the farm up at Gallapfel, pick a local girl to settle down with, have the family Ulbert had never had - until he had Lukitt - mapping out Lukitt's life for him, never truly believing other options would come to pass. That Lukitt had made up his own map as he went along was not a possibility he'd contemplated.

'What changed?' Ulbert asked quietly, sitting down in his usual seat by the fire, Lukitt taking his own, both staring into the flames, unable to look properly at one another for fear of what they might see.

'I don't think anything's changed,' Lukitt answered, for in his mind nothing had. Always his plan to get up and out.

'He only went and saved the Graf's son from dying!' Alameth shouted from his room, hearing everything, understanding nothing, Ulbert gripping the arm of his seat with agitated fingers.

'You…saved the Grafsohn?' Ulbert asked. 'But how?'

'He's young,' Lukitt explained, a sudden smile warming his face, 'a bit younger than his years, it has to be said; still has that habit of shoving anything and everything into his mouth.'

'And what exactly was it that he…shoved into his mouth?' Ulbert's despair momentarily distracted.

'Blister beetles,' Lukitt provided. 'Like the ones Hermistus hated having in his orchard. I knew them right away.'

'So what are you telling me?' Ulbert squeezed out the words.

'That this is our time,' Lukitt stated, looking steadily at Ulbert, as certain now as he'd been when he'd left the castle with instructions to get his gear together, get back soonest, all family matters to be resolved; him and Alameth to be packed and ready to start their new life. 'It's our time, Ulbert,' Lukitt repeated softly. 'I really believe it's our time.'

Nothing to be heard but Alameth in the next room, Alameth taking out one thing, putting back another; the singing of a blackbird out in the yard: a beautiful sound, one both Lukitt and Ulbert associated with Pregel, one shared but never spoken. Ulbert recognising the deed had already been done, and no undoing it.

'Then go with God,' Ulbert said, taking a breath, straightening his head, squaring his sagging shoulders. 'And if there's anything I can do to help, then so will I do.'

Words he'd said before and now – how had it happened? – was being called on to enact.

All day long carriages and carts, horses and ponies, rolled into the castle's courtyard, the animals taken away to be cared for in stable and byre, their owners divested of outer coats, cloaks and travelling blankets that were folded and stowed in one of the castle's store rooms, the woolly mountain growing hour by hour, threatening to topple into one vast damp undergrowth from which it would be impossible to extract a single identifiable item.

The various arriving parties led through the *Grafschwibbogen* and announced as they entered the Great Hall, the first thirty or so met with polite applause and general head-nodding as acquaintances and would-be acquaintances glanced up from their plates or drinks. The obsequy soon wearing thin, the general hubbub drowning out more announcements to which no one paid the slightest attention.

Tables constantly replenished by a relay of dishes brought up from the kitchens, the centrepiece to this unending banquet being an ivy-clad plinth surmounted by the most enormous cake anyone present had ever seen: a sugar work spectacular, the bottom layer three feet in diameter, bowed with ribbons and red roses, adorned with a scale-model of the castle whose sugar-spun arches and wood-dowelled colonnades supported the next layer, nine more tiers diminishing in size as they ascended, each with elaborate representations of the two families being joined in matrimony. The uppermost tier holding life-like mouldings of Groleshka and her Groom that would not be appreciated until much later, when the dismantling began and each cake separately displayed, admired, and finally devoured.

Only on close inspection could the painted cheeks, lips and eyes, the curls of hair, the latticed layers of the bride's nest of a dress, be truly appreciated, though this particular delight would never be eaten, its destiny to be marooned on a block of velvet, protected from humidity and dissolution by a heavy glass case. Kept by Groleshka on her dressing table beside her perfumes and powders to remind her how happy her life had been before she was transported to Italy where she was surrounded by jabbering maids, her torso tied up in the intolerable stays and corsets of fashions foreign to her; subject to dreadful heat, hordes of flies that bit and made her face swell up like a bloated pig-bladder, obliged to hide herself away from everyone - husband included, which was a blessing.

Even when the figurines went green with mould that grew back with a persistence her cleaning powders lacked the strength to combat, even after the noses and ears of the pretty manikins had melted away, their hands eaten by some species of filthy foreign weevil and the lattices of lace on her sugar-spun dress collapsed into a heap of broken fragments, even then, Groleska would polish the glass and run her finger over the bell-jar in future days. Sighing, remembering the wonder of her wedding: the adoration and excitement of all the guests, the cool mountain air that had blown through her window as she prepared to go down and make her breath-taking entrance; her brother Konrad making an arse of himself over his speech, her father making a better one that would sit with all her days – *my darling daughter, who has been both left hand and right to me for so many years, and for whom I would do anything, not the least of which being this wonderful marriage that has seen two countries, two families, united, never to be sundered.*

And Heddel, always little Heddel.

Many years later Groleshka would think on him, saved from the beetles long ago, but no one there to save him from the wars he later fought in. Dead and gone, as was Groleshka the moment she'd had to leave him behind. There'd be days to come when she'd stare at her thin face in the mirror, at her scraggy neck, her brown and broken teeth as bad as her father's had ever been, wanting to rip them out of her jaw to lessen the pain; Groleshka shuddering as she regarded the sad reflection of a life misspent and undone as if her skin already crawled with maggots, her flesh already disintegrating into drip-grease, artful worms playing a cannonade on her bones.

But all that yet to come.

'And now, Ladies and Gentlemen, *Damen und Herren*, puffballs and piecrusts, lollypops and lambchops,' the Master of Ceremonies hesitates, looks down at his script, uncertain of the gibberish, lacking the loud manner and foppishness his new post demands. He is Jansen, Head Huntsman who, up until two hours ago, had been happily sitting at his own table, glad for an early end to a long day, flexing his toes and softening his bunions in a bowl of warm water, busily laughing himself silly at the goings on of the wedding and, more specifically, the Groom-to-Be.

'He thought we'd caught the marmots in the Eberswald! Any piece of bum-fluff older than two could've told him they don't nest in the woods.'

His wife slapping his dinner onto the table in front of him.

'Twenty years ago you boasted you had a nest of them up your trousers, I seem to recall.'

Jansen professed his shock, but was laughing still.

'You should bite off your tongue and boil it, woman. But you're not wrong,' he went on, swallowing a great spoonful of cucumber pickle and a piece of dumpling. 'I was a pretty rare man in those days to be sure. Pretty rare. You'd not have done better and don't you think it. Strong and straight as a piece of picket fence, I was.'

Frau Jansen sighed, rolled her eyes before dunking her hands into the washing water.

'Picket, pricket,' she muttered, scrubbing a pan with unnecessary vigour, thinking of her three strong dark sons who looked so much more like Jörg the coachman, their lodger, than Jansen. Not that Jansen ever noticed; Jansen burping with satisfaction, happily replete, when the knock came at his door summoning him to the castle.

'Whad'you mean, Master of Ceremonies? I don't do stuff like that. I'm a master huntsman, not a ceremonial windbag.'

The messenger explaining that all available windbags of suitable status were unavailable, that the Announcer of Guests had finally croaked out his last name and gone to bathe his throat with what turned out to be a severely over-liberal dose of brandy. That, basically, there was no one else left.

'Master of Ceremonies,' Jansen grumbled. 'Bet he doesn't call himself that when he's at home,' tucking his ash-blond hair under his cap, buttoning up his jacket.

'Master of Ceremonies,' cooed Frau Jansen, once her husband had left, wiping her hands, taking off her apron, loosening hair and bodice, lifting the latch to her lodger's, her long-time lover's room, unaware how short-lived Jansen's role would be: his only duty to read off his card and introduce the entertainments procured for the wedding. Once he'd said his *Mein Damen und Herren* speech his time was over, going straight back home to find his wife and Jörg coming from the upper room at his interruption, mumbling their excuses, fumbling with their clothes. Jansen not thinking, Jansen grabbing up the crossbow he'd left preloaded by the door ready to knock off the fox that had been attacking the chickens; Jansen sending its vicious bolt through both wife and lover with the same shot, the two staggering with the blow before crumpling headfirst down the stairs into an untidy heap at his feet, bleeding all over the flagstones; Jansen wailing out the anger of his betrayal to all the world until all the world – at least those in the stables and cotts surrounding the courtyard – came to him.

Upshot being Jansen imprisoned for several nights in the castle's dungeons sobbing into his hands, everyone shaking their heads as they heard the news, wondering why he'd suddenly decided to break up the trysting that had started the moment Jörg had been billeted with the Krommers; all assuming he knew - that it was for him a convenience, a means to an end, a way to keep face and get the progeny he'd been unable to produce by himself.

A terrible deed he'd done, no doubting it, but one that had been a long time coming, as agreed the Graf a few days later when informed of the full circumstances, releasing Jansen without charge, appointing a new head huntsman – the one who'd shot the boar with the help of Lukitt's whistles and codes.

The Graf recognising a crime of passion when he saw one, mostly because he'd just committed one himself in handing Groleshka over to the Cockerel, both gone for Italy the day before. A crime for which he never forgave himself.

17

Marriage and Melodrama

Once the Master of Ceremonies had introduced the wedding's entertainments and departed, onto the stage came Lupercal and Jericho with a rangle and a jangle, back-flipping their bodies over the boards. Heraldo had abandoned his lute in favour of a *Tromba Marina* that gave an ear-splitting noise as of cleaver against bone, its weird twanging cutting all excess chatter stone dead.

Attention gained, Heraldo slung a hurdy-gurdy swiftly about his neck, tripping through tunes now sad, now gay, now leaping like Ludmilla and Longhella twirling their orange skirts across their stage. Over two years since Lukitt had seen them at the Abbey: taller, prettier; bronzed hair cascading down their backs, plaits interwoven with ribbons and spangles; bare arms slim and pale, their freckled expanses almost a match for Groleshka's face which - at that very moment – had undergone a lemon-juice bleach and now was being slathered in a paste of orris root and zinc-white bound with oil of violet, all to make her fashionably pale, ready for her entrance when the entertainments are done.

But done they are not, and onto the stage comes Kaspar Larriscarri, a stock character everybody knows, applause and cheers welcoming, enthusiastic as he takes his bows, fine silver suit sparkling in the light of the lamps. Kaspar soon regaling his audience with ludicrous tales of what went on at his own wedding, his vivid recollections acted out with every frippery and exaggeration by other members of the cast.

Folk stories and folk memories everyone enjoys.

'We have laughed, we have cried,' Kaspar announces as he reaches the end of his play. 'We've seen the worst of men but now, Ladies and Gentlemen, we are privileged to witness the best.'

He waves his arm and up goes the curtain, a silver shimmer revealing Bride and Groom seated on gilded thrones: Groleshka pale below a froth of veil, her dress fanned out about her; Udolpho a living, breathing rainbow: blue hat, yellow jerkin, red shirt, trousers the colour of wet spring grass. Before both kneels little Heddel, a golden oriole offering up a clutch of multi-coloured flowers; Groleshka's father and brother standing behind alongside the priest, two acolytes swinging thuribles that fill the hall with sweet and pungent incense, stage changed into church and altar, and no one can fail to be moved. Not even Groleshka, who is weeping quietly, streaking her painted face with tiny runnels, not that anyone can see them beneath her veils.

The marriage is made: speeches done, vows taken, Groleshka's father giving away his daughter with heavy heart. The women in the audience sighing, wishing they'd had a wedding as spectacular as this; the men clapping and striking their glasses with silver pencils or business-card cases, thanking God they'd not had to stump up for the same.

Bride and Groom removing themselves for the nuptial bed, stage abandoned, hall a-thrum with celebration, the music starting up again – no weird stuff this time, just regular tunes that soon have pretty slippers and polished boots dancing side by side, step by step. And on they went and on, right through the night, almost until morning, none of the guests knowing of the other small dramas playing themselves out about the castle.

Head Huntsman Jansen killing his wife and her lover;

Groleshka slowly denuding herself in her bridal chamber, ashamed of her body, ashamed of her tears, ashamed of her new husband;

Udolpho rampant and erect, aroused by his new wife's distress and evident ignorance of what went on between a man and woman in their bed;

Groleshka's father retiring to his room, down on his knees, begging God's forgiveness, wishing he could turn back the years, make a better match;

Lukitt and Alameth in Seiden See packing their bags for the fifth or sixth time, too excited to sleep, talking about all they would do in Italy, how the sea would look, neither having witnessed it before;

Père Ulbert ensconced in his chair by the dying fire in his manse, listening to the boys and their sporadic chattering, wondering what had been set in motion, fearing for Lukitt, fearing for Lukitt's family, fearing for himself.

No Kaspar Larriscarri to direct these small plays, point out the high points or the low, the right of them or the wrong.

No all-seeing director to set the stage to warn each and every one what might happen next.

18

How to Can a Bottler

The bridal party left the castle the following day, Lukitt and Alameth amongst their ranks. It was a mixed baggage, many of the Italian entourage still a little drunk and in good spirits, glad to be on their way; the Austrian element few and subdued, comprising only Groleshka herself and two longstanding maids eager for new horizons, unthinkable to abandon their mistress despite being given the option to stay.

The generally buoyant mood of the retinue continued, the Italians tilting their faces to the meagre sun, eager for home; Udolpho at their lead, jaunty and bright in attire and manner, singing Italian ditties and folk songs that might have been pretty, had they not been so dreadfully out of tune. Heraldo running to the fore to offer his services, the Pfiffmaklers travelling with the party - due to perform at the other end of the journey - but despite his skill on the lute there was no steering Udolpho into the right key, the Count crashing his way through yet another medley of discordant song.

Heraldo retreated to the back of the line, falling into step with Alameth; Lukitt a few yards behind, lost in a world of his own, studying the grasses, the late mushrooms, the lichens on the rocks, picking up small samples of minerals and stones he didn't recognise, stuffing all into his pockets for later study.

'He sings like a crow, that man,' Heraldo said with disgust. 'But you!' slapping Alameth on the back. 'You left the Abbey! What brought that on?'

'Well,' Alameth beamed a smile that had far more radiance than the weak sun shining down on them, 'it was sort of you.'

'Me?' Heraldo put a hand to his chest, genuinely surprised and somewhat mystified. 'Whatever did I do?'

'Your play, remember? The one with the boat when Lukitt did his turn?'

'His star turn,' Heraldo agreed. 'Of course I remember. Fair's folk have been talking about that ever since – getting booed indeed, and at a monastery! But why would that make you leave? I seem to vaguely recall you weren't far off from taking your final vows.'

'You're right there,' Alameth agreed. 'Supposed to take them that very Christmas, but had them put back to Easter because...well, after you were at the Abbey, Lukitt got all sort of shook up about us taking off together to see the world.'

Heraldo whistled softly.

'Is that right? Noble sentiments. But surely can't be all of it?'

Alameth shook his head.

'It wasn't. You won't know about this,' he took a quick glance over his shoulder at Lukitt, but Lukitt wasn't listening, was bending down to retrieve yet another wonder he didn't recognise, Alameth going on with lowered voice. 'Remember young Pregel? That boy Lukitt was so tight with?'

'Pregel,' Heraldo repeated the name. 'I think I heard him sing during the Christmas Service. Gap between his ears where the sun didn't shine?'

Alameth grimaced but agreed.

'That's him. Point being he fell off a roof and died, and that sort of turned Lukitt a little harder, got him real keen on getting away, got himself a plan, and me in it, and then...well, away we went. Been working the boats on the Seiden See getting on eighteen months.'

Heraldo was impressed, and it took a lot to impress the likes of Heraldo who'd seen things most men would never witness in their entire life-times.

'Still doesn't explain why you're here, travelling away to Italy with the ghastly groom and his ghastly bride,' he commented - always a lad who liked puzzles, putting back together the *Tromba Marina* proof of that – solution to this particular enigma eluding him. Alameth noting it, brushing his hair away from his forehead, grinning like he held the secrets of the universe in his hand.

'It was Lukitt again,' Alameth announced, neglecting to keep his voice down, Lukitt coming up beside his friend at the mention of his name, nodding at Heraldo, happy to see him, had been meaning to seek him out, ask how things were going.

'It was Lukitt again, how?' Lukitt asked, Alameth delighted to supply the answer, telling the tale gladly of boy and beetles.

'Well I'll be damned,' Heraldo announced, demanding more details of the hunt, for he'd never been on one. The only hunting he and his folk did being the kind that kept them alive when they were tramping from one place to another, from one town to the next, thrilled to the marrow by Lukitt's description of his close encounter with not one boar but two, and Alameth's antics in heading them off.

'Bravo!' Heraldo clapped. 'You two really know how to live. And then going on to save the Grafsohn! Who knew that a bit of education about beetles would actually have a use.'

'Knowledge always has a use,' Lukitt said, entirely serious, thinking back to the boats and how he'd measured mountains. 'See these?' he said, 'these are called Napier's Bones.'

Withdrawing from his pocket a leather holder the size and shape of a small tobacco tin and producing from it a set of jet-backed ivory sticks, each with an eyelet at the top through which went a thong so he could spread them out like a deck of cards.

Ulbert's parting gift.

'What are they?' Heraldo asked, taking them from Lukitt, fascinated. 'Some kind of travelling domino game?'

'A way of multiplying large numbers,' Lukitt happy to explain. 'It's kind of complicated and simple all at the same time…'

About to explicate when Heraldo held up his hands.

'Stop! I surrender! Don't think I can take it in while we're on the move, but show me later, when I can take notes.'

Lukitt coloured, but Heraldo was entirely serious.

'I mean it,' he went on. 'I love stuff like this. Wish I'd had a better bit of learning myself. Lots of measurement involved in making instruments, and it'd be real handy to know how something like this works.'

Lukitt happy now, tucking the bones away, already sketching out a few notes in his head about how best to explain their mysterious workings and how Heraldo could put them to practical use.

The cortege wound up the pass and through the mountains, lucky with the weather, lucky with their guide; skimming the Tyrol, crossing the neck of Switzerland.

At first all seemed the same: mountains and snow, lakes and trees, but gradually the vista changed, the mountains become hills dropping away into flanks of green, the slopes become tiers, stages for waving troupes of denuded olive trees, oranges and pomegranates; the last straggles of marrows and melons sprawling over the grass, left there after their last fruiting to rot back into the ground. They passed flocks of sheep being brought down for the winter, fat lambs still tugging at their mothers' withered teats, lambs soon to be sorted: execution for some, others to replace mothers turned into mutton; herds of goats nudging and wrangling for the last mouthfuls of purple swedes that were being gnawed down to their straggly roots.

Groleshka - in her carriage, ill with the travelling and sick to the stomach with the whole affair - sees those swedes as chewed decapitated heads, cursing the goats for not letting them be, not allowing them to be done with life in their own time, in their own way. She says as much to her husband on one of the few occasions he brings his steed alongside her carriage to check on his new wife, Udolpho scolding her for this pessimistic view.

'It's a new life we're heading into, and you really shouldn't talk of things you know nothing about. Those decapitated heads you're so fanciful about? *Rutabaga* hereabouts, or *scorzonera*: the peasants' purse - saved in summer, spent in winter. Keeps them all alive, one way or another, and peasants need keeping alive, my dear, for where would we be without them?'

Groleshka takes the rebuke without a word, irritated at the way Udolpho had wagged his finger at her as he spoke, a gesture he'd become fond of during this time of travelling.

It's not for pleasure Groleshka groans. The thought of spending the rest of her life with this man is appalling. She'd rather be down on hands and knees with the peasants, chomping on what the goats had left of the rutabaga than go on with this charade of a marriage: this terrible, unlovely and unloving union she's been forced into.

Oh my little Heddel, she thinks, leaning her head against the side of the carriage, uncaring of the bump bump bump of it as the wheels negotiate yet more pot-holes. *What are you doing now, my darling*?

Thinking too of the lad who'd saved Heddel from choking to death, aware he was travelling with them, obscurely glad of the fact, as if he might save her like he'd saved Heddel, deciding there and then that when they finally got to where they were going she would seek him out, if only to hear the story of his saving Heddel for herself.

A little piece of home.

Something she could hold onto and treasure, for Lord knew – as did she – there was little else to hang onto.

Lukitt had no inkling of Groleshka's thinking as they travelled overland into Italy. All he knew was that he was excited, happy to have Alameth by his side and with the added bonus of Heraldo too – for a short while at least. He'd garnered a few facts about the relationship between the Grafs and the Italians - the marriage between Groleshka and Udolpho merely the latest addendum to a deal that had been on-going for many years, trading partners from one country to the other; the latest jig being to open a canning factory on the Italian side, following Nicholas Appert's experiments with the autoclaves that promised to sweep into the past the bottling industry – no thought of what would happen to the bottlers and the makers of their glass.

Times were changing, as the Graf had previously surmised, the main message being *keep up, adapt, or get out*.

That Nicolas Appert had been thrown into a pauper's grave a couple of years previously was neither here nor there.

Villanova appeared deserted as the wedding party approached, its estates spread in a relaxed sprawl across the hillsides, the open cotts yawning around the demesnes to which they were attached, terracotta roofs warming in the meagre winter sun. Tangles of leafless trees led the eye through the orchards tipping smitter smatter down the surrounding slopes, a partially snowed-over track winding a lazy way alongside a river that well knew its way to the sea. And where river spilled into ocean, on a mist-licked horizon, was the port Udolpho's fleet plied from, tethered to the earth by a maze of main masts and white washed walls, looking to Lukitt's shaded gaze – hands cupped across his brows - like a mirage: the arc of the bay shivering by its shores, ripples of white breakers a gentle lace against the grey, an outline soon dissolved back into mist.

This strange peace extended far beyond the farmlands – for it was Sunday, and Service time – the cortege passing without encountering a soul, doors and shutters closed against them, several tatterdemalion dogs standing to attention on dirty paws, growling and hostile, the ropes keeping them to their homes stretched taut and tight.

Conversation in the party fell with the wind as they approached their destination and, by tacit agreement, everyone got into the given hierarchy of order: Groleshka's carriage and the Cockerel at the front, his men immediately behind, rank falling into rank. Tatters like Lukitt, Alameth and the Kunterbunt taking up the rear.

Udolpho took it upon himself to drum up the welcome he believed he deserved, taking out a large hunting horn, pursing his lips against its silver rim and blowing like the devil, the resultant caterwaul shrieking through the air, ripping the somnolent Sunday silence to shreds, the growling dogs reverting to throat-blown howling, chickens and pigeons squawking and fluttering in their coops, stones skidding under hooves as horses reared and snorted, spitting out foamy saliva in their alarm.

Within moments, the tocsin of Villanova church was pealing wildly, people spilling out of its doors mid-sermon securing shawls and scarves, buttoning jackets, shoving hats on heads, everyone in a scrum, eager to clap eyes on their new mistress for the first time, make a good impression. The returning wedding party soon engulfed by noise and tumult as they entered the courtyard of the Palazzo Villanova; children grabbing reins, pulling at saddle blankets the second the horses' riders had dismounted, vying for who should carry the returning travellers' bags; women rushing off to fetch buttermilk, wine, blackcurrant brandy, bread, curd cheese, baguettes soaked in olive oil and herbs, all of them wanting to impress with their gifts.

Udolpho and his new bride welcomed like returning heroes, a troupe of guests – who'd arrived the previous night in happy expectation - all geared up in their finery, emerging from the Palazzo, Udolpho laughing loud and strident, Groleshka's smiles strained and wan as she was led away by Udolpho's several sisters, Groleshka trying to keep up with this new idiomatic form of Italian she barely understood, heart-torn and grieving for the life she'd left behind, trying to please, trying to be pleased, but failing miserably, eyes and oxters wet with a regret that would never leave her.

And so begins another Wedding Feast, entirely different from the last: everything seemingly done on the hop, tables and chairs appearing from nowhere and set up in the covered courtyard; braziers hastily fetched and lit; every surface soon covered in earthenware bowls, jugs and platters; the palazzo's kitchen a hot fluster of roasting meats in ovens, pans and plates; maids fetching from the pantry food already prepared: great plaits of bread dusted blue with poppy seeds, or sprinkled with crisp sesame, dotted with olives and salt; multi-coloured peppers and aubergines glistening with oil, small yellow tomatoes preserved on their stalks like grapes, larger greener ones sweet as plums; oranges and lemons brought out from one of the Estate's several ice-houses, kept so fresh their zest made the maids' noses tingle; bowls of peaches, apricots and prunes soaked in brandy, plums soused in calvados; jars of honey so fragrant they'd have made Hermistus weep.

The courtyard soon animated with busy conversation, news being swapped and shared, everyone eating and drinking their fill. Lukitt and Alameth awed by this outdoor eating a mere few yards from the dirty snow outside the courtyard, looking up at the unbesmirched snow gleaming on hill-tops in the bright white moonlight as afternoon quickly shifted into night; seeing how warm and cosy the courtyard soon became, cocooned by the lime-washed walls of the Palazzo on three sides, the braziers doing their job, not a lick of wind to sway the lamps strung from portico to portico.

'It's kind of a marvel, when you think on it,' Alameth breathed contently, as the two removed themselves from the main event, stomachs filled, leaning back against one of the stable doors that had been closed up for the night, listening to the last snickerings of the horses within as they subsided into sleep, the warmth from the nearest brazier making their boots steam lightly as they held their feet out towards it.

'How so?' Lukitt asked, listening not to the gabbling of the many people about their tables, nor the Pfiffmaklers' subtle backdrop of music meant to fill the gaps in those conversations, not that those gaps ever occurred. Lukitt more attuned to the strange screechings of the birds that had chosen to settle here to bide their winter through, the noises of the horses settling in their stables, the whistling peeps and shreeps of a few bats woken by the company's activities and desperate for food.

'Well, that we're here at all, for one,' Alameth answered. 'And how all this got put together so quickly, how everyone sort of chipped in.'

''Cept for us,' Lukitt said, Alameth agreeing, laughing softly. 'Mind that flea circus we saw in one of Père Ulbert's books?'

Lukitt smiling, for Alameth always called Ulbert by his formal name, an Abbey habit he'd not been able to break.

'I do,' Lukitt replied, seeing the page before him: the tiny creatures miraculously jacketed in their even tinier clothes, somehow trained to climb miniature towers, crawl along ropes made from single strands of hair, dance tight circular jigs for their finale. He'd been disinclined to believe it was possible until Ulbert corrected him.

'Saw it myself through a magnifying eyepiece,' he'd said. 'They're not really trained. Just hopping around waiting for their next meal – females, blood suckers all. But makes you wonder what else there is in this world that beggars belief and yet exists all the same.'

Lukitt seeing what Alameth meant, how impossible this journey of theirs appeared, how inexplicable the series of events that had led them on.

And yet here they were. Faith solidified into fact.

About to say more, when he was hauled roughly aloft by his collar.

'You Lukitt Bachmann?'

Lukitt nodding, unable to speak.

'Thought so. You've to come with me.'

Lukitt given no option, feet scuffling along the cobbles as the large man drew him on, Alameth scrabbling up, about to accompany Lukitt until he was shoved unceremoniously back by the man's other hand.

Alameth shocked, making no move – not at first - had never been brave; but the boots on his feet had walked across country borders and felt worthy of more, and so Alameth followed, keeping to the shadows, but following all the same.

Lukitt entered the Palazzo under his own steam, following the big man, curious what would happen, where he was being taken and why. The Palazzo was impressive: three large rectangular blocks three stories high, stern facades punctured by lines of arched windows, each with bricked voussoirs and moulded spandrels to soften the regularity of their spacing, the whitewash shining under the pale light of the moon.

Gaining the interior was an odd experience, everything dark and hidden, their footsteps echoing on the flagstones, large tapestries on every wall, the glimmerings of the gold thread winding through their stories caught by the leap of light coming from the courtyard beyond its windows; the raucous laughter and chatter sounding far away, shielded by walls two foot thick.

'This way,' Lukitt's companion commanded, Lukitt following diligently, going along corridors, up a wide flight of polished marble stairs, the man stopping abruptly outside a doorway.

'Here y'go,' the man said, rapping sharply on the door before stepping away, moving quickly back down the stairs, disappearing into the gloom.

'Komme,' Lukitt heard from beyond the door: a thin, slightly querulous voice reminding him of the sedge warblers he'd heard so often back on the Seiden See. He did as bid and opened the door, saw before him the Countess Groleshka, her freckles glowing in the lamp set upon the side table next to the uncomfortable looking chaise longue she was perched on, a small picture frame clutched with skinny fingers to her breast.

'Hello?' Lukitt asked as he moved inside, closing the door behind him, aware of some faint movement in the shadows back in the hallway, Alameth's blonde head bobbing around a corner, telling him he was there; Lukitt smiling, glad of his friend's presence although surely there was no danger here. Only the new wife of the Italian Cockerel, though what she wanted with Lukitt he'd no idea.

'Come in,' she gestured, waving a pale arm to bring Lukitt on, Lukitt obeying, uncomfortably aware, as he approached, that Groleshka's face was anything but happy at her new circumstance, instead appeared tired and drawn, tear lines tracked down what was left of the powder on her cheeks.

'A little of the old country,' she said, as Lukitt came nearer, stood before her, saw her studying him as he was studying her, her stillness reminiscent of the insects he'd used to capture in jars when they'd realised there was no escape and ceased their struggling, choosing to cling to the glass looking out onto the world that had once been theirs. Small pang of pity, both for them and her.

'So you're Lukitt Bachmann,' Groleshka stated, 'the boy who saved my little Heddel,' Lukitt nodding, relieved, aware now what this was all about, trying to quickly think out angles that might work to his advantage.

'I am,' he said, voice as quiet as hers, both intimidated by their new environment, this stone carapace that held them tight within its midst. Groleshka shook her head, stood the picture she'd been holding next to the lamp, careful to make sure its leg was positioned correctly to keep it upright.

'I never thanked you,' Groleshka whispered, lowering her head. 'I don't suppose you've any idea what that boy means to me, that I raised him as my own.' She closed her eyes, shook her head slowly from side to side. 'I'd have brought him with me if I could. The thought of not seeing him again…well. It breaks my heart. But the fact that he's still alive,' she raised her head, looked at Lukitt Bachmann standing before her: a lad who couldn't have been much older than sixteen, ragged and dusty from his travelling, brown eyes so earnest and trustworthy.

She took a breath, went on.

'What I'm saying is this. The fact that he's still alive gives me hope, gives me my only hope in this godforsaken place. Hope that he'll grow up, remember me and come looking for his sister Groleshka, maybe even take me out of here, back to where I belong. And that is entirely because of you.'

Lukitt blinked, unsure if he should say anything or no, wanting to keep this woman on side, for advancement in a new country was a tricky thing and - no matter what Udolpho had said – his and Alameth's position on the Ligurian boats was not a foregone conclusion.

He bowed.

'I'm only glad I was there to do service,' he said, keeping to the formal, hoping it would please, which it did.

'As am I!' Groleshka answered fervently. 'As am I,' she repeated, fingering the portrait once again, looking back at Lukitt. 'And I gather that my…husband…' no doubting the contempt with which she spoke that last word, 'gave you a promise. Said he would put you on his boats.'

'He did,' Lukitt answered, a little hesitant, putting two and two together, fearing they were only going to make three instead of four.

'Well you can forget all that,' Groleshka said bitterly, confirming Lukitt's worst fears. 'He's a man who talks like a lion roars – all noise and teeth, but very little intention of springing into action. But let me tell you this,' she leaned forward, beckoning Lukitt in, Lukitt obeying, trying not to flinch as Groleshka put out a skinny finger and drew it down Lukitt's face. 'I will make sure it happens,' she went on, contradicting herself, resting her finger momentarily below Lukitt's chin before withdrawing it, withdrawing herself. 'You can't trust that man any more than you'd trust those marmots he's so in love with to make you breakfast. But I, Lukitt,' she straightened briefly on her uncomfortable chair, in her uncomfortable new life.

'I will do everything in my power to make it happen. You might need to be patient, but I will do my damndest to get it done.'

'What happened?' Alameth asked, the instant Lukitt appeared from the dark room and closed the door quietly behind him.

'Some good, some bad,' Lukitt answered, leading Alameth away – not in the direction they'd come from but further into the depths of the Palazzo, for no better time to explore what it might hold whilst all and sundry were out in the courtyard, the party apparently intent on staying there all night, or at least until food and drink had dwindled into crumb and dreg.

'Bad?' Alameth echoed, fear stark in that single syllable. 'How bad? What do you mean, bad?'

'No need to worry,' Lukitt said blithely, 'just that the Count is big on making promises but not so keen on keeping them.'

'But he brought us here,' Alameth countered, 'that's got to mean something.'

Lukitt nodded his head.

'Something,' he agreed, 'just not sure what. I'm thinking he might make us work out some kind of apprenticeship, and the good Frau back there is thinking the same. But,' Lukitt placed a hand on his friend's arm, 'like I said, not to worry. She's on our side. We might have to bide here a while, do as we're told, but she'll see to it. And as long as we're gone by springtime, well, No harm kicking our heels here for a bit, see what there is to be seen. It's a new country after all and...'

He stopped abruptly, cocked his head.

'Did you hear that?'

'Hear what?' Alameth listened, all he could hear being the faint undertow of the courtyard gathering that had accompanied them their whole way through the building. 'And where are we going anyway?'

'Ssh,' Lukitt urged, concentrating. 'Water. I can hear water, and voices.'

He moved towards the sound, found a wall covered by a large and heavy tapestry.

'I don't think we should...' Alameth began, but Lukitt was curious, lifted a corner of the tapestry, found a small door hidden beneath. He tapped it: no answer, so Lukitt gently turned the handle and pushed open the door, the two of them arrested on the threshold by the extraordinary sight beyond, the tapestry dropping back behind them as they took a step inside.

'Good God,' whispered Alameth, surveying the small fountain at the centre of the room. 'But aren't we one storey up? How...'

'Hydraulics,' Lukitt explained, dismissing the fountain, more impressed by the walls of the room that were composed of slabs of amber and mirrored glass, the effect dizzying, his reflections jumping as he moved further into the sparsely furnished room: one large sofa just beyond the fountain scattered with embroidered cushions and several stools placed up against the walls, where amber met glass, the wood of the stools' surface plainly made for a man kneeling, carefully chiselled and polished to make such action as easy as possible.

He went to the one on the right, figuring it to be the closest to the murmuring voices he'd heard outside, knelt down on the wood, soon spotting a small ledge placed across the interstices of the panel - rounded just so, to take a man's chin – locating a small spy hole carefully drilled through the wall a few inches above.

'Well I never,' he whistled softly, lifting himself up on his knees, the spyhole obviously intended for someone several inches taller than himself. He eased his eye to the hole and gazed through it – clear line of sight into a ladies' boudoir, several women on the other side of the wall adjusting various pieces of attire: one straightening a topiaried topknot of hair, another re-plastering a lip-smudged cheek, a forlorn lady sitting to one side weeping gently into a wisp of lace, another practising a smile and then a pleasing pout at her reflection in the mirror.

Lukitt withdrew, shifted his attention to the other stools, finding the same chin niches, the same occularities built into the walls above them. The one in the back wall opposite the door gave aspect onto a large thin room that was plainly used for wrestling matches, drinking contests, indoor *Pallone*, archery and boules, judging by the equipment that was scattered about its interior; a few men gathered at its farthest end and, although he couldn't catch a word they were saying, it struck Lukitt that these were men making deals, swapping letters and handshakes, and how useful a tool this spyhole might be to Udolpho, how advantageous to see who was doing business with whom.

'Ooh, Lukitt! Look at this. You're going to love it!' Alameth had followed his friend's lead and settled himself on the last stool, quick to vacate it when Lukitt came over.

'What is it? Lukitt asked.

'Just look,' Alameth said, and Lukitt did, Lukitt astounded as he put his eye to the spyhole to see another room stretching out before him, all in darkness, but no doubting the ranks of shelves that strode away into the shadows, the polished marble pillars, the polished marble floor.

'Oh my,' he whispered, knowing that on those shelves lay books – at least a hundred times more than Ulbert and Opapa owned between them - all that knowledge just waiting for him to ferret out, wanting right now to unfold the words from their pages, absorb the ideas they held within.

Thinking too it no bad thing they'd likely be spending their winter here before they left for the boats.

A catch of a different but superior kind.

19

Rosebuds and Recognition

The following day went on as had the night before, Wedding Feasts here in Italy apparently going on for several days. During which Lukitt had no problem seeking out the library next to the tapestry room, only to be confounded at the last to find the door locked. He crouched down and slid to one side the thin metal cover hiding the keyhole, gazing through it to make sure. Definitely the library; all he needed was to find the person who held the key and gain entrance, and the only person he could think of was Udolpho himself.

By now the party had shifted to the Banqueting Hall that took up the entire ground floor of the third arm of the Palazzo, a room of enormous proportions, pre-attired for the reception of the returning Count, last night's impromptu gathering in the courtyard being exactly that – impromptu, no one knowing exactly when he would return. By contrast the Banqueting Hall was lavishly furnished with wooden tables, an army of chairs, decorative colonnades holding up its roof from which hung five candelabra taking fifty candles apiece, the *piece de resistance* being a dancing floor and a stage to hold musicians or, as was the case now, the performing parts of the Kunterbunt who were in full swing when Heraldo brought Lukitt and Alameth around the back to witness the goings on.

'We've a new act,' Heraldo confided with some excitement, 'a man we met in Prussia last summer. He's a voice thrower. Calls himself Pompillio Parabolano, *Vocal Illusionist & Polyphonist Extraordinaire*. He's teaching me the basics. I'm not so good at the moment. Just about mastered the breathing control but my tongue can't manage the distant voice thing yet. Makes my throat hurt.'

'What's a voice thrower?' Alameth asked, eager with excitement, loving the already experienced Kunterbunt, keen for more.

'You'll see,' said Heraldo, winking, leading his friends to the wings where they could catch the end of the show, pointing to an unassuming man sat on a tall chair in the middle of the stage, the puppet of a pretty child on his shoulders and another of an ugly dwarf set between his knees.

'He's partway between ventriloquist and puppeteer,' Heraldo whispered, 'does all the voices and sound effects himself. Just about to do his finale, operates both puppets, tells everyone about how they met, and honestly – you'll not believe it – everything you hear is coming from him.'

Lukitt and Alameth arrange themselves by the curtains, from where they can see *Il Parabolano* operating his puppets: the top one with his hands, the bottom one with his feet, though how he makes their movements so realistic beggars belief.

'Will you just get on with it, you boring *bratwurst*. You're not on your own here, you know!'

It's the dwarf apparently speaking, and although he's made of plaster and crudely painted, when his eyes suddenly flick open his audience is amazed.

Pompillio looks as surprised as they do and becomes flustered.

'Why of course. I'm so sorry, so sorry. Let me introduce my travelling companions. This is Plashvit Koblingen…'

The dwarf bows between his creator's legs and interrupts.

'They call me The Cripple,' says he, in a voice so unlike that of his master it's truly astonishing to think they're made by the same person. 'They call me that,' he growls on, 'because I've a bloody great hump on my back,' rolling his eyes upwards to indicate Pompillio as his great burden, Pompillio pretending – according to his own script - not to notice and carrying on.

'And this delightful child on my shoulders is our little Rosebud and our delight;'

The child on his shoulders giggles and bats her eyelids, that carry a forest of black lashes.

'She's a pretty one, alright,' agrees Koblingen gruffly, 'plump and pink from top to tail.'

His lecherous laugh is so unpleasant that some of the audience gasp, Pompillio himself wincing and tutting in exasperation.

'Really, Koblingen. Not in front of our guests. We've a position to keep up.'

'Ha!' retorts the dwarf. 'From where I'm standing, I'm the only one keeping anything up!'

Laughter from the audience, for certainly it appears true from where they're sitting, Lukitt seeing otherwise, astonished when the Rosebud pipes up for the first time: a sweet falsetto voice with an occasional lisp:

'Oh dear,' says she, or rather the astonishing Pompillio says for her, 'I do wish I knew what our dear dwarf is talking about thome of the time; it thounds tho much fun!'

Pompillio shakes his head. 'It really isn't my dear, it's really not for your pretty ears. Koblingen, will you never learn?'

'Can't teach an old dog new tricks!' Koblingen gurgles;

'Are you so old?' tinkles the Rosebud;

'Certainly not!' growls back the dwarf, 'A mere sprig at thirty!'

'Thirty!' laughs Pompillio, 'More like sixty!'

'Thirty-five!' says the dwarf;

'Fifty!' laughs Rosebud;

'Fifty-five!' counters Pompillio;

'Forty!' shouts the dwarf;

'Forty-five!' laughs the Rosebud;

'Fifty!' yells the dwarf, confused;

'Done!' calls Pompillio and nods his head.

This swift altercation is greeted with an enthusiastic round of applause, Lukitt watching closely, but unable to figure how one man can utter three voices in such quick succession.

'He's amazing!' he whispers to Heraldo.

'Best is yet to come,' Heraldo confides, the two of them directing their gaze back to the stage as Pompillio makes the dwarf's head droop ever so slightly before suddenly bringing him back upright.

'But not so old I didn't get you lot out of trouble!' Koblingen apparently shouts.

'Ah yes,' says Pompillio, master of the understated voice, 'that you did;'

'Ah yes,' pipes up the Rosebud perched on Pompillio's shoulders, 'that you did. Tell them, Papa Pompillio, tell them our tale.'

'Might as well get it over with,' grumbles the dwarf, in patent false modesty, rolling his eyes unnervingly as Pompillio begins; Lukitt fascinated, the wedding guests leaning forward slightly, trying to see the trick, but Pompillio switches voices with such speed it's almost impossible not to see the puppets as having a life of their own.

Pompillio: I came across my companions in a town that had no name…

Mutters the dwarf: Never been a town doesn't have a name….

Rosebud interrupting: Sssh! Let Papa Pompillio continue.

Papa Pompillio does: Thank you, my dear. So there I am, and it's very late and very dark, the town already asleep. No people, no lights, no sounds, just me and my old horse clopping up the cobbled road

Inexplicably, Pompillio's audience hears the horse, Pompillio clicking his tongue inside closed mouth - in the distance at first, getting closer and closer until, with a scatter of tired hooves on loose pebbles, it comes to a stop.

Pompillio: It was past three in the morning, that I know, for I heard the church bells chiming: *klang, klang, klang*;

His audience hear the sounds of the church bell echoing through the crisp night air.

Pompillio: My horse is deadbeat; all he does is hang his head and snort.

They hear the snorts, and know the glue-factory is calling.

Pompillio: I look around me, but all I see is dark and empty windows. The snow has begun to fall, softly at first and then thicker and thicker as the wind grows stronger.

His audience hears the faint whisper of softly falling snow and the rising of the wind, the howling of it as it moves through the buildings of this unnamed town.

And then I hear something –

He cocks his head, looks upward, everyone instinctively following his gaze.

It's coming from a window, high up in the street!

His audience raise their heads for there is the house, there the window suddenly appearing, courtesy of the Pfiffmaklers.

And there's that noise again! Someone crying! Someone crying their heart out!

And there it is: quiet and soft, a girl sobbing in a distant attic.

Switch of voice, Rosebud now, piteous and quiet:

That was me; it was so cold, so cold.

Pompillio: Your daddy had locked you in your room for a week with no blankets, no comforts. Only a bowl of water, a stinking bucket, and a loaf of stale bread.

Rosebud : Ah yes, it was so cold, so very, very cold.

And again there comes the small distant sound of crying, nothing else, everyone concentrated on the stage, on what would happen next, knowing it to be a subterfuge yet willingly subjecting themselves to this alternate reality, this story that is not theirs, hoping it will have a happy ending.

Pompillio: I found the window, saw the girl pressed against it, her face pale against the glass, weeping in the middle of that dark and soulless night, so I started to throw pebbles at the window.

Plink, plink; plink, plink – everybody hears it.

But no way to reach the poor child.

Pompillio sighs.

Growls Koblingen: Until I came along.

The audience ease into their seats as the Dwarf comes dramatically back to life.

And I had a rope coiled about my shoulders - nothing bad about that, folks. Wasn't thinking on robbing anyone.

His argument unconvincing; everyone knows it, everyone so immersed in the story, so invested in the characters that they laugh a little at his attempted deception.

Pompillio: But with his rope and grapple - *they hear the scrape of metal on stone* - so was our little Rosebud rescued, *and convinced was his audience, hearing the distinct crash and tinkle of glass falling from the girl's prison into the street below, the little Rosebud jiggling on Pompillio's shoulders:*

Saved at last!

Pompillio swinging with ease into his final routine as he sings his *Song of the Three Unlikely Companions*, skipping from one voice to another in quick and sharp succession, the puppets seeming to move from side to side of their own accord as they get into the rhythm:

We are three in one and one in three,
There's me
And me
And me.
I'm on top,
I'm in between,
I'm on the bottom and you know what that means,
All the long day I carry this crew,
And I'm the one who gets the view!
I do the steering,
I do the cheering!
And I get a back askew
And bunions like balloons.
I've got curls & pretty manners,
I'm an earth with two moons.
I do the work!
I do the thinking!
I do the laughing & the lithping!
I plan the route,
I'm the look-out,
I'm the one who wears through his boots!
I've a crick in my neck – it's like carrying a vat,
I'm your acquired conscience;
You're a prick, I'll give you that,
And what are you, my little Rosebud?
I'm the sugar on the cake, the swan upon the lake,
Me below
And me betwixt
And upon us both she's sits.

Like what, Rosebud?
Like what, Rosebud, are you sat?
Rosebud tinkles, Rosebuds laughs, Rosebud states:
Why everyone knows: I'm the very prettiest kind of hat!

Last words of the act, the house behind them crumpling to the stage floor, Pompillio Parabolano standing up, extricating himself from the two puppets, holding them up, one in each hand, Heraldo's father Wenzel leaping onto the stage to take them from him.

'All his own work! Every word you heard! Every sound!'

'Bravo!' shouts Udolpho, 'Bravo! Bravo!'

'Hurrah!' shout the men, everyone clapping, Pompillio bowing deeply, taking his dues, his audience laughing and beginning to chatter: astonished, amazed, and truly amused, as had been the intention. Time now to bring on the musicians and get the wedding guests dancing once more; Lukitt seeing his chance, removing himself from the wings of the stage and down the stairs into the ballroom as Heraldo and Alameth clap their hands, Pompillio Parabolano bowing himself from the stage, wiping his brow.

'Good show, lads?' he asks, draining a flagon of water.

'The best!' Heraldo states.

'The absolute best!' Alameth agrees, looking around for Lukitt, but Lukitt is gone.

20

A Different Kind of Act Altogether

Lukitt keeps to the edges of the ballroom, dodging the groups of dapper men heading for the dance floor and the swirling skirts of the women. Udolpho is, naturally, at the top table attired in his customary yellow, face hearty and red with drink, slapping his hand repeatedly on the table as his fellows congratulate him on the wonderful performance of Pompillio Parabolano.

'Like you said, bravo!' his nearest companion was shouting jovially. 'An absolute coup, my friend, an absolute coup. I have to get these people to Turin. It will be an absolute triumph!'

Udolpho leaning back in his seat as Lukitt approached, waving him away, taking him for one of the serving boys.

'You're not needed. How many times have I told you all to keep your distance until you're called?'

He started chatting with the man to his left, Lukitt standing like a shadow at his elbow, waiting for a break in the conversation, Udolpho turning back irritably that the lad should stay despite his dismissal.

'Didn't I just tell you…' he began, before focussing in on Lukitt's face, recognition dawning. 'Oh it's you. I forget your name – but this is the boy, friends, I was telling you about. The one who shook that idiot Heddel up and down by his heels, and not a moment too soon! *My mouth burns! My mouth burns*!' Udolpho raising his voice to an unpleasant falsetto imitation of Heddel, a task almost anyone – let alone Pompillio Parabolano – would have done better and with less cruelty.

Surprisingly to Lukitt, several men turned their gazes upon him with evident curiosity.

'So this is the one knows so much about beetles?' asked one, Udolpho nodding with largesse, attitude switching in a moment as he recognised his fellows' interest, never mind that he'd almost completely forgotten who Lukitt was or why he'd bothered bringing the lad over to Italy.

'Pauper boy from the hills,' he answered vaguely, dredging his memory for details, imbuing his words with implied ownership, the men around this table being important folk. 'Thought I'd take him under my wing, so to speak,' Udolpho added for good measure.

'But plainly a pauper boy with an outstanding education,' another of the men said, looking to Lukitt for explanation.

'Père Ulbert taught me,' he said quickly, 'and I had some books from Opapa…from Brother Ommaweise, at the Gargellan Monastery.'

'Is that so?' another leaned forward. 'I know that man, have corresponded with him many times about the nature of optics.'

'So what're you here for?' Udolpho cut in to bring this boring conversation to an end.

Lukitt bowed his head quickly.

'Just wanted to ask if I could access your library while I'm here,' he said, 'think it might be a great opportunity for me, being under your wing and all that.'

He bowed again, not missing the brief exchange of glances between several of the men about the table.

'I see no objection,' said one of them. 'Udolpho?'

The Italian Cockerel sat back in his seat, toothpick in one hand, crystal glass filled with wine in the other, studying Lukitt, because if Udolpho's present companions were interested in this boy then so was he, momentarily at least. He'd laboured long and hard to get himself accepted into the intellectual *literati* of the area, mostly to boost his ego, get himself acquainted with a better class of men who could extend his contacts, the excuse of his wedding being the perfect foil; for here at his table were a load of Professors, not to mention Hans Trudbert - an important investor in his canning venture. All in all, a very illustrious presence that had been years in the cultivation.

'Well, well,' Udolpho says after a few moments, 'then why not, my young prodigy? But how about you do us a favour in return?'

Lukitt held his breath, prepared to jump through any hoops to get into that library.

'I'll give you one day,' says Udolpho, 'one day to come up with an interesting lecture for my friends here who are Professors and very important people.'

Waving his hand about the table, his companions smiling and nodding.

'Excellent idea!' agreed one.

'Show us what you're made of,' added another.

'A grand end to our visit, that would surely be,' Hans Trudbert enthusiastic.

Lukitt thanking them all, mind racing, Udolpho extracting a key-ring from a voluminous pocket and fumbling about to get the right one, finally managing to unclip it and hand it over, grabbing Lukitt's wrist tightly as Lukitt took it.

'Don't let me down, boy. I'll want something good, and it'll need to be more than just about bloody beetles. Understood?'

'Understood, sir,' Lukitt nodded, trying not to skip from one foot to the other in his excitement, knowing that if he could impress even one of these men then things might go very differently for him than merely learning how to sail a boat on the Ligurian Sea.

The following morning Lukitt rose early from the room Groleshka had arranged for him and Alameth – right in the eyrie of the single tower that grew up from the middle colonnade, the only part of the entire Palazzo exceeding the regimented three stories of the rest; built as a look-out post in earlier times when the Palazzo was under threat from neighbouring estates. The evening before, when one of Groleshka's women had fetched them from the stables and brought them here, both Lukitt and Alameth had been breathless with the view afforded them from the windows punctuating the stone façade: three hundred and sixty degrees all around, from the mountains and orchard terraces to the vineyards and lower fields; from the village and the winding road that led to a town a few miles distant.

And the sea.

Their first proper sight of the sea: a mere silver shiver out there on the horizon of the night, but they knew it all the same for there were the masts they'd previously been able to discern and, from this height, the bay that bore the boats.

'Will you look at that!' Alameth whistled, 'and to think we might soon be out there ourselves.'

Shaking his head in wonderment, not yet privy to Lukitt's latest plan – which was to bypass the boats altogether, dazzle Udolpho's apparently brilliant friends with his brilliant lecture and maybe, in consequence, be offered a teaching post, secure some kind of undergraduate tenure so he could continue his education without having to stink of fish every living moment of his days and nights.

Lukitt looked out of the seaward window this morning as he dressed quickly and quietly, felt the brass key secure in his inner jerkin pocket, saw how magnificent his dawn view was: the water an unsettled blue-green expanse, smooth in one place, ruffled in others as down-below currents swirled their way beneath, the wind causing white peaks here and there to rise and fall, a few boats already plied and distant, throwing out fishing lines, bright sails flashing in the sun.

Lukitt was appreciative, but didn't stop long, set out instead down the narrow winding staircase that went the whole height of the tower to ground level, selecting the first storey door and turning towards the library. The Palazzo at that early hour completely deserted, a few groans and sighs emanating from various rooms as he passed them by, their occupants sleeping deep from too much dancing, an excess of food and drink. He'd taken off his boots when he'd exited the tower, not wanting to wake anyone, reaching the library without incident, taking out the key, briefly worrying whether Udolpho in his cups had given the wrong one, but it turned, a little creakily, in the lock and Lukitt opened the door and went in.

Walked into a cathedral of tomes and folios, shelves stuffed from polished floor to a stuccoed ceiling painted with scenes of Academia: schools of putti being taught the arcana of mathematics, music, philosophy and theology, overseen by long-bearded men and clean shaven angels bearing harps. All guarded below by a legion of brass-runged ladders and several mahogany desks topped with green leather, and a barrage of lamps – all unlit. There were several vast armchairs dotted here and there, each of which had attached stools to rest the feet, and tables that swung from their sides to hold the absent scholars' port and cigars, and the odd book.

Lukitt was overwhelmed, felt like one of those nets the men on the boats in the Ligurian Bay were casting overboard at this very moment, hoping for a catch, no idea what he might be capable of finding and presenting in a coherent manner to Udolpho and his friends. What was clear to him was that it needed to be impressive, startling if possible, touching on each of the fields those eminent men held most dear. He wished he had Ulbert here to guide him, the man who'd done so much to set him on his course; and he thought too on his parents, who'd loved him enough to let him leave. Up to him to see them through their final days when they came, to carry on the farmstead - or provide them with the means to give it all up before that happened.

He closed his eyes, took a deep breath, for if ever he was going to help any of them – all of them – then this had to be his best option. His only way. Get himself on, shove himself up the ladder so he could go back and save them all.

He started with a brief survey of the library's layout, found it separated into themed sections, but those sections in no further discernible order; it becoming clear to him that this library had stood undisturbed for years, most probably a construct of Udolpho's father, a project Udolpho had not deemed important enough to keep up.

There was, though, one surprising shelf that had several recently published volumes on it, all penned by the men at Udolpho's table the night before – names Lukitt had gone to some lengths to discover, asking here and there, learning from the serving staff exactly who they were: Professors Elemossa, Franconelli, Grotanelli and Vannevar, along with Hans Trudbert who seemed not to be an academic but a business partner.

Udolpho maybe not the blockhead Lukitt had taken him for, having sought out those men's publications, researched their areas of specific interest. Lukitt needing to do the same, work into his lecture each of their individual areas of interest: history, social justice, natural science, industry and theology; tie them all up with some over-arching theme.

He conjured up Ulbert's cardinal rules for making a sermon interesting: *Intrigue, Entrap, Instruct.* Lukitt sticking to those principles during his next hours burrowing through Udolpho's library, looking through this book and that, making notes, getting his lecture workable.

And no better advice could he have had.

He chose not to give his lecture in the vast Banqueting Room that by now was entirely emptied of fops and females, everyone gone from the Palazzo that morning excepting Udolpho's intellectuals. Gone too were the Pfiffmaklers, although folk were still gabbling about Pompillio Parabolano as they departed for home. Time now for Lukitt to perform, the sides of his hands starting to itch with the stress, Alameth a jumping bean beside him tasked with illustrating Lukitt's lecture with one volume or another, several drawings Lukitt had made, or some object he'd picked up on his walks outside the Palazzo walls, Lukitt wishing he'd begged from Heraldo some handfuls of razzamatazz he could use to enliven the moment.

But Heraldo had gone.

Only Lukitt and Alameth left.

Only the next hour or so to dictate how their lives would go from here on in.

Udolpho was plainly not in the best of moods – no doubt from being three days drunk – but his learned friends were of better temperament, saving themselves for this end to their visit with some anticipation, and so Udolpho had no choice but to play along.

They're in the library itself – a place Udolpho has little familiarity with –Lukitt seating his audience in a small tier of chairs before a table, has set the scene, lit a few lamps, and Udolpho is obscurely impressed despite himself.

Lukitt clears his throat, glances down at his notes:

Title: *An Experiment in Envenomation*
Subplot - Nature: *Attack, defence and subterfuge*
Analogy: *Deborah v. Jael (Judges 4 & 5)*

Opening shock: The chicken

'I once murdered a chicken,' Lukitt began, drama and intrigue his intent. 'I found a wild bee-comb forming under one of the oaks on my great uncle's farm, probably established by one of his own overwintering queens. *Destroy it,* uncle advised, *our own hives are full and we don't need the competition.* I set to my task, smoking the alien hive drowsy in the cold of the night. I cut the neck of the comb and dropped it and the half-sized swarm into a pot. I sealed the pot with a piece of muslin and set it in the far field where an old chicken pecked in the dust. In the morning, I laid a trail of corn and put a pile of it on the muslin lid, and along came the old chicken. She clucked and pecked along the line, came to the pot, neck jiggling with greed, peck, peck, peck; pecking at the pile until the muslin broke. My thinking being that she'd get a wonderful treat in the form of the somnolent bees and their honey. But I'd not done my research, did not understand the behaviour of drowsy bees, for out they came, angry and disoriented, hardly able to fly, descending as one onto the enemy they deemed had attacked their nest, destroying themselves by destroying her. That poor old chicken,' Lukitt groaned, still disturbed by the memory, for it was a real one.

'I was watching from behind the woodpile, thinking my plan a grand one; and it worked to an extent, for certainly I'd destroyed the hive – all the workers dead, lives torn from them by their stinging, a few left in the pot, drowned in their own honey – but the chicken, ah the chicken, lay some yards from the pot, one foot still kicking, a single last bee buzzing in her gullet. Awful,' Lukitt said, shaking his head. 'A terrible lesson, and one that hasn't left me. From that day onwards I realised two things: firstly, that a person must plan carefully before putting any scheme into action; secondly that every part of nature carries its own mechanisms of attack and defence. For the chicken it had not gone well, but that chicken – during its lifetime – had murdered many worms and grubs as surely as I had just murdered her, although murder is not the word we usually use to describe such acts. We call them the entire opposite. We call them survival mechanisms, and every species - every plant, every insect, every mammal, every creature that lives in water, land or air - has its own specialized weapons with which to attack, subdue, or kill its enemies. Life is a hard game, and dying a natural death from old age incredibly rare – except in humans. Because for us, life and death have taken on a different aspect, our intellect so far exceeding those of our myriad companion species on this earth that we have gained a unique advantage.'

He glanced at his audience, pleased to see his stratagem had worked, for all of them – even Udolpho – appeared transfixed.

'The weapons and adaptations nature has equipped itself with are breath-taking,' he hurried on, 'as are the lengths every living creature will go to survive long enough to reproduce a further generation. Many of these methods are obscure, bizarre even, and yet entirely effective. Witness the worm that lives in a sperm whale's gut that can grow ten yards in length without killing the animal it has chosen as host, or the wasp that lays its egg in an ant's head, the larva eating it from the inside out, forcing that ant into behaviours unknown to it, making it climb a stem of grass so the wasp's pupa can hatch out and launch itself into the air that is its natural medium...'

Lukitt continued his lecture as planned, Alameth quick with Lukitt's chosen illustrations, bringing them up close so his audience can view the exciting, the bizarre, the apparently cruel. Lukitt finishing with a biblical example, just as Ulbert would have done, tying everything up within a moral argument.

'So, let me end,' Lukitt was saying, 'by citing an example to illustrate man's own exceptional capacities for defence, or not men in this instance but women: namely Deborah and Jael in Judges. Deborah an Israelite, patriot, prophetess and judge – the only female judge noted in the bible - deemed a honey bee by her friends, a stinging bee by her enemies, the bee at that time the sign of monarchy. She prophesied that Barak, despite his ill-equipped army of tribesmen, would be victorious if he rose up against the professional army of King Jabin, led by Sisera; so convinced of that victory that she went with Barak into battle and against the odds, and by Deborah's good stratagem, they succeeded; Sisera fleeing to the tent of his enemy's enemy, to Jael, wife of Heber the Kenite, thereby fulfilling another of Deborah's prophesies - or reasonable deductions as we might call them - that the Lord would deliver Sisera into a woman's hands.

'Jael was a woman of faith, with no love for the godless Canaanites whom Sisera had been aiding, but offered Sisera *leben* – a drink of curdled milk, still to this day given by Bedouin to their guests as both refreshment and soporific after their long days of travelling. She made him comfortable, allowed him to sleep. Then took up a tent-peg and hammered it through Sisera's head.'

Lukitt acting out the shocking deed with his hands.

'Deborah's defence mechanism being her intellect, her understanding of how Sisera would behave once defeated, and how Jael would react upon receiving him,' Lukitt explained. 'Getting rid of one's enemy by another's hand. Murder at one remove. Muddy waters, ethically speaking, but effective all the same.'

Alameth hurrying forward with his last exhibit: a section of water-hemlock Lukitt had dug up from beside the washing-pool only hours before.

'From this example I've learned that morality and intellect are my tools, as they are yours,' Lukitt pronounced. 'I could chop up this piece of root and put it in your soup, and two hours after ingesting it you would all be as dead as Sisera was when Jael spliced his brain in two with her peg. Life is both fragile and yet desperate to survive and replicate itself by any means necessary.

'Nature teaches us that to survive one has to adapt, that there are no limits to which it will not go to achieve that end. And my argument from this has to be a moral one, and that surely human beings – who have surpassed this imperative by the evolution of their intellect – are by now a species apart, who have to judge the measures of our living and dying by entirely different standards. Nature is a vast store-house of how to kill and be killed, present in a million different guises. Our strength, as human beings, is the ability to understand our weaknesses within that order, to figure out what can hurt us most and how to avoid those hurts. And these abilities give us a moral imperative to seek out what can do us well, to improve our society, to not be the drowsy swarm that kills the old chicken just because she happens to be there but to look around, spy out the real enemy - the one hiding behind the woodpile unseen.

'To murder, if we must murder, and go to war, if we must go to war, with reason as our tool and right on our side. We must be Deborah, who weighed up an apparently hopeless situation and yet saw how it could be changed, put to advantage, and by doing so achieved an enormous victory and liberty for her people, establishing forty years of peace in a place than had never seen a year of it.'

Lukitt checked his audience, wondered if he'd over done things, but it seemed not. Time for the last hoorah.

'But we must also be prepared to be Jael, murdering the man who needed to be murdered, carrying it out with a swift mercy those bees in the pot will never have the wit to do. Reason is the key. We are human beings. We are weak and we are strong, but recognition of our weaknesses is our greatest strength.'

And so Lukitt finished.

Took a short bow to signal it.

His audience stunned.

No need after all for Heraldo's magic mix of exploding powder in the flames.

Lukitt's words all the explosion necessary.

Udolpho the first to clap, soon followed by his fellows, and then they were all clapping like there was no tomorrow, and out came the wine and all were on their feet coming forward, looking over Lukitt's illustrations, studying his notes, following his deductions.

'Impressive work!' Udolpho was delighted, clasping Lukitt by the shoulders. 'A most interesting talk,' dropping his voice. 'And between you and me, I've sat through an awful lot worse.'

Shaking his head, shuddering slightly, recalling the truly boring and incomprehensible lectures he'd had to undergo to get these men into his home. Interrupted by Professor Elemossa coming up and shaking Lukitt by the hand.

'Thoroughly enjoyable, young man,' he stated. 'I was very surprised you knew about the *Nerium* oleander. I had to examine an entire family who dropped dead after eating goat meat skewered and roasted on their sticks,' Lukitt accepting the compliment, neglecting to add that he only knew about it because he'd read it in Elemossa's book that described several of the more outlandish deaths he'd investigated as *magistrato* for the Venetian authorities. 'A terrible affair,' Elemossa went on, 'one of my worst. The youngest child was only three.'

'And the Rabbit fish!' Franconelli broke in. 'Inspired, my boy. Why we've only just discovered that *Siganus rivulatus* has established itself in the Mediterranean, undoubtedly come from the Red Sea up the Gulf of Suez.'

'One of Ulbert's,' Lukitt admitted.

'Ah yes,' Grotanelli broke in, 'you mentioned him before. And was it he who introduced you to Brother Ommaweise?'

'In a way,' Lukitt agreed. 'Opapa Augen was…very kind to me,' he went on, 'made me look through the eye of a glow-worm, told me about his work grinding lenses, even after he'd lost most of his fingers and toes.'

Grotanelli looked back at Lukitt, astonished.

'He lost his fingers…but how? And how does he continue to work? How can he write me all his letters?'

Lukitt remembering how deftly Opapa Augen moved and manipulated objects.

'Frostbite,' he said. 'But he still had a good length of his fingers, only lost the last joint and fingertip on most of them. And he adapted,' Lukitt added, just as he'd said men should.

'Well, well,' Grotanelli commented, shaking his head, wriggling his own fingers as if to make sure they were all still there in their entirety. 'It just makes him a more remarkable man than I've always thought him. And be certain I'll mention you in my next missive. It's about time I wrote to him…'

'I'd be very pleased if you would,' Lukitt interrupted quickly and with enthusiasm. 'I should have thought to write to him myself. He'll be impressed to know I've made it to Italy.'

'And why exactly have you made it to Italy?' Grotanelli asked, looking hard at Udolpho's young prodigy. 'What's here that you couldn't get back at home?'

'More education,' Lukitt replied swiftly. 'The Count has promised me and Alameth work on his boats, and I mean to save enough to enter myself into an Academy, maybe even a university, if I can get myself accepted.'

Grotanelli nodded slowly.

'Well if anyone deserves such a place, it's you.'

Lukitt looked up expectantly, hoping for an offer of help, but Grotanelli turned away, went to speak to Elemossa. Lukitt dismissed from his mind and thoughts, though he did mention Lukitt a few weeks later in a letter to Opapa Augen:

I met your boy Lukitt. He's quite the little lecturer. Rough around the edges, of course, and not quite our stock. Might do well enough if someone sees fit to give him a chance.

Grotanelli not that man, Lukitt grinding his teeth as Udolpho's pals closed ranks, froze him and Alameth out as they poured themselves more glasses of wine, the two summarily dismissed by Udolpho a few minutes later, Udolpho careful to retrieve the library key from Lukitt, leaving him with none of the procurements Lukitt had hoped for, bar one.

'You did well, Lukitt,' Udolpho pronounced as he led them away, 'and because of it, and because my wife has so advised it, I'm sending the two of you off in the morning to the port. Two days from now you'll be doing as I promised, be out on the boats.'

'But maybe,' Lukitt started, in desperation, cut off by Udolpho who put a hand to Lukitt's shoulder and physically shoved him out the door.

'But maybe nothing,' Udolpho growled. 'You've had your chance, done your turn, so just be glad I'm sending you on the way you first wanted to go.'

Shutting the door in Lukitt's face.

'Well, at least we're on our way,' Alameth offered, running to keep up with Lukitt as he strode along the corridor away from the library, aware of the anger Lukitt was making no attempt to hide. Lukitt had never mentioned to Alameth that he thought his lecture might be a stepping-stone to better things, but Alameth was no fool, knew too that advancement would never be gained with such ease. The monastery proof of that – men like Caleb quickly rising through the ranks because they came from monied families; folk like Alameth having to try twice as hard and twice as long to catch up with them. Ability and aptitude having nothing to do with it. Lukitt having more ability and aptitude than anyone he'd ever met – apart possibly from Heraldo – was never going to be enough. Batten down and get on with it, was Alameth's philosophy. Everything took time, moved to its own measure. That Lukitt had expected so much more was no surprise, but the vehemence of his resentment certainly was.

'Who the hell do those bastard men think they are? And what've they got that I haven't?' Lukitt asked as soon as they were out of earshot of the library.

'Well, money, for one,' Alameth offered, trying to be light-hearted, not achieving it.

'But that's precisely it!' Lukitt couldn't stop himself. 'What I said today should've been enough to get me into any of their shitting universities! But no. I'm not the *right calibre*, not from the *right family*, just a pauper boy from the hills. It's outrageous. It's…it's just not right!'

'But that's always how it's been,' Alameth mollified. 'Doesn't mean we won't get there in the end, only that it'll take us a little longer. And you heard what Udolpho said – off to the boats tomorrow! That's got to be a start.'

And it was a start, though Lukitt smarted at the injustice; might have reconsidered if he'd known what lay down the line.

21

Bad Times, Bad Decisions

Two years after Lukitt's lecture they were still working on the *Ligia Liliana* - one of Udolpho's fishing boats - no advancement in sight. Spending weeks at sea catching fish, salting them down into barrels, expected to stay on board once back in port. The pay pitiful – deductions made for the food they'd eaten while abroad and for their so-called apprenticeships. Trapped within a service they couldn't get out of. And so much worse for Alameth – handsome boy that he was – some of the crew believing it their right to take what they liked when on the water as a substitute for what they were used to on land. Alameth bullied, abused, frequently bruised in places he couldn't admit to; Alameth's faith and personality in tatters in consequence, which situation Lukitt was finding hard to bear.

They'd hit landfall, Lukitt busy rolling a barrel of pickled herring the few yards from the jetty to the door of the canning factory, when a man appeared out of a small ginnel and grabbed at Lukitt's arm.

'Lukitt,' he said, nearly sending the barrel scudding off down the street. 'Let me buy you a bottle. I've a matter of importance to discuss.'

Lukitt recognized Hans Trudbert immediately.

'What the hell do you think we have to discuss?'

Bitterness in his throat, hatred in his heart. Hating every minute of every day he and Alameth spent on the boats, both desperate for escape, especially Alameth - which was the worst of it all.

'I want you to help me,' Trudbert said, not understanding the lad's anger.

'And why would I do that?' Lukitt shot back. 'You'd the chance to help me all that time ago and you did nothing, just like the others. Absolutely nothing.'

Trudbert pinched his face into a frown, clutched at Lukitt's shoulder and pulled him around; Lukitt had filled out, grown a few inches, but was no match for Hans Trudbert, twenty years his elder.

'Listen to me, you little blow-by,' Trudbert hissed through his teeth. 'You might think you're the cleverest little fisherman in these parts, but a clever little fisherman you'll remain unless you hear me out.'

Lukitt set his feet on the cobbles, set his face in defiance, despite the truth of what Trudbert had said.

'So what do you want?' he asked shortly. 'And what are we going to get in return?'

Trudbert rocked back on his feet, loosening his grip on Lukitt, aware they'd hit a truce, baiting his line, reeling Lukitt in.

'I can get you away. Get you into an Academy,' Trudbert said. 'Secure you a teaching post to pay your way. In exchange, I need you to do one thing for me. One small thing, and thereafter your life will be what you make of it.'

Lukitt narrowed his eyes.

'How soon? And I'm telling you it needs to be soon because Alameth…well…he's to come with me, wherever I go.'

Trudbert spat in irritation, shaking his head, though part of him admired this loyalty and, after all, the small thing he wanted Lukitt to do was no small thing at all, and so he agreed.

'Him too. But be warned, my slippery young friend,' he added, 'once this deal is done I want no more to do with you and yours. I don't want to see or hear from you ever again. Is that understood?'

Lukitt wanting the same, nodding curtly.

'So get it out then,' he said, Trudbert's reply being to lead Lukitt down the dark and empty street into a dark and crowded tavern of the lowest sort where dockers and stevedores drank away their wages, shouted and swore, bulging forearms hooked around their mates' shoulders or the waists of women who'd seen better days, disease and poverty in every crook and cranny. A place where anything went and nobody overheard or, if they did, would never admit to it.

'So it's a bargain?' Trudbert said, after he'd laid out his proposition, Lukitt's throat dry at the prospect of what he'd been asked to do, only merit being a quick way out for him and Alameth. Particularly for Alameth.

'It's a bargain,' he agreed.

'Mind what I said. Use what you've got,' was Trudbert's curt reply. 'And I need it done quick.'

Plan already forming in Lukitt's head, given what Trudbert had told him.

The chicken and the bees, he was thinking. Got to be the chicken and the bees.

Lukitt sits by the pool in the forest.

It's just past dawn and the day will soon be hot, though not yet, mist still lying a breath above the water. In the shallows he sees an otter playing, several grebes tacking through the reeds, a black stork combing out its feathers, a dragonfly trying to lifts its wings, subsiding, waiting for the warmth of the sun.

By mid-morning all is change and call, rustles and whistles, splash landings, dives, flies and bees. By noon, with the sun high in the sky, he spies what he's here for: a wasp come to collect water from the lake to cool the nest. He waits, and before long there are more at the task and he carefully scoops them up, puts them in a jar, screws on the lid. He watches the last wasp heading back into the trees, cranes his neck until he loses sight of it, sets off in the same direction. When he judges the moment right he takes out his jar and unscrews the lid a little, allows the release of a single scout who buzzes angrily around his head for a moment, then sets off towards its home. Lukitt follows until he loses sight of that one too, when he releases another and then another. Five wasps later he's found his quarry, and is leaning against a fallen linden trunk watching the workers come and go through a small hole in the ground in the sorrel-carpeted glade. He bides his time, lays out his tools: a small spade, a length of tubing, a funnel, a ball of clay, a bottle of water, a pair of thick leather gloves, a canister of benzene – a compound isolated by Faraday twenty years earlier, Lukitt well versed in its varied uses.

He spends another hour or so calculating the height of the trees surrounding his little grove for amusement, clicking away on Napier's Bones, working out that the ash is twenty-two metres tall, the medlar barely five, the aspen seventeen and a half. He looks at the bones themselves – given to him by Ulbert, that had so impressed Heraldo. He wonders briefly where Heraldo is now, if he ever found his own set, if he's discovered any more wonderful instruments like the *Tromba Marina*. He wonders too on what Heraldo would think of him doing what he's doing now, the carrying out of the deal Trudbert had laid out for him, doubting Heraldo would see any righteousness in it, as surely Alameth would not, despite their situation.

Which was precisely why Lukitt had never told Alameth the truth.

'Remember how angry I was after that lecture in the library?' Lukitt had asked Alameth after he'd returned from his meeting with Trudbert.

'Hard to forget,' Alameth said dully, no longer a lad who laughed, who spent his time picking at the callouses growing over his palms where the skin had been shredded by the ropes they constantly pulled up from the Liguria; the Liguria no longer a friend or an adventure, instead an enemy that had stripped away from Alameth far more than his skin.

'Well I'm angrier now, and I'm going to get us out of here,' Lukitt had stated, but there'd been no faith in the eyes Alameth turned on him, his gaze instead moving towards the half-addled cook Jacques, and his one-eyed monkey, who'd been the only one on board to give either any aspect of friendship, and Alameth some shielding from the worst.

The sun began to drop, a breeze coming off the sea cooling the air, the return of the wasp workers from their foraging all but ceased. Lukitt pours a little water onto the clay and begins to knead it until it's soft and pliable. He loosens the lid on the canister of benzene and puts on his gloves. He takes the tube and carefully inserts it into the mouth of the hole in the earth between the sorrel plants, pushing it in gently, finding the direction of the tunnel that leads to the nest. It takes a couple of minutes, during which time three or four guards exit on patrol, giving Lukitt's gloves a few stings before he bats them off. Eventually he finds the passageway and, slow as a cooling lizard, slides the tubing in. Time for action. He fits the funnel into the tube and takes the lid off the benzene, pours it quickly into the funnel, down the tube and into the nest. The ground starts to thrum and rumble, Lukitt whipping out the tube and stoppering up the hole with the softened clay before legging it away into the trees. Despite his efforts part of the angry hive is up and out, but doesn't find him. No looking behind the woodpile for them.

More waiting now; no certainty his plan will work, despite previous research and preparation. No way to know until he puts the final part into play.

Night falls, and still he waits.

Night goes all the way through until the first glimmerings of dawn, when Lukitt can see again what he's about, when he takes up the spade and returns to the nest, starts digging, finds the cavern in which the wasps have slung their paper nest that's the size of his head. There's a few all-nighters returning from the field, but it's cold and they're sluggish and he gives them a whop with spade or glove and down they go.

No survivors in the nest, so he carefully removes it, wraps it in a sheet, trying not to destroy it too much in the process, for it's a beautiful thing. At the bottom of the excavated cavern there's a heap of dead wasps dusted in the paper flake detritus he's shaken from their nest, and these he shovels up and puts into a large jar, and then he's off.

Once back in the room Trudbert has rented temporarily for him, Lukitt strews the dead wasps on the sheet and gets out pincers and scalpel. It's an easy thing, once he's got the hang of it, to slice off the tip of the abdomen and snip out the poison sac, dropping them into the solute that will extract the venom. Next, he excavates the valuable wasp honey that lies within the nest, hidden in the comb like a treasure in a fennel-stalk box. It's dark and viscous and Lukitt can't resist, dips the point of his tongue into the honey cells where the wax caps have broken, the wasp honey slightly acidic, very different to that of bees', with a distinct taste and aroma that is tantalising. There won't be much, but there'll be enough, Lukitt loosening the rest of the caps and setting the combs at an angle to the collecting bowl, hearing Hermistus's hard voice in his ear that self-poured is by far the best. He leaves it dripping for several hours, collects as much as he can, adds his solute, stirs it, decants it into a small jar, seals it, places it in the hamper he's been provided with, along with a short note he's scratched out with pen and ink in his best writing.

All done.

Alameth's deliverance almost at hand.

'God forgive me,' Lukitt whispers, as he wraps the hamper, gets it labelled ready for the off. 'God forgive me.'

22

The Wasps do Their Worst

Jasanoff Diderik takes his lunch alone and at his desk as always, has important letters to sign, important decisions to make. He grunts over his large belly, leans forward in his chair to reach the ink-pot – expensive ink, slightly pink, scented with cardamom – and shuggles the wax in its little brass pot, the candle below wavering with his efforts. He's lined up his four official seals and ponders over which to use. This the best part of his job as secretary to the Duke, and he never tires of the enjoyment of selecting the seal he deems most suitable, folding the document carefully, pouring on the wax, making the impress quickly and with a flourish, not forgetting the slight sigh to show that he does this every day and it's really rather a bore.

He's proud of his position - insufferably so, some have said - earned not by merit but inherited from his father who ground on interminably until the age of seventy two, insisting on doing his duty to the last. And now it's all Jasanoff's. He's had years to prepare and plan, to preen and expand his flesh to the regulation portliness of size. He's even taken a wife - albeit from a contract forged by his father years before – who's just turned sixteen and rather beautiful in a wan sort of way. At night, when he feels inclined – which isn't often - he has to take her from the side so his overlying weight doesn't crush out of her what little life she appears to possess. And if no son appears then there's his nephew from his sister's side – young Hans Diderik - to take his place.

Jasanoff frowns to think on his nephew, who'd not gone the way either he or his father would have liked: mincing around with his university pals in Italy before coming up with that madcap scheme of the canning factory: a rickety venture financed by the family and a couple of other investors, despite Jasanoff's explicit disapproval.

His valet knocked at the door, bringing in a basket.

'What's all this?' Jasanoff asks, as the valet places the basket on the quickly cleared desk.

'Card says it's from Herr Frücklestein, Master of the Gold Workers Guild,' his valet informs, Jasanoff rubbing his hands in anticipation. The Gold Workers Guild! Things were looking up; his buttering up of important men having at last yielded something of value.

Get yourself a good broad back and a thick hide, his father had always advised him. *Lots of scratching to be done.*

And here was his first itch about to be satisfied.

He'd had the stonemasons round a few months before, but saw no use in a couple of grinning gargoyles or, God forbid, *the best sorrowing angel in the cemetery this side of Heidelberg.* Stonemasons be damned. Goldsmiths was more the mark; a smart clock perhaps – he'd seen one with the hours inlaid with opals. Or maybe a decent ring, one with a seal hidden inside a spring-hinged lid.

He undoes the buckle and opens his gift, mildly disappointed to find no intricate gold-work but soon diverted as he spies a rather good bottle of Anjou wine, another of Kümmel, and an exotic-looking coffee liqueur.

'Fetch me a couple of glasses, a plate and some cutlery,' he commands his valet, who is hovering at his shoulder. The valet disappearing, returning a few minutes later to find his master laying out the contents of the hamper onto his desk, already salivating at a pot of cured eel sautéed in lemon; spaghetti and asparagus tips in green olive sauce; some French Rum Baba still in their Turk's head moulds.

'Well, look at this!' Jasanoff is clearly pleased. 'A feast! I think a long lunch is in order after a hard morning's work.'

His valet rolling his eyes - though not in view of his master - retiring discretely, leaving Jasanoff to his greed.

'And - oh my Lord!' the valet hears vaguely as he shuts the door behind him, cutting off the end of Jasanoff's sentence. 'I can hardly believe it! A pot of Damascene Velvet! Certainly to be saved until last, perhaps with some of these salted Florentine biscuits…'

An hour and three quarters later, Jasanoff is filled to the gills and suffering a little heartburn because of it. He rings for his valet, who fetches from the medicament chest a solution of chalk and lime water that Jasanoff swallows, though feels no better for it.

'Can I get you anything else, sir?' his valet enquires, concerned at how clammy his master's skin looks.

'I'm…not sure…' Jasanoff says, trying to stand, his valet rushing forward because Jasanoff seems unable to bear his own weight, his gait peculiar, Jasanoff starting to lift his feet as if the carpet was littered with small objects.

'Sir!' the valet shouts as Jasanoff's eyes lose focus, lowers his master back down into his chair with trembling hands.

'I don't feel…' Jasanoff whispers, an alien tingling radiating through his arms, listlessly aware he no longer seems to have a body below his waist. He's finding it hard to breathe, can feel his heart palpitating. Can't think clearly. Tries to reach for the bell to summon back the valet, even though the valet is still by his side looking around for help, unsure whether to stay or go, shouting at the top of his voice for someone to come and aid his master. Jasanoff misses the bell pull completely and is terribly frightened, feels drawstrings pulling tight about his neck, his valet pulling him upwards as he slumps forwards in his chair, releasing him suddenly as diarrhoea pours out of Jasanoff's breeches, soaking into the brocade as he loses control, windpipe swelling itself shut, no more passage of air from out to in, Jasanoff's head slumping to the desk top.

'Help! Help!' the valet shouts uselessly, but there's no one near to hear him, hands held to his face in horror, no doubt in him that he's watching his master dying and completely unable to prevent it, smelling the faeces and urine dripping through the horsehair of the chair and collecting in a foetid pool on the floor below.

'My God! My God!'

The valet can't bear it, turns and runs for the door, wrenches it open, tearing down the corridor shouting for assistance.

But Jasanoff Diderik is already dead.

Use what you've got, Trudbert had said to Lukitt, after running through several salient points of Jasanoff's lifestyle and health. Badly allergic to wasp stings ever since he was young, almost dying once, throat swelling shut for over a minute before admitting a tiny gasp of air, and then another and another; Jasanoff terrified, rarely venturing outside during warm summer days ever since.

And how much more poisonous to him the envenomated honey Lukitt had prepared, the Damascene Velvet, ingested by Jasanoff with such delicious delight, delivering that venom straight from stomach to blood, setting off a cascade of reactions that could not be stopped.

Two weeks later - when all funerary flummery has been done – Hans Diderik Trudbert formally takes up his uncle's office that has been so precipitously and tragically vacated, unhappily leaving the canning factory in Italy to attend to this urgent family emergency. Count Udolpho angry, but grudgingly understanding. Far angrier and far less understanding when he learns of several pending lawsuits that have followed the unmitigated disaster of Trudbert having miscalculated how much lead was needed to seal the cans, a mistake that has already resulted in six deaths, and certainly more to follow, Trudbert bailing out in the nick of time.

On Jasanoff Diderik's grave the angel gifted by the stonemasons' guild poises its stone wings and blows a trumpet into a rain spattered heaven, the two gargoyles - who might best have represented Hans Trudbert and Lukitt Bachmann - nowhere to be seen.

23

GETTING OUT, BUT MAYBE NOT GETTING ON

Alameth and Lukitt were sitting on the poop deck, quite literally – two evacuation stalls constructed from old packing crates having been built out the back of the boat in the style of an old carrack. They're watching Jacques' monkey dance a pirouette in a small pool of lamplight to the creaky wheezes of an ancient accordion Jacques manages to squeeze a tune out of. The night is calm, a few porpoise streaking through the water beside them, swirls of fish winking about the stern in the threads of their own blue lights. There's only the three of them – Jacques, Lukitt and Alameth – celebrating their last night on deck, the rest of the crew gone to carouse in nearby taverns. They've had a bit to drink and have waded through Jacques' terrible turbot stew, and soon the monkey has had enough of dancing and Jacques of playing, so they lie on the planking and stare up at the stars, talking quietly and sporadically, Jacques occasionally breaking into song

'The English hung a monkey once, for a spy,' says Lukitt, as Jacques' one-eyed companion scampers about the boat, intoxicated with the freedom of being let off his rope. 'And the French garrotted cats early on in their Revolution, before moving on to the aristocracy.'

'Seems a sensible thing to do,' Jacques commented. 'Don't hold much with cats. Always yowling and turning into witches when you least expect it.'

Lukitt smiles.

He'd been taken aback when he'd first come on board and become acquainted with the superstitions sailors were capable of.

'Cats is no good,' Jacques went on, spitting over the side of the boat, ''cepting in a casserole. Never know what the buggers are thinking. If they find you on the stairs they're like enough to trip you up as walk past you, make sure you break your neck.'

Lukitt laughed.

'You think that's funny?' Jacques sounds angry but is not, Lukitt knowing him well enough by now to discern the nuances in his voice. Jacques has spent all his working life in Italy but despises the place, clinging to his French accent though he's no need to. He's enjoyed the company of these young lads this past while, done his best to warn the others off the pretty one, not that it had done much good. Glad they've got somewhere else to go. He roused himself, took up his accordion, coaxed it back to life.

'Got a great song for you,' he said. 'Might be a trifle racy for the monastery boy,' Lukitt wincing, looking over at Alameth who was no longer the innocent he'd once been. He shivered in the darkness, Jacques' monkey returning to his master's side prompted by Jacques' accordion wheezing out its tune, Jacques clearing his throat, ah-ah-ing a couple of times to get the right pitch and then heading right on in.

Ooooh, the five-legged humpy-backed camel,
He came from the sands of the East.
Could carry a half-ton of spices and was a most magnificent beast.
He caught him a spot of heat-stroke and swore to get out of the sun,
Said it was time for a holiday and a couple of weeks of fun.

He loads his boat with silver, sacks of silk and spices,
Crews it with scorpions, desert rats and mices;
Sails his way to Italy and lands in Naples fair,
Ties up at the harbour and goes to sell his wares.

Oooh, the five-legged humpy-backed camel stops off for a drink at a bar,
Finds it crewed with women, that it's a Casa di Malaffare.
He hires himself a pretty one, and up they go to peg.
Says she, 'Oh my, but you're the handsome one,
Though you seem to have five legs.'

'My dear,' says he, getting down to it, 'I think you'll find you're mistaken;
It's the dark, my dear, your eyes aren't yet taken.'

They writhe and bounce, they kiss and cuddle
Until she screams in delight and starts to say:
'I was wrong! I was wrong! It's two foot long!'
Before moaning and fainting away.

Oh, the five-legged humpy-backed camel became the toast of the day,
Mobbed at the bar by women begging him to go all the way.

Jacques stands and bows to take his fellows' appreciation, for this song always goes down well; but doesn't get the reception he'd expected.

'That's disgusting,' Alameth says quietly.

'Alameth,' Lukitt tries to intervene, but Alameth is already moving himself away, wrapping his blanket about his shoulders, tears leaking sporadically from his eyes, shutting himself off from everyone and everything but the darkness of the night.

'Might've gone better,' Jacques comments, watching Alameth go, all gaiety relinquished, realising his gaff.

'It's not your fault,' Lukitt says, the two getting to their feet, celebrations over.

'Just promise me one thing,' Jacques says. 'Come visit me when I'm old and grey. Show me what you've made of yourself. Gonna get me a little plot in Sansonnet, spend the last of me life seeing to me cabbages and beans. Be good to have a cupla guests to look forward to.'

Lukitt promised.

'And thank you, Jacques,' he adds. 'I know you did what you could.'

Jacques sighs, his monkey chittering by his side.

'We tried,' he said. 'But trying's not always enough.'

Alameth lies on his blanket, gazing up towards the stars.

Lots of things in life are disgusting, Alameth had said to Lukitt when they'd first realised what they had to do on the boat: the many, many hours spent sitting on upturned barrels as they slit slimy white bellies from gill to tail, chucking the guts to bickering gulls; deprived of their seats one by one as the barrels filled.

But never had Alameth imagined how disgusting those things might be.

Monastery boy, Jacques had always called him.

But Alameth was no monastery boy now, and never could be again.

Such shame for Alameth, and such guilt.

He doubted he'd ever feel clean again.

24

A Curious Education

Lukitt and Alameth left the following morning, Trudbert's prepaid tickets in their hands, his letter of introduction in Lukitt's pocket. They caught the coach to Turin and from there to Switzerland, alighting in the octagonal *Hauptplatz* of Lenze that was that town's main square.

'We're finally here,' Alameth's joy muted, blunted by his hellish time on the boats, but had a faint rise of expectation in his chest. Lukitt encouraged by Alameth's soft enthusiasm, the two moving away from the coach as several people spilled out behind them and the holding ropes were undone, bags and cases unloaded.

Together making their way across the square, shoulders back, heads tipped to the sky, breathing deeply of the warm air as they crossed over the *Stagenbrücke* that spanned the broad sweep of river - its down-below waters mumbling along in slow brown eddies, grumbling against the banks as every few yards it accommodated yet more sludge and filth from the small canals running parallel to the streets - the stench of their waste masked by the drift of chestnut leaves that whorled along their surfaces, and the curls of smoke from the bridge braziers cosseting sausages and small ribs of beef, slabs of pig cheek, twirls of dried ham dipped in water and set to cook slowly on skewers.

Lukitt glad to see Alameth smile as they stopped to take a ladle of kidney soup and a bag of dumplings rolled in butter sauce. They wiped their hands on their trousers before heading off to the Old Town, Lukitt rechecking his sketchy map, taking them off down a strange high-walled street that had small corridors reaching across from attic to attic, roof to roof, the balconies of the houses sagging with ivy, the light down below a shadowing, shifting green. The street suddenly opening onto another square: a fountain in the middle dribbling water through a mask of verdigris, and pigeons that cooed and thripped.

A place of calm, of soft echoes, their footsteps fading into whispers. They washed their faces in the fountain and set off again, soon finding their destination, slowing up, straightening their jackets, combing their hair, taking the few brisk paces to the door of *Die Neugier Kultur Akademie von Lenze* - the College for the Culturally Curious.

They rang the bell, were met by the woman who ran the establishment who demanded to see their papers and credentials, upon which Frau Ingpen ushered them in like long lost family.

'Oh but you're so welcome!' she exclaimed. 'Come in, gentlemen, come in!'

Taking them straightaway to their quarters up top of the house, a room they were to share.

'It's such an honour to have you with us,' she twittered as she rushed over to their beds to make sure everything was shipshape and in order. 'It's quite a while since we had any new tutors.'

'Aren't we to be students, then?' Lukitt asked, discombobulated, Frau Ingpen smiling broadly.

'But of course, young gents!' she answered. 'That's how things work around here. We've paid tutors – as you are – and we've paying students. But everyone teaches everyone else. That's the way of it,' bustling off, closing the door behind her.

'Odd set up,' Lukitt commented, the moment she had left.

'Who cares?' said Alameth, throwing his pack onto his allotted bed. 'At least we're away from the boats and have somewhere to kip. Can't be that bad.'

And bad it wasn't, if a tad peculiar, the academy's principle being that one person's area of expertise was another's deficit, meaning a group of bright students under care of competent tutors could teach other bright students what they didn't already know, pursue their own areas of interest whilst absorbing everyone else's; the tutors obliged to give one lecture a week on whatever subject they chose, then both tutors and students debating and exchanging views, accommodating the learning tools Plato had employed a couple of thousand years before.

Rules that worked well, Lukitt throwing himself into the programme with fervour over the following months, relishing the debates, finding a natural aptitude in reasoned argument, constantly refreshed and challenged by his colleagues, and with an excellent library at his disposal. Slipping into the life quicker than an otter into water. And as far as otters were concerned, he'd recently learned what fascinating creatures they were, courtesy of fellow tutor Kumpel Guaarde's lecture.

'There's been recent studies conducted with the very latest microscopes,' Kumpel informed his audience, 'showing how complicated are their pelts: double layered, with upwards of seventy thousand follicles to every square centimetre.'

'That can't be right,' put in Kumpel's brother Roelof. 'How could anyone count something so small?'

'Ah, but,' Kumpel raised a finger, 'one couldn't previously, except for the new microscopes available and a person dedicated enough who has done exactly that. See here?' He produced the paper in which he'd uncovered this gem and handed it round. 'And not only that, but close observations of the animals have noted the extreme dexterity of its digits, so precise they can unpeel a toad from its unappetising skin in less than five minutes.'

'That I can understand,' Lukitt put in, 'for toad skins can be poisonous. Ancient Romans are recorded using them to be rid of unwanted pregnancies, or spouses,' he glanced around him, thrilled with the entrancement on the younger boys' faces. 'And in Haiti the medicine men throw several Bouga toads into a stew that, when ingested, can cause catatonia. Some folk have been buried alive on account of it, everyone thinking them dead, only to emerge a few hours later scrabbling from the soil, no idea who they are or what's happened to them.'

'Good job they didn't bury them very deep!' chimes someone, to general amusement; all except Alameth, who finds the prospect of being buried alive deeply disturbing, having several times back in Liguria contemplated the dreadful sin of suicide, shuddering to think how close to the brink he'd come, for here in Lenze he's beginning to relax, return to his core, recover his self-worth, to the point that he now adds his own opinion.

'What's really interesting about catatonia,' he offered, 'is how it brings into focus the very real division between the body and the mind, the possibility that the latter can appear to exist independent of the former...'

Rewarded by smiles and instant chatter, the debate cascading from otters and toads to theology, one discipline spilling into the next, everyone talking at once until Kumpel brought them back to relative order.

'Speaking of spirits,' he announced, neatly diverging from someone's mention of Descartes' theory of mind-body duality, 'what plans do we all have for Christmas? Me and Roelof are stopping here for the season. Anyone else?'

Apparently only those two, and one Holger Lucknaught, along with Lukitt and Alameth. Kumpel clapping his hands in delight, quick to draw up an action plan for the festive season that he laid out before the others a few days later.

'We've got to have a discussion on St Nicholas...'

'Light-hearted, I hope,' Roelof butting in, Kumpel raising his eyebrows in exaggerated surprise.

'But of course light-hearted! It's Christmas!'

'Oh but he's so interesting,' Alameth leaning forward, 'no other saint like him. Benevolent in some countries, malign in others, downright evil in Finland and Spain.'

'Then you're to be the one to give it,' Kumpel slapping Alameth lightly on the back, Alameth fighting a wince, not liking to be touched.

'I didn't exactly mean...' he began, Lukitt stepping in quickly.

'I'd like to help with it.'

Kumpel laughing:

'But of course you would! Stuck to books like a fly to shite, is our Lukitt.'

'Not that flies ever actually stick to shite,' Roelof stated pedantically, Kumpel shaking his head, rolling his eyes, going on with his plans. Everyone relaxed and excited by the coming season.

Even Alameth, who saw the sacred as the others did not; Advent the true beginning of the ecclesiastical year, an echo of its rhythm still within him. Celebration of the birth of Christ a holy duty, recalling too the verses of Saint Simeon the New Theologian spoken at the Abbey's

Advent Service:

Rejoice my Brothers, for He will soon be amongst us to heal our bruises and wounds, break our bonds, sweep away our sins, render us all to shining.

'And oh My Lord, My God,' Alameth prayed that night, tears slipping from eye to cheek to pillow, 'if only You would render me shining, I'll ask of You nothing more.'

A visit to the *Christkindlmarkt* in Lenze was the first part of Kumpel's plan, one Lukitt and Alameth were happy to oblige.

'I can't tell you how glad I am we're here,' Alameth said, halfway across the Stagenbrücke bridge, the two of them leaning their elbows on the parapet as they gazed down into the river.

'Me too,' Lukitt agreed, glancing surreptitiously at his friend, certain he's seen some change, some relief, in Alameth this last week that he can't put a finger on. Maybe it was just Christmas, but he hoped it was something more, something deeper. They could hear a street puppeteer doing an atrocious Kaspar Larriscarri sketch not far away.

'Wonder where Heraldo and his crew are performing this year,' he speculated, peeling another chestnut, holding it between his teeth to cool it down.

'Probably not the monastery,' Alameth replied. 'Think you shot them in the foot, far as that goes.'

Lukitt looking over at Alameth but seeing no bitterness there, only an odd sort of peace, about to answer when a groan of snow slid from one of the arches below the bridge, disappearing with a whump into the black water, the lights of the *Christkindlmarkt* dancing across the ripples before they were washed away. Some carollers screeched into action at their backs, pitching their voices too loud and high before subsiding into a relatively harmonious rendition of *Bethlehem, Holy City.*

'Come on,' Lukitt advised, Alameth falling into step, both buttoning up their jackets against the icy wind that had begun to thread its way through the Christmas streets; Lenze not caring, Lenze alive with stalls and booths, groups of people dancing to hurdy gurdies and half-stringed violins, folk singing and laughing, baskets creaking with their wares, fires and lanterns sizzling, the *Christkindlmarkt* buzzing despite the late hour and insidious creep of the wind, children running everywhere: between people, in and out of stalls, their many legged ways marked by a litter of abandoned mittens, hats and scarves, the remnants of snowballs and the tall hats they'd knocked off that hadn't been retrieved.

The noise tumultuous and comforting, constantly changing, bells ringing out from churches, hand bells from stalls, jingle bells from sleighs.

Surrounded by the scents of gingerbread, roasting nuts, mulled wine.

The two engulfed by the crowds, bartering with store owners for small Christmas gifts. Alameth buying a large bag of sugared almonds before announcing loudly that he was about to throw them away – chucking them into a crowd of children, laughing as they tried to catch them in their mouths and then went scrabbling in the snow to find the rest.

'Are you back, then?' Lukitt asked, as they walked through the snowy streets, Alameth not answering immediately, Lukitt shivering, fearing what might come, what guilt Alameth might put his way.

'Not yet,' Alameth finally said, 'but getting there. And you're not to blame yourself,' he added, pausing, shuffling his feet in the snow. 'I never did.'

The two walking on, Lukitt hesitantly linking an arm through Alameth's, Alameth not shrugging him off.

'But I always did,' Lukitt whispered. 'And I always will.'

Alameth shaking his head, stopping again, looking at Lukitt square on.

'It'll never be right,' Alameth got out, 'what happened.' Lukitt's face pale as the snow falling about them. 'But I still believe in my God, and I still believe in His redemption. So leave yourself out of it, Lukitt. It's between me and Him.'

Lukitt dismissed from the equation, a pair at truce returning to the Academy, greeted by Kumpel Guaarde and his brother Roelof:

mouths already full, spoons digging into a communal bowl of kippers mashed with scrambled eggs and potatoes, Frau Ingpen poised beside them adding a ladle of fried pancake strips and bacon to the steaming mound. Holger Lucknaught - a little drunk - trying to pour brandy into his bowl of coffee, co-ordination suffering, all he could do not to drop the bottle.

'Take the bloody top off, idiot!' Kumpel advised, leaning forward, taking the bottle from Holger, uncorking it, pouring a glug into Holger's cup, taking a quick swig himself before handing the bottle on to his brother.

'Lukitt!' Holger was effusive, taking his feet off a chair so Lukitt could sit down, Roelof doing the same for Alameth. 'Just in time for the feast! Come on, man, sit down. We've an hour or two before we're off to the dancing, need to get ourselves fortified and oiled, prepared for the fray!'

'Happy Christmas to you all,' says Lukitt, face pink with the warmth, unloading his satchel. 'For you, Frau Ingpen, from me and Alameth,' handing her a velvet pincushion that for some unfathomable reason was shaped like a large strawberry, with white headed pins for seeds. Frau Ingpen glowed, overwhelmed, never given a gift by any of her boys before.

'Grovelling little toadspittle,' Holger muttered, Frau Ingpen immediately deciding who was going to get the best of tomorrow's Christmas meal and who was not. Lukitt explaining, undeterred.

'I know we decided that tomorrow would be the day of gift giving,' holding up his hands to bat off argument, 'but both myself and Alameth would like to present ours to you now, just as we used to do at home on Christmas Eve, as a very sincere token of how much we appreciate every one of you, and how welcome you've made us.'

'Oh, the tears, the tears,' Holger groaned, pretending a finger drawn across his eyes, but not when he saw what the two were giving him: a bottle of the apricot liqueur he'd once talked of, but never tasted.

'Got it from an Italian trader,' Alameth chipped in.

'Oh my!' Holger exclaimed, as he brought the bottle up to the light. Real tears now, no simulacrum, Lukitt smiling.

'There's everything and anything to be found out there. Just got to know what you're looking for.'

And have the bartering skills he and Alameth had learned at the fish markets, and never thought of value until now.

'A thousand thanks!' Holger slurred, truly moved, as were the brothers Guaarde and Roelof when given a box of Dutch chocolates to remind them of home.

'This is some celebration!' Frau Ingpen said, bringing more food in on her tray, lifting the almond sponge ring onto the table, piling into its empty centre little knobs of sugar soaked in a hedgerow liqueur of her own devising, all set to flame with a triumphant flourish that had her lodgers excitedly clapping, no longer wanting to head off to the dancing but happy here, happy with her and her cooking, about to make this her best Christmas ever.

As it was Lukitt's and Alameth's, who'd never experienced such pageant before, and after food and drink came the telling of tales around the Christmas fire – Lukitt unanimously elected to give the first, Lukitt sweating, not expecting this, but something popping to the fore.

'Well, it's not exactly a story,' Lukitt began, 'seeing as how it actually happened to Père Ulbert many years ago when he was travelling in the Holy Lands.'

His audience settling in, including Frau Ingpen who'd subsided into a seat next to Lucknaught, entirely against her usual habits, eager to hear what would be said.

'He'd a guide with him,' Lukitt began, 'an Arab who'd devoted his life to visiting deserts in search of solitude and spiritual release. Been to China, India and Russia before returning to Egypt where he met Ulbert. So what of it, you might ask. One desert is much like the next, except no, each is different, has its own character: one filled with vast dunes of sand constantly shifting and singing in the wind, another an ocean of littered rocks, black and hard, smooth as glass, jagged and cruel, fissures deep as the deepest mine. Others mere stretches of scrub land, mile on mile, nothing green, only spikes and spines, where rain falls once a century when the entire place erupts into a massive bloom of flowers, bushes that seem to spring up overnight, swarms of butterflies appearing from tiny holes in the banks of wadis that have become torrential with the rain.

'And it was in this last type that Ben Ali ab'bouthai, an Arab, yes, but a Coptic Christian, found himself one Christmas Eve,' Lukitt pauses for a moment as the fire crackles briefly, the light jumping about his face, all candles by then extinguished, Roelof rolling the hard caramel centre of a chocolate around his mouth as he listens, Guaarde gazing out the window, seeing himself there in the fabric of Lukitt's story, Lucknaught snoring quietly, beginning to doze, murmuring every now and then as Lukitt's words interrupt and influence the course of his dreams.

'It was a terrible place he found himself,' Lukitt continued. 'What people in those parts call ten days empty, meaning you're ten days march from any habitation. A hard rocky plain bounded by crags, their black shadows gnawing at its edges in the moonlight. A place where a knocked stone, the clack of a stumbling hoof, a single camel cough, sounds like the rumble of thunder, so devoid was that place of life.

'So it was with shock that he saw before him a boulder and a single dusty sandaled foot straddled at its edge. He thought for certain this person must be as dead as everything else he'd encountered during the long miles of his trek, the face of the man leaning against the other side of the boulder so dark and cracked with sun and dust it was hard to make out any distinctive features. But he was alive – although only just.'

Frau Ingpen, sat opposite Lukitt, raised her hands to her cheeks, enthralled. Never had she been in such intimate contact with a storyteller; never had she been to a theatre – except those encountered on street corners; never had she read a book, being practically illiterate outside of doing the household accounts. Yet here by the fire, on this Christmas Eve, Lukitt's voice was drawing her into another world she'd never considered might exist.

'Our Arab, Ben Ali,' Lukitt went on, the caramel in Roelof's mouth now small enough to swallow, not that he did so, hanging onto it as he was hanging onto Lukitt's every word , 'was a kind man and good. And although it was plain this stranger would soon die – for he had no pack with him, no animal, nothing but the ragged clothes that barely covered his body – Ben Ali took out his last provisions: the very last of his bread, the very last of his dates, chewed them up and coaxed them down the stranger's throat with the very last of his water. Then Ben Ali sat down beside the unknown man, leant his back against the same boulder, took the man's hand in his own and prepared to die.'

'No!' Frau Ingpen cried out, the single word of protest muffled by the knuckles she was holding against her mouth, Alameth beside her, patting her arm.

'It can't end like this,' Alameth comforted, looking over at Lukitt for confirmation, Roelof of the same opinion, swallowing audibly, casting a quick glance at his brother who was still staring fixedly at the window, at the snow perhaps, that was falling thick and quiet.

Lukitt held up a finger, shook his head, surprised his story had evoked such strong emotion, learning the trade of telling quite by accident: from Ulbert's sermons, the Pfiffmaklers' performances, the tales told on boats on sleepless, restless nights.

'I'm telling you this,' he went on, 'exactly as it was told to me, and never fear, Frau Ingpen, for Ben Ali survived long enough for Ulbert to learn the ending, though it's an odd one, as many of Ulbert's travelling tales were. Ben Ali told Ulbert this: he held that man's hand throughout the terrible cold of the night, didn't bother getting out his blanket knowing neither of them would see the morning and wanting life to go from them as quickly and painlessly as it could. Throughout the blackness of that dark night the stranger mumbled a single phrase over and over: *If ever you were in the presence of God, then it is now.* But when Ben Ali awoke in the morning - the sun as terrible and hot as the night had been terrible and cold - he was completely alone. Nothing near him but that single sandal he'd spied the night before by the boulder. And then, in the sky, he saw great billows of dark clouds rolling from out the blue horizon, and soon the rain began to fall, became harder and harder, running in rivulets about his feet, washing away the dirt and stink of travel. He was weak, but got his water canister filled, drank his fill, began to stumble onwards. Yet still he might not have survived had not a band of horsemen arrived out of nowhere and took him up, bore him away, brought him back to health. Told him the tale within the tale.

'*It was the Sufi saved you*, they told Ben Ali, *the one who appears to travellers when they're lost. Treat him well, and he will save you. Walk past him and he will have you die.*

'And then they bade Ben Ali look upon the sole of his foot, Ben Ali astonished to see there a henna tattoo: two dates in the Arabic script, the first being the day he was found, the second unknown to him. *The day when you will die*, he was told. And so it was, as it happened, though not until Ben Ali was very old, at the very time Ulbert was with him, when Ben Ali – assuming his time was up – went out into the desert, slung up a hammock between two olive trees, and sure enough had expired by morning.

'But,' Lukitt added, 'what no one could explain was that over Ben Ali's body lay a drift of the purest, whitest snow.'

The ensuing silence interrupted by Lucknaught grumbling, half asleep.

'A load of bloody hooeh.'

'Exactly what I thought,' Lukitt responded, 'but when you pull all the bizarre elements apart it's easily explained.'

'How so?' Roelof asked.

'Figure it out for yourselves,' Lukitt replied. 'Maybe it's just a Christmas fable.'

The party moving on, Lukitt remembering how he'd arrived at his own explanation of the tale, having thought about it for several days.

'I think I've got it,' he'd said, Ulbert smiling, putting his hands behind his back, nodding for Lukitt to go on.

'I think we can assume there really was an old man, but that after Ben Ali found him he crawled away in the middle of the night, probably delirious.'

Ulbert nodded.

'Exactly my thinking. He crawled away, and died. But how did Ben Ali not see his body?'

'Because of the rain,' Lukitt went on. 'The fact that it only falls once in a few generations was a massive stroke of luck, but it's not so unlikely that when it does someone is saved by it, as Ben Ali was, and that someone isn't. The rains sweeping away the old man because he'd fallen into the wadi, leaving only the sandal that had previously fallen off.'

'And the horsemen?' Ulbert asked.

'Well obviously they're there because of the rains – the one time they'd ever seen it and probably never would again. Who wouldn't go riding off to see what they could see? I'd have gone just for the novelty, but maybe they wanted to collect some of the plants or butterflies for one of the Expeditionary…'

'And the tattoos?' Ulbert interrupted.

'You said yourself they were henna,' Lukitt switched tack, 'so they were put there by the horsemen when Ben Ali was recovering. They knew the day they'd found him, and picked a distant date for his future death at random. The fact that he lived to a grand old age might even have been influenced by him believing he would do exactly that.'

'But to die on the exact date?' Ulbert raised his eyebrows, pleased with his pupil.

'Ah,' said Lukitt, 'that's the interesting part. Look at this,' he got out a book reporting the exploits of several British Expeditionary Forces in the area at the time – a book purchased by Ulbert for the exact same information. 'It's here,' Lukitt held out the page. 'That particular night the temperature – always cold in that part of the world, especially in the desert - plummeted well below zero, and sporadic snowfalls were reported in various oases where it was coldest, freezing the water content of the air. Most melted soon as the sun rose, except where places were in shadow – as it was beneath the olive trees between which Ben Ali had slung his hammock.'

'Very good!' Ulbert exclaimed. 'A man convinced he's going to die allows himself to freeze to death rather than admit half a lifetime's belief could be wrong.'

'Exactly,' Lukitt agreed. 'But it does rather take the shine off the whole story.'

Ulbert studied Lukitt's serious face.

'I'm not sure that it does at all. What's at the heart of it, Lukitt? What's the most unusual part, now that you've taken all the fairy out of the tale?'

Lukitt frowned, not understanding.

'It's the kindness,' Ulbert said quietly. 'It's the fact that a man was prepared to die rather than allow another – a complete and utter stranger – to die alone.'

Lukitt mentioned none of this logical explication to his fellows that Christmas Eve in Lenze, the silence and wonder left by his tale soon overtaken by others, by Frau Ingpen giving a hesitant recital of the Twelve Princesses Who Danced Their Shoes To Pieces, Roelof telling an old Dutch tale of Saint Nicholas and how, in a time of famine, he found the bodies of three small boys pickled and salted in a fish barrel ready to be sold off for food, and restored them instead to life; Alameth reverting not to a biblical story but to the bird who moved a mountain by taking it apart piece by piece with its tiny beak.

'Know what I found most extraordinary about tonight?' Alameth said later, when all tales had been told, and everyone had retired to their beds.

'What's that?' Lukitt asked, standing at the window, watching the snow falling outside, the lights in their neighbours' windows going out one by one, feeling a little drunk, not quite ready for sleep though it was almost two in the morning.

'Your Ben Ali,' Alameth said, as he climbed into his bed, removing the warming pan that had almost gone cold, so late had they all stayed up.

'Not my Ben Ali,' Lukitt corrected, 'but Ulbert's.'

'But he was a real man?' Alameth asked. 'And that was a real tale?'

'It was,' Lukitt answered, turning back from the window, 'told by Ben Ali to Ulbert except, of course, for the end.'

Alameth sighing as he moved himself onto his back, put his hands beneath his head, eyes open, staring at the ceiling as the candle flickered on the cabinet by his bed.

'I just think,' he went on slowly, 'that if it's true...'

'It's true,' Lukitt said, moving to his own bed, beginning to disrobe. 'I could tell you the how of it if...'

'Please don't,' Alameth remonstrated quietly in the near darkness. 'I know you'll be able to take the mystery out of it, but I don't want you to.'

Lukitt stopped in the middle of taking off his socks.

'What do you mean?' he asked, obscurely offended, Alameth turning onto his side, looking at Lukitt in the glimmering light.

'You wouldn't have let it lie,' he said. 'You'd have found it all a load of bloody hooeh, as Lucknaught put it, as would Ulbert. The two of you would have gone ferreting out the whys and wherefores of how it really happened. But me? I'm happy with the tale as it is. I want to keep the extraordinary alive.'

'Even if it's not the truth?' Lukitt countered, Alameth closing his eyes, Lukitt seeing a small shrug of Alameth's shoulders as he pulled his coverlet about him.

'I mean,' Alameth said, replicating Ulbert, 'that the most extraordinary part of the story was Ben Ali himself, willing to lay down his life for a man who wasn't even his friend.'

Lukitt continued removing his socks.

'Would you have done it?' he asked quietly.

Alameth didn't answer, a long exhalation indicating his slip into sleep.

But Lukitt knew the truth of it: Alameth would have stayed, and would still stay despite all that had happened to him; whereas Lukitt would have walked on into the night and left that rallion old man to his fate.

25

Life, Luck and Fortune

Christmas Day, and they went *en masse* to mass, returning to find Frau Ingpen hauling a fat-dripping goose out of her oven, nutmeg-infused potato scones spitting in a pan, a mound of shredded red cabbage in another.

'Whoah!' shouted Kumpel Guaarde, his cheeks red with cold, small blinks of ice in his beard as he came in on his brother's heels. 'This is what I call food! My darling Frau Ingpen, I think I want to marry you!'

'Just like my mother used to make,' Lucknaught added nostalgically, 'or no. A lot better, as it happens, if smells are anything to go by.'

They ate well, and were soon calling out toasts in traditional manner in the dimming afternoon, each armed with a tipple of the *Aprikotenschot* Lukitt had presented Lucknaught with the night before, that promised - according to the label - to be the perfect festive tipple, fragrant and delicate but with a decided kick, and did not disappoint. Standing at the head of the table Lucknaught toasted the season, welcomed in the winter, wished it well but God's speed away again.

'Hurrah!' shouted Kumpel and Roelof in unison.

'To Life, Luck and Fortune!' Alameth exclaimed, getting into the spirit, the cry going around the table, the taste of apricot on everyone's lips.

They entered into a round of word games, Kumpel and Roelof presenting their pre-planned entertainment with lightning speed.

Why is the man throwing himself off a cliff like Adam?

Because he lived before the Fall.

Why should a clergyman receive a wage?

Because otherwise he's good for nothing.

Why does a donkey prefer thistles to oats?

Because he's an ass!

Why does a writer wield more power than a king?

Because he can choose his own subjects.

Who make the worst correspondents?

The prisoners who spend a lifetime on a single sentence!

Then it's Lucknaught's turn, who's decided on a game he calls Fizz, Bang, Wallop, and suits his mathematical bent.

'Call out a number, any number,' he proclaims, 'and if it's a multiple of seven I will say *Wallop*; if a multiple of five I will say *Buzz*, a multiple of three then *Fizz*. If you challenge me and I'm right then I give you a forfeit of my choosing and *vice versa*.'

Neither Lukitt nor Alameth had heard of it before; Kumpel and Roelof in the know.

'Just try it,' they encourage, and Alameth does just that.

'Twenty one?' he asks hesitantly.

'Wallop Fizz,' Lucknaught came back straightaway. 'You'll need to do better than that.'

'Two hundred and seventeen,' Lukitt offers.

'Wallop!' Lucknaught barks, after barely half a second.

'Surely not,' Lukitt remonstrated, but too quickly, adding up in his head, seeing his error.

'Forfeit!' Lucknaught announces. 'Go do a handstand against the door.'

Lukitt laughs, but does as told. It takes him a couple of goes and he feels a little sick, but he manages.

'Five hundred and thirty six!' Alameth jiggles in his seat, Lucknaught remaining quiet, whipping his thumb across his lips.

'But I felt sure, with the six at the end…' Alameth trails off.

'Do you want to challenge?' Lucknaught asks, with raised eyebrows, Alameth frowning, uncertain.

'Three thousand four hundred and eighty nine!' Roelof breaks in, unable to stop himself, despite having been caught out by this game on numerous occasions.

'Wallop!' Lucknaught answers after a couple of seconds, Roelof madly calculating, but unwilling to challenge.

'Thirty eight thousand nine hundred and fifty five,' Lukitt offers, sensing there's a trick to this game, though he's damned if he can see it.

'Fizz Bang Wallop!' Lucknaught announces dramatically. 'The Holy Trinity. I'll give you one minute before I challenge you to challenge me.'

Throwing a pencil at Lukitt who quickly takes out a notebook and his Napier's Bones and begins scribbling.

'Thirty seconds,' Kumpel warns, having taken out his impressive fob watch. 'Twenty…ten…'

'No challenge!' Lukitt announces, looking at his lines of workings out. 'That's astounding! How on earth do you do it?'

Lucknaught shakes his big head and waves a hand.

'It's a gift, my boy, a gift. Had it since I was small. Throw a handful of spills on the table and I'll be able to tell you how many are there in a few moments. It's like the numbers sing to me, form themselves into patterns.'

'But it's a trick, surely,' Lukitt argues, going to the mantelpiece, grabbing up several handfuls of the rolled spills Frau Ingpen has made out of broadsheets, flinging them on the table, watching Lucknaught as Lucknaught studies them.

'Sixty nine,' Lucknaught announces, Lukitt pulling the small heap apart into piles of ten and finding there to be exactly that number.

'That's extraordinary!' Lukitt exclaims, Lucknaught shrugging his shoulders.

'Extraordinary, but true,' he says, Lukitt remembering Alameth's words the night before, and how Lukitt had to pull everything apart to see how it worked, how others – like Alameth, and maybe Lucknaught – merely accept the mystery and got on with things.

'So what's your party piece?' Kumpel put in, pulling at his beard, Alameth leaping to his feet, fetching the equipment he and Lukitt had previously prepared.

'Extraordinary too,' Alameth volunteers, though Lukitt was not of the same opinion, about to enact a simple trick of chemistry when what Lucknaught had demonstrated was beyond his ken. Alameth bringing to the table a bowl of household salt, setting it over the spirit lamp that had previously been heating the last of their coffee, the only source of light now coming from the fire.

'Observe,' Lukitt announces, producing a vial of ethanol and pouring it over the salt, put a lit spill to it and immediately a flame shot up from the salt, bathing the entire company in an eerie yellow light that made them all look horribly like revenants newly risen from the grave.

'And that's not all,' Lukitt said, producing an egg from his pocket, Alameth adding to the mix a quill pen filled with quicksilver stoppered at each end by hardened wax, Lukitt warming it briefly in the yellow flame before jamming the quill into the egg and laying the egg on the table when – to general astonishment – the egg began to jump and move and kept on rolling – apparently of its own accord – for several minutes.

'And you accused me of trickery!' Lucknaught exclaimed, impressed.

'I could explain…' Lukitt began, before catching Alameth's eye, 'but in this instance I will not. You've to puzzle it out. Make it one of our New Year lectures.'

'A very good suggestion,' said Lucknaught, standing up, refilling everyone's glasses. 'This has been a most entertaining year, the Academy for the Curious certainly standing up to its name.'

Not long after - by which time they were all wrung out of games and demonstrations, settling into drinking too much and eating too much – there came a knock at their door, a small boy handing over to Frau Ingpen a letter she handed on to Lukitt.

'Maybe a Christmas greeting from your family?' she asked, though the seal on the back suggested otherwise.

'Maybe,' Lukitt said, smiling as Frau Ingpen returned to her well-deserved seat by the fire, Lucknaught placing a cushion behind her back and a glass in her hand, Lukitt taking the missive she'd handed him and breaking the seal.

'We've still the carol service to go to if we want to,' Lucknaught yawned, but no one wanted, all safe and secure where they were, happy in their own company.

'Anything in your letter, Lukitt?' Alameth asked, Lukitt unsure how to answer, having scanned through the contents.

'There is,' he answered. 'It's from that Professor Vannevar, the one we met at the Palazzo. He's offering us a few months sabbatical in a place called Kutná Hora, wherever that is.'

'Snatch it up!' Lucknaught advised. 'It seems our toast to Life, Luck and Fortune has worked its magic. Chances like that don't come along every day.'

Lucknaught right, and the following morning Lukitt wrote off to accept the offer, Kumpel and Roelof getting out books, discovering Kutná Hora was in Central Bohemia, a mere stone's throw from Prague.

'Prague!' Lucknaught announced. 'Now there's a place I'd like to see. There's an Englishman, Edward Thomas, just set up shop in the city producing steam engines. You've got to promise me you'll go see him, Lukitt, because I'm telling you steam engines are the future. None of that horse-hauled railway rubbish they've got running from Essen to Nierenhof. I honestly don't know why they bothered! It only runs for a Prussian mile.'

He snorted with contempt and Lukitt smiled, promised he would go see the Englishman first chance he got.

'Kutná Hora,' Alameth put his book down on the table. 'Says here it's an old silver-mining town. King there used to be the richest man in the whole of Central Europe. They even had a resident Italian Court – maybe we'll bump into Udolpho again.'

'I hope not,' Lukitt replied, shuddering at the thought.

Would have shuddered a whole lot more if he'd understood the premise behind Vannevar's invitation, would have shuddered and thrown his invitation on the fire, stayed in Lenze where he and Alameth now felt they belonged.

26

The Spurs That Push Us On

Surprise is a startle of sunrise that sweeps across your horizon, waking in you the realisation that the world is glorious. Like back in the Vorarlberg one night when the welkin was alive with stars that fell and swooped, his father shining a lamp to show Lukitt the million mayflies emerging from the ground, winging their way into ghostly whorls above their heads, the Bachmanns sat on the steading porch eating sugar fritters, a brief respite from the harshness of their toil.

Shock is quite different, makes the sun sink in an instant, drags its darkness with you into the depths of the earth. Like when - a few days before Lukitt and Alameth were due to leave for Kutná Hora - a letter arrived from Ulbert. Previous to its receipt, Lukitt had been sauntering through the quietness of the fountain square, satisfied with the day. He'd just demonstrated the anatomy of hedgehogs at the Academy, Roelof piping up some wild tale he'd heard about them stealing milk from recumbent cows at night.

'It's nonsense,' Lukitt had remonstrated. 'A myth arising from entirely opposite circumstance, namely that certain farmers – my father included – wean their calves early by tying a piece of hedgehog skin, spines and all, to the ends of their noses so their mothers push them away.'

He couldn't figure how it was that he'd just been talking of his father only to learn – two hours later - that his father was dead.

Lukitt going to his bed after reading the letter, clutching it to his chest, weeping to know he'd never see Nethanel again, and how awful Trudl's situation must be without him, stranded alone with the black hard sticks of Hermione and Hermistus. How it could be that Nethanel had died before either of those two old termagants. The thought imperative in him that he had to save his mother, do well, better himself, get her out, give her a better life.

It made leaving Lenze all the harder, going once more into the unfamiliar, but he'd Alameth with him and Lukitt's melancholy soon brightened to observe the coming in of Spring as they went on their way, the leaves of honeysuckle growing green in the hedgerows, early purple orchids coming up between new blades of grass. Waiting for their coach by the river they watched people passing over the bridge in their new hats, their light coats and cotton cloaks; trunks and cupboards having swallowed the thick worsted of winter. The two lads twiddling daisies between their fingers, watching the silver skins of fish bursting through the water sending ripples running into one another, the river flowing clear and pure since the melt waters had coursed between its banks, swept away the accumulated rot of leaves recently released from the ice.

'What do you think it's all about?' Lukitt asked Alameth. 'Life, I mean.'

Alameth shaking his head, aware how acutely Lukitt felt his father's loss.

'I guess it depends on how you view the whole of it,' Alameth answered. 'Back at the monastery I'd've said it was all about pleasing God, making Him proud that you were spending your days in a way of which He would approve.'

'But not now?' Lukitt asked.

Alameth shrugged.

'I still believe the Lord has a plan for each of us. I'm just not sure He's watching over us every second of every day. I think there's too much going on; that at some point we have to be trusted to make our own way, take our own decisions. See where they take us.'

'And you're happy this is our way?' Lukitt asked, feeling that with Nethanel gone from the world some anchor had been cut from beneath him, that he was drifting, unable to determine the logic of his next move, that he'd let Nethanel down. Let Alameth down too.

'You know what Lucknaught said,' Alameth assured. 'These kind of chances don't come along every day. And we won't be gone for long. Back here by Autumn.'

'Back here by Autumn,' Lukitt murmured, as the coach drew into the square and they got their baggage loaded. Lukitt nodding, content with the answer, feeling the sun warm on his face as they waited for several other passengers to board before boarding themselves.

They spent the first part of their journey discussing Professor Vannevar and his work, Lukitt having dug out the notes he'd cribbed from Udolpho's books.

'He did his early work on the Bone Chapel at the Monastery of St Nicholas of Flüe,' Lukitt said.

'Know all about him,' Alameth chipped in, eyes gazing out of the window. 'Illiterate Swiss farmer, went off to fight a couple of wars; came back, married late, had ten children, before he got the call.'

'Kind of unusual, isn't it?' Lukitt asked. 'Best of both worlds. And can't have been easy on his wife.'

'The call is never easy,' Alameth retorted sharply, 'whichever way it takes you.'

Eyes darkening, fingers rubbing at his temples, bad memories resurfacing, refusing to be consigned to the nightmares where they belonged, no matter how he prayed and hoped. Lukitt waiting a moment before he spoke, twining his fingers hard together on his lap, not oblivious to these brittle lapses in his friend, nor of why.

'So what brought him to sainthood?'

Alameth sniffed a couple of times before answering.

'Saved his country,' he said dully, quoting by rote. 'Moved just down the road from his family, became a bit of a wise man, got called on one day by the authorities in Lucerne when the cantons were on the verge of civil war. Gave them such sound advice they encoded it in law – the Compromise of Stans. Can't remember when. 1481 maybe.'

Alameth losing interest in the conversation and Lukitt didn't push it.

'I know you think the religious life is an abdication from the norm,' Alameth said, a few minutes later, to Lukitt's surprise. As far as he knew he'd never said as much, though now his opinion had been voiced he recognised the truth of it; Ulbert and Opapa exceptions to the rule.

'But it can be a good life,' Alameth went on, more to himself than

Lukitt, Lukitt hearing regret in the words, and accusation. 'Sometimes a great one. Setting yourself apart lets you see the world as others don't, like looking down from a mountain, the everyday laid out before you, easier to make out its rights and wrongs.'

Lukitt unsure how to answer, stopped anyway by the sharp jab of an elbow in his ribs by the old woman next to him who didn't mind a bit of talk about saints but was hanged if she was going to allow a couple of whelps to yap the entire journey through.

'Will you two numbskulls never shut up? I can't take another hour of it,' she shook her head dramatically. 'All an old woman wants on a journey like this is to get a bit of sleep. You can blab all you want after I've got to where I'm going. But until then, please, give it a rest.'

Everyone, Alameth and Lukitt included, complied; silence kept by all as they bumped along pot-hole by pot-hole, the old woman soon snoring loudly until she disembarked an hour and a half later, the coach having drawn into an ostlers to get the horses changed, allow its remaining passengers to grab something to eat and drink while new passengers were loaded into place.

A few hundred miles – and four more days of travelling – ahead of them, both Lukitt and Alameth spending most of it in in silence. No more talk of saints, nor mention of monasteries; conversing inconsequentially about the weather, the countryside they were passing through, how much further was left to go.

27

Present Worries, Ancient Studies

Arriving in Kutná Hora in the middle of a thunderstorm, the crack and splinter of lightning on the horizon impressive, but soon as they alighted from their coach they were drenched to the skin, holding their bags above their heads as they ran for the nearest coffee house, ducking beneath its awnings.

'Good grief!' Alameth said, words all but drowned out by the heft of raindrops falling fat and heavy on the canvas, the late afternoon prematurely darkened by the heavy roll of yellow-bellied clouds above the small town, obliterating the normal routines of its citizens, all barricaded inside home and house, or stranded at work places, no one wanting to venture out into the angry spleen of the storm.

'Anyone meant to meet us?' Alameth asked, shaking out his sodden cap, squirming in his wet clothes, cold despite the humidity of the quickly falling night.

'Don't think they'll have hung around in this,' Lukitt answered, 'but we've an address. Can't be hard to find. Let's go inside, get ourselves warmed before we go looking.'

Alameth agreed, the two having reached some kind of truce during their silent travelling, and soon had pushed their way through a crowd of men hiding out as they were, managing to secure seats before a roaring fire, steaming gently as a flask of coffee was set on the table between them alongside a platter of hot pastries oozing butter and the black-grape jam secreted within their folds.

'Well, this is more like it,' Alameth shivered. 'Maybe we should take a room here for the night, go find Vannevar in the morning.'

The rain continued to pound the streets outside, droplets splashing a full six inches up from the cobbles, continuing even when most of the storm had passed – the splinters of lightning less violent, the low rumblings of following thunder coming at greater intervals.

'No point trying to find him in this,' Lukitt agreed, 'and no harm asking,' beckoning over one of the lads employed as waiters. 'Got rooms available?' Lukitt asked, receiving an affirmative nod. 'Ever heard of a Professor Vannevar?' he tried, at which the lad scrunched up his nose and shook his head before being yelled away to a neighbouring table. 'So tonight we stay here.' Lukitt decided, and both content with that.

A man with his back to Lukitt rustled the broadsheet he'd been reading, folded it, laid it on his knees before turning in his chair and tapping Lukitt on the shoulder.

'You're enquiring about Professor Vannevar?' he asked politely, spectacles fogging up with the soft mist rising from Lukitt's clothes.

'I am,' Lukitt said, turning to his interlocutor. 'Do you know of him?'

The man took off his glasses, rubbed them clean, perched them back on his nose, where they instantly fogged up again.

'You're somewhat damp,' he observed, pushing two thumbs over the interior of his spectacles, Lukitt perceiving the problem and pulling his chair back.

'We got caught in the downpour,' he apologised, 'but we're very pleased to make your acquaintance, Herr…?'

'Herr Obermann,' said Herr Obermann, 'and yes, I know of Vannevar. He's well known in these parts. A little eccentric…I think we might say. But he's done us a great service here, with his reorganisation of the Bone Chapel.'

'At St Nicholas's?' Alameth asked, turning his chair into the conversation, the travelling having ground away the edges of the rage that – despite himself - welled up every now and then, a rage directed at Lukitt, illogical and unpredictable he knew, but there all the same; forgiveness a gift from God he sometimes couldn't help throwing back in God's face.

'Did that one first,' Obermann agreed. 'Then moved on to Sedlec. This town's a bit of a treasure house of detritus left by the Ancient Knights who mined our silver to build their strongholds, and the Sedlec Ossuary is the jewel in the crown, so to speak.'

Obermann leaned forward, accepting the cup of coffee Lukitt offered him, eager to tell the tale he told anyone who would listen - being curator of the Ossuary and knowing his stuff.

'All started in 1278,' he began, 'when Otaker, the second King of Bohemia, sent the Abbot of Sedlec to Jerusalem; came back a few years later with a jar of Holy Soil from Golgotha and sprinkled it over the cemetery. Consequence being that the great and good of the whole of Central Europe paid good money to be buried there.'

'Must've got filled up pretty quick,' Alameth commented, knowing monastery cemeteries were small, calculated according to the number of their monks.

'Quite right, young man,' Obermann nodded in approval. 'They expanded it, of course, but during the plague years of the following two centuries it filled up faster than fish in a dragnet…'

Interrupted by a young man in his mid-twenties hauling his stool unbidden into their circle.

'Obermann likes that phrase,' he said, Obermann wheeling his head around.

'This is my area of expertise, Jan Golinski, and I'll thank you to remember it.'

Golinski grinned, but held up his hands.

'All yours,' he said amiably, winking at Lukitt and Alameth, who smiled back, three young men in the presence of an old windbag – a place they'd all been before.

'As I was saying,' Obermann huffed, 'all full up. Only thing to do being to build a church, and a chapel to take the bones…'

'Employed a half-blind Cistercian monk to do the deed,' Golinski interrupted again. 'Sorry! Sorry! But it has to be said. Shocking piece of work, shocking…' shaking his head sadly.

'Built a chapel,' Obermann pointedly repeated, 'that later had its charnel house remodelled by a very well renowned architect of Italian extraction – who might be your namesake, Golinski, but that's where the resemblance ends – Jan Blažej Santini-Aichi.'

'This is where Vannevar comes in, you'll be pleased to hear,' Golinski informed, Obermann closing his eyes briefly, taking a deep breath so he didn't leap across the table and strangle the lights out of the young whippersnapper, something he'd longed to do ever since Golinski had been assigned an internship at the Chapel on Curator

Obermann's watch.

'Precisely,' he said tightly. 'This is where Professor Vannevar comes in, because by then the ossuary contained the bones of around forty thousand people...'

'Forty thousand!' Lukitt whistled. 'That's a lot of bones.'

'You'd better believe it,' Golinski agreed.

'It is indeed a lot of bones,' Obermann continued loudly, 'and something needed doing with them...'

'And Vannevar's certainly done that,' Golinski finished for him, Lukitt fiddling with his own set of bones, namely Napier's, thinking that Lucknaught could have calculated all in a second.

'But that's eight million, two hundred and forty thousand,' he provided, 'given two hundred and six for each person.'

'How'd'you do that?' Golinski looking over at Lukitt.

'It's all to do with this instrument here,' Lukitt began to explain, but Obermann had had enough of being upstaged.

'For pity's sake,' he growled, exasperated, his broadsheet falling to the floor as he took his leave. 'Pay the place a visit tomorrow, if you choose. I'm sure Jan here will have all the time in the world to give you a tour.'

Jan Golinski stood up deferentially as his putative employer rolled his broad head on his broader neck and barged his way through the coffee house out into the night, the drizzle that had replaced the stair-rods of rain coming as something of a relief, calming his blood, slowing his angry steps as he counted down the weeks, the days, before the insufferable young Golinski was out of his hair – out of his chapel – for good.

'I think you've upset Herr Obermann,' Alameth said, care creasing his handsome face, never liking to upset anyone.

'Pffft!' Golinski dismissed Alameth's worries. 'Obermann gets worked up if I put the visitors' book a half inch out of place. Last week he chastised me for a knucklebone – a single knucklebone! – being a hair's breadth to the left instead of the right!'

'Forgive me,' Lukitt said, 'but given all those bones, what was it Vannevar did to put them in order? Aren't they just stacked in the charnel house? So how can a knucklebone – single or otherwise – be put out of place?'

Golinski studied Lukitt with a look Lukitt could only interpret as sly.

'I believe we've a thinker here,' he commented.

'You don't know the half of it,' Alameth sighed, words out before he could stop them, unable to meet Lukitt's eye.

Jan Golinski fetched up outside the coffee house at nine sharp the following morning, Lukitt and Alameth ready for their tour.

'Come on,' Golinski was enthusiastic. 'Got to get you there early, before all the gawkers arrive. Folk come from all over to see our chapel.'

Golinski gave Lukitt a skewed smile, Lukitt ignoring it, beginning to agree with Obermann that this Jan Golinski was a little too full of himself.

The streets were wet from the previous night's storm, but Kutná Hora had come back to life, thronging with folk hurrying to catch up with whatever they'd been prevented from doing the day before: carts pulled by horses, mules and thick-haired mountain dogs jostling for space as their drivers strove to get down whichever side of the street they were plying; housewives with full baskets gossiping and chattering as they made their way back from market.

When they reached the chapel it seemed neither as ugly as Golinski had implied nor as miraculous as Obermann believed: a square, four-turreted building with skinny arched windows – nothing remarkable, until Jan Golinski unlocked the doors, when Lukitt and Alameth stood transfixed upon the threshold.

'Well, look at that!' Alameth couldn't have opened his eyes wider if he'd tried, and even Lukitt's usually immobile face showed signs of astonishment. 'The entire place is made of bones!' Alameth went on for them both.

'Not entirely,' Golinski corrected, 'but certainly decorated with them. Up there,' he pointed towards the chandelier hanging from the centre of the nave, a beautiful construction rendered mainly from femurs and skulls, 'contains every single bone in the human body, all two hundred and six of them,' he added, for Lukitt's benefit. 'Although of course in total there's many more than that.'

'So many more,' Alameth murmured, following Golinski's finger.

'And over here to the left,' Golinski went on, 'is the family coat of arms of the Schwarzenbergs.'

More skulls, more femurs at top and bottom, the rest of the heraldic elements intricately defined by vast amounts of smaller bones. More impressive still, to Lukitt's mind, were those arranged in the form of bells at each of the four corners of the chapel. He didn't think he could be more agape, until Golinski took his visitors down to the crypts where entire tunnels were lined with thousands upon thousands of skulls, a sight that should have been morbid but oddly was not, in fact was rather comforting, invoking the thought - that many had spoken, though few had demonstrated as dramatically as was being done now - that all men were equal, that life inhabited rooms of every kind, from the most palatial to the most squalid, but death, the ruffian on the stair, could not be stopped, could break into their habitats at any time to steal away their occupants.

Lukitt starkly reminded of a passage he'd read in one of Ulbert's books on how to deflesh a corpse preparatory for a class in anatomy. At the time of reading it had seemed a mere intellectual exercise, a text illustrated by one of Rembrandt's props for his art classes: a skeleton of a man mounted on a skeleton horse.

Not so now.

Firstly, call in the fertilizer men so nothing goes to waste;

Secondly, open up the abdomen, take out all internal organs and intestines (better sooner than later, before the soft tissues begin to rot);

Thirdly, remove the brain from the top of the cranium;

Fourthly, excise the muscles as well as you are able;

Fifthly, boil the bones until any remaining flesh has fallen away;

Sixthly, run the bones beneath running water, making sure to repeat the procedure a minimum of three times;

Seventhly, prepare your hand drill and have the correctly gauged wire ready, along with your stand.

Staring down that long tunnel entirely lined with skulls, lit by hour-candles at strategic intervals, both Lukitt and Alameth felt a profound sense of peace, though for entirely different reasons.

Lukitt understanding the mechanisms behind the cleansing of bones, appreciative of how they'd been organised, the quiet revelation that everything was transient, that every single person on this earth would die, himself included, the concomitant reality of random injustice that had taken Pregel from him, and his father. The only unknowns being the when – unless you were Ben Ali - and the why.

Alameth thankful that forty thousand people still had their bones in one place, ready and available when Christ took his last landfall on earth to gather them up into Heaven, appreciative of the beauty in which their resting had been encased; comforted that so many believed Heaven an absolute reality, for if so many did then why shouldn't he? He'd certainly good reason to hope it so.

They left the chapel in comparative silence, the only sounds being Obermann and Golinski bickering about something or other neither Lukitt nor Alameth were listening to, taking no notice of the diminutive, bearded, bespectacled man bustling up the path towards the chapel, his steps quick and animated as if he was already late for some important meeting, a tension to his face that hinted he was a man of deep thinking.

'Aha!' he said, closing on them, words rapid and staccatoed. 'I was told you'd be here, assuming one of you is Lukitt Bachmann. I'm Professor Vannevar. Quite something, our chapel. Hope you were impressed.'

Lukitt and Alameth ceased walking, both recognising the man from Udolpho's.

'I am, and we were,' Lukitt replied.

'I'm trying to do the same elsewhere,' Vannevar went on in the quick, clipped tones Lukitt would soon be used to, Vannevar swiftly turning and leading them back down the hill. 'Got a few more monasteries lined up with their own ossuaries, not that they're all so receptive to change and decoration. But that's a small matter,' Vannevar shook his head. 'Bigger thing is that you're here to help me sort what I need sorting. I've thousands of artefacts to catalogue and sketch that I've collected on my travels: old bootlaces, snatches of songs preserved in the margins of hymn books, amber scavenged from various waysides that might have served as buttons or rosary beads or sucked as lozenges on cold winter marches. Oh, those Ancient Knights! Such an interesting lot!'

Lukitt and Alameth exchanged glances, raising their eyebrows, the exact nature of their sabbatical now apparent: their days to be spent ordering Vannevar's extensive Cabinet of Curiosities, much as Vannevar had ordered the bones in the Sedlec Chapel.

A project not unappealing.

'I need to get everything sorted and packed for moving,' Vannevar went on to explain, once he'd brought them to his house. 'My new wife is due here shortly, and the last thing she'll want is her prospective domicile cluttered up by all my carryings on.'

Lukitt and Alameth had to agree, for Vannevar's house resembled a kingfisher's nest: dark burrowed, lined on every side by the bones and detritus he'd collected over the years that filled every corridor, every room. And it smelled bad, Lukitt crinkling his nose as he entered, following Vannevar into his study, a room that had no room, every surface filled with all manner of weird collectibles - or rubbish, if a visitor was feeling unkind.

'This is she,' Vannevar said, parting the silk ruffles about his neck and drawing out a large gold locket, flicking it open.

'She's very beautiful,' Alameth commented, looking at the pale oval face that smiled out at him, the russet curls, the kind dark eyes.

'She is,' sighed Vannevar, 'not that I've ever met her. One just has to hope the portrait is true to life.'

Alameth frowned.

'So you've already married someone you've never met? How is that possible?'

Vannevar snapped the locket shut.

'It is as it is,' he retorted. 'Contracts swapped, signed and returned to each family, one part needing one thing, the other needing another.

But either way, and whatever you think about the matter, this place needs tidying up, and you two are going to help me do it.'

And so they did, Lukitt and Alameth keener at their duties than Vannevar had hoped - every object catalogued, described and put away from the house into travelling chests; every paper from every journal organised into chronological order and into yet more crates; books stacked and packed. Even the shelves removed from the room designated to Lady Julida, who had no learning at all and had specifically stated she wanted none of the like when she finally moved in, coming as she did from a very prominent family: the Klagenfurts, closely tied to the Prince Bishop of Gurk who was in charge of the mint that produced money for the entire principality.

No wonder Vannevar wanted to impress.

When everything was ready for the off, Vannevar cornered Lukitt in his study while Alameth was off to book the wagon that would take it all away a few days hence.

'Well done,' he commented, looking around him at the sparse empty room with regret, leaving Lukitt to ask the question that had been puzzling him.

'But how do you intend to carry on your work?'

Vannevar put his hands behind his back and looked studiously out of the window.

'And what exactly do you know of my work?'

'I read your book,' Lukitt confessed, 'at Udolpho's.'

'Did you now?' Vannevar turned, fixing his eyes on Lukitt. 'So you know how it important it is.'

A statement.

Lukitt answering in kind.

'I do, sir. By following the heritage of the Teutonic Knights from their origins to the Crusades and Acre, then from Acre back to Venice and from Venice to Prussia…'

'And from Prussia to the east,' Vannevar interrupted, 'to Lake Peipus, where the Brotherhood unaccountably fell to Nevsky and his Russians on the ice. Well, go on, boy.'

Lukitt flustered, trying to visualise the notes he'd made.

'From there right back to their origins, to the Teutoberg Forest,' he got out in the nick of time. 'And Arminius's destruction of the Roman forces in...'

'In 9 AD,' Vannevar finished for him. 'Arminius abducted as a child, brought up a Roman soldier and citizen who reverted to his roots, returned to being Hermann, Chief of the Cherusci. The man who united the tribes of Germany against Roman advances,' Vannevar's eyes a little wet, as if he'd been there, part of the extraordinary vanquishing of the Romans on German soil only nine years after the birth of Christ. Three legions of Roman soldiers annihilated by an ambush in the Forest of Teutoberg, Vannevar closing his eyes as he sees the trail of his forebears, runs it down to its roots.

'Cherusci, Hermiones, Angrivarii and Longobardi to the north,' he recites, 'Bructeri to the west; Semnones and Calucones to the east; Chatten to the south.'

'Ah, the Chatten!' Lukitt seeing where this was going, remembering the epilogue to Vannevar's book, the exegesis of the whole rambling lot of it, and rambling it had been. Ulbert would have pulled it apart in a moment, but not the time to mention it. 'Progenitors of the Lands of Hesse,' he continued, with as much seriousness as he could muster, eager to please, eager to flatter. 'And therefore your direct ancestors. Your heritage.'

Vannevar smiling, breathing deeply, eyes closed. It was one thing to burrow through the molehills of history, blind to the world above as he sifted the soil of centuries, quite another to hear someone else voice his conclusions out loud.

'Right past St Odilo and the Cluniac reform,' he murmured, 'right back to Boniface, past Arminius and further still, further still. But there my family is. The heart of Germany. My family, the heart of Germany.'

Lukitt said nothing, plain as day to him that Vannevar was madder than a box of frogs to believe this very personal trajectory of greatness that could never be proved, not that Vannevar would ever be convinced of the opposite, Vannevar believing his interpretation absolutely, the pursuit of its truth his life's goal.

Only obstacle being the ghastly, quotidian, and rather squalid fact that he'd run out of money to take his work any further.

But he was a far-thinking man who'd come up with a solution, a solution about to arrive in Kutná Hora, at his family's behest.

28

The Ripping Off of His Wings

'You're very quiet,' Alameth said to Lukitt as they were getting ready for bed. 'Everything all right?'

Lukitt rubbed his face with his hands, not wanting Alameth to see his expression, the incipient tears. He'd sat through dinner with Alameth and Vannevar, Vannevar droning on about his favourite subject, the Teutonic Knights – apparently in the best of humours - reciting a line or two from the *Livländische Reimchronik.*

'Penned four hundred years ago by a rhyming Soldier Knight,' Vannevar explained, delighted with himself. 'Scribbled with one hand whilst swinging his sword with the other against the pagans of Livonia. And compare that to a passage of the account of *Die Schlacht bei Blut Ballade - The Ballad of the Battle of Blood...'*

Alameth feigning interest, coming out with the relevant conversational inserts as Lukitt was unable to do.

'Is that so? Do tell us more...'

Which, naturally, Vannevar did.

'I'll soon be publishing my own translation of the *Battle of Blood,* alongside the definitive table of my findings, when I will prove that the Monastery of Nicholas of Flüe was built on a Holy Fort of the Knights Teutonic as the headquarters for their early Conquests, vital to the cause of Christendom...'

On and on and on.

'Just a little tired,' Lukitt answered Alameth's enquiry vaguely. 'Been a busy couple of weeks.'

'At least we've got the stink out of the house,' Alameth replied, 'along with just about everything else, apparently ourselves included.'

Referencing Vannevar's last pronouncement of the night that they'd soon be following their packed crates out of town.

'Can't figure why he wants to go so soon, with his new wife due to arrive any day,' Alameth added, Lukitt blinking, knowing more than did Alameth and that this was precisely the point.

'I'm glad you grasp the import of my work,' Vannevar had said, when he'd Lukitt alone in his study. 'But to further it I need to call on your own particular…area of expertise.'

Lukitt perplexed.

'Your manner of business,' Vannevar stated, staring at Lukitt, the light from the window bouncing from his spectacles so Lukitt couldn't see his eyes. 'Your particular method of advancement.'

Vannevar standing motionless, head to one side, hands grasped behind his back, waiting for the penny to drop, which it did not.

'I don't know what you mean,' Lukitt replied. 'I've never…'

'Oh come now, my lad,' Vannevar continued briskly. 'No need to be coy with me. I know all about your little agreement with Hans Trudbert.'

Blood draining from Lukitt's face, legs bowing like reeds in the wind. He'd all but forgotten Hans Trudbert, indeed had wilfully forgotten everything about him, which hadn't seemed that bad at the time, murder at remove.

Nothing to do with him.

'Whatever Hans Trudbert did with…' he started.

'No point denying it, my young sir,' Vannevar cut him off. 'Myself and Trudbert have corresponded for quite a while. We've letters, him and I; letters that state categorically that he believes you, Lukitt Bachmann, might have misinterpreted certain *rapprochements* he made to you,' a sly shake of his head as he went on sadly. 'Letters that state he believes you responsible for killing his uncle. Oh, you'd weep to read them, my young sir, weep at the heartache he spilled out because of it.'

Lukitt couldn't move, couldn't react, couldn't do anything; a moth with its wings ripped off.

'And now's the time for you to do the same for me,' Vannevar announced blithely, swiftly stepping across the room, jabbing a finger at Lukitt's chest. 'And don't think for a moment you can wriggle out of it. One word from me,' Vannevar spoke slow and deliberate into

Lukitt's ear, 'and your world will come crashing down. I'll see you in prison before the year's out, you and your pretty little friend.'

A wave of nausea swept through Lukitt, thinking back, trying to find a loophole.

'And I need it done at a distance,' Vannevar continued, casual as asking for the loan of a pen. 'Isn't that what you talked to us about at Udolpho's? And we're to be well away when it happens. No suspicion whatever must attach to me, for if it does – even a whiff of it – out will come those letters and I'll personally drag you into an open grave by your heels and see you buried. Understand, Lukitt?'

Lukitt understood, nodded, put his hands over his stomach to stop himself from vomiting, blood sluggish in his veins as his heartbeat slowed, body momentarily in shutdown as Lukitt simultaneously refused to believe what he'd been asked to do and yet knew he had to do it. Mind flashing back to his stepping out of the Sedlec Chapel with his new grasp on the truth of life's ephemerality.

No idea then he'd be so fundamentally implicated in proving that truth beyond reasonable doubt.

29

Bad Smells, Sound Plans

'Any objection if we take a look about the town?' Lukitt asked Vannevar the morning following that awful conversation, at a breakfast Lukitt could hardly touch.

'None at all, my young helpmeets,' Vannevar answered, shaking crumbs from his napkin. 'You certainly deserve a little time off after all the hard work you've done. There's some very ancient and interesting architecture to be seen, ecclesiastical and secular alike, not to mention the mint-house and mines that made this place what it is. And,' he added, shrugging, looking pointedly at Lukitt, 'who's to say what you might find on your wanderings?'

Threat unspoken, but there all the same, Lukitt acutely aware that time was short, expected to present his solution – Vannevar's solution – as soon as possible.

'Where to start?' Alameth was saying as they stepped out of the house. 'How about the mint?'

Lukitt agreeing, though not enthusiastic, trying to figure a way out of the trap he was in – and Alameth with him - how to extricate them both, get them back to Lenze.

But when he got to the mint-house he was impressed despite himself: a huge fortified, white walled, slate roofed castle.

'*Sentry guarding the trade route between the capitals of Bohemia - which is Prague - and Moravia*,' Alameth reading aloud from the board erected at its gates, '*suborned into housing the Royal Mint, only place fortified enough to keep it safe. Birth place of the Prague Groschen instituted by Wenceslas II, that unified currency across the Empire.*'

Lukitt not listening.

Lukitt jolted by a sudden surfacing of his parents' faces like fish from water in his cluttered head, remembering his father's recitation of the origins of the Herrnhuter in precisely those places and those names: the Bohemian and Moravian Brethren who'd followed the teachings of Lukaŝ of Prague, not without criticism, saved from annihilation by Von Zinzendorf inviting them to join forces with his own Herrnhuter - Lukitt's father's Herrnhuter - thereby guaranteeing them all survival.

Lukitt having the sudden urge to write it all down, send off a letter to his bereaved mother:

I'm right here, he would say, *right on the cusp of where it all happened, where father's Brethren took in other Brethren and became the stronger for it. I'm standing on the same paths they might have taken, treading the same stones of their exile. And, by the way, I'm coming back for you as soon as...*

Cut off by Alameth pulling him on, dragging him into the mint-house proper, into the lower, impregnable cellars of the palace, looking at all the tools and implements the mint-workers had used right up until the day in 1727 - the information boards were specific - when the mint proper was shut down, not that the Mint Authorities immediately abandoned it.

Far too grand a place for that, hanging on there for as long as they could.

Hanging on like Lukitt was hanging on, which was by a thread.

Next place they went – by natural logic – were the old mines outside of town at Kaňk, its mines now depleted, its former use indicated by huge piles of waste that Lukitt had to stop Alameth from climbing haphazardly over.

'God's sake!' Lukitt said, grabbing Alameth's arm. 'Don't even think about it! There's arsenic in there,' he warned, 'and that's not good stuff.'

Privately working out how much spoil he might need to make anything of it: maybe half a sackful of rock, but only if he could somehow get it crushed, heat out the arsenic. An impossible task, no way he could do it without anyone knowing, least of all Alameth.

'Can we at least check out the museum?' Alameth asked, pluffing air through his lips, he and Lukitt ducking into a small building that had once been a worker's cottage, the exhibits haphazard, some in locked cases, others open to view, curator nowhere to be seen – if there was one.

'It's a little dull,' Alameth commented, moving quickly from one display case to the next. 'Although these coins look interesting. An original Groschen here…ooh, and look at this! There's a diorama here of an actual working silver mine!'

Lukitt didn't answer, for Lukitt was standing by one particular exhibit that caught his interest, quick glance around, no one looking, two parts of it stowed swiftly without notice into his handkerchief and stuffed into his pocket.

Lukitt now a thief, upon everything else.

Not that he was inclined to gripe about it.

'So we can really do it?' Vannevar asked Lukitt later that night, after Lukitt had approached him with his suggestion, Vannevar excited, rubbing his hands together, eyes too bright.

'Maybe,' Lukitt answered, hating to be included in that 'we', small hope in him that Vannevar would've baulked at his suggestion, bow out at the last moment.

But Vannevar not a man for bowing out.

'How soon can we start?' Vannevar's words crushing that small hope like a mustard seed beneath his boot.

Lukitt hesitating, trying his best to put Vannevar off.

'The most of it will rest on you,' Lukitt stated bluntly, 'on how you present it. And you'll need to be careful about which jeweller you go to.'

Thinking he maybe had one weak exit strategy, a glimmer grown from Alameth's reading of that board outside the mint, that if he could get himself to the Herrnhuter he might be saved, protected, whisked away.

But no.

That wouldn't do.

He'd have to give up his father's name for reference and the reasons why, and he couldn't bear for Trudl to know her boy had turned out a murderer, no matter he'd been strong-armed into it. The thought ticking in his head that he should just murder Vannevar and be done with it.

'Don't you worry about that,' Vannevar was saying, unaware Lukitt was rushing various scenarios through his head: lure Vannevar to the top of a tall building and shove him off; pretend a robbery, stab Vannevar in his bed, but too many risks of him crying out, of Lukitt being covered in blood – even if he had the stomach for something so immediate and visceral, which he did not. Food poisoning a possibility – but no, too long and complicated, Vannevar certain to tumble to the ruse, Lukitt not doubting for a moment that Vannevar – and Trudbert with him – had lodged their carefully constructed correspondence with lawyers in case of just such occurrence.

One last option, namely that Lukitt freely gave himself up for one murder to save him from perpetrating another; but he was too young for that to be a viable possibility. Life too precious, and too much more of it to be had. And also Vannevar's threat that if Lukitt went down then Alameth would go with him.

No choice then but to go on with their plan.

His plan.

'Maybe in Prague. A jeweller in Prague,' he said.

'No need to repeat yourself,' Vannevar snapped. 'Instructions. Exact measurements. Long chain. I've got it. Stop fussing.'

Dismissing Lukitt, Lukitt not able to sleep, Lukitt burdened by the guilt of his cowardice, writing letters that night to his mother, to Opapa Augen that he might have retracted if he'd thought too long about it.

But he did not, and done was done.

Sent off the following morning.

A letter not exactly a confession, but not far off.

30

Plans Put Into Action

The following day was full and busy, for this was the day Lady Julida arrived at the Vannevar household – not that Vannevar had bothered to inform Lukitt and Alameth this was so. Julida arriving mid-afternoon with a small retinue of maids to whom Lukitt arbitrarily allocated rooms in Vannevar's absence, Vannevar being off in Prague. Alameth and Lukitt sent by the cook-come-housekeeper with a list of ingredients to be fetched for dinner when Vannevar finally showed up to meet his wife for the first time, and she her husband.

An awkward moment, when Julida and her three indispensables swept into the dining room in full evening dress, bodiced and bejewelled, exuding a cloud of perfume that had Alameth coughing uncontrollably, Vannevar standing stiffly, making formal introductions before bowing and kissing Julida's hand.

'It's such a pleasure to have you here, my dear, at last, after all these years of promise.'

'And my pleasure also,' Julida replied, a quick tight smile conveying the exact opposite.

'I'm so sorry,' Vannevar went on, 'that myself and my two acolytes cannot be here to settle you in. We're due in Quedlinburg tomorrow,' Vannevar sighing as he shook out his napkin. 'But no getting out of it, I'm afraid. Duty is duty after all, and must come first.'

Both knowing the meaning of duty, this matrimony one of them. It had benefits for both: Julida getting away from the stiflement of her parents' household, Vannevar having the promise of Julida's money once she'd gone, so both smiled graciously at one another across the table. They'd known they were unlikely to be well suited, a view strengthened by the night's proceedings, the two irritating each other from the off. Vannevar finding Julida's conversation insipid and irrelevant, a woman who talked much but said little, her main topics being fashion and the latest hits in the theatre or opera houses, chatting inconsequentially with her ladies-in-waiting who apparently viewed their mistress with some awe. For her part, Julida found Vannevar an insufferable bore who never conversed but lectured, Julida never having heard of the Teutonic Knights before and never caring to hear of them again.

But both understood the terms of their contract, and so they smiled and nodded, ate and drank, tolerated each other whilst in company, the company leaving them to it after dessert so they could talk privately.

'One child, if we must,' Julida said. 'But I will not suffer more.'

'One child,' Vannevar complied, though privately doubted they'd ever get that far.

'And this house is to be my own,' she went on. 'I'll not brook interference. I'll hire who I like, fire those I do not.'

Vannevar nodded, no sympathy for the woman who'd cooked and kept house for him the past sixteen years, nor that she was likely to be thrown out into the street.

'And likewise,' Vannevar added to this verbal contract, 'it must be accepted that my work is my primary objective. I've already packed up everything to do with it and will spend the greatest part of my time in Quedlinburg, returning only if absolutely necessary.'

Julida agreed, completely unaware exactly how important Vannevar's work was to him, but mightily relieved to hear he planned to not live in the same town, let alone the same house.

'We can maximise this situation to mutual benefit,' Vannevar said, 'if we're both willing to abide by each other's terms.'

'I agree,' Julida said, after a pause, Vannevar taking off his glasses, cleaning them with his handkerchief.

'Just one thing I would ask of you,' he said, replacing his glasses, not meeting her eyes.

'Only ask,' Julida was quick to reply, wanting this meeting over, now everything needed saying had been said.

'You know how people gossip, how they will most certainly gossip about us now you've arrived,' Vannevar slowed his voice, tried to stop his heart beating so fast. 'My standing in this town is high,' he went on, 'and I will not jeopardize that standing. It must not be said of me that because I'm away so much I have no caring for you.'

Julida creased her brows but understood, had been expecting a short lecture on what and what not to say as she sewed herself into the fabric of this town's high society – if it had one – and if not here, then in Prague, that was only a stone's throw away.

'My occasional nights here must be seen as between husband and wife. I'll not tolerate you stepping out with another man, nor any rumours of such,' Vannevar stated starkly. 'And I would like to give you this,' unexpectedly removing from his pocket a small jewellery case, Julida leaning forward with surprise and anticipation, a woman always swayed by pretty baubles, if not by pretty words.

'Wear it always,' he asked, taking from the case an unusual pendant that held as its centrepiece what looked to Julida like a sphere of solid silver.

'From our mines here,' Vannevar explained. 'My promise to you of my fealty while I'm away, and of yours while you remain here.'

Julida smiling her only true smile of the evening.

'But of course!' she agreed, taking up the necklace, immediately clasping it about her neck. 'I confess I never thought, I mean…but it's so generous.'

'It's no more than you deserve,' Vannevar said, colouring slightly at the words, at the guilt behind them; Julida misinterpreting, thinking that perhaps this marriage might not be such a disaster after all, not if lavish jewellery was to be the order of the day.

'It will not leave me,' she promised, just as Vannevar had hoped. 'I'll wear it night and day and perhaps, in time…'

'Perhaps,' Vannevar agreed, after a few moments. 'Perhaps, my dear. We've been poorly served by our beginnings, you and I, but that's no reason it shouldn't end well.'

He stood then, Julida smiling, fingering her pendant, feeling its weight, happy at how things had gone; both retiring to their separate bedchambers, both believing the day well done.

31

Opapa Believes Too That All Is Well

A few weeks later, Opapa Augen received a letter from Lukitt Bachmann, somewhat surprised to get a missive from him out of the blue, along with a small sample of metal Lukitt had apparently found on his travels. Opapa Augen rolling the metal bead from the muslin it had been wrapped in, taking a deep sniff of it – as was his wont - and felt a tickle in his throat at the faint odour of rotting fish. He rewrapped the bead and picked up the letter, tilted it to the lighted candle, then held his head quite still to one side as he caught the melody of a young boy's voice, thinking inevitably of Pregel, before returning his attention to Lukitt's letter.

Uncovered this in the spill heap of the Kutná Hora silver mine - a small lie on Lukitt's part. *Thought it might amuse. Here's what I read about another sample kept in the museum:*

Metal, Osmium, found in a nickel-platinum deposit at Trudgarr, three miles south-south-east of the needle shaft on 31 Nov 1827. Treated with aqua regia, the refined ore revealing a large amount of nickel, a small amount of platinum, (see #72a) and a smaller amount still of osmium – this last first discovered by the English chemist Smithson Tennant in 1804, his life soon thereafter cut short by a fall from a horse. Osmium, common to the Urals and Americas, very rare to our soils and having many interesting properties. Named for the Greek *osme*, smell, on account of its very nasty odour, present to warn us of its habit of extreme toxicity, its exposed surface quickly besmirched by a highly toxic oxide that should on no account be touched or inhaled as it will produce severe illness - as the first discoverer soon had cause to know, and who surmised – as experiments have since proved – that prolonged contact over a short length of time, will result in death. When joined with gold, its poison is quickly quenched and gives great strength, reminding us that like the marriage of a repentant soul to Christ from badness can come great good.

We're doing well, me and Alameth, have ended up in a place that suits us both.

Another lie, not that Opapa Augen knew it, Opapa removing his spectacles, pleased to think the boy he'd loaned his books to had after all, and against the odds, made something of himself.

Opapa Augen shaking his old head, remembering the night he'd shared with the boy in the snow.

Opapa Augen sighing, perhaps not so surprised after all.

32

Ancient Trees Still Living, Julida Not So Long

They arrived in Quedlinburg by chance on the day of *Lindenblütenfest* – the festival of the lime-blossoms - and, finding the main streets impeded, departed from their carriage to investigate, making their way on foot to the town centre: a cobbled square humped and bumped in every direction by the bulging roots of the magnificent tree growing at its centre. Just in time to see the Mayor climb the staircase that had been hewn in a spiral around the giant bole to access the platform built amongst the spreading branches and, once up, he began his annual spiel.

'Welcome, Ladies and Gentlemen,' he shouted, 'to the wonderful town of Quedlinburg! We're here today to celebrate our lime tree and thank it for the spring. Take a look, Ladies and Gents! It's eighty two feet high, twenty three in diameter. And regard its enormous circumference that, at seventy-eight feet and thirteen inches, makes it the second biggest lime tree in the whole of Germany.'

'I wonder where the biggest is,' Alameth said to Lukitt.

'Staffelstein in Bavaria,' spat out an old man next to them, along with a wad of spittle-soaked chewing tobacco. 'Got another few inches on ours, so they say, but ain't never believed it.'

'Its centre is entirely hollow,' went on the Mayor, 'all sixty three square foot of it, and inside there's a plaque with the legend *Gepflanzt im Jahre 760*: planted in the year seven hundred and sixty, Ladies and Gents. And if that isn't worth dancing about, then I don't know what is!'

Alameth whistled.

'That's some age! That makes it over a thousand years old. Can trees really live that long?'

'They can,' Lukitt affirmed. 'They reckon there's a yew somewhere in Scotland that's at least five times that ancient, and probably a lot more.'

'Where the beggaration is Scotland?' demanded the old man as he stuffed more tobacco into his cheek and puffed, not liking the tree he regarded as his own property – if communal – to be upstaged.

'Up north of England, sir,' Lukitt supplied, winking at Alameth who grinned back.

'Might as well be in bloody France,' muttered the old man, having no idea of anywhere outside his own regional borders, Alameth stifling a laugh.

'It's also our *Gerichslinden*, our Justice Tree,' the Mayor was going on unperturbed, 'so let's see no bad behaviour, folks,' the crowd duly laughing, except the ones who had been sentenced for their crimes beneath this very canopy. Though no one hung here – at least not in living memory - as was the case in other towns, from other lime tree boughs.

'But enough of history!' finished the Mayor, holding aloft his hands. 'Let the dancing begin! Into the tree, those of you who've been chosen, and off we go!'

And off they went, the crowd dissipating about Lukitt and Alameth, dividing into couples as the band struck up a tune.

'Are they really going to dance inside the tree?' Alameth asked, propelled forward by the surge, but the old man was no longer with them to provide an answer, gammy legs not up for dancing, heading instead for the makeshift drinking stalls that had sprung up about the square, the two young visitors forgotten.

Lukitt and Alameth pushing their way through the crowds – no idea where Vannevar was, and not caring - soon immersed in the general stramash of people dancing and singing, stamping their feet, laughing, waving tankards and bottles, the band playing on a little out of tune and a little out of time. The entire square soon a riot, Alameth and Lukitt retiring to its edges, sampling food from the street vendors, wondering how on earth they were going to find Vannevar in this human medley.

'Didn't he tell you the place we're supposed to be going?' Alameth asked through a mouthful of Pompillior bread, enjoying the hint of rosewater, cardamom and almond, which combined flavours he'd never tasted before.

'He didn't,' Lukitt agreed. 'But he did say it was nearby *Nikolaikirche.*'

'Another church of St Nicholas,' Alameth commented. 'I suppose we might have guessed. But got to be a different St Nicholas, hasn't it?'

'I should think so,' Lukitt said. 'This town's very old, at least as old as that tree, any rate.'

'So maybe *the* St Nicholas!' Alameth laughed. 'Der Weihnachtsmann himself!'

'Maybe,' Lukitt said, remembering the warmth and wonder of their Christmas spent at Lenze, the awful thought that Julida would never see another one, nor another spring, nor smell again the lime blossom that was so sweet on the air. He had the idea that he should write to her, warn her, tell her to take the pendant off, throw it into the river. An impossibility, for they'd been two weeks getting here - going from Prague to Dresden, from Leipzig to Quedlinburg – any letter travelling the same route back undoubtedly arriving too late, creating for Vannevar the perfect alibi, just as Vannevar had required.

Julida's doctor was mystified. He'd not made much of it at first, her waiting ladies informing him without prompt that she was prone to migraines, had an enthusiastic leaning towards hypochondria, a need – as he'd interpreted it – to be the centre of attention. Coming to Kutná Hora hadn't been all she'd hoped: no immediate welcome into high society as she'd imagined and, despite her frequent trips to Prague no success in that city either, Vannevar's name – contrary to what he'd implied – carrying no weight there at all.

The doctor had made note of all her symptoms, which at first were nothing out of the ordinary:

An obscure malaise, that hadn't stopped her travelling to Prague to purchase an entire new wardrobe to suit her new life as Professor Vannevar's new wife;

A bout of headaches and stomach cramps, that hadn't stopped her going to events and functions she'd not been invited to;

A dislike of the food she is being given, resulting in the sacking of Vannevar's cook and the hiring of another to provide meals more to her taste, though these had apparently not satisfied either.

So much, so ordinary, he'd thought. Merely a hysterically-inclined woman not settling into her new environment.

Yet two weeks in he was becoming seriously worried.

He consulted his latest notes:

Skin pale, easily sweated;

Chest tight;

Throat burning;

Ulcered mouth;

Odd smell emanating from her, similar to rotting fish;

Stools slimed with blood.

He shook his head.

He couldn't understand it.

He'd given her all the medications he had at hand: a curative mixture of antimony, mercury and Indian Hemp; tinctures of myrrh and nutmeg; iodide of potash and powdered opium; a silver nitrate stick to treat the ulcers.

Nothing aiding her in the slightest.

He added the new symptoms he'd noted that morning, having not long left her:

Skin unbearably itchy, so much so that she's scratched the centre of her chest raw with fingernails that have an odd blue sheen;

Lips thin, a deep purple colour;

Coughing that racks her ribs, ends in spitting blood that's dark as tar.

Julida is very ill, the doctor knows it, and fears there's nothing more he can do.

Time to call on priest and husband, let them know the worst.

He's sick at heart, for it will not look good on his résumé, but more so because this woman – a newcomer to Kutná Hora - is about to die, and he can't for the life of him understand why.

But die she does, mewling like a drowning kitten as she goes – a terrible sound, high-pitched and pained, her maids about her bedside weeping wildly, though only one taking her hand to comfort her, the others fearing contagion.

And straight into the ground went the skinny scraps left of the Lady Julida, before anyone had the chance to mutter about the plague.

A woman who'd apparently died for no reason.

A doctor who'd done his best, who spent his next few years trying to puzzle it out.

Three women-in-waiting insisting she be buried in her finery as befitted her, including the necklace her husband had bade her wear: the pendant with the long chain that meant she'd to tuck it beneath her clothes to stop it catching and swinging, the dark oxide forming on the metal constantly polished off and absorbed by her skin.

Finery and pendant going with Julida's body six foot under.

No one making the connection or crying murder, although murder had certainly been done.

33

Outrage All Round

They settled into Quedlinburg without qualm, Vannevar cossetted in his new study, all his books and artefacts unpacked and placed about his new abode. His initial leanings had been to leave the most of them crated up, ready to take back to Kutná Hora when the inevitable happened. Reminded by Lukitt this was not a good idea, that he needed to be seen to be here for the duration. So unpacked everything was, Lukitt and Alameth busied with the tasks of erecting shelves on any wall that could take them and, once this task was done, sent off hither and thither into the local countryside to seek for more signs of the Teutonic Knights, a task Lukitt and Alameth were happy to perform.

They didn't discover an enormous amount about the Knights, but they enjoyed trekking through the nearby Harz mountains, their guide-book a well-worn copy of *Die Harzreise* by Heinrich Heinrichson, Alameth fascinated by the tales of the Brocken Spectre mentioned therein – the vast ghostly being people reported seeing whilst high up in the mountains.

'It'll be a glory,' Lukitt confidently informed him. 'A reflection of themselves seen in fog or clouds due to raindrop refraction.'

Alameth frowning, disliking Lukitt so casually dissecting an age-old mystery with the ease of an otter peeling a toad.

Only once did they come across something that might be of interest to Vannevar, when they visited Gernrode. Hard to miss being the enormous church of St Cyriacus, harder to believe what they saw when they pushed its door open and stepped inside, found its vast interior being used as a storehouse by local farmers: great heaps of potatoes in every corner, stacks of baled straw down the main nave, sacks of flour piled haphazardly on broken pews, boxes of turnips and dried peas teetering on and about the altar.

They nevertheless wandered about for a time, having been informed by a small and badly engraved plaque by the door that this church was one of the finest examples of Ottonian ecclesiastical architecture in existence, its foundations laid in the 950s.

'Almost the same age as that lime tree,' Alameth commented.

'Stone and wood,' Lukitt murmured, gazing up into the empty heights of St Cyriacus, 'growing up span by span, long before Vannevar's Knights existed, and going on long after.'

'Opapa Augen had a piece of fossilized wood,' Alameth added. 'Really strange, it was. Looked like bark – all the crevasses there to see, but cold and hard and black.'

Cold and hard and black, Lukitt thought, like Vannevar's heart. Maybe like his own after what he'd done, having a sudden shocking vision of that lime tree at the heart of Quedlinburg being sliced through like a criminal's neck by an axe, the Justice Tree revealing a thousand years of corruption in its inner circles.

'Let's take some sketches,' he said, to rid himself of the thought that he might one day swing from its branches.

They went in separate directions, stepping past boxes and bales, noting down all they found of interest: details of the internal decoration, of the reliquary that may or may not still be protecting various body parts of the Saint after whom the church had been named; of the vast stone font, some ancient sarcophagi - one purporting to contain the remains of Geru and Hathui, dating back to 1014 - and a great many emblems in the wall-shields that indicated the Knights Teutonic must have occupied the church at some time. Which would please Vannevar no end.

'Hey, you two! What the hell d'you think you're at?'

Lukitt and Alameth turning to find a crook-backed man hobbling towards them, waving his stick. 'This here's private property,' the man continued as he closed on them. 'And if you'm thinkin' on pinching owt then you'd best think it right out your heads!'

Lukitt stepping forward to greet the interrupter, holding up his sketchbook in defence.

'I'm sorry,' he said quickly. 'We were just passing through and thought the place worth investigation.'

'Investigation, is it?' the man said. 'I'll give you investigation,' his tone less belligerent, tilting his head to accommodate his squint as he studied

Lukitt's sketchbook, straightening as much as he was able, coming to a stop, leaning heavily on his stick. 'Well. So it seems. Investigation, eh?'

'It's very impressive,' Alameth came up beside Lukitt. 'A crime it's no longer used for worship. I don't understand how that can be.'

'A crime, eh?' echoed the man. 'Well, you got that right. Centuries and centuries it's been here, then became a convent so it did, run by nuns till they fell foul of the Protestant creed what did for `em. Didn't last a hundred year after that, which serves `em right. Bloody women. Empty then for ages, just a few services held by a local pastor, till it got sold off and deconsecrated.'

'But how? No one has the right to do that!' Alameth morally outraged, prepared for godless people using the place as a grain store, but not deconsecration.

'Well there's the rub,' the man said, easing himself into a pew, looking about him, eyes a little rheumy - maybe from his squint, maybe not. 'Can't believe it anymore'n you can, lad. But happen it did,' shaking his head sadly at the thought. 'Got sold by the church to private buyers back in `31. Can't quite get over that I ain't never gonna hear another proper sermon here. Prays here all the time, I does.'

Lukitt scribbling all these facts down in his notebook, not that the old man noticed.

'Least they left Saint Cyriacus,' the old man said, jutting his chin towards the altar. 'No matter what folk says to the contrary. Spent most of his last years in a cave that man did. An' I kinda feel this place is a cave now, so maybe there's summat fitting in that.'

They left him to his meditations, Lukitt pausing at the plaque by the door, wondering if this man, this old refugee from the past, had been the one to make it; wondering how a building, even one so old, could provoke such attachment. Alameth providing the answer as they stepped back out into the late spring afternoon.

'They're all still in there,' Alameth said as he gazed at the vast stone walls of the no-longer church. 'All those women, those worshippers; all their prayers, all the songs they must have sung. Almost a thousand years of them. Like the stones have drunk them in.'

Alameth raised his hand to shield his eyes from the sun, aware of

Lukitt twitching beside him.

'Don't say it,' Alameth pleaded, without shifting his gaze. 'I know you think it nonsense. That stones are just stones. That you could pull this place down, build a thousand houses, put them to better use.'

'I wasn't going to say anything,' Lukitt protested. 'In fact I…'

'But that's exactly your problem!' Alameth shouted, colour rising in his cheeks, the rage back in him, the rage that couldn't be stopped, no matter how many times he told it go boil its head, and instead boiled his. 'Everything is all facts with you!'

He whirled on his heel, head thumping, heart going too fast, seeing Lukitt's face, seeing its shock, its mendacity, seeing it like a mask, wanting to rip it off with his fingernails to reveal the true nature of what lay beyond, needing to blame someone, needing to blame Lukitt, and desperately wanting not to.

Took a deep breath.

Took another.

Took another.

Subsided.

'The world isn't like that,' quieter now, withdrawing, moving away from Lukitt, fixing his gaze on St Cyriacus, some peace in those stones, knowing how long they'd been there, how long they'd had people within praising the Lord his God with not a tremor to their faith, no matter the consequences.

'That man in there?' Alameth's voice tremulous, tears on the brink. 'He knows it. I know it. And there's nothing you can say to make it any different.'

Hating the fact that this ancient place of spirituality had been demoted to a mere storehouse; hating the fact that only one old man with a crooked back and a bad squint seemed to care; hating most of all the fact that he himself cared so much about it and Lukitt couldn't, that with Lukitt every mystery was only there to be dissected, studied and, even if put back together, would always be wrong.

The news Lukitt had been dreading reached Quedlinburg that same night: a black-edged letter propped on the mantle informing Professor

Vannevar his wife had died, already buried for fear of contagion. Vannevar telling the news bluntly to his two assistants as he poured a glass of wine, sat down at his desk to work out how best to use the money he'd soon receive.

'But how can she be dead? And you act like you don't care!' Alameth emboldened by his earlier anger, Vannevar even angrier, banging his fist on the table.

'How dare you take the moral high ground with me,' Vannevar growled. 'You hardly knew her! I hardly knew her and she was my wife!'

Alameth looked to Lukitt for support but Lukitt had bowed his head, closed his eyes.

'I'm sorry, I'm so sorry,' Lukitt croaked, kneading the skin of his forehead with his fingers, Alameth perplexed by Lukitt's reaction but going straightaway to his side.

'Oh for God's sake,' Vannevar muttered. 'It's like being at some dreadful Weber opera...*enter bear stage left.*'

'Come on,' Alameth said, shooting Vannevar a black look that Vannevar ignored, Alameth leading Lukitt away, closing the door behind them.

'It's just life,' he said, unused to being the leader, trying to find the right words to say. 'Sometimes we're here and then, for no apparent reason, we're gone. Just like Pregel,' he added. 'You couldn't have stopped that any more than you could have stopped this.'

Lukitt swallowed a sob, bleakly aware of the truth of the first half of that statement and the absolute falsity of the last.

'Let's go back to Lenze,' Lukitt whispered, swiping at his eyes with his finger knuckles. 'Let's leave tomorrow; beg our way back if we have to.'

'I'm with you on that score,' Alameth agreed. 'Never liked that Vannevar. Streak of something vicious in him, I always thought.'

'You don't know the half of it,' Lukitt whispered; Alameth frowning, not understanding.

'And let's not tell him about St Cyriacus,' Lukitt added, to cover his slip. A small revenge, but revenge all the same.

'Absolutely not,' Alameth fished out a smile he didn't feel. 'Let's not tell that blackhearted man anything ever again.'

34

Swivelling On a Sixpence

Lukitt and Alameth going down to breakfast the following morning with light hearts, bags already packed, decisions made, plans afoot.

Until the black-hearted man changed the rules, called Lukitt to his study.

'I'm off back to Kutná Hora,' Vannevar stated, 'as is only right. But for you and your lackey I've made other arrangements.'

Lukitt frowned, shook his head.

'No,' he said. 'Me and Alameth have talked. We're back off to Lenze, with or without your help.'

'Oh but you're not,' Vannevar stated. 'I knew straightway I met you this time around that you were weaker than I was led to believe, and your antics last night proved it. I'll not risk you having an attack of conscience once you're so far away, back in the bosom of your friends. No, my young sir. I will not.'

'You can't stop us,' Lukitt tried, though saw the hardness in Vannevar's eyes and knew otherwise.

'That's where you're quite wrong,' Vannevar went on - *vicious*, Alameth had diagnosed, and he'd been right. 'I specifically told that jeweller in Prague it was you who'd designed the pendant for my wife and sourced it. Named names, of course. And expressed my utter joy at my marriage. One word from me will raise doubts enough to get the thing examined: *But how can she be dead?*' Vannevar's voice changing pitch to imitate Alameth's previous outrage, becoming piteous, distraught. '*It's so sad, so tragic, and she so beautiful, so excited about our new life together. So…unexplained.*'

Lukitt's scant breakfast curdling in his stomach, seeing it all unfolding: Vannevar getting back to Kutná Hora, raising a stink, finishing Vannevar's mock sentiments for him: '*And I know who's responsible. Trudbert warned me, but I couldn't believe it of such a promising young scholar. Chose to give him a chance, and look what's happened because of it.'*

'I'll dig her up,' were Vannevar's actual words. 'Both her and her pendant, if it's gone with her. Don't you think I won't. Ha!'

Vannevar sneered, seeing Lukitt shrivel before him surely as a slug scattered over with salt.

'What more do you want of me?' Lukitt whispered, unable to look at Vannevar, bile hot and bitter in his throat.

'Why I want to reward you!' Vannevar said effusively, 'and of course ensure your silence, and it wouldn't be unwelcome if you wrote to me every now and then to tell me of your progress. Of the work my acquaintance is engaged in.'

'Can't you just let us be?' Lukitt pleaded. 'Let us make our way back to Lenze? I'll not say a word, I prom…'

'Promises are not my purview,' Vannevar cut Lukitt off. 'You can promise anything you like but I'll not have a sword hanging over my head for the rest of my days, no matter the precautions I've put in place. You're a sad case, Lukitt,' Vannevar shook his head. 'You start by saving someone's life, and look where you've ended up. Grab, grab, grab. That's all the youth of today ever do. You didn't have to give that lecture at Udolpho's, but you did. And you didn't have to accept Trudbert's offer, but,' he shrugged his small shoulders, 'you did. And now you have to live with the consequences. And the consequences will be these: you will do as I say, or hang.'

'We're going where?' Alameth asked, when Lukitt announced their sudden change of plan.

'It's to an acquaintance of Vannevar's,' Lukitt said, trying to sound cheerful. 'Wants to make up for us not spending the rest of the summer with him, on account of…well. You know.'

Alameth knew, but couldn't fathom this sudden change in direction.

'But why can't we just go back to Lenze?' he asked.

Lukitt shrugged.

'Says it'll be a big help to us. Look good on our Curriculum Vitae.'

'Curriculum what?' Alameth knew the words from his Latin letters but not their application.

'Help us academically,' Lukitt attempted. 'This Züstraubben being a well renowned scholar. Could do us good.'

'Could do you good, you mean,' Alameth retorted. 'I thought we only left to have adventures. *See the world*, you said. But you don't want that at all, you just want…'

'Please, Alameth!'

Such beseechment in those two words, and such distress, that Alameth stopped his argument, seeing a reflection in Lukitt's face of the same inner turmoil he'd been undergoing himself. Terrible pain, and such terrible shame writ large on Lukitt's face. He'd no idea the reasons, but recognised the signs all the same and acquiesced. Off again to God knew who and God knew where, but Alameth would go with Lukitt, Alameth's faith obscurely bolstered by the fact of Lukitt's evident suffering, irrationally cheered by Lukitt maybe having something worse in him than Alameth had in himself. Alameth needing to stay with him, dog his steps, until he found it out.

The Vannevar household parting company without regret on either side, Lukitt and Alameth standing in the street, formally shaking Vannevar by the hand, him thanking them for their help, and they thanking him for his.

'It's no more than you deserve,' Vannevar said, smiling brightly at Alameth, less convincingly brightly at Lukitt, Alameth interpreting Vannevar's words as a compliment, Lukitt as a threat.

'Do right by Züstraubben,' Vannevar added, 'and he'll do right by you.'

Bowing curtly, turning his back on them and closing the door, gathering his necessaries together for his return to Kutná Hora and the tedious bureaucracy he'd need to wade through before he got his hands on his dead wife's estate.

'Well good riddance to bad rubbish,' Alameth said, hoisting his pack onto his back, striding off into the early summer morning. 'And a grand day to be ditching it.'

He was right. It was a grand day. Bright, blue and warm.

Lukitt agreed, heartened to be out of that house, out of Vannevar's immediate grasp, heading off into the Harz Hills towards Nordhausen, a direction they'd not been before. Glad to see the bees upon the thistle heads that lined the track, and the butterflies that flitted from one flower to the next: one grizzled skipper, several common blues, a couple of early swallowtails, several burnet moths out before their season.

Reminding him strongly of that first talk he'd given when he'd been new to Seiden See, when he'd first had the chance to peruse all Ulbert's books and collections; when he'd first met Pregel.

'Do you really believe in God?' Lukitt asked, a step behind Alameth, not noticing that Alameth had taken the lead when on all previous journeys Lukitt had been at the fore. 'I mean really and truly believe?'

'I do,' Alameth replied after a moment. 'You know I do.'

Thinking back to St Cyriacus, that reflex stab to the heart to know it had been so ill-treated, how for him it could never be other than what it had been built for. You could smash it down and take all those stones and put them to other use, but each and every one of them would still remain part of the whole, of that much he was sure. He mightn't have started this way, pushed into Gargellan as a youngster to ease the weight on his family's shoulders, but he'd grown into it, soaked it up, needing the certainty of belief more than ever.

'And you're certain he's a forgiving God?' Lukitt asked, for it seemed to him that God had smited folk with uncomfortable regularity - and very little reason - from Genesis right through to Revelations.

'How else would Christ have forgiven Dysmas?' Alameth asked simply.

The Triungulin Mosaic at Gargellan, Christ and the penitent thief both racked against their crosses, only a few tortured hours until both would die.

At my right side, today in Paradise, Lukitt recalled, and its illogic, the lie spoken by Christ immediately before he descended into hell.

35

DISCOVERING THE OSTROGOTHS

The Oberharz, when they got there, was entirely different in character to the areas of the Harz they'd already encountered. There the foothills had been rolling and green before rising up to the Brocken; here the Harz was wooded, hiding narrow rocky valleys and tiny hamlets. Having only the vaguest of directions and not knowing the way, they veered severely off track, eventually set right by a few charcoalers. Nevertheless it took them the entire day instead of the few hours it should have done.

'Can't miss it,' they were told by a boy driving his pigs through the forest. 'Bloody great place just over yonder.'

And a bloody great place it was, as they discovered when it suddenly hove into view as they surmounted yet another ridge and saw Züstraubben's homestead laid out in a cleared plateau below them: styled like an extravagant log cabin, the body of it extending to right and left, low to the ground, two arms curving slightly back upon themselves to shelter an open courtyard behind the main dwelling; two squat towers at their ends to mark a grand entrance from the other side.

They descended towards it, scrambling down the wooded slope, the last of the sunlight filtering orange through the leaves, finding the place at once enticing and forbidding – warm and cosy from the front, but then those two great flanking arms curving away as if to keep themselves from the forest and something in the forest from them.

'Well, here we go,' Alameth said, knocking politely on the wooden door, knocking a little harder when no one came, the door soon opened by a solid-bellied man peering suspiciously at them out of small eyes that had the quality of an ocean wave: a sandy grey flecked with scintillations of green.

'Lukitt and Alameth,' Alameth introduced themselves. 'Here to see… I've completely forgotten his name.'

Lukitt stepped up beside Alameth, the light almost gone, swallowed by the hills and forests at their backs.

'Herr Züstraubben,' Lukitt supplied.

'Professor Züstraubben, I think you mean,' said the man a little stiffly, emphasising the first word. 'Professor three times over, if you must know. And he's not in residence at the moment, though I suppose...' he glanced briefly over the strangers' shoulders at the malevolence of the forest, and ushered them in.

Immediately the door closed behind them they were elbow deep in young boys who'd previously been clustered behind it.

'Well, well!' Alameth said, delighted, truly pleased, shaking each one by the hand, asking their names, establishing them in descending order of age - from fourteen to five - as Filip, Rudiger, Jochen, Jakob and Edric, who were equally delighted at Alameth treating them like adults, sweeping him away, all noise and questions, constantly interrupting each other as they vied for Alameth's attention.

'*If children are as arrows,*' Lukitt murmured, '*then happy is the man who has a quiverful.*'

'You know your bible, then? Or the psalms at least,' said the pot-bellied man, eyeing Lukitt with some interest.

'I'd my education with Père...with a minister in Seiden See,' Lukitt explained. 'Boarded with him since I was young.'

'That's a start at least,' said his companion, warming to the young man, introducing himself. 'Anke Mingelstrosser, father of the tribe, chief helper to the Professor, and Elder of our little chapel.'

'Lukitt Bachmann,' Lukitt replied, the two following the children's chatter into a large dining room, hearing one of them telling a breathless tale of how he'd nearly drowned in the lake last year trying to net a dragonfly, immediately upstaged by another informing Alameth he'd almost been crushed by a tree two of the foresters had been felling that had come down the wrong way.

'Ah,' said Alameth wisely, 'forests can be dangerous places. I should tell you about when my friend here,' he paused as Lukitt entered the room, 'was only a second away from being gored by two fighting boars in a forest far away from here.'

'Gored by a boar?' asked Jochen, taking an audible breath.

'He said two boars, you nincompoop,' said Jakob.

'And not gored, but almost gored,' corrected the oldest brother, Filip, no less enthralled. 'So how'd it happen?'

'We were fishermen then,' Alameth began, relaxed, at ease, leaning back in his chair, 'and I was just fresh from the monastery...'

'A monastery!' Rudiger put in. 'What were you doing in a monastery?'

Alameth putting his hands behind his head, seeing in these young boys' faces what had once been in him, bad times forgotten, for the moment at least.

'I was about to take my final vows,' he began, 'but then the most extraordinary thing happened...'

Interrupted by Anke's wife Ishbella bustling into the room, placing a large bowl of pumpkin soup down in the middle of the table, a swirl of sour cream spiralling about the soup's centre as she got out her ladle.

'Guests!' she said, clocking the two newcomers without batting an eyelid. 'Well, how wonderful! I presume you have names?'

'Alameth,' Alameth said promptly, 'and over there's Lukitt Bachmann.'

'Alameth was telling us a story,' Filip begged his mother, 'please, let him go on with it!'

Ishbella ladling out her soup, fetching extra bowls.

'No reason not to,' she said, smiling at Alameth, for what a handsome boy he was, and so few their visitors. She was all for it, and Alameth eager to tell his tales, felt them bubbling up in him like a spring desperate for release. Forget the bad, the bad could wait for the confessional, for here were people who wanted to hear what he had to say, suddenly aware he had wonderful stories for them, that his life since he'd met Lukitt had become extraordinarily enlivened; Alameth turned into a storyteller and, like a true teller of tales, taking intense delight in getting them told.

Supper a boisterous affair, the food tasty and plentiful, the two strangers absorbed into the large Mingelstrosser family without making a dent, served by two girls, the oldest children - Annely and

Lata – who laid out battered ox knuckles along with paper-thin slices of white veal, and garlic spinach wrapped about the blackest of blood sausages in a rich plum sauce.

The Mingelstrossers a lively lot, the scrimmage of boys focussing their attention on Alameth, this large family so like his own - bar the novelty of him being the oldest boy instead of the youngest. Alameth reappropriating his youth, commanding attention, become a bear amongst an army of squirrels all eager to impress.

Lukitt envious of Alameth's obvious ease, slotting in as he could not.

Anke Mingelstrosser seeing Lukitt's discomfort and weighing in.

'You must excuse my boys,' he said. 'We're such a long way from town and have few neighbours, none with children. So you're here to work with the Professor? I confess it's not been mentioned to me.'

'It was a sudden decision,' Lukitt explained. 'We were to spend the summer with Professor Vannevar in Quedlinburg, but then he…had to return home… his…wife, well…she…died very suddenly, so he sent us here instead.'

Hard to get out those last words, give them form and substance.

'I see,' Anke murmured, glancing over at Ishbella - the beating heart of his family, unable to envision how he would cope without her, nodding his understanding. 'And so he sent you here, and quite right too, seeing as we're on the doorstep, so to speak.'

Lukitt's blood quickening, seeing a chance for escape.

'We certainly don't want to impose. If you rather we left we could…'

Interrupted by Anke putting a fatherly arm about Lukitt's shoulders.

'We wouldn't hear of it!' he exclaimed. 'No. Absolutely not. And in truth the Professor could do with a little help, so you're both very timely. Ishbella!' Anke raising his voice, shouting above his children's chatter. 'These lads are to be here with us all summer, so what do you think of that?'

Ishbella's answer a wide smile, a short inclination of her head as she stood to fetch dessert, any words she might have said drowned out by her boys clapping loudly and speaking all at once.

'That's brilliant! All summer!'

'Can Alameth come with us with the goats?'

'Let's go fishing tomorrow. You said you used to be a fisherman, didn't you?'

'Alameth could show us how to hunt boars!'

'Let's give the poor boy some peace,' Ishbella's voice cutting through the crowd as she placed a lemon-infused posset on the table, nodding at Annely – her oldest girl – to do the dishing out, noting the blush on her cheeks as she served Alameth. No one giving a second thought to Lukitt at the other end of the table, who felt sucked down to the marrow by the bargain he knew must have been made to secure this post.

Udolpho to Trudbert, Trudbert to Vannevar and now Vannevar to this unknown Züstraubben.

No way out.

No exit.

No forgiveness.

But seeing Alameth's happy face in this sea of Mingelstrossers, Lukitt swore that whatever was asked of him, whatever he'd next to do, he'd make damned sure that if he went down – when he went down - he'd not take Alameth with him.

They were taken, after supper, to a couple of chilly guest rooms, it seeming odd to both to say good night and depart each to his own, and for a few minutes Alameth hung at Lukitt's door, talking about the Mingelstrosser boys and how good it had been to hear their chatter, hear their stories, tell his own. Lukitt smiling vaguely as he went about the business of unpacking his bag, putting a couple of shirts in the small wardrobe, the rest of his clothes into a rickety chest of drawers.

'I'm sorry for going on about it,' Alameth said, leaning his shoulder against the jamb. 'It's just so grand to be back in a family again. I'd forgotten how much I missed it. I mean I know the monastery was a family of sorts, but not like this. And d'you know what I've realised? In all the time I've known you I've never asked about your family, if you have brothers and sisters.'

Lukitt paused, his hand resting on the drawer he'd just pushed shut.

'No one,' Lukitt said. 'Just me, mother and father.'

Hermione and Hermistus not counted in the mix.

Alameth looking at his feet; the fact of Lukitt learning of his father's death a few days before they left Lenze given new proportions. A third of his family scythed down long before his time.

'I'm sorry,' he said. 'I never realised how few you were, your family, I mean.'

Lukitt didn't turn around, coming only now to the same conclusion, unable to decide if it was good or bad.

'I guess if we'd stayed with the Herrnhuter,' Lukitt reflected, 'then I'd have had a huge family, if not related. But on the other hand,' he made a vague gesture, 'if we'd stayed with them I'd probably be a religious bigot and never have rocked the Gargellan boat, never have met you, never have ended up here.'

His attempt at humour was lost, Alameth looking on Lukitt, seeing his dark hair, his dark eyes, the same dark shadow of serious studiousness that always accompanied Lukitt wherever he went, keeping him away from the crowd. It occurring only now to Alameth that this had been Lukitt's abiding characteristic for all the years he'd known him: that wherever they'd gone, whatever they'd done, Lukitt was always his own person, more apparent now than ever; Lukitt not taking to people lightly, sticking rigidly to the few friends he'd made: to Pregel, and then to Alameth, and no one else. Even at the Academy in Lenze he'd kept his distance.

'Are you hating it here?' Alameth asked. 'Because we can leave tomorrow if you do. Go back to Lenze, or somewhere new?'

Lukitt raising a smile.

'I'm happy here if you are,' Lukitt answered, knowing how impossible that would be. 'Let's just wait and see.'

'All right then,' Alameth answered. 'But say the word,' he added, 'and we're off.'

Lukitt closing the door to his room, to Alameth, putting his face to the damp pillow on his bed, made damper still as he lay down and wept.

36

At the Lodge

Lukitt didn't sleep well, despite the long day's trek through the Harz. He'd not closed the shutters – had never liked being closed off from the outside world – and woke soon as the sky was lightening, listening to the birds in the trees: a lone blackbird soon joined by the piping of coal tits, several wood doves forming a soft backdrop. The blackbird overtaken by a mistle thrush and next a couple of vying robins, all soon subsumed by a congregation of rooks rising from their nests in black riot, dissipating across the fields that lay beyond the lower fells.

Lukitt dressed, tiptoed through the house and out the front door, went walking not back into the forest but off to the south where the woodland was varied and deciduous, water dripping through the leaves from a pre-dawn shower of rain, wisps of mist wreathing the tallest firs behind the house, the air calm and crisp, cobwebs slung from brambles that were throwing out their runners, wild quince flowers sprinkling reds and whites amongst the undergrowth.

He followed a grassy track, heading for the sound of water spilling over rocks and the bubbling crescendos of black grouse in lek. Miner bees began to emerge from the rocks and banks about him, woodcock whirring low through the trees, woodpeckers tapping out their semaphores above him, wrens sprightly through the mounds of honeysuckle that were abundant with leaf, if not yet with flower.

He breathed deeply, felt utterly at peace, sat a while on a willow stump once he reached the river, throwing twigs into a recessed pool, watching them swirl in slow circles before the current took them off to wherever the river would find its end; wishing he could go with them, wishing himself away, tilting his face to the rising sun, a remnant of last night's tears trickling unbidden from the corners of the eyes he'd closed against the glory of the sun.

'Well, that's a first,' said one of the Mingelstrosser girls, standing a few yards away from him, a shallow basket hooked onto her arm, feet so sure upon the grassy track he'd not heard her approach. Lukitt hurriedly rubbing his fingers to the corners of his eyes.

'Come here often?' the girl asked lightly, smiling at Lukitt, her own eyes having that same odd mix of grey flecked with green her father had.

'Not often,' Lukitt managed. 'You should maybe consider becoming a professional assassin, the way you creep up on people.'

'Oh, very funny!' the girl said, coming up to him. 'As if such people really exist.'

Lukitt could have corrected her on that front, but did not.

'You're out very early,' he said instead.

'As are you,' right back at him, laying down her basket. 'Although at least I'm doing something useful. Got bitter cress, bistort leaves, wild garlic, alexanders and morels. What about you?'

Lukitt held up his hands.

'Nothing,' he admitted. 'Just like being out when no one else is around.'

The girl frowned, went to pick up her basket.

'I didn't mean to disturb you,' she began, Lukitt cutting her off, motioning with his arm for her to sit, liking that she was here, that he'd someone to talk to, the burden of last night's thoughts slipping away.

'I didn't mean that,' Lukitt said, taking off his coat, putting it down so she didn't have to sit in the damp of the rain. 'I just meant there's so much here, by the river. It's like just being next to the water can wash you clean. And I'm really sorry,' he added, 'but I've forgotten your name.'

'Annely,' Annely supplied, sitting down on Lukitt's coat, adjusting herself, getting comfortable. 'Oldest of the Mingelstrosser clan and yes, it's beautiful this place, and old Züstraubben's very generous with his Mingelstrosser employees and all that stuff, unless you'd like to see what else the world has to offer.'

Lukitt didn't move, kept staring at the river pool, at the fish jumping for early-morning flies.

'Don't you like it here, then?' he asked.

Annely turned her head away from Lukitt and spat on the moss-covered rocks.

'Might do,' she said vehemently, 'if I weren't about to be married off to the nearest old professor who'll have me, and with father's consent.'

Lukitt took a moment to absorb what the girl was saying.

'Marry you off? But to whom?'

'To that rat-bag Rausgarten, of course,' Annely sighed. 'I mean I know all about family duty and that, but Rausgarten? He's practically in the grave! Nearly sixty, for heaven's sake. Although,' the girl reflected, Lukitt looking at her, gauging her to be maybe sixteen or seventeen, 'I suppose that means he won't last too long.'

Lukitt appalled. Groleshka with Udolpho was one thing, Julida with Vannevar another, both done voluntarily as far as he knew. But that this young woman, this girl, about to be married to someone three times her age seemed unforgiveable, and so he said.

'It is,' Annely sighed, 'but no getting out of it. Got to be done. Rausgarten's Züstraubben's boss, and if Züstraubben loses his job then we'll all be out on our ears, and that's Rausgarten's bargain: me for the job.'

She plucked up a yellow celandine and twirled the flower with her fingertips.

'But doesn't Züstraubben own all this? Surely he's got money of his own?' asked Lukitt.

'All gone,' Annely said. 'Mostly went into building this place, with my father's help, not to mention his blasted collection.'

'His collection?' Lukitt echoed. Annely shrugging, holding the flower below her chin, Lukitt watching the soft yellow reflection of it skim her skin.

'Father'll show you it later today,' she said. ''Sposed to be the best collection of whatever it is he's collecting this side of the Harz.'

Lukitt interested, imagining a fine cabinet of curiosities like Ulbert had, as so had Vannevar, only twice as big and three times as grand.

'Not your thing?' he suggested, Annely laughing a little shrilly.

'I'll say not. My thing, as you put it, is to learn how to be a good little housewife. They've even got me learning the harp, for crying out loud. To soothe Rausgarten's troubled brow.'

Smiling a straight-lined smile that meant no smile at all, then stood up, picked up Lukitt's jacket and brushed off the stray lichen that had caught in its fibres, let out a deep breath.

'Best be off,' she said, handing the jacket over, Lukitt taking it, several new ideas tumbling through his head as the water tumbled over the rocks in the river.

'This Rausgarten,' he asked, 'what's he a professor of?'

'History, or some such,' Annely sighed, straightening her skirts, retrieving her basket. 'Dry as sticks, just like him. But in charge of the university's money. The reason why…well, you know why.'

And yes, Lukitt did. Annely about to be married off to the man who could safeguard Züstraubben's job and finance his work; Vannevar sending Lukitt here to help Züstraubben with his own problem – maybe this Rausgarten himself.

All his life Lukitt had wanted to learn, get on, be useful to society; that he'd learned and got on was not in doubt; that he'd been useful to society was debateable; but if Züstraubben's aim in having Lukitt here was what Lukitt suspected then at least it might free Annely from a future she dreaded.

'Are you any good at it? The harp, I mean?'

Annely paused and looked back at the lad perched upon his rock, and smiled a proper smile.

'I absolutely stink at it,' she said. 'If I'd pignuts for fingers I couldn't be any worse. My plan is to play for old beardy Rausgarten on our wedding night, hope he has an aneurysm from the shock.'

'Good plan,' Lukitt said as Annely went back up the grassy track towards the house, *though give me a little time*, he was thinking, *and I might come up with a better one.*

After breakfast, Alameth was spirited away by Annely's brothers to fetch the goats and pigs from their stalls, take them into the forest, all the boys pushing each other out of the way to show Alameth how to whittle a branch for swishing at the animals to keep them in line, pointing out the plants that went into the wormicide and drench needed to keep them tiptop, especially now, when they were all dropping young.

Frau Mingelstrosser was clearing the debris from around the dining table when Anke downed the last of his coffee and stood up, motioning Lukitt with him.

'Time to show you the collection,' he stated, 'come on.'

Lukitt did so, following Anke along the gallery leading to the towers at the back of the colonnade, passing above the courtyard, noting it of curious aspect, the cobbles appearing coloured, laid out in some pattern obscured by animal droppings. He switched his gaze to the towers: wooden, like the rest of the building, three storied, circular and squat, almost as wide as they were tall, pierced with small arched windows on first and second floors, third floor by contrast seeming secretive, unassailable. And between these two towers Lukitt saw an enormous beam of wood sided by handrails, below it a rolled-up winchable portcullis that presumably could be dropped in time of attack, though what that attack could be Lukitt had no idea.

'Towers are copies of Theoderic's mausoleum in Ravenna,' Anke said. 'King of the Ostrogoths,' Anke going on with the lecture he always gave to visitors. 'Fearless leader of his people, taking his entire nation across the Alps from Pannonia into Italy, and thence to victory over his enemy Odovacar. Born a true Goth and Barbarian,' Anke's voice loud but monotonous, 'of noble blood, abducted by the Romans, brought up in the Byzantine court as a scholar and an aesthete, member of the alien Roman horde. Nevertheless,' Anke paused his lecture to take out a keychain as they reached the first tower, finding the one he needed, 'on his release and return to his homeland he immediately rebelled against the Romans and took power for his people. A man to be admired and imitated.'

'Just like Arminius,' Lukitt commented, not all of Vannevar's words in vain.

'Indeed,' Anke said, slotting in the key. 'And Theodoric's mausoleum still standing in Ravenna fifteen hundred years after being built, capped by a single stone five hundred tonnes in weight, eleven metres in diameter; a cap-stone shipped with terrible difficulties from Croatia and almost,' Anke emphasized the last word, 'sunk into the depths of the Adriatic Sea.'

'But wasn't that mausoleum only two stories tall?' Lukitt queried. 'Ravenna, you said? I'm sure that…'

'Well spotted, young sir,' Anke answered with surprise, turning the key, opening the door. 'But we needed the space, so made our roofs hollow, wooden shells within a skin of stone.'

Lukitt hadn't missed the proprietary pronoun.

'You built this place?' he asked.

'I did,' Anke answered proudly, Lukitt about to congratulate him on his achievement – which was undoubtedly great – but had stepped inside the opened door to find himself in the centre of a diorama of Natural History: there was a porpoise, a crested penguin, the neck and head of a giraffe, an elephant trophy complete with trunk and ivories, its feet placed below by the hearth for foot-stools. A fox glaring glassy-eyed at a wolf-cub, innumerable birds rainbowing through the eaves, stoats and mountain hares peeping from trees and bushes growing from pots standing at the base of the walls. Closer inspection revealing niches and cornices that held tiny panoramas of massacre – snakes curled and poised over lemurs and lemmings; a puffin and a petrel burrowing into sand dunes, the marram grass above them halted, below them glass rockpools shimmering, anemones holding inanimate feet above their heads, barnacles opening up the petals of their shells, a crab lounging from a part-sloughed carapace, a clutter of seaweed divided to reveal this secret world, the graceful wave of their fronds forever stilled. There was a chair made from whalebones, a bactrian armchair snug between the humps of a camel, rugs of zebra fur, a tiger with its head still growling in its doom; strings of shark teeth hanging from the mantle, sharp in their disuse, yellowed by age and smoke. A platypus hanging from its tail, looking shy and small, a little moth-eaten. A line of cabinets displaying row upon rows of eggs, moths, bones: the fragile skeleton of a shrew, a vole, a dormouse, the sternum of a hummingbird, the femur of a rat, the extended fingers of a bat; ears from llamas, cats, leopards and – shockingly - a man, a Tasman aboriginal, according to the label, an ear small and black, pinned against the velvet. A diorama of a Roman funeral, a strange figure prancing behind the bier.

Depiction of the Archimimus, Lukitt read, *integral part of the funeral procession, employed to proceed behind the coffin imitating the person who is now deceased. He adopts their mannerisms, wears their clothes, acts out the stages of their life. He roams from place to place, taking on the guise of other people's lives and is not known for himself. In the end he is an empty construct, a buffoon, paid to fulfil his function and then moves on and is forgotten.*

Lukitt flabbergasted, turning slowly on his heel, surrounded by corpse-clutter: an assassin ensconced within a cemetery inside a mausoleum.

'It's…I don't know what it is,' Lukitt started, before stuttering to a stop.

'Takes a lot of folk like that,' Anke Mingelstrosser said softly, proud at Lukitt's back. 'Guess I'll leave you a while, let you take your fill. Here,' he added, placing something in Lukitt's open hand. 'Key to the library. It's in the other tower. Hope you don't get vertigo, got to go over the wooden beam to get there unless you go the whole way round the building to the other side.'

'Thank you,' Lukitt mouthed the words, though hardly had them out. This place was too extraordinary, and it was only after Anke left that Lukitt properly registered Anke's words, eventually wobbled his way out of the door on the other side of the tower and took a single step onto the vast beam of wood slung between the two towers, gripping at the hand rails, taking a deep breath, smiling broadly, detecting Anke's boys chittering like goldfinch somewhere in the nearby woods, and Alameth's voice too.

'Well, would you look at that! That's extraordinary!' Lukitt had no idea what Alameth was looking at but echoed his words, felt them beating with the blood in his veins, because this place was just that. Extraordinary.

'I'll tell you, lads,' Alameth was saying, 'if I'd known there were things like this to see I'd've left the monastery a long time ago!'

'There's more! There's more!' the young lads clamoured as they took Alameth further into the woods, their voices soon lost to Lukitt as he took his next few steps from one tower to the next, revelling in the slight breeze, the warmth of the sun, the scents of the forests; air above him, empty air below, Lukitt stepping into the unknown, feeling unutterably privileged to be here, to see what he'd seen, quickly stepping across the beam and unlocking the door to the second tower to find it crammed top to bottom with books, Lukitt running up the stairs to find the next floor and the next: all three the same. He ran back down again, almost tripping in his excitement, pulling out one volume and starting to read but then was up again as his eye was caught by another title, and another and another.

Feeling suspended from reality, dropped into another world; couldn't stop smiling, couldn't stop reading, couldn't stop thinking that everything had been worthwhile because it had led him here.

Lenze be damned.

He could spend his whole life sorting through these books, absorbing their knowledge, soon sullying the empty surface of the polished circular reading desk with his stacks, finally noticing a small sheaf of papers lying flat on one of the several shelves immediately above. He picked it up, read the title: *The Carolingian Crypt of St Wigbert and a Clerical Conspiracy of Silence*, saw that the author was Professor Xavier Englebaum Züstraubben and sat himself down, read the paper carefully, trying to build a picture of his new employer, took a few notes.

It seemed that Züstraubben and Vannevar had similar interests, and perhaps similar personalities, for the article was long and verbose, neatly written with tightly packed letters but many crossings out, corrections rewritten above the lines. The basic gist being that Züstraubben had centred his work on Quedlinburg, excavating the area about the 12th-c church of St Wigbert. His conclusion: it was built on the site of a long line of earlier places of worship, and that if only he could dig directly around and below St Wigbert's he was sure he'd find signs of Roman occupation – potsherds, bones, possibly coins and jewellery – and, if he went further still, he'd find the real prize: evidence of a pre-Romanic sacred site, a *Viereckschanzen*, a rectangular settlement enclosed by a V-shaped ditch, a well at its centre, a repository for ritual offerings and, with any luck, preserved timbers from pre-Christian temples and habitations.

Lukitt sat back.

So Züstraubben was a real scholar, someone who didn't mind getting his hands dirty. By comparison Vannevar's work seemed vain and trivial, obsessed with using the bones of long dead people to make what he considered art, and money - if the Chapel of Bones at Kutná Hora was anything to go by. Lukitt paused in his note-taking as he re-read the conclusion to Züstraubben's article:

If it can be proved that beneath St Wigbert's there is a Viereckschanzen, *it will be one of very few so far found, and the first in these Northern parts. Such a discovery could and should change our history, for it will prove that our ancient originators - the Jastorfs, who lived long before the birth of Christ, pre-dating the Romans, going right back to the Iron Age - lived in harmony with other ancient Celts in other parts of Europe and shared their cultures, ideas, rituals and funerary rites. In short, that we lived in peaceful cohabitation with our neighbours and, far from being divided – as we are now – the peoples of Europe lived in peace, came from one stock. And if we could do it then, why can't we do it now, when we have most need of it? We are on the brink of an apocalypse of war, and I for one have seen more blood and battle than I care for, and it behoves the church – in the forms of Bishop and Kompter – not to conspire against my work but to encourage it, for all our sakes.*

Lukitt's skin was tingling. He'd stopped taking notes, had instead chewed his pencil right down to its core and it was bitter on his tongue, and still he sat, fingers outspread on the paper before him, on that last page, that last conclusion; unable to figure how the man who'd written this paper could be contemplating murder, which must be the case. No other reason Vannevar would have sent him here.

Unless Vannevar only wanted rid, and Züstraubben the nearest person to fob Lukitt off on.

A small glimmer of hope, then.

If not for long.

37

THE FEEDING GROUNDS

'Time to take the goats to the summer feeding grounds,' Anke Mingelstrosser announced at breakfast, the boys immediately up, Anke laughing at their happy disarray, their eagerness to be off, this being one of their favourite times of year: a few days of untrammelled freedom.

'Can Alameth come with us?' Jakob asked excitedly, glancing over at Alameth who raised his eyebrows.

'And me!' Edric, the youngest Mingelstrosser put in. 'You promised, papa. My first time. You promised!'

Anke wiped his mouth with his napkin and looked over at his wife who smiled, gave an almost imperceptible nod, for this indeed had been their promise on Edric's last birthday – provided that from that time to this he'd behaved himself, performed his chores, stopped grumbling at his school work. The room went quiet as Anke deliberated, though in truth the decision had already been made.

'You can, my boy,' Anke said, holding up his hands to stop the whoops of congratulation coming from his other sons. 'But you've to do exactly as Filip tells you. In my absence, he is head of the household,' Filip dipping his head, acknowledging the honour. 'As for Alameth,' Anke went on, 'that is entirely up to him.'

'I'd be absolutely delighted,' Alameth said, immediately surrounded by the boys who dragged him away, no one but Lukitt noting the small smile passing between Alameth and Annely, the slight rise of heat to both their cheeks. Lukitt uncomfortably annoyed by the exchange and that Alameth had been kidnapped by the boys again. He'd wanted to show Alameth the treasures of the two towers today, unveil them like a Pfiffmakler spectacular.

Then again, it would give him more time to go through the library, and he was on his way there when the Mingelstrosser boys took the goats away in a bleating herd under the lifted portcullis: a great gush of animals noisily flooding through the courtyard, hooves clopping, bleats and brays, switches swiping through the air, the boys whooping and yelling as they got the animals on their way and, at the back, Alameth – already dishevelled, straw in his hair and in the pockets of his jacket, a boy upon his back, hat down over one eye - laughing the loudest of the lot.

Out came Annely and Lata, who began sloshing the courtyard clean of excrement with pails of water from the fountain, Lukitt watching, reminded of Longhella and Ludmilla in the way they worked together so fluently. Still watching as they left, the sun catching the glint of the cobbles, Lukitt seeing the pattern that had been hidden by the now scoured away dirt. He squinted, went to one of the books he'd been looking at the day before that contained the famous portrait of Theodoric the Ostrogoth from the Ravenna church where he'd built his mausoleum. Picked it up, held it to the window. There was a slight difference to the original - not in the layout or colouring of the tiles, or cobbles in this case, but in the aspect of the face itself: the features of Theodoric subtly changed, the eyes smaller, the face wider, a beard and moustache where they shouldn't have been. Lukitt feeling a sudden chill to realise this had to be a portrait of Züstraubben himself, all the kindly thoughts he'd had of that man slipping away, thinking the obvious: that he'd been delivered from one megalomaniac right into the hands of another.

All hope gone.

The bitterness of the discovery tainting the rest of his day and the day that followed, shutting himself off from the remnants of the Mingelstrossers; taking his meals in the tower, brought to him by one of the girls. Spending his time burrowing through the drawers of Züstraubben's desk, uncovering as much of his work as he could. The outcome bleak and without comfort. In order to complete his researches on St Wigbert's, Züstraubben needed three key supporters:

Professor Rausgarten, his immediate employer at the University of Leipzig, to whom Annely was betrothed for the good of the family – for the good of Züstraubben;

Bishop Frenk, who oversaw the See in which St Wigbert's lay –

presumably the Bishop named in The Conspiracy, as was the next name on his list;

Hieronymus von Kronberg, Komturei of the Teutonic Order, in whose bailiwick was the church and the land immediately surrounding it where Züstraubben suspected the most part of the *Viereckschanzen* lay buried.

A dispiriting catalogue of possible victims, Lukitt hoping to God he wasn't expected to bump off all three.

I can't do this, I can't do this again.

The thought there every second, his head empty of anything else; distracting himself, gaining apparent control by gathering all the information he could on these main players, desperate to uncover some chink, some argument against the confrontation he knew must come when Züstraubben arrived and charged Lukitt with the inevitable.

He needed to find another option to present to Züstraubben, needed leverage, some way of getting these men on side as they obviously weren't already, given that Züstraubben hadn't started the archaeological dig that was apparently the singular focus of his life's work.

He got out papers and back-journals, went through the library, wrote down all he found.

- *Stephan Rausgarten*: Professor of Archaeology, Classics and Linguistics at Leipzig University, Dean of Appointments and Finance. Publications: History of Roman incursions into Germany; of *Hoch Deutsch* with all its variants, literature of the 12th and 13th centuries: *Minnesinge*r – Songs of Love - by the Lyric poets;

- Bishop Frenk – next to nothing found, blameless and selfless, overseeing his diocese with care and devotion;

Hieronymus von Kronberg yielding most: extant *Komturei* of the Teutonic Order, direct descendant of the famous von Kronberg, Grand Master of the Order in the 1500's. Many volumes in the tower's library referring to the Order and Lukitt making best use of them, got their history nailed down to various significant points:

- First and proper name: the *Fratrum Theutonicorum Ecclesiae S.Mariae Hiersolymitanae,* confirmed by Papal Bull on February 6th 1191, emerging during the early Crusades, primarily as Hospitallers and later as a military order of Germanic noblemen

- A military force for hundreds of years, vanquishing heathens wherever they found them, abiding by the Order's laws of poverty, chastity, obedience - and the slaughter of barbarian hordes; a gradual diminishment of opponents leading to an increase in wealth but a decrease in power

- Early 1800s and much of their property has been dispersed to various sovereigns, a great many of their monasteries disbanded

- March 1834: a decree of Empire dramatically reversing this decline, returning their rights and lands to them – including St Wigbert's - declaring them an Autonomous Religious and Military Institute under protection and suzerainty of the Emperor himself

At this reversal of fortunes a new era had begun, and therein lay Züstraubben's main problem. Lukitt found copies of several recent petitions to the *Komturei* in Züstraubben's correspondence together with their replies, each less encouraging than the last: Kompter von Kronberg would consider the petition in due time; Kompter von Kronberg couldn't entertain Züstraubben's questions at the moment; Kompter von Kronberg was suffering from an unspecified wasting disease that meant he couldn't be disturbed; Kompter von Kronberg was dying, and any further petitions must wait until they could be sent to his successor.

No wonder Züstraubben believed there was a conspiracy against him.

Looking further through Züstraubben's letters – specifically those exchanged between Züstraubben and one Rueland Klopstock - Lukitt uncovered the three candidates for that succession, the decision to be made later this same year at the Annual Assembly of Knights.

Lukitt summarising what he'd found:

Rueland Klopstock: pious, austere, close to the old Kompter, undoubtedly keeping to the old Kompter's line that St Wigbert's was not to be disturbed;

Thaddeus Münzenberg: surely too old. Has served the Order for almost sixty years, man and boy;

Cornelius Steggle: progressive, energetic; wants to regenerate the Order along ancient lines; favoured by many in the Order, particularly the younger members and – according to Klopstock himself – very likely to welcome Züstrabben's dig, prove the Order's links to the earliest settlements on German soil.

Steggle obviously Züstraubben's man, and the clear front runner.

Until Lukitt read one last letter - dated a month back – in which Rueland Klopstock put all in doubt:

It won't be long, old friend, before I take on the mantle I was born to. I've been told in confidence that once von Kronberg makes his last address to the Assembly in September – and God willing he will hold on that long, as both I and his doctors believe he will – he will endorse my candidature publically, and I will be elected the new Kompter of this region when von Kronberg sadly leaves us for a better place.

So there Lukitt had it.

Züstraubben needing the old Kompter dead before he could endorse Klopstock in September, for without his explicit recommendation Steggle would undoubtedly be elected without dissent.

Lukitt leaned back in his chair, lacing his fingers across his chest, incredibly relieved; expected of him only that he help a dying man on his way. It might even be considered a mercy, providing an easier death than the man might otherwise have. He'd several ideas, consulted a few more books, went back into the museum and thereby came across a method that was almost laughably simple: a pufferfish staring at him from the wall.

All Lukitt needed was access to the Kompter, Züstraubben presumably orchestrating that particular detail right now.

An assumption substantiated that very afternoon when Lata brought him a missive from Züstraubben inviting Lukitt to meet him in the town of Brummsberg, just the other side of the Harz. One of the places Lukitt knew from Rueland's letters that the old Kompter was visiting on his way to the Assembly in Kwydzyn; taking his time getting there, taking one last tour of the places he loved, places true to the Brotherhood.

So now Lukitt had the who, the how and the where.

A slim chance of success, if not of salvation.

38

Out of the Mausoleum

'So you've come back into the fold!' Anke Mingelstrosser exclaimed as Lukitt joined him for breakfast the following morning.

'You look pale, my lad,' Ishbella admonished. 'Stopping yourself up in that library for two days hasn't done you any favours.'

'I was trying to get to grips with your Professor's work,' Lukitt smiled feebly. 'It's not an area I know well...'

Ishbella rolled her eyes dramatically.

'Who does, my dear? But splish-splash, so much for that. What I want to know is how to put some colour back in your cheeks. Fancy some fried pig's ears? Or no, wait. I've some wonderful spicy sausages that need eating up. Sound good?'

'Sounds wonderful,' Lukitt enthusiastic, as was his stomach - rumbling soft and low as pixie thunder.

'Very well then. Lata!' Ishbella called loudly as she strode off towards her kitchen. 'Fetch those good sausages from the pantry and get that pan back on the heat!'

'She likes to feed, does Ishbella,' Anke said, pouring dark bitter coffee into their cups. 'She's missing the boys. Used to cooking for an army, and with just myself and the girls, well, we can't do her justice. So tell me, did you find what you were looking for?'

Lukitt nodded.

'I think so. I'd no idea how accomplished a scholar Professor Züstraubben is. His work is incredibly interesting, and the library an absolute cornucopia.'

Anke's oddly coloured eyes glittered as he put his head to one side and looked at Lukitt.

'So you really didn't know anything about him when you came here?'

'I didn't,' Lukitt admitted. 'But I truly hope I can make myself useful to you both, myself and Alameth that is,' he added hurriedly.

Anke laughed.

'Don't think you need worry on that score,' he said. 'My boys will make sure on that. They'll have him out the back glade clearing the new vegetable patch they're planning for next year, building new coops for the chickens and well…I don't know what else. But once they've the bit between their teeth there's no stopping them.' He smiled indulgently. 'They're good lads,' he went on, 'but have hands need keeping busy. Take after their father on that score. Taught them all the rudiments of carpentry since they were knee-high to gnats.'

'That's very admirable,' Lukitt said. 'Every man needs a trade.'

'And what is your trade exactly, Lukitt?' Anke asked, leaning forward, trying to puzzle this boy out, none of the easiness to him that Alameth had.

'Well I…I'm not sure it's a trade…exactly,' Lukitt stuttered and then revived. 'But I've a quick mind, eager to learn and be helpful.'

'Helpful, is it?' Anke said. 'Well, that's all to the good. Professor could do with a bit of help. You've no reason to know it, but that library of his? Never been catalogued,' he shook his head at the tragedy. 'Now me, I like to know where everything is, what I've got, how many of this or that. This type of nail, that kind of tool. Got all mine ordered and inventoried. But him? Got his head in the clouds half the time and down some dirty godforsaken crypt the other.'

Lukitt smiling at the oxymoron of a crypt being godforsaken, interrupted by Ishbella bearing down on them with a platter of spiced pork sausages, Lata on her heels with a hot potato and mustard mash.

'Are you joining us, my dears?' Anke asked hospitably, Ishbella raising her eyebrows, shaking her head.

'Ate two hours since,' she chided. 'Three kinds of people in this world,' she began her favourite proverb, Anke chuckling as he speared a sausage onto this plate.

'I know, I know: women, priests and professors; women waking first, followed by the priests, followed by the professors. So all we're lacking is the priest.'

'Maybe not now Alameth is here,' a new voice, Lukitt looking up as a basket of warm barley bread and a crock of butter were put down on the table.

'Just because he came from a monastery doesn't make him a priest,' Anke corrected Annely, slicing into his sausage. 'But priests be damned. This food's heaven on a plate!'

Annely tutted.

'Best not say that in chapel,' she commented, 'or to Mama,' unrolling her father's serviette and tucking it beneath his chin, Anke smiling gloriously, breathing deeply.

'Never confuse piety with puritanism, my lass,' said he. 'God gives and God takes away, but God tells us quite precisely that priests are not to be the anchors of our belief.'

Annely leaned over the table and spooned some potato onto Lukitt's plate, Lukitt uncomfortably warm at the scent of her sweat as she moved her arm, the delicate way she made the mash fall, the way she moistened her lips as she got ready for her riposte.

'He told me about you, you know,' she said, looking directly at Lukitt as she straightened up, eyes glittering like her father's, though brightened by her youth.

'Told you what?' Lukitt asked, his face reddening beneath her scrutiny, Annely smiling suddenly to reveal small white teeth, two crooked incisors Lukitt hadn't noticed before and found suddenly enchanting.

'About you hounding out the monks, of course!' she answered, twirling her skirts as she turned to leave. 'And if anyone needs hounding out,' she added as she went through the door to the kitchen, 'it's monks.'

Lukitt watching her go, wondering firstly what she meant by that enigmatic statement, secondly when she and Alameth had talked about such things, and thirdly why his heart was racing faster than a horse running helter-skelter down a hill.

'She's right about that,' Anke went on oblivious. 'Our chapel doesn't hold with such hierarchies. *The Body of the Faithful Comprises a Universal Priesthood*,' he quoted from his chapel's handbook.

'You practise Pietism?' Lukitt asked, prodded by the words, finding a suitable calming stratagem. 'The…*Pia Desideria*…and *Das… geistliche*?'

Anke dropped his fork in rapt amazement, finishing Lukitt's sentence for him.

'*Das Geistliche Priesterthum*. But how on earth do you know of such things? Have you made a study of theology?'

'No, sir, but I had a good teacher. And my father was of the Herrnhuter Brethren who…'

'The Herrnhuter!' Anke interrupted, pushing his plate to one side, leaning in excitedly. 'You don't need to tell me about them. A great inspiration. Well my! Chuck a stone into deep water and see what comes to the surface! They're from the same stock as us. Same roots, different branches, both growing the right way to God.'

Lukitt choked momentarily on a bite of sausage.

'I'm not sure my father would have seen it that way,' he finally got out, voice a little strained.

'Left under a bit of a cloud, did he?' Anke chuckled, Lukitt frowning at both the accuracy and implied levity of this question.

'He married out. My mother…'

Anke raised a hand.

'No need to go on, my boy. I hear they can be rather strict, those older sects. Ishbella! Ishbella!' he shouted for his wife, who appeared a few moments later, crossly wiping floury hands upon her apron.

'You yelled, my lord?' she enquired politely, sarcasm in every syllable.

'Indeed I did, my dear,' Anke went on regardless, waving a hand across the table towards Lukitt. 'This lad's a Herrnhuter, would you believe.'

Ishbella turned her head slowly from her husband to Lukitt, her eyes narrowing, an unfriendly jut to her chin.

'I'm really not…' Lukitt protested feebly, Anke going on anyway.

'And guess what? Father married out, just like I did, but got booted for the pleasure. What a turn up!'

Ishbella regarding Lukitt with less animosity, rubbed her nose with a finger, leaving a smudge of flour there.

'Left for love then, did he?' she asked, Lukitt frowning again, uncertain what he'd set in motion, Anke shaking his head.

'Women!' he said, in a loud stage whisper that had Ishbella bearing down upon him and giving the back of his head a smart slap.

'Anke,' one slowly drawn out word, one awful note of warning, and then she looked over at Lukitt and unexpectedly smiled. 'Just be glad your parents got out when they did. Religion is a terrible divider and good for nothing, in my opinion. Let men have their gods, but don't inflict them on me and mine.'

'Including monks?' Lukitt asked, emboldened, remembering Annely's earlier comments.

'Especially monks,' Ishbella said, with some vehemence. 'Men belong with women and women with men. How else is the world to move forward?'

Anke shrugged, winking over at Lukitt as Ishbella excused herself and went back to the kitchen to beat her bread to a pulp.

'Kind of did the same myself,' he explained. 'She was a Catholic back then, though not so much now. Didn't go down too well with my lot either. Women, priests and professors,' he sighed theatrically. 'Not a one of them easy to figure out.'

Lukitt had a few hours before he was due to leave for Brummsberg, went into the first of the towers to secure what he needed before he left, still trying to figure out the dynamics of the Mingelstrosser household and his own family, how it had gone for his mother and father to leave all they'd known, just because of him. Ashamed he'd never thought to ask, when Annely arrived, his heart jumping at the sight of her: that smile again, that revelation of her crooked teeth, her fingers pushing a few strands of hair back into her bonnet.

'Time to leave for Quedlinburg,' she said, without preamble. 'Coach for Brummsberg leaving there at half past two, so get your wriggle on.'

Lukitt nodding dumbly as off she went, Lukitt's heart thumping, but not for the same reasons as before; Lukitt rubbing his hands up and down his thighs, feeling for the small vial in his inner jacket pocket, thoughts scattering this way and that like winter hares disturbed by a fox upon a hillside.

So here it is.
Can't be a coincidence.
Got to be the old Kompter.
Got to be my cue to act.
And I like it here.
And Alameth likes it here.
He doesn't want to leave.
And I don't want to leave.
And I like Anke and Ishbella.
And I like...I think I like...I do like...Annely.
So it's got to be done.
I've got to get it done.

39

Brummsberg, and Misdeeds Abounding

A pus-green moon looked down on Lukitt, cursing his mission as he entered the low arch and through the walls of Brummsberg. He passed below the campanile housing the ancient *Kummerglocke* - a vast iron bell forged in 1518 to mark the deaths of one hundred and fifty six miners, including women and children, when the shafts collapsed due to heavy rain; its clappers clad in velvet ever since, moments later sighing out a warning that it was late, the gates about to be closed.

Lukitt finding the subdued peeling ominous and unnerving.

The streets were quiet as he approached the town square, the last of the market-stall holders tossing their few remaining wares into sacks, collapsing their trestles, loading them onto carts and heading for home. Music leaking from several taverns that masqueraded as theatres on market days to keep the surplus population amused, and in one of these taverns Lukitt was to meet Züstraubben, though no idea which.

Uncertain, he hangs at the edge of the Dorfplatz, watching the stall-holders empty themselves into the night, his several shadows extending beyond him, cast in differing directions by the lamps lit at each corner of the square.

He knows nothing of this place, knows nothing of its history; that it was first mentioned in a manuscript back in 867 AD: a wooden church erected here, its steeple a crude structure mounted on four stone plinths; a coal-mining village since 1113 and very likely long before; mining and mining injuries leading to the establishment of one of the first ever documented hospitals, a training camp for Crusader Hospitallers before going over to the Holy Land; the unassuming village of Brummsberg therefore considered by a great many of The Order as the birthplace of the Knights Teutonic.

And no wonder the ailing Kompter had put the place on his itinerary, and no more wonder that Züstraubben had chosen this place to meet with the Kompter – via his friend, Rueland Klopstock – one last chance to state his case about St Wigbert's, get approval for his dig.

The two friends holed up in the tavern closest to the old Ritterhaus, where the Kompter was staying.

'How's he doing?' Züstraubben asked, he and Rueland hunched about a small wood-burning brazier, for the night had turned cold; neither liking the acrid smoke that pervaded the air, nor the candle-lit darkness of this place that leant their meeting a subtle note of misplaced conspiracy.

'He's been very badly,' Rueland said, recalling their journey here in the confines of the carriage: the sharp jut of the Kompter's bones thrown against him as they rounded a bend, the pervading bitterness of sweat that saturated his clothes, his intermittent fits of shivering, the small groans he tried to suppress.

'I'm sorry to hear that,' Züstraubben said quietly, 'and not just on my account. Will he make it to Kwydzyn, do you think? Will you get your endorsement?'

Rueland Klopstock took a sip of the harsh wine that was the best Brummsberg had to offer, if the bar tender could be believed.

'Actually,' Rueland smiled over at his friend, 'since we arrived here he seems to have revived a little. Feels connected to the place. Calls it his spiritual home. And yes, to both your other questions: I believe we'll get to Kwydzyn, and that my future is assured.'

'Well, I'm very glad to hear it,' Züstraubben smiled also, raising his glass, the two clinking a toast, both grimacing as they knocked their drinks back in celebration. 'But you haven't changed your mind? About St Wigbert's, I mean?'

Klopstock's face clouded, lowering his head, unable to meet Züstraubben's gaze.

'I'm sorry, old friend. I know it means a lot to you, but I've got to abide by the Kompter's wishes, and if he doesn't want it done then no more must I. But I have managed to get you your audience.'

'Oh thank God!' Züstraubben raised his head heavenward, rubbed a hand about his chin, pouring them both a large glass of the appalling wine. 'I can't thank you enough! Are you sure? Will it not be an imposition?'

'Always the same Xavier, always ready to thank God when it suits you and vilify Him with the next breath,' Rueland laughed, remembering the arguments they'd had as students, Xavier insistent that one day science would sweep all necessity of religion from the face of the earth. He expected his friend to smile, to remember, make a quip, but Züstraubben was entirely serious, shaking his head.

'I've never disregarded your calling, Rueland,' said Züstraubben, 'and I can't tell you how proud I am of how far you've got. The next Kompter of the Knights Teutonic, from Braunschweig to Kwydzyn... well, sir, however it plays out...' he held his hand out over the small wood burner to Rueland Klopstock, a hand taken and shaken. 'It's been a real honour. And thank you for giving me the chance to state my case one last time, and in person.'

Two men who'd known each other thirty four years, two men on opposite sides of a divide, two men with lumps in their throats uncertain what next to say, two men interrupted by a young man hoving into view proffering a short, badly rehearsed speech, Lukitt having battled his way from one tavern to the next, his shadows following him, shifting their courses, moving boundaries, but reaching his goal; recognising Züstraubben from the painted cobblestones, making sure by asking the bar-tender, pushing his way through the fug of men and their drinking and cigars - everything prepared, wanting to get it done, get it over with.

'Excuse me sirs, but my name is Lukitt Bachmann,' he stated. 'I was told to meet you here?'

'Aha!' Züstraubben said, relieved at the interruption, deep emotions not his bent. 'Lukitt Bachmann!'

He stood up and grabbed a rickety stool, snatched an empty glass from the tray of a passing serving girl and ordered another bottle of wine before settling back down again.

'Well, Lukitt Bachmann, such a great pleasure to meet you. Professor Vannevar sang your praises when I met him in Prague,' dividing the last of the wine between their three glasses. 'Let me introduce you to my very dear friend Rueland Klopstock,' Züstraubben went on cheerily, Lukitt choking on his drink to see in the flesh one of the names on his list.

'The wine is rather bad,' Züstraubben misconstruing Lukitt's reaction, 'but it's all we've got, and we've several reasons now to celebrate.'

Rueland Klopstock smiled at Lukitt over his spectacles, and Lukitt had to put down his glass, fearing the tremor in his hand might be seen.

'So what brings you in search of Xavier?' Rueland asked kindly, attributing the flushing of the young man's cheeks to the warmth of the inn, the slight wet glazing of his eyes to the haze of smoke.

'Um, well, I rather gather the Professor here has need of my services,' he said, in a hoarse whisper.

Züstraubben laughed.

'Well, you could put it that way. It's more that Vannevar was praising you to the hills, how quick and apt you were at your books, how useful you'd been to him. I confess it made me rather jealous he'd such a studious helpmeet. *And good with his hands too*, he told me, *designed for my wife a most beautiful pendant to celebrate her arrival at my home*. Said you might be just what I needed to further my archaeological researches.'

Lukitt swallowed.

'I'll do what I can, of course,' his fingertips beginning to pinch at his trousers that were clammy against his thighs, several drops of sweat forming in cupped palms.

'And he may very well need help if his audience tonight with the Kompter goes well,' Rueland chipped in. 'He's a persuasive fellow, is Xavier.'

'It's been known,' Züstraubben added happily, 'and here's the proof,' the serving girl at that moment plonking another bottle down on their table, pocketing the coins Züstraubben handed her, the act reminding him of putting money into church platters, becoming suddenly sombre. 'But of course,' he added quickly, 'I was very sorry to hear about the circumstances that have brought you to me and mine.'

'The circumstances,' Lukitt repeated dully, his mind buzzing with what was to come: the meeting with the Kompter at some unspecified time, Züstraubben's expectations, what would become of Lukitt and Alameth if he couldn't carry it off, what would happen to this man in the spectacles if he did not, Züstraubben hammering the point home as if Lukitt was a dullard who'd not the wit to realise the gravity of the situation all by himself.

'Well, his wife dying so unexpectedly,' said Züstraubben quietly, 'his return to Kutná Hora and all that entailed. I gathered from his letter he'd have kept you for a lifetime if not, but offered you to me instead, for which I'm immensely grateful.'

Lukitt swallowed, needing to be sure, needing to verify his duty without asking directly.

'But why meet you here?' he asked. 'In Brummsberg, I mean. Do you have a dig going on nearby you need my help with?'

'Ah,' Xavier replied easily. 'A very perspicacious question, young man.' Leaning forward to uncork the new bottle. 'Apologies for the travelling. The road to here is bad enough to knock the bones out of your joints. But there's a few very interesting sites I'd like to point out to you on our journey back to Leipzig, give you the lie of the land so to speak, not that we'll have the time to inspect…'

Interrupted by the bell in its campanile pealing out the hour, a soft sound and yet somehow perceived, Rueland Klopstock taking out his pocket-watch, glancing at it, putting it back.

'I'm afraid this second bottle will have to wait,' he said, pushing his spectacles up his nose, looking ruefully at Xavier Züstraubben. 'It's time, old friend. Last chance. Whatever he decides I will abide by, so do your best.'

Züstraubben sighed.

'This is it then, do or die,' downing the last of his wine, glancing over at Lukitt. 'Will you come, lad? It's not often you'll get to meet a Kompter of the Knights Teutonic. A saint in the making, so Rueland assures me. Vannevar would spit kittens for the chance of it.'

Lukitt nodding dumbly, interpreting the request as a command.

All three leaving, Lukitt's heart beating hard within his chest, reminded of the hares he'd coursed as a boy in the hills of the Voralberg, his father panting at his heels.

My Lord, lad. If you've a head as fast as your legs then you'll go far.

And far he'd come, farther than Nethanel could ever have envisaged, Lukitt sick with how it had come about, the small vial in his jacket pocket reminding him what must be done, what Züstraubben had brought him here to do. Züstraubben as clear with his instructions as Hans Trudbert and Vannevar had been before him, leaving Lukitt no way out. The mention of Julida and her pendant had seen to that, reinforced by those words: *Last chance. Do or die.*

His stomach in knots as they came out of the maw of the tavern into streets glistening with a gentle drizzle of rain; turning into a narrow ginnel leading them to the *Ritterhaus* where the original coal workers' hospital had begun, where the Kompter was now.

'He's been my mentor for so long,' Rueland Klopstock said as they went, pushing his glasses to his forehead as he checked his tears. 'I'm going to feel completely rudderless when he's gone.'

Züstraubben wrapping an arm about his friend's shoulder in such a blatant display of amity and hypocrisy Lukitt almost ran at that moment for the hills.

'He's not gone yet, friend,' Züstraubben comforted. 'And you said he's been better since he got here.'

'He has, though it won't last,' Rueland sniffed, softened by the wine. 'So please, Xavier, don't expect too much. Don't push him too hard.'

'I won't,' Züstraubben said gently. 'That's not at all my intention.'

Lukitt hovering at their backs, knowing Züstraubben's intention all too well.

Arriving at the *Ritterhauser* Rueland knocked, made himself known, led them in, bowing to the Brothers who were sat on chairs just inside the doors to keep uninvited intruders out.

'There's been a constant stream of visitors,' Rueland explained. 'Not just here, but at every stop on our journey. People wanting blessings, last wise words...'

He cleared his throat as they gained the stairs that were tight-packed, the wood of the risers sighing beneath their weight.

'He sees as many as he can, of course, no matter how it tires him, how early or late the hour.'

Züstraubben frowned, being one of these late visitors, it being past eleven, so surely he must be the last. But even as he thought it he heard another knock on the door down below, a shiver of pity passing through him for the old Kompter to have his nights so plagued by hangers-on, people needing his favour in one form or another, himself included.

'We should go back,' he said. 'Return in the morning,' feet stopping on the stairs.

Rueland sighed.

'He's people booked in all tomorrow, Xavier. I'm afraid this is the best I could do.'

So up they went, Rueland ushering them down a narrow corridor, through a low-beamed door.

The room is dark, lit only by a single lamp, day being as night to the old Kompter, eyes unable to bear the strength of sunlight despite his love of it, the shutters at his windows – in whatever place he's in - at all times hard-drawn and latched.

He sleeps a great deal, wakes as he's bidden to greet the folk who've come for his blessing. His attendant sits on a chair by the lamp, reading, or taking dictation for the Kompter's correspondence. He looks up as the door opens and Rueland, Xavier and Lukitt enter. He doesn't get up, but nods at Rueland who motions Züstraubben to the bedside, Züstraubben kneeling on the hassock placed there for the purpose, Züstraubben taking the old man's hand in his, kissing it, as Rueland has instructed. The skin is dry and cracked; the half-moons of the Kompter's nails receded into his skin as if they've given up growing. The Kompter flickers open his eyes and breathes his benediction, Rueland at his other side, helping the old man lever himself up against his pillows.

'This is my friend,' Rueland says quietly. 'The one I was telling you about. The one who believes there's an ancient *Viereckschanzen* in the environs of St Wigbert's.'

'My name is Professor Xavier Züstraubben,' Züstraubben says.

'You've written to me before,' the old Kompter creaks.

'I have,' admits Züstraubben. 'And I know you've always refused permission for me to dig there, but I wanted one last chance to state my case.'

The Kompter takes back his hand, closes his eyes, nods briefly, Rueland looking over at Züstraubben who licks his lips and begins.

'I don't mean at all to disrespect you, in fact only want to further your cause, demonstrate the Knights' linkage to times long past, trace your history, place it in historical context, prove that at the start their ancestors were the making of our nation, the reason all our ancient tribes came together against a common enemy, became the foothold of what we've become today.'

The Kompter moves against his pillows.

'And what have we become today, do you think?'

Züstraubben clears his throat. He'd expected dissent, not a detour through political philosophy but, given the opportunity, he wasn't going to waste it, got to the thrust of the argument Lukitt had read in Züstraubben's as yet unsubmitted paper.

'I believe we've become a nation divided,' he answered. 'A nation that will continue to divide unless we can bring it back together. And we can do that, you and I. If you give me leave to excavate St Wigbert's I can prove that at heart we were all one, that we should be one again, that we are all Knights Teutonic, and their predecessors, at our very root.'

Lukitt standing beside Züstraubben, right next to the jug of water on the Kompter's bed-stand, his hands loose by his side, in one of them the small vial extracted from his pocket, unsure he can do what's expected of him, desperate for the Kompter to agree to Züstraubben's last plea, casting his eyes about the room – the attendant disinterested in the petition, reading his book; Rausgarten and Züstraubben concentrated entirely on the shrivelled man in his bed; Lukitt's thumb-nail poking open the lid of the vial, hanging on the Kompter's every word.

'But the digging up of your *Viereckschanzen,* Professor Züstraubben,' the Kompter gets out, 'will that not also entail digging up crypts and all the ancient graveyards that surround St Wigbert's? Men and women buried in that ground for centuries?'

Züstraubben paused, looked over at Rueland, both knowing his time was up, that his argument was lost.

'It will,' he admitted, 'but I will make certain that every single…'

'But by doing so,' the Kompter stated, 'you will happenstance deny those people – and they are people, no matter how long deceased - the chance of the resurrection when it comes.'

'We could make a bone chapel like at Sedlec…I'd take every care,' Züstraubben begins, but knows it's useless, as does Lukitt, the Kompter breaking into a wheezy chest-racking cough from the exertion, everyone immediately distracted, Züstraubben getting up from his knees in consternation, opportunely blocking all view to Lukitt who takes his chance, tips the contents of his vial into the Kompter's water jug, wiggling his finger in it to disperse the contents.

'Pour him a glass of water,' Rueland commands Züstraubben as the coughing continues, Lukitt stepping smartly to one side as Züstraubben does as bid, passing the glass to Rueland who raises it to the Kompter's purple lips.

Züstraubben taking a few paces backwards, aghast at the fit he's provoked in the old man that thankfully is subsiding, surprised when Lukitt steps forward and kneels down on the hassock, lowering his head to the old man's hand where it lies listless on his coverlet.

'I'm sorry, father, for I have sinned,' whispers Lukitt, 'and I hope you will forgive me.'

The Kompter's feeble finger marking the sign of the cross on Lukitt's forehead as Züstraubben places a hand on Lukitt's shoulder.

'Come on, lad,' he says quietly. 'Time we were gone. Thank you for seeing me, Kompter, and thank you Rueland. I know your time will come but, God willing, it will be a long while yet.'

Rueland acknowledging his friend's gracious speech with a short bow, the old Kompter raising a small smile, wiping his fingers against his lips.

'Not so long, I fear,' he whispers. 'And I'm truly sorry. Your union of peoples is…' *cough*, 'a righteous wish…' *cough*, a few more sips of water. 'I'll pray for it…' *cough*, 'as will Rueland after me – for…' *cough cough*… 'Lord knows,' more coughing that maybe contained a thin thread of humour, 'our country needs what you are trying to provide.'

Lukitt and Züstraubben tread a soft and careful retreat from the room and down the stairs, two more visitors already on their way up, squeezing close by them in the narrow cloistered stairwell.

They regained the street, the mizzle in the air like a sheet of gauze descending all around them.

'I'd no idea he was so badly,' Züstraubben said, shaking his head. 'I'd not have bothered him for a moment if I'd realised.'

Lukitt frowned, but wasn't about to quibble, fell into step beside his new master, stuck to his part.

'I'm sorry you didn't get the permission you needed, sir,' he said dutifully.

Züstraubben shrugging a few drops of rainwater from his broad shoulders.

'As am I,' he sighed. 'But there'll be other places I can excavate. It's just going to take a bit more time. And now I have you, it might not take as long as I'd assumed.'

You've got that right, Lukitt thought, closing his eyes briefly, glad for the benediction of the rain, a faint tingling on his forehead where the old Kompter had blessed him, forgiven him, no matter he'd no idea what he'd been forgiving.

They arrived at their lodging house and went straight to their beds, by which time the velvet-stoppered bell had rung out another hour and the Kompter had blessed his last few guests, been allowed to take the uninterrupted rest he so evidently needed, Rueland Klopstock remaining by his side, dismissing the attendant to his bed.

At five in the morning the old man wakes briefly as the hour is wrung from the ancient bell - muffled and sad in the early morning air.

'Not feeling too good,' he murmurs, Rueland roused from his dozing, taking the Kompter's tablets from the drawer in the bed-stand, the old man so weak Rueland has to place them on his tongue, dribble in the last dregs of water from the jug, wiping the old man's face with a sponge after he has swallowed.

'My fingers...' the Kompter whispers, 'pins and...pins and...'

'Pins and needles?' Rueland asks, panic rising in his chest. 'Left or right?'

'All...over...' the Kompter mouths the words, Rueland snatching up the hand -bell and dinging it hard to fetch the doctor.

'Do you mean the tingling is all over, or that it's...?'

He can't even get the possibility out, grasps the old Kompter's left hand with his own, can't find a pulse, feels the skin cold, unresponsive.

'Help! Help!' he shouts wildly, then kneels down beside the bed, taking the old Kompter's hand in his own. 'Please don't leave me. It's too soon, Lord. It's too soon.'

He sounds like a bleating child, and has begun to weep, the old Kompter fluttering his other hand across the bedding and lowering it onto Rueland's head.

'I'm sorry,' he wheezes, Rueland struggling up again as the doctor pushes open the door, dressing-gown untied, tripping as one of his slippers falls from his foot in his haste.

'He's not well,' Rueland whimpers, brushing the tears from his eyes. 'A heart attack I think. What can I do?'

'He's had his tablets?' the doctor asks, coming forward, glancing at the empty water jug. 'He's drunk all that?'

'He was thirsty. Coughing a lot,' Rueland says, 'and yes. Tablets, just a minute or so ago. What can I do?'

But there's nothing to be done.

Within the hour the old man can no longer breathe, his diaphragm no longer able to lift. It happens agonisingly slowly for Rueland, the doctor and the old Kompter, his muscles paralysing inch by inch; the doctor shaking his head sadly, diagnosing the heart failure Rueland has feared, nothing he can do to intervene, nothing Rueland can do either.

Nothing anyone can do

Rueland continues holding the old Kompter's hand as he slips away, last breath taken, still holding the Kompter's hand a few minutes later because astonishingly he's certain he can feel a pulse there in the old man's veins - albeit slug-slow and hardly there at all – just a faint intimation of the life the man has led still there beneath Rueland's fingertips, an echo of what has been, a stone skimming across the water, a stone that inevitably ceases and sinks.

A sign of sainthood, Rueland thinks, Rueland believes, as he will go on believing and proclaiming until the end of his days.

40

BACK TO THE LODGE

Xavier and Lukitt leave early: ten thirty-five and already two hours on their way to Leipzig, Xavier in good spirits, pointing out strategic places to Lukitt as they pass them by.

'Got to have them envisioned in the mind's eye,' he was saying. 'Not the same at all as viewing illustrations.'

Lukitt nodding dumbly, making notes in his head, wondering if he'd succeeded, how quickly Xavier would throw him to the wolves if he had not.

Ten thirty-seven, and the Kompter is washed, dressed and laid out for the many visitors Rueland Klopstock knows will come.

Ten forty-four, and the ancient *Kummerglocke* bell of Brummsberg begins its mourning, the bell-ringer pulling slow and regular on his rope - a solemn tolling the townspeople understand, taking off their hats, lowering their heads, before carrying on with their day.

Rueland finding it hard to concentrate, filled with the injustice of having his mentor snatched so suddenly from him given the Kompter's apparent recuperation since being in Brummsberg.

'How it goes sometimes,' said the doctor, trying to ameliorate Rueland's distress. 'Often the case that folk rally just before the end…'

Rueland shaking his head.

'I should've stopped people coming in, shouldn't have subjected…'

'Twaddle,' the doctor interrupts, never one for melodrama. 'Whatever either of us did wouldn't have mattered a jot. We've all been with him on this journey and knew – as did he – that it was only a matter of time. He was the one insisted on seeing so many people, especially here in Brummsberg.'

'But maybe…' Rueland started, the doctor cutting him off again.

'Maybe nothing. What's done is done. No point mulling over how it might have gone. What's needed now is for you to decide whether he's buried here or taken on to Kwydzyn.'

Rueland rubbed his forehead.

'I just can't think...'

'What would he have wanted?' the doctor asked, more gently. 'And what would be best for The Order?'

Rueland shook his head, took off his spectacles, closed his eyes.

'I'm not sure I'm the one you should be asking,' he murmured, the doctor frowning.

'But you're the favourite elective for Successor,' he said bluntly. 'The Kompter's right hand man.'

Rueland sniffed, took a deep breath, put his glasses back on.

'I know. But all...this... I don't think...I mean, I can't be him. I can never be him. And without him I'm just...' he shrugged, let out a breath with awful realisation. 'I'm just a man who wants to go home.'

'Home!' cries Xavier, flinging himself from the cart. 'Smell that air, Lukitt! I keep a little jar of pine resin whenever I travel to remind me of it.'

Lukitt having no time to answer, for here came the Mingelstrossers: Anke at the lead, boys behind him; Alameth – already an honorary Mingelstrosser – on the step, waving at Lukitt.

'You're back!' Anke announces cheerfully, Xavier marching on to greet him, a swarm of Mingelstrosser boys taking down the heavy baggage.

'More books, Professor?' asked Filip, with a hint of laughter.

'More books,' Xavier agreed happily. 'Can never have too many. But look at you boys! Have you been trampled underfoot by a herd of elephants?'

Filip looked down at his mud spattered jerkin and smiled.

'Just back from taking the goats up the Harz. Bit of a job trying to stop the new bocks from fighting. But Alameth was a great help.'

'Alameth?' Xavier queried. 'Who's Alameth when he's at home?'

'Why, Mr Lukitt's friend, of course!' Rudiger retorted. 'You should hear the tales he's told us! Might've been in a monastery most of his life, but you should hear him!'

Xavier looked questioningly at Lukitt and Lukitt looked questioningly back.

'Didn't Professor Vannevar mention him in his letter?' Lukitt asked, not understanding the omission, not knowing Vannevar had penned that letter long before he knew Alameth went with Lukitt like a shoe on a foot, that he and Trudbert had talked about Lukitt after his lecture at Udolpho's, or rather how Lukitt might be useful to both down the ensuing years. A humorous conversation at the start, until both divined in the other what he knew to be in himself; long-term stratagems put in place to do both well, if not Lukitt – not that they cared a whit about the clever little fisherman from the Voralberg Hills.

'He didn't,' Xavier said. 'But what the ho! The more the merrier. Come along, my little family. Let's go see what Ishbella has made us. I've sorely missed her cooking.'

All piling off inside the lodge, leaving Lukitt on the outside, Alameth stepping forward, hugging Lukitt, releasing him.

'You should've come with us,' Alameth said. 'It was the greatest. Goats galore, and the boys – well, quite a wild tribe when left to their own devices. Had me building catapults. Tried to take down a mountain hare or two,' he chattered on, 'without success, I admit. But Jocken and Jakob, they're masters! Had an animal shot, skinned, gutted and roasted on the fire in no time.' Licking his lips at the memory. 'But instead you've met our Professor. Seems a friendly chap.'

'He does, doesn't he?' Lukitt answered, though had his reservations.

'So where did you go this time, Uncle Xavier?' they heard as they went inside to join the others.

'Uncle?' Lukitt asked, Alameth shrugging.

'That's what they call him; seems they've known him all their lives. I've a really good feeling about this place, Lukitt, really good.'

'Brummsberg,' Xavier was saying. 'But Goslar just down the road before that, and very promising as it happens.'

'Ooh, didn't they used to have a big palace there?' Rudiger put in, squirming in his chair, eager to make his learning known, Xavier laughing merrily.

'That's right, my boy! So at last, some of my teaching sticks! Built by whom?' he prompted, Rudiger chewing his bottom lip.

'One of the Holy Roman Emperors? One of the Henrys?' he offered, dubiously.

'You're right!' Xavier agreed. 'Henry II built the palace, but Henry III more attached to it, added on most of the ecclesiastical buildings. Born 1017, died 1156 right here in the Harz in his hunting lodge, his heart taken to Goslar – by his own asking..'

'His heart?' young Edric piped up. 'Why just his heart? What happened to the rest of him?'

'He wanted his body buried in Speyer Cathedral,' Xavier explained, 'next to his father. But his heart belonged to Goslar. Placed in an octagonal gold casket, later buried at the base of his tomb in St Ulrich's chapel. Though doubtful it's still there, the whole place…'

'So who put it there?' Edric couldn't get why anyone would choose to have himself buried in two separate places.

'Ah,' Xavier lifted a finger, 'now there's a story. Chapel wasn't built then, St Ulrich's the creation of one of his successors, Frederick Barbarossa - or Redbeard as he was known – another great ruler; forty years in power over Germany, Poland, Hungary, Denmark and Burgundy. Led fifteen thousand men - including three thousand knights - on the third Crusade against the mighty Saladin; fought and won several big battles before being swept away whilst swimming in the river Saleph in Armenia - then called Cilicia. Never brought home. Buried in Antioch.'

'It's true,' Alameth vouchsafed, as they took their seats about the dinner table, 'and also that Barbarossa's early battles were against the pope himself. Got excommunicated, set up his own anti-pope in remonstration, then changed his mind; the reason he built St Ulrich's chapel, buried Henry's heart there before setting off on his own Crusade by way of reparation.'

Xavier looked at the newcomer with surprise.

'Said he had tales,' Rudiger put in, sitting next to Xavier, Xavier patting Rudiger's knee.

'You did indeed,' he said, and to Alameth, 'That's very impressive, young man…'

'Alameth,' Alameth supplied.

'Alameth,' Xavier repeated, Annely and Lata appearing with the first of the food: a wonderful mushroom soup flavoured with wild garlic and sweet cicely, the faint aroma of aniseed pervading the room as the girls set down their bowls, Annely paying particular attention to Alameth, making sure he had the fullest bowl, the best of the bread.

Lukitt ignored.

Lukitt left on the side-lines, uncertain whether to be pleased or hurt.

Lukitt dreaming that night of Annely, waking to the unpleasant realisation that he'd ejaculated, and not only in his dreams; a new kind of guilt pervading him, and a new kind of desire, one he knew would not be reciprocated, that Annely's desires lay elsewhere - Rausgarten or no Rausgarten.

He got up, washed, dressed, stood at the window, the rooms on this side of the lodge catching the morning light.

A short knock at his door.

'Lukitt? Are you awake?'

Alameth.

A tinge of jealousy rising briefly before being quashed. Alameth might be popular with the Mingelstrosser clan but Lukitt was the one asked here to aid Xavier, and aid him he'd done. And now maybe Xavier would aid Lukitt, get him a placement at Leipzig University, if he could prove himself useful and apt.

'Up and ready for action,' he called back to Alameth, Alameth opening the door and bounding in, big grin on his face. And no wonder Annely found him so appealing, Alameth filling out these past few years, growing taller, stronger, his fine cheekbones more delineated, hair blonder from exposure to sun and sea, eyes clear and bright.

They'd dimmed a little after they'd left Liguria, but not so now, Lukitt's brief animosity towards Alameth slipping away.

You and your pretty little friend, Trudbert had threatened.

Not if Lukitt had anything to do with it.

Alameth's friendship a treasure Lukitt swore he would not relinquish, under any circumstance.

41

The Tapestry

'I've started a preliminary catalogue of your books,' Lukitt was telling Xavier, 'and once finished with the library I could do the museum.'

'Could you now?' Xavier said, lips twitching, admiring the lad's ingenuity if not exactly the lad himself; something about him he didn't quite like, couldn't put his finger on, as if Lukitt was a step aside, not quite in tune with the world. Unlike Alameth, to whom Xavier took straightaway, Alameth getting on with the Mingelstrosser boys like he'd been born into the family. Perhaps not as intellectually gifted as Lukitt, indeed had opted out of coming to the library immediately he was offered an alternative – Filip and Rudiger taking him off fishing, or gathering raspberries, or hoeing a new strip of vegetable patch. But Alameth's knowledge about St Ulrich's had impressed him, and he was wondering which of these two unknowns – sent to him by Professor Vannevar, a man he didn't care for, who pursued the same lines of investigation he did, if not in the same way, nor for the same purpose – would prove the better helpmeet when push came to shove.

But he was a fair man, open to having his mind changed by evidence, as Vannevar was not.

'So how've you ordered this catalogue?' he asked, Lukitt eager to explain, proffering over a box of cards he'd uncovered in one of the desk drawers.

'We create a master,' Lukitt said eagerly, 'with author, title, general subject, provenance and so on, then make multiple cards from this first – one filed by title, another by author, another by subject, more for sub-subjects – and give each book a specific code within its subject group so you'll be able to locate any single book by multiple means.'

'Very comprehensive,' Xavier said. 'But won't it take a huge amount of work?'

'I've calculated five minutes per book,' Lukitt answered quickly, 'and given you appear to have around six thousand volumes that's two months, at eight hours a day. Less if we all work together, you, me and Alameth. We'll certainly be finished by the end of the summer, even if I do it all myself.'

Xavier let out a short laugh.

'Well my! You've really worked it all out. And I confess there is something appealing about being reintroduced to my library.'

He rubbed his hands, glanced around him.

'And if everything is ordered as you suggest then it will make the next stage of my work so much easier. All right, my lad. Let's do it!'

And so they did, spending the next few weeks – starting at the top of the tower and working downwards – taking armfuls of books off shelves and onto tables, Xavier and Lukitt doing the cataloguing, Alameth branding the spines of each book with their cataloguing marks using a small hand-burner Xavier had dug out from his museum; slowed up occasionally by Xavier coming across one volume or another he'd entirely forgotten he owned, or Lukitt finding one he wanted a better look at. Piles of books on a spare table put aside for later study.

'*The Natural History of Frogs*. Now why on earth would I have purchased that? And here's a book on electricity by Joseph Priestley. I wondered where that had got to. Thought it might offer a new way of studying the…oh now wait a minute…' and off Xavier flitted to a new one.

Lukitt enjoying these diversions, exactly like when he and Ulbert opened up the crates of books from Opapa Augen all those years ago. But one particular day was different, one discovery momentous.

By then it was late July, the last two weeks of which had been atrocious weatherwise: every day cloudy and grey, hardly any sun, far too much rain for anyone to enjoy; the boys' vegetable patch suffering and looking miserable – too many caterpillars, slugs and snails, picked off by the dozen every night and stamped into obliteration. But the army kept on coming.

'Maybe a volcano's exploded somewhere,' Lukitt offered, as they got to work that day, each looking up glumly to the sky, seeing no summer, only more rain about to fall.

'It's possible,' Xavier agreed. 'The Lisbon earthquake of 1755 did tremendous damage over in Morocco on the other side of the water; tremors felt as far north as Scotland.'

'Happened on All Saints' Day,' Alameth murmured, remembering his lessons. 'Half past nine in the morning, every church and cathedral filled to bursting. An example of God knowing, but not interfering...'

'Or not caring. Or not being there.' Lukitt interrupted, finding such an excuse for the Godhead's neglect monstrous.

'Or possibly,' Xavier put in, smoothing the waters, 'Alameth's God understanding that by presenting such a moral conundrum it would move mankind's thoughts onwards, seek out the mechanisms of the world in which they live, begin in earnest the study of what we now call geology, when otherwise...oh but, just a minute...'

He'd been flicking casually through a book on the history of the Mongols and now sat down, spread the book out before him, ran his eyes over the text and hurriedly turned the page, lifting his fingers from it in utter surprise.

'But this is extraordinary! Look at this...' unfolding the right hand page to reveal a depiction of a tapestried frieze. '*Die Schlachtdenkschrift*,' he read. 'A Battle Memoir,' he explained. 'The author states he saw this tapestry at Goslar, suggests it illustrates the Mongol Invasion of Poland... Battle of Leignitz... 9th of April 1241.'

'Hard to believe they got so far,' Lukitt said, looking over Xavier's shoulder. 'I mean I knew about China, but this far west?'

'You're mistaken,' Xavier shook his large head. 'They almost had us, almost had the whole of Europe.'

'That can't be right!' Alameth exclaimed. 'Means we might all have been, well, whatever the Mongols were. Certainly not Christian.'

Xavier tapped the page.

'Think on it, Alameth, for that was very nearly the case. The greatest attack on our civilisation since the Romans. Twenty miles outside Leignitz the Mongols utterly destroyed the army of Henry of Silesia, twenty thousand men strong. Henry sent his knights in first – two thousand of them, Knights Teutonic, Templar and Hospitaller - completely outwitted by the Mongol *Mangudai,* trained in feigned-flight tactics.'

He moved his finger to the start of the frieze and pointed to the battleground: three blocks of Henry's army in blue basket-stitch over-threaded with gold, before them the scattered *Mangudai* with flanking cavalry arched behind them, another at the back – all blood red.

'The *Mangudai* weren't supposed to win,' Xavier explicated. 'They pretended fight before fleeing, setting up a smokescreen – quite literally – so when Henry's army came blundering in they couldn't see what was happening, first part massacred, the rest turning and retreating in confusion.'

'And after them went the Mongol cavalry,' Lukitt added, following the history laid out in perfect detail before of them.

'Cut down the lot,' Xavier said, 'but that wasn't the worst. Look on.'

Alameth and Lukitt looked on. The following scene appearing bucolic: a small town by a river, vines and corn growing along one side, forest the other. The detail astonishing: a dog picking at a bone, women grinding corn, others tending fields, a man and boy cutting the throat of a wild boar they'd captured and subdued.

The river ran on into the next scene, but all had changed: same river, same town, same miniature figures - right down to the dog - but here houses and crops were burning, people leaping into the water, one scrambling up the bank on the other side, another reaching the outskirts of the forest, the rest – in the next scene, further on down the river – massed up dead by its sides like logs.

'According to the script this is Hermannstadt, five hundred miles to the south,' Xavier explained, completely immersed in this miniature world, seeing the depiction of tiny stitches as real people in real terror. 'Attacked on April 10th – just a day after Leignitz - same tactics, same results; the army of Transylvania completely routed. Real mystery being how the Mongols managed to arrange such attacks so tidily.'

'Hermannstadt. Named after Arminius,' Lukitt murmured, finding the resonance disturbing, wondering if the Mongols understood the significance as these townspeople must have done, although Arminius's momentous battle with the Romans had taken place many hundreds of years before.

'Like I said,' Xavier said, 'very impressive strategists, those Mongols, their next inroad...'

'11th of April,' Lukitt read on excitedly. 'Hungarian army on their tail from Buda to Mohi...'

'Where the Hungarian army in turn was destroyed and their country in ruins,' Xavier took over again, eyes leaping to the end of the frieze where the river from Hermannstadt turned from blue to red, then to a wide dusty road into a wider dustier plain, men on horseback showering a corralled battalion with silver-stitched arrows that appeared like falling rain, if far more deadly. Arrows piercing their foes in arms and legs, between gaps in armour, in throats, eyes, in horses' eyes, in horses' flanks.

'What's this near the end?' Alameth asked.

'It's what it looks like,' Xavier sighed. 'The vanquishers filling their sacks with the ears of the vanquished. Something the Mongols were rumoured – though not proven - to do. But all in all, those three days saw the massacre of three armies by the Mongols, maybe a hundred and fifty thousand men dead, though very few on their own side.'

'And left the rest of Europe wide open,' Lukitt observed, puzzled. 'So why didn't they take advantage, flood in on the bore?'

'By the merest chance,' Xavier answered, feeling the threat as if it were still upon them. 'Ogudei - ruler of the Mongols, son of Ghengis Khan - dying, and Batu...'

'The one who'd organised this campaign in the west,' Lukitt put in, reading down the page.

'Precisely,' Xavier nodded, 'Batu, along with all the other princes of the realm required to return to base to elect a new Khan. And Batu going with speed, being a mere grandson of Ghenghis and needing to state his claim against his uncles.'

'And so we were saved,' Alameth breathed loudly.

'And so we were saved,' Xavier repeated. 'And thank God for it. But this illustration is very puzzling.'

'I don't see how,' Alameth said, standing up as the bell in the courtyard rang out, instructing them that food was about to be put on the table, and Ishbella's food was not to be left waiting.

'I'll need to check a few things,' Xavier concluded, shifting his eyes back and forth along the little path of history laid out before him. 'But if this author, this illustrator, is correct, if this tapestry really came from Goslar, then there's some link I must have missed.'

The bell rang out again, insistent, Xavier's hand havering over the illustration like haar over sea when the day has been hot.

'So all is not lost,' he said to himself, Alameth and Lukitt already on their heels and partway to the door, Xavier following, a beatific smile on his face.

So night is changed into day, he thought, *just as Job had it. And all because of Lukitt*; shuddering to think of this book laying buried in his library and him none the wiser.

Damn the crypts of St Wigbert's.

Goslar was the place to be, his mind a busy warren of what needed doing, which loose ends to tie up and which to leave behind to fray and blow in the wind.

42

Plans, and Pigeon Pie

The household thrown into upheaval the following morning by Xavier announcing he was off to Leipzig for a week, maybe two.

'No!' Filip argued, unwilling to let Xavier go, not when he'd promised to be here for the rest of the summer.

'And you haven't even looked at the vegetable patch,' Rudiger more pragmatic. 'You said you'd help us get the soil better for next year…'

'And I was going to show you how good I've got with the catapult,' Jocken added.

'We'd a tournament arranged.' Jakob attested swiftly.

'That they had,' Alameth seconded, for it had been his idea, quick to notice how much these boys looked up to their nominal uncle and how keen to impress, gain his praise and admiration as much as they did their father's.

'Can I ask why?' Anke ventured for them all, Xavier surveying his family - not his by blood yet one he considered his own.

'I've Lukitt to thank for it,' Xavier said with exuberance, Lukitt feeling anything but thanked as the entire Mingelstrosser family narrowed their focus in his direction – including Alameth – all looking less than pleased. 'If it wasn't for him,' Xavier went on oblivious, 'I'd never have discovered what has pointed me in a new and unforeseen direction. And this time I need no one's approval.'

He smiled broadly at Lukitt.

'No need to look so perplexed, my lad,' Xavier went on, Lukitt's confusion plain on his face. '*Die Schlachtdenkschrift*? That depiction of the Goslar tapestry we looked at last night?'

'Well yes,' Lukitt replied, 'the battle of Leignitz and the rest. But what about St Wigbert's? Isn't that the place you need to excavate?'

Xavier's turn to look puzzled.

'Not an option, you know that. The Kompter couldn't have been clearer.'

'But your article,' Lukitt said slowly, 'the one left in the library. I'm sorry if I...I mean, I thought you'd meant me to find it.'

Xavier hesitated a moment, before remembering chucking the essay onto an empty shelf in disgust after one rewrite too many. He chuckled, scratched his ear.

'That risible paper I drafted for the Transactions? My supposed clerical conspiracy of silence? Good heavens! Such drivel! Thank the Lord I never sent it, especially with what we've now discovered.'

'But it seemed so...logical,' Lukitt argued, a heat growing in his chest like an angry flower bursting from the confines of its bud.

'Logical, maybe,' Xavier agreed with nonchalance, 'but a logic badly argued and badly flawed. To think the old Kompter and his cohorts were conspiring against me. It's laughable! No proper evidence, my lad, and evidence is the keystone to comprehension.'

But comprehension was running riot through Lukitt at how badly he might have misconstrued the situation from first to last: the paper not left out for him specifically; no clerical conspiracy, so no need to have it dealt with; Lukitt's calling to Brummsberg nothing more than pleasantry so Xavier could offer him the honour of meeting a great man – the Kompter – and show Lukitt some of the sites Xavier had worked on as they returned to Leipzig and then the Lodge. Maybe all in order to get to know his new assistant a little – and why wouldn't he? Why would Xavier take Vannevar's word on anything? Lord knew, as Lukitt did, and likely Xavier too, that Vannevar wasn't the most trustworthy person on the planet. Maybe he'd feared a spy in the camp just as Vannevar had asked Lukitt to be, not that Lukitt had acted on it.

But if all that were the case then...

'Tell you what,' Alameth interposed. 'Why don't the boys set up the tournament right now? And take your uncle to visit the vegetable patch? We could have a good bye picnic by the lake. Meanwhile I'll nip down to Quedlinburg to book his place on the afternoon coach. I'm assuming there is an afternoon coach?'

'There is,' Xavier said, 'and that all sounds grand!'

'But I'll go for the coach,' Lukitt got in, his insides squirming. 'And Alameth will stay.'

The boys clapping their hands in ecstatic agreement, everyone getting up in excitement, Ishbella and her daughters disappearing into the kitchen chattering about what they would cook up for the picnic and for Uncle Xavier to take with him on the not-so-long trip to Leipzig, Xavier laughing loudly as he was borne away by his adoptive sons.

'I'd like to see you better the catapulting skills of my youth! I was quite the champion…'

Doors slamming as they left, the air stilling, Lukitt sat alone at the table, no part of this happy family; Lukitt slipping unnoticed from his chair, from the room, from the lodge. Lukitt hitching up a horse and making his way along the lane leading towards Quedlinburg, tears tracking down his cheeks, chest heaving with sadness and self-recrimination, fingers of one hand clutched so tightly about the reins he was depriving them of blood just as surely as he'd deprived the old Kompter of his last few months of life. An act he now understood had no reason behind it.

No reason at all.

He'd added two and two together and made nineteen.

The tournament was a great success – sun coming out for the first time in weeks - catapult targets of apples and summer squashes set upon rocks, in the lower branches of trees, everyone taking their turn; Jakob coming out on top, Xavier a shabby fourth, Alameth at the bottom, even Edric doing better than both. They surveyed the vegetable patch, Xavier admiring the lines of salad mustard, potatoes, onions, winter cabbages, skinny leeks, the great tangle of rain-bedraggled squash plants taking over one edge and trailing out across the grass with their yellow trumpets and broad hairy leaves; Ishbella and the girls joining them for an early lunch by the placid blue waters of the lake.

'While I'm away,' Xavier was saying to Alameth, 'I'd like you and Lukitt to finish up in the library then catalogue the museum, see if you can find anything relating to Goslar or early artefacts from the area.'

'Speaking of Lukitt,' Alameth said, 'shouldn't he be back by now?'

No one having given Lukitt a second thought, nor noticing his non-return, Xavier flipping open his pocket watch. Getting on for half past one.

'No matter,' he said, happy and replete. 'I'll set off anyway, meet him on my way down.'

'And after Leipzig,' Anke asked, 'what then?'

Xavier rubbed his hands together.

'It rather depends,' he said, 'but ideally I'll take a sabbatical for the rest of the year. I'm sure Rausgarten will approve,' a quick glance at Annely who studiously refused to meet his gaze, Xavier clearing his throat. 'Then on to Goslar, only a hop, skip and jump away from Quedlinburg, so we'll be able to return here every weekend.'

'Every weekend! But that's wonderful!' Filip answered for them all.

'And by we?' Alameth queried.

'You and Lukitt, of course!' Xavier smiled with largesse. 'I'll need as many extra hands as I can get. Got to dig through every last brick and stone that's left.'

'Sounds a bit drear,' Ishbella commented, Xavier barking out a laugh.

'To you maybe, my dear,' he said brightly, 'but food and drink to me and mine. Speaking of which - any of that pigeon pie left?'

'Best pigeon pie this side of the Harz,' Anke said, handing Xavier the last of it.

'Only this side?' Ishbella chided, Xavier patting his ample stomach.

'That remains to be seen,' he said. 'But I shall certainly report back when I have the answer.'

43

Goslar, Then and Now

Goslar, Early Summer 1200AD

You come down the wooded slopes of the Harz mountains along the wide track-ways used by the royal huntsmen for their sport. You come out of the forest and see before you the collegiate church of St Simon and St Jude, its limestone walls glistening in the sunlight, octagonal towers alive with swallows and martins who've made their nests there. You admire its sturdiness and breadth, having once before walked through each of its naves and the three eastern apses, witnessed for yourself the massive statues in the narthex you hadn't really believed existed, and the sculptured stone panels cradling three sides of the great bronze throne on which successive kings of Germany have been crowned, some of them Emperors, anointed by the Pope himself.

You smile as you pass by the porch with its painted saints serene above the arched windows below. You see the Benedictine cloisters and refectory to your right, gaze up the large grassy slope that leads to the Imperial Palace - the Kaiserpfalz – a building so large and impressive it always takes your breath away. You remember surging up this slope years ago with a crowd of townsfolk eager for a glimpse of the Emperor Barbarossa through the openings in the lower façade. A queen of days, because against all the odds you'd actually seen him. And his beard had been as red as his name implied.

You're here to visit the chapel he's added to the left hand side of the Palace – the chapel of St Ulrich - a small bauble comparative to the church of St Mary's connected to the Palace on its other side. But it's a bauble beautiful in its simplicity: two storied, round at its base, upper floor octagonal - reserved for royal guests only - the whole looking like an Imperial Crown. And, as you approach - the dew seeping through the badly stitched seams of your boots - the steepness of the grassy slope makes you breathe a little harder, reminding you why you've come here: to make a prayer for your father who died with Barbarossa on the 10th of June ten years earlier to the day, both swept away by the fast flowing waters of the River Saleph, as they crossed the Taurus mountains heading for the Holy Lands on their Crusade. Here to say your prayer at Henry's tomb inside St Ulrich's, evoke the blessing of his heart which lies within its golden casket.

No holier place than this, you think as you push open the door of the chapel and step inside. *The heart of Henry the heart of Germany*, as your father often said, and although you've not followed your father's path as knight and crusader – there being no need since the peace agreed between Saladin and Richard a few years back - you still feel the calling in your blood.

Would follow that path in a beat if you could.

You move forward, you kneel, lay your hands upon the stone sepulchre. You bow your head and murmur out your prayer.

No notion that in exactly two years and four months – on the 10th of November 1202 - your calling will be enacted and you'll be one of eleven thousand men setting off from Venice on board one of two hundred ships going for Zara on the Adriatic coast.

No idea this Fourth Crusade will destroy every aspect of the chivalry and righteous destination of its predecessors, that its first act of warfare will be to take Zara for the Venetians – Christians murdering Christians – and go on to sack Constantinople, take part in pillaging of such ferocity and violence it will make you weep.

And will make you weep long after you've returned, will bring you back here to Goslar, will make you walk back down these royal trackways through the trees and out of the forest. That by then you'll be so bone-weary and sick of life you won't tarry by the church of St Jude and St Simon, won't notice the magnificence of the Imperial Palace atop its grassy knoll; this time will take your way directly to St Ulrich's and into the chapel, where you'll lay your head against the cold stone of that sepulchre and beg your God, and the heart of Henry, to forgive you.

Because – Christ knows – you can't forgive yourself.

Goslar, Late Summer 1848

Xavier stepped through the ruins of the collegiate church of St Simon and St Jude: in disrepair for years, sold at auction to a craftsman in 1819 who'd used it as a quarry for its stones. Only parts still standing being the porch – the upper statues blanched and weather-beaten into non-recognition – and part of the narthex, with several of its own outsized statues. These last toppled and broken.

'A tragedy,' he murmured softly, kicking at several stones, glancing up the grassy slope towards to the *Kaiserpfalz* that had fared a little better, the townsfolk liking its majesty, and the Sheriffs of previous centuries loving the Imperial Hall in which to hold their ceremonies. More extraordinary was St Ulrich's chapel, the least part of the whole complex, being completely intact, employed as a prison house for a couple of centuries.

Xavier's previous visit had been rather on a whim, but he was back with purpose and stood at the bottom of the unkempt slope - a wilderness of wild flowers and grasses beaten low by the unseasonable rain, where once there had been clipped green lawns – began to erect the ruined buildings stone by stone in his mind with the eye of a practised archaeologist; turning through the compass as he slowly surveyed the scene, planned the order of his excavations, eyes agleam with expectation of what he might find, inwardly blessing the old Kompter, not to mention Lukitt, for indirectly leading him to this place.

'What d'you reckon this is?' Alameth was asking, holding up a clever piece of carved stone that looked like a frog sitting on a miniature snowshoe.

Lukitt noted the hole in one end of the shoe and the bowl built into the frog's back.

'Think it might be a pipe,' he said, jotting it down in his inventory.

Alameth put it to his lips and blew.

'Nothing,' he commented. 'Are you sure?'

'Not that kind of pipe,' Lukitt smiled, glancing at a flute made from some ancient femur bone. 'The kind you smoke tobacco with.'

'Now that makes sense,' Alameth laughed. 'He's got some load of stuff in here. Where d'you think he got it all?'

Looking around him at Xavier's hoard: the obscure astronomical devices, stuffed animals, pinned insects, preserved body parts, eyes lingering on the Tasmanian example that was all the more shocking since they'd seen the depiction of the sacks of ears supposedly collected by the Mongols.

'Do you reckon Xavier's right?' Alameth added, turning an ancient globe of the world with his fingers, 'about our entire civilisation nearly being wiped out?'

Figuring the places the Mongols had already conquered before they'd reached Poland and Hungary, realising it encompassed almost half the globe, the speed with which they'd done it frightening: only fifty years to take China, Russia, Persia and Syria, almost to the Mediterranean coast.

'Reckon he's not far wrong,' Lukitt said, looking up from yet another tiny label he was attaching to yet another exhibit. 'Not that far from Leignitz to Leipzig, and not far from there to funnelling through Germany and into France and Spain. Though guess they'd have had to stop sometime. Takes a load of feed to keep that many horses on the run.'

Lukitt shook his head, concentrating on his next task, Alameth unable to grasp the concept in its entirety, needing to break it down into isolated facts.

'So no Gargellan monastery,' he frowned. 'No Triungulin Mosaic.'

Lukitt pausing, remembering the stained glass window that had so beguiled and bemused him.

'Maybe no monasteries at all,' Lukitt's gaze fixed on Alameth's hand stretching out across the globe, wondering what really might have happened if Batu hadn't returned East after his victories at Leignitz, Buda, Mohi and Hermannstadt, if he hadn't had to fight his claim for the Khanate. The idea deeply unsettling. 'Maybe no more Catholicism,' he stated, watching Alameth spin the globe slowly beneath his palm. 'Maybe no Reformation, no Renaissance, and none of the art or architecture that went with it. Probably no great humanist philosophers either, so no shift towards the sciences. Maybe no discovery of the Americas.'

It didn't seem possible world history could be changed so dramatically by one person – one single person – having to return East instead of battling on into the West.

But there it was.

That was the truth of it.

Lukitt tortured by his own decisions about what might have happened if only he'd let things be.

Got to get a grip, he thought. *Got to swallow down this guilt, grow my forgetting over it like a gall on damaged leaves.*

Remembering the old elm tree that stood out back of Ulbert's house as it groaned in the wind, the witches' brooms sprung thick and wild where its limbs had been torn off by previous winter storms; fixing the image in his mind, willing himself to do the same: replace loss with growth, seal his wounds from the world, create a thicket over their scars that no wind, no storm, could ever breach again.

Annely and Lata were dancing - dinner over - Mingelstrossers having collectively decided to put on a little show for Lukitt and Alameth as a leaving do, even though they'd be back in a couple of weeks. It was mostly for Alameth's benefit Lukitt knew but did not begrudge, Alameth having apparently recounted every detail of the Pfiffmakler's entertainments to the Mingelstrosser children who – from youngest to oldest – were enthralled and keen to replicate as much of them as they could. Annely looking magnificent in her swirling skirts, taking every opportunity to brush up against Alameth's chair, the table having been shifted to one side to provide a stage of sorts. Lata too was enthusiastic, if not so graceful; the boys providing a cacophony of mismatched accompaniment from their various musical instruments of choice knocked up out of scraps from Anke's workshop; Alameth leaping up at one point to fetch the femur flute from the mausoleum – Lukitt wincing, reminding Alameth it was at least a couple of thousand years old. Alameth laughing, doing a jig as he blew through it: a sound like waves pushing through a cave.

'If it's lasted this long,' Alameth argued, 'then another pair of lips isn't going to do it any harm!'

He'd also retrieved a mouth harp that Anke had a go at, neither his nor Alameth's contributions improving the chaotic symphony. Annely and Lata taking no heed, sticking to their prearranged choreography, Ishbella banging out the beat for them on the bottom of a pan.

Lukitt strongly reminded of that small room back at Udolpho's palazzo, whose ambered and mirrored walls had thrown out his reflection in vertiginous multiplicity, merging those other selves with the flashing rainbowed sparkles coming from the fountain at its centre: the embodiment of random chaos then as now, unless you understood the underlying order. Just like that old riddle Ulbert had illustrated one of his sermons with, running it by Lukitt before giving it out the following morning:

I saw a glass fifteen feet deep,
I saw a well filled with men's tears that weep,
I saw wet eyes quick as a flaming fire,
I saw a horse bigger than the moon and higher,
I saw the sun, and at midnight
I saw the man who saw this dreadful sight…

'Can you figure it out, Lukitt?' Ulbert had asked, Lukitt studying the verses for several hours, only getting it when he murmured them out loud: once, twice, three times…when all became plain.

'I have it!' he'd shouted, jumping up from the desk, taking a few quick steps to where Ulbert was sat by the fire, Ulbert's face glowing with an echo of Lukitt's pride.

'I saw a glass,' Lukitt had begun.
Fifteen feet deep I saw a well
Filled with men's tears that weep, I saw wet eyes;
Quick as a flaming fire I saw a horse;
Bigger than the moon and higher
I saw the sun, and at midnight…

'The first interpretation,' Ulbert had homilised the following day in church, 'is confusing, inexplicable – and how the world appears to most of us. The second is how it appears to God and the wise.'

Fine words, but never any explication of that man at midnight who rounded off the riddle, no shift of meaning for him, no happy ending.

'I don't understand where he fits in,' Lukitt had said later, Ulbert studying his young pupil's earnest face.

'There's always room for mystery,' Ulbert had replied, an unsatisfactory answer if ever there was one, Lukitt harrumphing, retiring to his desk, determined to work it out. Not that he had, and he'd been grumpy with Ulbert the following morning because of it.

'Have I become your enemy because I've not told you the truth?' Ulbert had asked, twisting St Paul's words to the Galatians - a reference Lukitt was not unacquainted with – Ulbert twitching out a smile as Lukitt served him a rather dry bowl of scrambled eggs and some less than perfect toast. Lukitt replying by taking the damned riddle and putting it in a drawer, slamming the drawer shut, Ulbert raising his eyebrows.

'Sometimes, Lukitt,' Ulbert had said, closing the conversation, 'a man has to discover the truth for himself.'

But where that truth was, Lukitt didn't know. He'd not thought on any of it – the riddle, the dry scrambled eggs, Ulbert's annoyingly pithy explanations, his own slamming shut of that drawer – for years. But lying on his bed tonight, listening to the faint sounds of the Mingelstrosser party going on downstairs, there came that riddle again, and Ulbert's words latched upon its heels:

Have I become your enemy because I've not told you the truth?

Lukitt shivered in his bed with the truths he could never tell, all the enemies he would make if he did.

Lukitt sleeping badly that night, dreaming of the man at midnight who'd seen his dreadful sights. Lukitt shivering in his sleep, because that man - within his dreaming - was himself.

The day following their leaving-do, Lukitt and Alameth joined Xavier in Goslar.

'Welcome, lads!' Xavier holding his arms open wide. 'We've so much to do! I've been over the ruins with a toothcomb, found a lot that's going to be of use.' He dropped his voice to a whisper. 'Think

I've found part of the imperial throne in the rubble,' looking over his shoulder as if anyone was listening, which they weren't. 'And St Ulrich's chapel,' Xavier went on, taking them up the path he'd made in the overgrown acre of meadow that had once been the lawn of the Kaiserpfalz. 'It's amazingly extant and, more to the point, Bishop Frenk was free with his permission to dig beneath it. Got to go at it sideways, of course, so we can check out the foundations, that we don't collapse the chapel, but archaeology's always been a dirty job.'

He rubbed his hands together in happy expectation, and wasn't wrong, Lukitt and Alameth spending the next few weeks excavating a tunnel leading from the outside world into the undercrofts below St Ulrich's, dragging out basketfuls of the soil, mud and debris that had accumulated since the Kaiserpfalz and all its associated buildings had fallen into disuse. Dirty work indeed, but satisfying in the extreme when they'd the last of it out and rested in the cavern they'd unearthed. The space square, with the remains of several stoved-in sarcophagi, one of which must presumably have at one time sheltered the octagonal gold casket containing Henry's heart. It was also apparent that there were several tunnels leading off at the four points of the cross, though more digging and excavating would be needed to see where and what they led to – ossuaries the most likely answer. And then there was the bottom half of a squat stone staircase that presumably led to the chapel above.

'We should go top-side, see if we can dig out the last part of it from above,' Alameth suggested, Lukitt examining the circle of supporting pillars that seemed completely unmoved by the years; nevertheless he examined them for cracks and stress-lines, as instructed.

'They seem sturdy enough,' he commented, 'but I think we should get Xavier down here before we do anything else.'

Reluctantly Alameth agreed and volunteered to fetch him, Lukitt meanwhile studying and sketching the underground crypt: organised on a Greek Cross, just like the layout of the chapel above, with five sarcophagi placed within the circle of pillars, one at its direct centre.

Has to be Henry's, he thought, tempted to start sieving through its rubble for the golden casket - though the likelihood of it still being there was remote. Instead he took another long look about him, noting an anomaly in the east facing wall, that it was smoother at the top than the others, with none of their lumps and bumps. Curious, and having time to kill, he took up a stout-bristled brush and began to remove the caked compacted dust of centuries, choking as plumes of it came up and drifted through the air before settling to the floor. His eye catching a dull distinction of tone in the leftmost corner, taking a softer brush to it, dislodging the last layers of silt from the bedrock. Stopped, opened his mouth in shock, started again, stopped again: for there in front of him was a distinct incision, unmistakably the uppermost part of an heraldic emblem soon revealed to be a single-headed eagle etched into the stone: symbol of the Holy Roman Empire adopted by Frederick Barbarossa.

'My God,' he breathed – never mind the dust that caught in mouth, eyes and throat - moving hastily on to the next section of the wall, brushing at it inch by inch, foot after foot, finding ten yards of inscriptions scrolling out to the right of the eagle. The man who'd seen dreadful sights pushed into nonexistence, replaced by one witnessing the wondrous for here, in the stone walls below St Ulrich's, Lukitt was uncovering a crude rendition of the Goslar Tapestry; *or maybe*, Lukitt was thinking, regarding the hesitation marks, the slips, the shallow and apparently hasty incisions in the stone, *not its replica but its original template.*

He ran his fingers over the engravings that in some places were barely more than scratch-marks, imagining its creator down here with hammer and chisel, a couple of candle stubs burning – just as they were doing now – desperate to make a permanent record of the terrible events that had happened not so far away; events that must have appeared at the time apocalyptic, signalling the End of Days: the heathen hordes at their very doors, nearing Leipzig – a stone's throw from Goslar – only days away from being as utterly destroyed as Buda, Mohi, Hermannstadt and Leignitz had so recently been. One man down here in these undercrofts – maybe a man who'd escaped from Leignitz and the others, given the detailed knowledge of those battles - believing all was done for.

But not done so for these inscriptions; still around to be found by Lukitt Bachmann six hundred and seven years later, tracing the panic and desperation gone into their making, his fingertips mapping their contours, their wobbles, their mistakes; seeing here before him the complex swath of the tapestry in Xavier's book: the river that ran first blue and then red, that single man's face coming out of the forest.

'I hope that was you,' he whispered. 'I hope that was you.'

He moved his fingers over the tail-end of the depiction – the sack overflowing with ears - whorled them around and around in ever increasing circles as he thought about the implications, what this would mean to Xavier and therefore to himself and Alameth. And by doing so he found the final revelation of St Ulrich's hidden in the gloom beyond his candle's light, discovered by his touch, uncovered by his brush: the maker's mark: the who, the when, the why:

Excud Josephus mandatus Hermann Von Salza vulneratus non victus Aprilis VII Ides MCCXLI

Made by Josephus on order of Hermann Von Salza, bloodied but unbowed, 7th of Ides, 1241

44

Great Discoveries, Great Regrets

Alameth hadn't found Xavier at any of the expected haunts: not at the old porch, nor where Xavier had been scrutinizing the 11th century stone screens that had once surrounded the imperial throne – part of which he had indeed found; nor at the guild houses of the Bakers, Tailors or Pewter-makers whose archives he'd been patiently burrowing through for records of the town's earliest history; nor at the Rathaus, where Xavier had been studying the *Huldigungssaal* – the Hall of Homage.

At this last place Alameth lingered, moving in slow circles upon his heels on the flagging of the floor as he gazed up at the painted panels completely covering the Hall's walls and ceiling; the experience magnificent and overwhelming, the colours so rich, the scenes so vivid he felt he could step into any of them and become a living breathing part. The Triungulin Mosaic back at Gargellan paltry by comparison.

'If only you could see this, Opapa Augen,' he whispered, 'you'd die a happier man.'

As will I, he thought, nothing impressing him so much since he'd left the monastery, except perhaps Annely Mingelstrosser whose face - he was embarrassed to realise - he saw at every turn, superimposed on each depiction of the Magdalene or the Blessed Virgin, or any number of the other female participants in this extraordinary and epic pageant of history, biblical or no. He shivered with his guilt, tried to throw it off, concentrated instead on Xavier and where he might seek him next. Thought on Lukitt in that damp undercroft: Lukitt, who'd taken him out of the monastery to experiences such as this; Alameth aided in his endeavours by a council official coming into the hall and chucking Alameth out.

'Don't know what they was thinking letting you in in the first place,' said the man. 'You ain't no professor, even if you works for one; an' this place is special. Ain't for just anyone's eyes.'

And yet Alameth's eyes had seen it, and would never forget; he still had the images in his mind as he crossed from the Rathaus through the market that was busy with stalls and traders and into the square, where he washed his face in one of the two bronzed basins situated below a gilded imperial eagle rising up from the water.

Never had Alameth been so happy, never had Alameth felt so free, that life was his for the taking.

I've a good feeling about this place, he'd said to Lukitt, and by God that feeling had got stronger with every day, his interactions with the Mingelstrossers easing his shame, erasing his anger, replacing both with a self-worth that might otherwise have been lost forever.

In short, the Mingelstrossers making of Alameth a happy man.

At the lodge, Anke Mingelstrosser was glad for Xavier's new interest in Goslar. During past excavations they'd maybe not see Xavier for months, everyone missing him, the children most of all; but Goslar not so far away. Xavier had rattled the cages of folk at his chapel, but Anke understood him skin and bone as the elders did not, and that Xavier's only purpose was to unite the German people, aid their understanding of shared roots, a common past, bring them into a single fold. And if Goslar was to be the proof of it – as Xavier's latest missive indicated – then so much the better.

My dear Anke, that letter had read, *wonders here abound! After several weeks of work – and forgive us for not returning during that time, but we must get our groundwork done – we've made several key discoveries. The Palace at Goslar was indeed first envisaged by Henry II, then properly begun as an Aula Regis by Henry III around the middle of the 10th-c, as I supposed. I've got work records from the guilds that allude to its rebuilding after its partial collapse in 1132. I've also confirmation of the dates of the other ecclesiastical buildings, but I won't bore you with those. Of greater importance is that we've excavated from the rubble part of the Imperial Throne and this, together with the original stone tablets that surrounded it, are making interesting study. But the greatest discovery has been made by Lukitt Bachmann this very day...*

Lukitt Bachmann, Anke thought, straining to recall the lad's face, realising that once out of sight he'd also slipped from mind. Undoubtedly an impressive young man, but one who lacked life and substance in the household, always quiet, at arm's length, more akin to books than people, grey-scale comparative to the luminosity of Alameth who had life and laughter leaking from every limb. Anke shook his head, went on reading, bracing himself for some dry discovery Lukitt had made, immensely surprised to find the exact opposite.

He's uncovered – quite literally - a link, and a very substantive one. He's found the origins of the tapestry I was telling you about. And there's more! And so much more. It's going to be the culmination of my life's work! The inscription at the end of the engraving he's found has a very specific origin, stating unequivocally that it was made by one Josephus on the orders of Henry Von Salza himself, who I've spoken to you about previously. Von Salza! Can you believe it! Here's what he found: Excud Josephus mandatus Hermann Von Salza vulneratus non victus Aprilis VII Ides MCCXLI.

Anke Mingelstrosser sat down on the first chair he could find, holding the letter out in front of him, re-reading the passage, long enough in Xavier's service to understand the significance: Hermann Von Salza, first grandmaster of the Order of Teutonic Knights, the Order going deep into Prussia to defeat and convert the pagan tribes there; Von Salza, loyal supporter and intimate friend of Frederick II – Frederick's moniker *Stupor Mundi:* the Wonder of the World - who'd gathered flocks of learned men about him as a sheep grows wool. Including Von Salza.

So you can see where this is leading, Xavier went on, *it means we've proof positive the Knights were at Leignitz when the Mongols struck, and the Goslar tapestry an accurate depiction of that historic event, its details recorded by someone actually there – namely Von Salza himself. We've always wondered why and how he'd died at Barletta, and now we know.*

Indeed they did. Anke could make the deductions all by himself: Von Salza dragged from the battlefield of Leignitz, *bloodied but unbowed,* as the Goslar inscription informed them; taken behind the lines to the Imperial Palace at Goslar to heal his wounds, pass on how very real the Mongol threat had become. Von Salza directing Josephus to inscribe it on the walls below St Ulrich's, Von Salza troubled enough to journey on to Italy – despite his wounds, and later dying of them - to deliver his dire warnings direct to *Stupor Mundi* who was about to leave Italy on his own Crusade to the Holy Lands, ignorant of the fact that his entire Empire was about to fall to an enemy much closer to hand: the Mongol hordes that had been diverted by the merest chance.

This discovery of Lukitt's will be the first of many, Xavier had written further, *and because of it we must hold a feast in his honour.* Anke letting out a laugh, for a feast meant just that, and Ishbella would be ringing like a bell to throw herself into such a task. Lukitt Bachmann might be an enigma to Anke Mingelstrosser, but if he'd furthered his master's cause of uniting Germany steadfast and strong in the shared precepts of its history then Anke was happy with that.

Genius develops in quiet places, as Goethe had it, Xavier's letter concluded, *and genius is developing here in Goslar. Über allen Gipfeln. It's been a struggle up this mountain, old friend, but at the top we shall find peace.* Anke smiling at this reference to Goethe, taken from his *Wanderers Nachtlied*, hoping Xavier's wanderings – both intellectual and actual – were truly about to find their goal.

Only blight on his horizon being Annely's upcoming marriage, and that Xavier couldn't reach his goal without it.

45

ÜBER ALLEN GIPFELN

'I can't begin to express how proud I am of you two,' Xavier was saying, radiating warmth and bonhomie as he sat at a desk far too small to accommodate all the papers he'd accumulated since arriving in Goslar. 'All that digging! All that shifting of dirt…'

He took off his spectacles, rubbed them clean of several tear splatters that had besmirched their inner surfaces.

'Just glad to be of service,' Lukitt said, Xavier finding Lukitt's quiet restraint a tad irritating, given the circumstances.

'*Glad to be of service!*' Alameth parroted, bringing the joy back into Xavier's world. 'Honestly, Lukitt,' Alameth went on, putting an arm about his friend's shoulders. 'Anyone would think you'd merely done a bit of housework instead of finding something really important to Mr Xavier's work!'

'Well put,' Xavier said, replacing his spectacles. 'If you'd not thought to brush down that wall then…well...'

Lukitt allowed himself a small smile.

'We'd have found it sometime,' he demurred, 'once we properly looked at the place.'

'Oh tush!' Xavier chided. 'We'd have started on the sarcophagi, you know we would, and then on the staircase and tunnels. No reason at all to think there'd be anything on the walls. Don't forget I spent the whole of yesterday down there, Lukitt, and it took a very mindful eye to spot what you did. Brabarossa's eagle...' He shook his head. 'To think we might never have found it,' a riffle of fear passing through him, blinking several times, besmirching his glasses all over again.

'But find it we did!' Alameth exclaimed, 'or rather Lukitt did.'

Xavier standing up, rolling his shoulders, stepping towards them.

'That he did,' he said, making a formal bow in Lukitt's direction. 'But if Lukitt doesn't want my thanks, then so be it.'

He turned away towards his desk, Lukitt frowning, fearing he'd offended, Alameth catching his breath, about to speak in Lukitt's defence when Xavier swivelled on his heel, chest heaving with laughter as he took a couple of strides and caught the two of them in an unexpected hug, slapping at both their backs with large and calloused hands.

'But I'm joking!' he said expansively, slapping them once more before releasing them, gazing on his protégés, opening his arms wide as if about to conduct an invisible orchestra. 'My two young scholars,' he said more soberly, 'sent to me by providence, who have dug themselves into Goslar's soil like moles, and who are going to get my thanks whether they like it or no!'

'Hoorah!' shouted Alameth, clapping his hands, Lukitt too feeling a sudden lurch of relief.

'I could go back right now,' Lukitt said, in an enthusiastic garble, 'see what's on the other walls. And maybe there's more in the tunnels…'

Xavier brought his hands together against his breastbone and smiled like he was God Almighty Himself watching the Israelites entering Canaan.

'Well yes,' he conceded, nodding slowly, brows furrowed, lips puckered in apparent agreement. 'Yes, you could do that, Lukitt, or,' he went on, mouth twitching into a broad smile, holding up a finger, 'or we could cordon off the lot, say goodbye to Goslar for a couple of days, go back to the Lodge where Anke and Ishbella have already been tasked with creating a feast in your honour!'

'Oh let's do that!' Alameth could hardly contain himself. 'A feast! And at the Lodge. The perfect reward.'

'All right with that, Lukitt?' Xavier asked, raising his eyebrows, gratified to see the lad unbend, straighten his shoulders, a stab of sunshine permeating his habitual seriousness.

'All right with that,' Lukitt conceded, smiling now, 'in fact more than all right,' the clock tower chiming two at that precise moment, Lukitt lifting his head, counting the beats. 'But if you both want to go ahead, get the three o'clock back to Quedlinburg I'd be more than happy to…'

'To do what?' Xavier laughed, winking over at Alameth. 'Go through all my papers? Start cataloguing them with the wall inscriptions in mind?'

Lukitt frowning, because that was precisely what he'd had in mind; Xavier's smile dropping, cocking his head as he looked at Lukitt, realising the truth of it. Remembering his own first big discovery – a dig in Eythra in Saxony that uncovered the petrified wooden remains of water wells and the tools that had made them; Xavier estimating them to be at least seven thousand years old, which meant before the first recorded instance in Europe of metal tools – not a popular opinion, his peers and superiors arguing vociferously against his dating strategies. Until Xavier had proved his point, engaged a skilled carpenter – one Anke Mingelstrosser - to recreate those bone and stone-tipped wooden-shafted tools, and with them recreated the well structures: a proof that had set Xavier Züstraubben on the road to academic success. The thrill of that first discovery, that first battle won against established opinion, never leaving him; recalled too how he'd needed time alone to absorb it. How he'd returned to the site at Eythra after receiving his professorship at Leipzig on the basis of that work, bivouacked beneath the stars, imagined the tribe that had resided there millennia before and all the complex networks of their lives with neighbouring tribes; how they'd survived against the odds.

The single reason he'd pursued his theories for so long.

And understood.

'All right then,' Xavier agreed. 'Let's do exactly that. Me and Alameth will go, leave you to your own devices overnight. But tomorrow, Lukitt, tomorrow,' he emphasised the word, wagging a finger, 'you're to come to us at the Lodge early evening, where you'll be welcomed as a hero. A hero, and don't you forget it.'

Taking off his glasses again and having to re-clean them, reassessing Lukitt Bachmann: not so cold and distant as he'd first seemed, Lukitt no longer an enigma. Lukitt instead a seeker dedicated to scholarship just as Xavier was, Xavier giving Lukitt the leeway to enjoy his victory any way he chose, which was alone - exactly as Xavier had done himself.

And so it went.

Lukitt left to his own devices in the crypts below St Ulrich's, several candles spread at regular intervals below the inscriptions on the wall, their flickers lending the scenes depth and shadow, making them jitter into life. Lukitt leaning against the broken sarcophagus at the centre of the cavern, thinking big thoughts, thinking that at last he'd found someone to admire and follow in Xavier Züstraubben, but recalling too the cost to Annely that hadn't seemed right before and seemed no righter now. And, while going through Xavier's papers – that lay in un-neat piles upon the desk back at their lodgings – Lukitt had a notion how it might be made moot. No certainty it would pan out - and he'd need to carefully structure the logic of his argument - but, if it did, then so much better for them all.

He took his carriage as planned the following afternoon, getting to the Lodge to find it eerily quiet; went inside and up to his bed chamber, depositing his bag, taking out his notes and going through them one more time, despite having memorised every shaky point on the journey over.

Distracted himself by looking out of the window, seeing immediately why the place was so empty for there, by the lake, the whole family was gathered, engaged in erecting some kind of tent, Anke directing his troops like a would-be Pfiffmakler.

Lukitt sat watching by the window, listening to the happy sounds of Mingelstrossers making preparations: the boys getting charcoal barrels burning; the girls tending tables, laying them with clean linen, setting pots of wild flowers at their centres, small bowls of condiments appearing here and there along with jugs of lemonade, elderflower cordial, wine and beer; muslin draped over their tops to keep out the flies. Shouts coming up from the river as fish were caught.

'Something's biting!' came the cry, 'and this one! Come on lads, help me reel `em in!'

Lukitt's breath catching in his throat, envying this easy belonging, yet slightly repulsed at the same time. He remembered saying to Alameth that if his parents had stayed with the Herrnhuter he would have been just like this - an individual, certainly, but defined and bounded by the whole, one number in an equation that needed the rest to give them meaning and sense. Remembered that Christmas Eve of Fizz, Bang Wallop – a trick he'd never been able to figure out – and how the spills had been spread out on the table - always one outlier, one that fell further than the rest.

And that outlier, Lukitt knew, was himself.

He might envy this togetherness, these binding ties of family, but understood at his core that its claustrophobia was not for him. No matter how long he stayed with Xavier and the Mingelstrossers – and he hoped it would be a long time – he would never be one of them, would always be that single ash he'd seen at the Eberswald growing alone, away from the rest of the trees in the wood.

'You're back!' Alameth out of breath, having run from the lake and through the Lodge and up the stairs specifically to see if this was so.

'I am,' Lukitt agreed. 'Looks like all's going well,' waving towards the window, Alameth coming up beside him, face falling to see the whole surprise party in full view.

'You weren't supposed to know,' he said, turning toward Lukitt, such beseechment on his face. 'Please don't spoil it. They've gone to so much trouble.'

'This is all for me?' Lukitt asked, flabbergasted, proud nonetheless to know it.

'Xavier's idea,' Alameth rushed on, 'but please don't say you knew, please don't say.'

Lukitt laughed, a true and merry sound he did not often give, touching his finger to his lips.

'I'll not say a word. Just lead on, friend, lead on.'

And lead on Alameth did, bringing Lukitt out of the Lodge blindfolded, as previously agreed by the Mingelstrossers, Lukitt stepping with staggering gait over the grass down towards the lake, tripping on several stones, nothing to be heard but his own stumbling steps and the tits and flycatchers piping in the trees, and Alameth's soft breathing. And then the unmistakeable titters of several young boys trying to remain unobtrusive.

'Shhh, Edric!'

'I am shhhing.'

'Not very well.'

'Quiet, Jakob. Here he comes!'

'Quieter than a field mouse…'

'I said quiet, Jakob…'

And then Alameth whipped off Lukitt's blindfold as they reached the makeshift pavilion.

'Home is the hunter!' Xavier shouted, clapping his hands, everyone following suit, the entire Mingelstrosser family lined up before Lukitt outside the tent, clapping their hands with ever more enthusiasm.

'Home is the hero!' Filip shouted on cue, Lukitt not having to feign his surprise for he was overcome, had to be ushered to a seat where he was uncertain whether to laugh or cry, ended up doing both, all his previous misgivings about not belonging swept away in a rush of gratitude.

'But this is too much,' he protested. 'What's all this for?'

Xavier sat beside him, filling a glass, pushing it towards Lukitt.

'It's only what you're due, Lukitt,' Xavier said, sniffing back his own emotion. 'Only what you're due.'

'But I…'

'No buts, my lad, not tonight. I told you before what I thought of your discovery, that it's sent me leaps and bounds in new directions. So lean back, enjoy. And you'll never believe it, but we not long back caught three fat brown trout that are already sizzling on the burners. Three, I tell you! Never been done before!'

And oh, but they had a night of it, those three brown trout only the least, Xavier not wrong when he'd said that Ishbella would revel in the feast-making, she and her girls providing exactly that and the boys not slacking either, presenting a slapdash play under Alameth's shaky direction that had their audience splitting with laughter – and not only at the terrible jokes, but at the terrible manner in which they were performed.

It was late into the night, fireflies blinking in the trees, when Lukitt had a chance to talk to Xavier alone.

'I've been thinking,' he started, a little tentatively.

'Do you ever stop?' Xavier asked, pleasantly drunk, marking this evening as one he would never forget, the women back to the kitchen, the boys and Alameth away chucking themselves into the lake for a late night swim. Lukitt silent a moment, thinking maybe this was the wrong time to broach the subject, until Xavier turned to him, bade him spit it out, Lukitt swallowing and began.

'I went through all your work at Goslar,' he started.

'But of course you did,' Xavier breathed deeply of the night air that was still warm with the last hints of a late autumnal summer. 'What else would you do?'

Not irritated. Anything but.

'You might think this a bit of an imposition,' Lukitt began again, Xavier waving a hand through the air, dottling his pipe.

'I'm prepared for an imposition on this perfect night,' Xavier replied amiably, Lukitt nervous, steeling himself, recalling all those notes, all those arguments he'd memorised from Goslar to Quedlinburg.

'Well it's this,' he said, hoping he could get everything out the way he wanted. 'I don't think you should present any of the Goslar findings to Leipzig University. I believe there's a better alternative.'

Xavier halted his pipe-filling, swivelled in his seat, fixing his gaze on Lukitt, Lukitt rushing out his argument in one long line without hardly pause or breath.

'There's grounds, sir! Honestly there are. I've looked into it. Barbarossa built the Goslar chapel and took knights from the area on his Crusade in 1189; then there's his grandson, *Stupor Mundi*, who granted the charter making Hamburg a city, and there were Hamburg Knights at Leignitz with Von Salza, and we know Von Salza was the originator of the Goslar inscriptions that were later turned into the tapestry - probably by order of *Stupor Mundi* himself to celebrate the dead Von Salza; and then there's the throne – seat of power and their inscriptions too – and I haven't even started on all the burial sites at Luneburg, not to mention the Illyrian connection…'

'Stop a moment,' Xavier interrupted, bemused. 'Just stop a moment. What precisely are you saying?'

Lukitt breathed out, lowered his head, got to the nub of it.

'I'm saying,' he explained, 'that if you present your findings - the inscriptions, the tapestry, the throne - to the University in Hamburg, pointing out all that city's connections to your work, they might give you a post, make Leipzig a non-runner, get you out from under Rausgarten's thumb.'

Xavier raised his eyebrows.

'And how do you know I'm under Rausgarten's thumb, as you so elegantly put it?'

Lukitt cleared his throat.

'Annely,' he said very quietly, Xavier nodding slowly, understanding.

'So she told you,' he sighed. 'Not my finest hour. And not a decision any of us took lightly.' He considered Lukitt and his arguments, small smile on his lips, head to one side. 'I have to admit it's appealing. Releasing Annely from her promise would bring a great deal of happiness to many people, including me.'

'Excepting Rausgarten,' Lukitt said, after a beat.

'Excepting Rausgarten,' Xavier repeated, a chuckle growing in his throat as he leaned back in his chair, took off his glasses, wiped his eyes. 'You're quite something, Lukitt, you know that? Quite something,' a catch in his throat as he took it all in. 'And it just might work, by God. It might just work…'

Great smile on his face then, great lump in his throat as he placed a hand on Lukitt's shoulder and gave it a quick squeeze, unable to stop a few tears trickling down his cheeks.

'Welcome to the family, my boy,' he croaked, 'for if anyone has earned a place here then it's you.'

And if anyone could have been prouder at that moment, Lukitt didn't know who it could be.

The next few days taken up with Lukitt, Xavier and Alameth preparing Xavier's petition to Hamburg University, the Mingelstrossers to a body disappointed that the three of them chose the days after the Great Feast to huddle themselves up in the library, until they convened for dinner on the third evening.

'I can't tell you what's going on exactly,' Xavier announced, not wanting to give hope where it might not be warranted, 'but be assured it's for the good of us all.'

That created a buzz, questions firing in from every side.

'How for us?'

'What d'you mean?'

'Is it to do with Goslar?'

'Good in what way?'

'So we're not leaving here?' Jocken's voice broke through the mêlée, shrill with anxiety, silencing the storm, Xavier puzzled, seeing Jocken's lower lip trembling.

'Why would you think that?' he asked.

'Well, you talked about school. Last year,' Jocken whispered, 'about sending us down the valley.'

'Oh Jocken,' Ishbella was stricken, remembering the conversation she, Anke and Xavier had had about what might happen if Xavier didn't get St Wigbert's, if he was forced to some other site further afield. Marrying Annely off was bad enough, but if Xavier was not here to give the boys their schooling it would mean splitting the family up for good. How Jocken had heard about it was anyone's guess.

'Absolutely not!' Xavier gave comfort, St Wigbert's entirely forgotten, not a man to dwell on fights lost nor regret the losing. 'No, Jocken. Nothing like that. And in fact that reminds me: I must draw up some new plans for your book learning now I've a couple of helpers.'

Winking at Alameth and Lukitt; Filip and Rudiger exuding audible sighs, rolling their eyes, wishing Jocken had kept his mouth shut.

'So what's the big secret, Uncle Xavier?' Annely had her chin propped on her hands, looking at him intently, Xavier blinking under her scrutiny, the intensity of her gaze, that extraordinary combination of clear grey eyes flecked with green she'd inherited from her father, eyes that had floored Rausgarten the first time he'd met her when she was only thirteen, that would floor many more suitable men if only they were given the chance. Xavier uncomfortably hot about the collar, wanting to blurt it all out, reining it back in.

'I can't tell you,' Xavier said, shaking his head. 'At least not yet.'

Another barrage of questions:

'Not yet - so when?'

'You've got to tell us!'

'At least give us a hint.'

Xavier wishing he'd let the mystery lie and never brought the subject up, Lukitt coming to his rescue, nodding briefly at Xavier to assure him he wouldn't say too much.

'We're preparing a petition,' he stated, 'that might keep you all – and I mean all - in your home.'

Magic words reaching their target, everyone ameliorated; curious, but satisfied for now.

'Thank you, my boy,' Xavier said later, when they'd retired back to the library. 'I don't think I'll ever be able to thank you enough.'

Lukitt smiling – which he did a lot these days – but getting straight back to work.

'We've not nailed it yet,' he said, Xavier knowing it, slumping down into a chair, putting a hand over his eyes.

'But it's not such a risk,' Lukitt went on. 'Even if Hamburg refuses; and if Rausgarten gets wind of it he's surely far more likely to want to secure you at Leipzig and not the opposite.'

'Let's hope so,' Alameth put in, more serious than Lukitt had ever seen him. Alameth looking at Lukitt with the same intensity, the same hope he'd done all those years ago when Lukitt had first suggested the two of them leaving.

What if you could see the world, like you've always wanted to do?

Alameth remembering, Alameth remembering more than Lukitt suspected.

'Lukitt will not let us down,' Alameth stated, more for his own benefit than Xavier's. 'You'll not, Lukitt. I know you'll not. You didn't before and you won't do now.'

Lukitt couldn't answer. Lukitt went back to his books, a whole pile of them scattered open-faced on the table before them - their previous cataloguing and cross-referencing proving its worth.

'Have we enough, do you think?' Xavier asked, unable to

concentrate, his mind constantly skittering to the bad scenario of Anke having to give Annely away to Rausgarten and the boys to school down the valley. It hadn't seemed real when they'd previously discussed it, Ishbella aghast, Anke pragmatic, Annely wavering before stoically accepting her duty if it meant Xavier keeping his job and thereby keeping the family in the Lodge, together and safe.

'I think we've enough,' Lukitt said. 'I really do, but it would help if …oh, wait on!'

He jumped from his seat and ran quickly up the stairs to the second floor of the library, returning a couple of minutes later with yet another book, stumbling down the last few steps as he stabbed at one particular page with his finger, scanning the text before him, reading it out loud for the benefit of his companions.

'*Frederick the Second,*' he said, 'that's Stupor Mundi, *granted both Lübeck and Hamburg city status in 1226 and 1266 respectively, a century after each had been founded under the reign of his grandfather, Barbarossa. Between those two dates, however, a most momentous event occurred…* and this might just nail it!' Lukitt exclaimed, mind running ahead of his tongue, tripping over the next few words before getting back on track. '*…namely that in that year…Lübeck and Hamburg …formed an alliance to protect their Baltic trade routes, an alliance later joined by Lüneberg, along with Straslund, Wismar, Rostock and Greifwald…*'

Alameth frustrated by all the names, by too much history.

'Just get it said!' he pleaded, Lukitt smiling, nodding, laying the book out on the table, running his fingers along the next lines as he read them out.

'*Many scholars believe this initial alliance between Lübeck and Hamburg to be the true beginning - the birth - of the Hanseatic League, and therefore the founding moment of our country as a single nation, uniting itself by trade, if not by dictate.* And that year,' Lukitt concluded, face flushed, lips twitching, voice quiet and reverent as he pushed the book over to Xavier, who hardly dared believe what he was hearing.

'That year,' Lukitt went on, 'was 1241; same year as the Battle of Leignitz, the inscriptions in the Goslar crypt; this alliance the undoubted product of its aftermath.'

'Oh my!' Xavier finding it hard to get out words. Leaps and bounds, he'd said to Lukitt previously, but this a leap and bound he'd never have found by himself.

'Meaning what?' Alameth asked, not getting the gist.

'Meaning,' Xavier said, taking his time, ordering his thoughts, Lukitt ahead of him, willing Xavier to make the same deductions he'd done himself, Xavier doing precisely that.

'Meaning,' Xavier went on, blinking spasmodically behind his glasses, 'that there's a solid argument for Goslar and its contemporaneous depiction of the battle of Leignitz being the trigger for the formation of the Hanseatic League, and therefore the start point, the beating heart and soul of not only Hamburg but the unification of Germany. The final piece.'

He took off his glasses, laid them on the table and rubbed his tired eyes, Alameth looking from Xavier to Lukitt and back again.

'So you'll get your post at Hamburg?' Alameth breathed the words out, the desperate hope not passing Xavier by, Xavier not entirely ignorant of the growing intimacy between Annely and Alameth over these summer months; Xavier looking over the desk at his own small *Stupor Mundi* in the form of Lukitt Bachmann, who might just have saved them all.

'I think so,' Xavier agreed. 'I really...'

Interrupted by Alameth jumping wildly from his seat, swiftly crossing the room and kissing Lukitt on first one cheek and then the other – the monastic expression of brotherly benediction not made since he'd left the Abbey.

'I knew you'd not let us down,' he whispered. 'I knew it.'

46

Brandy and Wine

It's weeks since that day down by the lake when Annely plucked up a slender-stemmed, simple-petalled flower - Grass of Parnassus – and remarked how beautiful it was, Alameth daring to hold out his hand and place it to her cheek.

Not so beautiful as you.

Both blushing, both looking away.

And it's more weeks since Xavier's petition has gone to Hamburg, and now Anke Mingelstrosser is roaring up the steps into the Lodge clutching the letter he's just fetched up from Quedlinburg - where he's been waiting anxiously at the post depot every morning, since Xavier finally let him in on the secret before departing with Lukitt and Alameth back to Goslar.

Don't tell the family, Xavier had warned, *because if it doesn't come off then it will be too cruel.*

But come off it had, by God, and Anke couldn't keep the news in a moment longer, running through the Lodge towards the kitchen, almost bowling Ishbella over as she came out the door rubbing floury hands on floury apron at the commotion.

'Annely,' Anke gasped, breath coming short now he'd stopped moving. 'Where's Annely?'

'She's doing the laundry down at the lake,' Ishbella answered, concerned for her husband who looked about to have an apoplectic fit, face blotched with exertion and far too red, eyes too bright. But he quelled her fears, caught her by the waist and danced a sort of jig that had her corns throbbing, before thrusting Xavier's letter of acceptance to Hamburg University into her hands and leaping off again towards the lake.

And there was Annely, back bent above her washing-board, scrubbing a bed sheet against its rough surface: rinsing and pummelling, pummelling and rinsing. Anke stopping a few moments on the rise above, wanting breath enough to say the words he'd been longing to say ever since that wretched marriage agreement had been made.

'If you say no,' Xavier had said then, eyes wet with self-recrimination to even be suggesting the bargain, 'then so be it.'

'But if you lose your professorship then we'll also lose the Lodge?' Annely keeping her gaze steadfastly on the floor, hands twisting in her jam-smeared apron as they sat about the kitchen table, the pan of wild strawberries bubbling and burning on the stove.

'That's the size of it,' Anke had agreed miserably. 'If Mr Xavier doesn't get his post renewed next year then we're all at an end. Boys will have to be palmed off on my sisters and your mother's brother. And Lata, well…'

He'd glanced over at his wife for help but Ishbella couldn't speak, the thought of leaving the Lodge, dispersing her family, the worst of all possible scenarios.

'I'm so sorry,' Xavier whispered. 'I'd no idea how much debt I was in. My stupid museum. My stupid library…'

'But they're not stupid!' Annely had lashed out, her voice louder than she'd intended, but not the words. Not the words; lifting her face – flushed and furious, eyes flashing, enhancing exactly the features Rausgarten so desired – Annely looking from father to mother to Xavier, who was a third parent as far as she was concerned.

'They're not stupid, Uncle Xavier,' she'd ended with. 'They're not stupid at all. And one day someone is going to come along and make you realise it. And so of course I'm going to marry your stupid Rausgarten,' unable to find another adjective, 'and we'll all stay here. You'll stay here. And I'll be back the second stupid old Rausgarten kicks the bucket.'

Such fortitude, Anke had thought then, *such resilience*, prouder of his daughter than any of his wooden constructions, the Lodge included.

And now she'd been proved right; someone really had come along and made Xavier see the worth of his collections, put them to a use they could none of them have foreseen. Anke recalling his first encounter with Lukitt Bachmann, when the lad and his handsome friend had emerged from the forest, how he'd almost sent the two packing, how instead he'd brought them in.

And thank Christ for it.

He gathered himself as he made his way down the knoll towards Annely, seeing her arch her back, turn herself towards him as she heard him advance.

'Oh Annely,' Anke said, heart tumbling inside his chest as he moved towards her. 'I've the best of news, my dear. The very best of news.'

Two separate celebrations soon ensuing: one raucous, saturated with smiles and toasts of goodwill, the Lodge ringing with laughter, overflowing with food and drink, Lukitt a glowing and adored lamp at its centre, blessed and kissed and blessed again and again. Only Alameth unusually quiet and thoughtful.

And near Hamburg a more modest affair in the offing: Xavier meeting up with Rueland Klopstock who resided now in Lüneburg just outside the city, theoretical overseer of the Lüne Abbey Nunnery, though in practice he had very little to do.

'It's all women,' Rueland sighed, pouring his friend a drink, Xavier nodding sympathetically, both having decided early on in their careers that women were not for them, their studies too all-consuming to allow the restraints that came with marriage and the inevitable children that would follow. That Xavier had ended up with a large family – if by proxy – seemed not worth the mention.

'Why did you withdraw from the Komptership?' Xavier asked, perplexed, Rueland's recent letter unforthcoming, stating only that he'd retired to Lüneburg, should his friend ever be in the vicinity, as Xavier was now. Rueland adjusting his glasses as the tears welled up afresh.

'The Kompter died before he got to the Assembly,' Rueland answered quietly, unable to look up, fingers trembling about the stem of his glass. 'And he was such a good man, Xavier, such a good man. Every minute with him was as an hour spent with anyone less…'

Rueland broke off, upheaved by the grief that was raw in him now as it had been in Brummsberg, a plough he couldn't stop from churning up the same sorrow again and again.

'I didn't know,' Xavier said, mortified he'd not followed up on the old Kompter after their meeting, it never occurring to him to enquire, and hardly headline news. 'When did it happen?'

Rueland sniffed, rubbed his nose with his hand, took a large swig from his glass.

'That very night,' he sighed. 'That very night you saw him. Or rather, the morning after. His heart. Nothing to be done.'

He swept a hand across his forehead, attempting a smile.

'But let's not talk of that. You said this was to be a celebration?'

Xavier's returning smile as unconvincing as Rueland's, both recognising the need to move away from Rueland's deep bereavement.

'Well, well,' Xavier said, joviality aimed for if not achieved. 'Do you remember the young man who met with us in Brummsberg?'

Rueland creased his brows, Xavier grimacing at his mistake in mentioning Brummsberg and moving swiftly on.

'Well I set him to cataloguing my library – and there's things I need to tell you about that, but it can wait – but while doing so we came across an unknown exemplar called the Goslar Tapestry…'

And so the night went on, Xavier singing Lukitt Bachmann's praises, spelling out to Rueland all their researches and the pursuant excavations that had led them to this point.

'I'm finally on my right path,' Xavier finished. 'And without that lad I'd not be, and if that doesn't merit celebration then I don't know what does. Meet a newly appointed Professor of the University of Hamburg!'

And now Rueland genuinely smiled, some light at last penetrating his gloom.

'I'm so very glad,' he said, 'so very glad, Xavier. I felt terrible you were denied St Wigbert's, so terribly bad, but the old Kompter...'

Xavier put back his head and would have laughed had his friend not been so earnest. Instead he delved beneath his chair, brought a bottle from his knapsack, placed it on the table.

'Do you know what this is?' Xavier asked, Rueland shaking his head, regarding the fine string that been laid around the bottle's neck like a fisherman's net.

'This,' Xavier informed Rueland, 'is a bottle of apple brandy made by my grandfather. It's over sixty years old and we, my friend, are going to drink it.'

Xavier ceremoniously breaking the net, popping the cork, pouring a generous measure into their two glasses.

'To our futures,' Xavier happily announced. 'Me at Hamburg and you, well, you right here, amongst all the nuns.' He lifted his glass. 'May you find one who meets your favour.'

Xavier and Rueland clinking glasses, drinking, savouring the deep tones of the apple brandy, unaware of the festivities taking place at that same moment at the Lodge, where a not so old bottle had just been broken open.

'I gathered the fruit for this last autumn,' Annely was saying, glugging a small measure of blackberry wine into all their glasses – very small, in the case of her youngest brothers. 'Back then, I thought they might be the last blackberries here I'd ever pick but thanks to God,' she nodded at her father, 'but mostly thanks to Lukitt and Alameth,' - bigger nod, broader smile- 'there'll be no Rausgarten, and I'll be here – we'll all be here - to pick blackberries for as long and often as we choose.'

And if that didn't merit celebration…but of course it did.

47

Resolution

Xavier back at the Lodge a few days later, eager to organise his papers and research materials. Lukitt and Alameth had not been idle, Xavier greeted by the sight of several tidy towers of books lined up like a city roof-scape on his desks, all extracted from his library if even vaguely relevant to the work they would soon be undertaking.

'What's all this, lads?' he asked, delighted, rubbing his hands together, his eyes running over a few of the titles. *Castle and Tower: the archaeology of power in early Teutonic Buildings; Kingdoms and Crusaders; From Silk Road to Salt Mine - a personal exploration of the routes followed by the Mongol Khans; The Neolithic chambers of Lower Saxony; A Handbook of Ecclesiastical Stitch-work...* 'Well my! Haven't you been busy!'

'We've found every single book that might have relevance to Goslar and its surroundings,' Alameth was quick to explain, a little in awe that Lukitt's cataloguing system had thrown up so much. 'I don't know how we're going to get them all to Hamburg.'

'Oh we'll manage,' Xavier assured, 'even if I have to carry them on my back. And we've a fine work space waiting at the university. They've been very generous. I fear we might have ousted some ancient emeritus professor for the room they've allocated us is quite grand, with an entire wall taken up with shelves on which all these books will soon be rehomed.'

As if they were pigeons returning to their rightful roost.

Still there several hours later when the bell in the courtyard rang, Alameth away on a run having something urgent needed doing, Xavier and Lukitt lingering, tacitly electing to remain until the second gong called them.

'I've so much to thank you for, Lukitt,' Xavier said quietly, lifting sheaves of papers from his drawers to keep himself occupied, deep emotions coming to the fore about Annely and not easily dealt with;

glancing over at Lukitt, whose eyes were glittering oddly in the light of the single lamp left them, Alameth having taken the other to guide his way.

'You've done so much,' he went on, 'without you I'd've...'

He interrupted his thanksgiving, eyes automatically scanning the latest paper delved from out his drawer.

'Without you I'd've...' he repeated absently, before stopping short. 'But what's this?' Xavier shuffling through a few pieces of paper, singling several from the rest, holding up first one and then the other, brows drawn together as he studied them, his expression as baffled as it had just been thankful. 'Have you being going through my private correspondence?'

Sweat prickling from Lukitt's armpits, dread in every pore, recognising immediately what Xavier had ferreted out, cursing himself for not covering his tracks when he'd had the chance, when he'd first realised his mistake. Xavier laying down those several sheets covered with Lukitt's own accusatory handwriting, Xavier's eyes roving over them, lips reading out several key passages:

First and proper name: the Fratrum Theutonicorum Ecclesiae... *Rueland Klopstock: pious, austere... Thaddeus Münzenberg... Cornelius Steggle... Züstraubben's man... It won't be long, old friend, before I take on the mantle...*

'I don't understand,' Xavier said, scratching his neck in consternation. 'Why would you be going through my letters? And why on earth would you be making notes about Rueland and the Kompter's possible successors?'

Lukitt had no answer, couldn't find the words, couldn't look at Xavier.

The second gong ringing out into the silence that fell between them, neither reacting, both waiting until it was done, taking the time of its doing to come to their own conclusions.

'It was an...intellectual exercise,' Lukitt got out with huge effort, 'after I read your paper on St Wigbert's... and because Vannevar led me to believe... well...led me to believe...that you...'

Stuttering to a stop.

'So you read my paper on St Wigbert's,' Xavier repeated dully, a chasm opening up through which approached a torrent of fear and comprehension that would not be stopped. 'And your conclusion,' Xavier went on, tapping a finger on Lukitt's notes, 'before I told you what utter rubbish it was, was that Rueland or the Kompter…were standing in the way of my work?'

The torrent snaking through its narrow walls, funnelling towards the rapids, thundering over the stones of understanding, washing them clean. Xavier shaking his head slowly from side to side, pushing his fingers below his glasses, rubbing at his eyes. Thinking on Vannevar; Lukitt sent to him from Vannevar, a man whose ambition so far exceeded his aptitude it was as a bird pecking at a mountain; Vannevar, a man who needed money to further his ludicrous pretentions to luminary ancestry; Vannevar, whose wife had so inexplicably died.

'I can't believe what I'm thinking,' he whispered, 'and that I'm thinking it of you.'

But thinking it he was, remembering Rueland telling him the old Kompter had died not long after they'd been to see him, how close Lukitt had been to the water jug before Xavier himself had passed that same water to the old Kompter.

'Please tell me you didn't…' Xavier clung to the hope. 'Please tell me…'

But Lukitt could not.

He could have lied, could have pleaded, was about to explain the whole set of convoluted circumstances that had led him from his unremarkable past to this unwanted present; how he'd been manipulated by first one person and then another; how because of them he'd been primed to see what wasn't there; how his purpose had been good, to keep him and Alameth safe.

He opened his mouth to get out his defence but Xavier was quicker, saw the appalling truth writ large on Lukitt's face and hammered both fists down on the desk, making the papers shiver with anticipation.

'So you've made of me a murderer!' Xavier shouted, voice hoarse with rage and despair, whipping up from his seat and striking Lukitt a hard blow across the side of his head that sent him staggering to one side, Lukitt so shocked by this deviation from Xavier's everyday character that he made no move to defend himself, fell hard against another section of the desk, hands dislodging a pile of books as he fought for his balance and lost, crumpling to the floor, the books falling with him, muzzy thoughts of alarm to see them settle in a haphazard muddle, pages torn and caught, spines cracking, eyes randomly flicking from one title to another: *Hidden Tribes of the Dark Ages; The Cherusci and the Celts; The Early...*

And then he was on the move again, Xavier catching Lukitt up by his collar and hauling him to his heels, Lukitt's head a-swirl with internal maelstrom, bile in his throat, Xavier pushing him backwards onto the now emptied desk, Lukitt's head hitting the wall behind as Xavier gripped a hand against Lukitt's throat to keep his enemy upright, strong shovel-wielding fingers itching to squeeze and squeeze and squeeze…

'You made me kill a man,' Xavier's words soft, face pale and clammy as a fish belly.

Lukitt struggling to focus, head pounding, but such rage he registered on that still face, and such disappointment, the grip about his throat tightening like a vice, like Lukitt was a bad slice of wood that needed cutting off. He didn't fight it. An end for an end. A life for a life, or three lives if he had to be exact - and Lukitt had to be exact, even to the last.

He let out a long sigh, allowed his tears to slip out without any notion to stop them.

All done now, words falling through his head with abandon, like sunlight through trees, glad the subterfuge was over.

Forgive me, he mouthed, Xavier reading them, remembering Lukitt's soft words to the old Kompter - *forgive me father, for I have sinned* – and the Kompter's finger on Lukitt's forehead tracing out the sign of the cross, Xavier closing his eyes, regaining his moral compass, dropping his hand, stepping away, eyes leaking – not with anger now but sorrow for all that had happened, and for what must come next.

48

Followed by Realisation and Retribution

Alameth had run swift as a Mongol messenger from the library and over the walkway linking the towers to the lodge, heart and soul burning within him, knowing this had to be the night if they were to leave for Hamburg tomorrow as planned.

Got to be tonight, the words looping through his head over and over, hardly able to believe he could have reached such a point to be considering what he was considering, had been considering ever since Xavier had gained his professorship at Hamburg.

Oh my Lord, give me strength, he whispered as he left the outer gallery and gained the corridor. He could hear the family chatting animatedly in the dining room below, hesitated at the top of the stairs, breathing deeply, trying to hold his nerve, focussing on the morning after the Feast when they'd been sitting together by the lake…the flower…his fingers touching her cheek…

But not as beautiful as you.

Alameth desperately hoping he wasn't wrong, that he'd not misinterpreted the signals, that he could go through with it, that she would understand when he told her all – and he would have to tell her all. The whole ghastly lot of it. And if she would be repulsed, disgusted, or able to see him for what he was: a boy plucked from the monastery just as she'd plucked up…

And then there she was: Annely, just returned from ringing the gong and checking on the goats; Annely standing as elegant and graceful as that flower, gazing up at him, a look of curious expectation on her face.

'Alameth,' she breathed out his name as he flew down the stairs to greet her, heart and body in a flurry, all reason gone, needing to get it done, however it went, tripping down the last two steps and almost toppling into her.

'I'm only going to ask the once,' he said, getting his balance – though how he got the words out he didn't know – 'and if you refuse then you refuse, but if you'll have me then…then…'

Annely laughing, Annely crying, Annely laying her head upon his shoulder and winding an arm about his waist.

'It took you long enough,' she whispered, Alameth folding into Annely, Annely folding into him, Alameth whispering into her ear, *there's things I have to tell you first*…Annely not caring and saying so, neither spying Anke Mingelstrosser standing on the threshold, smiling broadly, slipping himself back out through the open door, holding up his face to the gentle rain, whispering *Hallelujahs* to his God.

'You've to leave,' Xavier said, nothing in those three words to give Lukitt any hope, and no more afterwards. 'And you've to leave tonight. I can't bear to look at you, can't bear to have you under my roof.'

'Alameth…' Lukitt began, everything about him broken, head aching, throat sore from Xavier's hard grip, feeling like he'd been shoved headfirst into a cellar and unable to crawl his way out.

'Alameth,' Xavier barked out a laugh that was anything but. 'If you tell me you've dragged him into any of this then…'

'I haven't,' Lukitt whispered. 'Not this nor…before.'

'Before!' that harsh laugh again, Xavier ahead of him. 'Vannevar, no doubt, or rather Vannevar's wife. And to think I gave that man my sympathy, took you on because of it.' He shook his head before going on. 'Any more you care to confess?'

Lukitt an empty shell, hearing the clicking of Napier's bones deep inside him as he added up his options, rattled out his answer. No point lying now.

'Only one,' he whispered. 'Some relative of Hans Trudbert. I never met him.'

'And that makes it all right?' Xavier shouted, his anger back in a flash, staring daggers at Lukitt who thankfully had his head down or Xavier might not have been able to control himself, Xavier forcing himself to stay calm, keep himself in check, needing to understand. Unable to understand. Speaking quietly now.

'What made you think you had the right to do any of this? What on God's good earth could make you think you had the right?'

Lukitt stared at his feet, unable to lift his head. One chance, and only one.

'I'd no right,' he murmured. 'No right at all. But I was given no choice. Not the first two times.'

Xavier took off his glasses, rubbed his face with his hands. He'd no knowledge at all of Hans Trudbert, but Vannevar was a different matter. He could well believe such a man could manipulate without compunction a lad like Lukitt, place him in an impossible situation, especially if he already knew what Lukitt had apparently done for Trudbert. But whatever the reasons, however it had started, the choice to act or not had to lie with Lukitt.

And the Kompter…well, that he could not forgive, not given the consequences for Rueland. He breathed deeply before reiterating what he'd said before.

'You've to leave. And tonight. You may have had no choice before but neither do I now.'

He replaced his glasses, looked at Lukitt, felt a stab of pity to see the boy so shattered, to see him nod his head in abject acceptance, as if he'd always known it would come to this.

'And Alameth?' Lukitt asked, lifting his head, trying to meet Xavier's gaze and failing, letting his eyes drift off towards the small window to Xavier's right, nothing to be seen but the darkness of the night and the deeper darkness of the forest beyond.

'Alameth will be taken care of,' Xavier said shortly. 'Alameth will stay here with us. You've no fear he'll come to harm.'

'And me?' Lukitt asked, more of himself than of Xavier. 'What will become of me?'

Xavier did not respond immediately, let his eyes rest upon his desk, upon the piles of unspilled books, the papers, the boxes of cataloguing cards Lukitt had so assiduously arranged and ordered, representing all Lukitt had done for him and his own. He cleared his throat, made a decision.

'I'll give you one week,' Xavier announced, his voice catching in his throat. 'One week for you to get yourself away before I inform the authorities with all I know.'

Lukitt nodding, Xavier giving him more than he had a right to.

Lukitt leaving.

Lukitt heading out across the open walkway blindly, without a lamp, the rain falling upon him.

Lukitt looking down upon the courtyard below, seeing Anke Mingelstrosser sitting on the edge of the fountain, seeing the blurred outlines of the Theodoric portrait in the wet cobbles, Lukitt's heart lurching, Lukitt's heart tearing itself apart inside him for all he'd done, all he'd now never do.

Lukitt throwing his few possessions into the same bag he'd brought with him from Lenze and before that from the Seiden See.

Lukitt thinking on Père Ulbert, on his mother, wondering if she could save him. But no. To return and confess would be unbearable for both him and her.

One week to get away, to get ahead, to save himself.

Stealing his way across the courtyard – Anke having thankfully deserted – hearing some loud Mingelstrosser voices from inside the Lodge, unable to make out what they were apparently celebrating, but oddly glad he wouldn't have to hear them celebrating ever again.

Lukitt still the outlier, always the outlier.

Not sure it would be enough.

49

And Celebration

Entering the dining room, Xavier fought to keep his nerves under control, though it wasn't immediately necessary. The entire place was in uproar, Alameth having apparently just asked Annely to be his wife, proposition rapturously accepted by Annely and the entire family.

'But we've got to tell Lukitt!' Alameth exclaimed. 'Where's Lukitt?'

Alameth looking over at Xavier with gleaming eyes that could not have been happier, Xavier havering, but only for a moment.

'He's had to leave rather suddenly, I'm afraid,' he stated baldly. 'Family problems. Got a message a while back.'

No one questioning the ruse, everyone accepting it, getting on with their perfect joy.

'It's got to be a winter wedding!' Ishbella ecstatic, her daughter's leanings towards Alameth old news to her.

'And a pageant!' put in Filip.

'With real fireworks!' Rudiger enthused.

Xavier switching himself off, no one noticing except Anke.

'Everything all right, Professor?' Anke asked, Xavier feeling the tears again, the awful loss, the awful waste. Conjuring up a smile.

He'd have to give them all an explanation, but not now.

Oh the Lord, Anke's perfect God, not now.

50

On the Trail of the One-Eyed Monkey

From the moment Lukitt left the Lodge he found it hard to think straight, mind rolled up like a hedgehog in the face of danger, little prickles of thought repeatedly coming to the fore: what will Ulbert think when news reaches him…what will his mother think?

Terrible guilt at all he's done, but terrible anger too.

Absolute rage towards Hans Trudbert and Vannevar of how they'd exploited him, exploited Alameth's suffering towards their own ends.

But no chance of help from either quarter, they'd made sure of that.

Mad thought of tracking down the Pfiffmaklers, hiding within their peripatetic anonymity, but no. That wouldn't do. No earthly way of finding them. No last chance of hearing Heraldo play his lute, seeing Ludmilla and Longhella doing yellow cartwheels in the snow going faster and faster, skirts burning orange like St Catherine's wheels. Remembering the origin of the phrase: of Catherine's persecutors trying to break her on a spiked wheel, a punishment still used in some parts of this land.

He comes out of the tree line, heads the opposite way from Quedlinburg.

It's the middle of October, a tingle of frost in the air; Lukitt seeing the round speckled body of a little owl going quick down from its perch to pluck up a cockchafer, thinks of Pregel falling – his bitterness from back then distilled into the poison he has become.

One week to get ahead.

It isn't long, not on foot, but the drive to survive is strong and won't let him be. He gets as far as he can that night, guided by the lamps in the windows of outlying farms until the last is extinguished, when he hunkers down in a barn. Can't sleep, spends his time scanning the sky for the arrival of a dawn he doesn't want to come. Forms a plan: head for Dortmund, a city large enough to get lost in, find his way from there to the North Sea, disappear on the boats that ply about the Frisian Islands where surely no one would expect him to go. He could grow a beard, gain passage on a vessel to Scandinavia. But his navigation skills are rusty and, four days in – when he deems it safe enough to hitch a few rides, takes a few carriages with the meagre supply of money he has to hand - discovers he's drifted too far south. Changes plans, decides he may as well aim for the Rhein, get over the river into another country, maybe another life.

He's surprised at the evident civil unrest as he goes deeper into the countryside to the south-east of Dortmund, where crops have failed again and famine is rife, cholera decimating villages, castle storehouses being ransacked, ransackers slaughtering any animals they can find for food, including several exotic menageries: a grim humour in the thought of starving men and women laying out the carcasses of lions, bears and ostrich in their makeshift fire pits.

Lukitt at first welcomes this chaotic interruption to the norm, until he realises that each minor insurrection is being stamped out with maximum force, soldiers and militia flooding to these outbreaks of revolution to squash them down, put the bickering peasants in their place.

But no news of any hunt for him, even though it's two weeks into his travelling, for here in these lands of unrest he's but one murderer amongst the many, so a little hope yet, unless he's put down accidentally with the rest.

Time to be moving on, and with rapidity.

He steals a skin-thin horse – not so hard in these desperate times – abandons it before he crosses the water at Montebeliard, setting off on foot again, not a coin in his pocket and only one place - one name - to head for: Jacques, from the boats in Liguria, who'd treated him and Alameth with such kindness, who'd said that when he retired – and he surely must be retired by now – that he'd be back home quick as he could, spend his days gazing over familiar landscapes, dipping his fishing rod into the Rhein. Lukitt scouring his head for the name, eventually has it, for it had been unusual and Lukitt had always liked unusual: Sansonnet-St-Genès, first part meaning starling, second referring to the martyr Genesius the Actor, some old legend having it that he'd taken part in a mocking version of a Christian baptism – an Archimimus in the making – until he'd been struck by the truth of it, the holiness of the sacrament - converting on the spot, rewarded by immediately having his head chopped off.

Either way, it was Sansonnet-St-Genès Lukitt reached two days before the end of October, directed to Jacques' cottage, easily distinguished, being the only one backing directly onto the village cemetery, the rest neatly sewn on either side of the main street.

It's dark, moonlight making the dew-frost on the gravestones sparkle.

Lukitt knocks hesitantly on the door of the tiny cottage; hears nothing at first, and then a shuffling followed by the door opening, Lukitt blinking in the light of the lamp Jacques is holding up to see who is his visitor.

'It's me,' Lukitt says, 'Lukitt Bachmann. From the *Ligia Liliana*.'

Jacques frowns. It's been years since he's heard that name or seen this boy, this man - two weeks bearded and not looking like any Lukitt Bachmann he ever knew - but he recognises the provenance and motions Lukitt in.

'Lukitt?' he asks. 'But what on earth? How are you here?'

'It's a bit of a yarn,' Lukitt sighs, reverting to ship-speak as he steps across the threshold, looking about him for the one-eyed monkey, but the one-eyed monkey has long since died and been buried at the edge of the graveyard where Jacques can visit him every day. Not that the villagers know – God forbid.

Jacques pulls out a chair for Lukitt about a sparse table, Jacques studying Lukitt and realising that yes, it really is him, the greenhorn on the *Liliana* whom he'd taught how to gut and split bloaters before loading them into barrels of salt.

'Well then,' Jacques says, fetching a bottle from a cupboard, poking at the fire, 'if yarns is involved, then I'm your man – as you'll no doubt remember.'

'I do,' Lukitt avers, sitting down, dog-tired, yet eager to tell his story, state his case, spill it all out, too much held inside him for too long. And no danger here, no judgement, not with Jacques; Jacques pouring out his drinks late into the night as Lukitt pours out his soul.

'Well that's a tale and a half,' Jacques exclaims when Lukitt has finished, but knowing all too well the Alameth part of it: pretty boys on rough-crewed boats never ending well. 'Seems like good luck's brought bad with it every step of the journey,' he added philosophically. 'Happens like that sometimes, had an uncle the same. Used to say his good fortune had a shadow it just couldn't shake.'

Lukitt skews a crooked smile at the analogy, thinking it apt, a little cheered he's not the only one.

'Anyone see you arrive?' Jacques asks, scratching his grizzled chin.

'Only a man I asked directions of. Pedlar, I think. Had a cart of stuff he was pulling behind him.'

Jacques nodding, assessing the situation.

'All to the good. That'll have been Simeon, and he'll be moving on in the morning. So, my young friend, time to get you hid whilst we thinks ourselves up a solid plan.'

Lukitt so relieved he finds it difficult to speak, his whispered thank you hardly adequate for the occasion but Lukitt so very weary and grateful he can get out no more, Jacques' acceptance of his situation given with a grace Lukitt finds so reassuring he almost nods off straightaway into sleep.

'Been a rough ride you've had,' Jacques says mildly, helping Lukitt to his feet, steering him towards the door. 'Let's see if I can't lighten the load.'

And so it's to the Lanterne des Mortes Jacques takes Lukitt under cover of night.

'No one to find you here,' Jacques murmurs, as he leads Lukitt to the stone steps that spiral up the inner wall of the tower, settling him by the broken bowl of the bell, bringing up blankets, some straw for bedding, a small supply of food and water, a pail.

'Get yer head down,' he says kindly, as Lukitt settles on his makeshift bed, Lukitt grabbing Jacques' hand before he leaves, closing his own about it.

'I can't thank you enough,' Lukitt says, eyes brimming with tears, Jacques gently shaking him off, brushing away his thanks.

'Got to look after our own,' he says. 'Did it back on the boats and no reason not to do it now. Hush you down and get yourself a good kip. Let tomorrow bring what it will bring.'

Lukitt sleeping well and deep for the first time since he's left the Lodge, dreaming fragmented scenes of Mingelstrossers, of Xavier, Alameth and Pregel, and in the morning Jacques arrives with good news.

'Got a scheme to get you out,' he says, holding a finger to his lips to stop Lukitt yelling out his relief. 'Gotta keep it quiet, lad. No one's to know you're here if it's gonna work.'

Lukitt nods, takes the bread, cheese and sausage Jacques hands up to him.

'Good,' Jacques says, casting a quick glance over his shoulder in case they're overheard, which they're not – the two ensconced in the Lanterne des Mortes that is Jacques' purview, and his alone. He'd wanted a farm, Lukitt remembered, but apparently that hadn't panned out, Jacques' job now to care-take the tower and its graveyard.

'All Hallows Eve tonight,' Jacques went on, 'so the whole of St-Genès in a bit of a flutter. Superstitious lot,' he added with a soupçon of disgust, Lukitt smiling, for a more superstitious lot than sailors was hard to imagine. 'Once everyone's gone,' Jacques went on regardless, 'that's when we'll make our move. I'll come calling when it's safe and we'll get you out of here. Should have some papers by then, new name and a bit of cash to get you on your way.'

Jacques begins to duck his body down from the casement but Lukitt stops him.

'Wait,' he says, 'just a moment.'

Jacques obliges, his head popping up again into view, Lukitt seeing Jacques' embarrassment writ plain across the parts of his face between cap and beard.

'This is a big thing you're doing for me,' Lukitt says, 'and I'll not forget it, and if ever I make good I'll bring it back your way three fold – seven fold - soon as I'm able.'

Jacques smiles awkwardly, tipping his cap in brief acceptance.

'Just do what I say and let's hope this piece of good luck don't come with the bad tripping on its tail.'

Then he's away, Lukitt listening to Jacques' slow retreat down the tower, navigating the stone steps badly, smiling when Jacques swears as vile an oath as ever he'd mouthed on the *Ligia Liliana* when he misses his footing. Hardly able to believe he'll soon be down those same steps, heading off into the night, never to be heard of again by anyone who knows him; excepting Jacques, for that's a promise he means to keep.

All Hallows Eve and late, the ghosts and their descendants having departed a while since from their festivities. The bowl-light flickers across the walls and Lukitt waits, wishes the moth that had visited earlier would return, but of course it does not. Why would it? It's escaped once into the night and once is enough. Lukitt shivers, wonders how much longer he can stand his life, how much longer Jacques will be. It's cold, ice forming on the rim of the bell-bowl, tippering into the oil below, silver slivers of it in his badly grown beard. His gloves are frozen solid with his breath, housing fingers he can no longer feel. He's nodding, almost dreaming, when he finally hears Jacques, the sound that heralds his passage into a new and better life.

'Lukitt,' Jacques' call is soft, just as they'd planned, not wanting to arouse any residents of the village who might still be abroad, though the possibility is slim, it being almost three in the morning.

Lukitt prises himself up from his blankets, stumbling into a crouch, tries to straighten his knees.

'You've to hurry,' Lukitt hears Jacques. 'Not much time!'

His voice is urgent, Lukitt lowering himself from the hatchment, a horrid moment as he thinks he's seeing the shade of the one-eyed monkey glaring at him from the stone, but it's only Jacques' shadow pulled into a point as it curves around the wall.

He takes a breath, gets his feet planted on the stones of the staircase, slipping on the ice that has formed in the small curves made by frequent usage, hands braced against the wall. He hears a noise outside – the snickering of a pony unpleased to have been put into action so late in the night, or early in the morning, depending on how you looked at it. Either way Lukitt is relieved, and takes the final steps with happiness in his heart, feet meeting the earth of the tower in utter darkness, a hand immediately cupped about his elbow as Jacques tells him once again to hurry, Lukitt obliging, stumbling in the darkness, only Jacques to guide him to the door of the Lanternes des Mortes and outside.

'Ready, old friend?' Jacques' voice is subdued, croaked, as befits the mission.

'Ready,' Lukitt replies, as Jacques flings open the door to the tower, gives a shove to the base of Lukitt's back that sends him sprawling, Lukitt making out in the darkness beyond something barring his way, no time to register that it's not a cart, not a horse, nor any means of rescue, but a man in heavy boots, and not only one man: two soldiers grabbing him, hoisting him up by the armpits, slamming his face into the rough stone of the tower as they throw ropes about his wrists, have him hogtied in thirty seconds and on the ground.

'Jacques!' Lukitt's shout muffled by the frosty mud, not understanding what's occurring.

'Jacques!' he yells again as he's dragged across the short-tipped grass, is picked up, thrown into a waiting tumbrel like a slaughtered side of beef, cheek and shoulders cracking as they hit the cold tar of its boards.

'Jacques!' Lukitt screams, his panic and confusion interrupted as the tumbrel jerks forward, the pulling pony's flanks getting into unsteady motion, whipped on by the soldiers walking an easy pace beside it.

'Keep it shut,' one of them growls at Lukitt. 'Ain't gonna go better for any yelling you can do.'

'I don't understand,' Lukitt whimpers.

'He don't understand!' the soldier beside him mocks, poking him in the back with his whip.

'I bet he don't!' says the other with glee. 'Thought you'd gotten away fancy free, didn't you? But ain't that the way? Friends just ain't what they used to be, an' that's a fact.'

And that indeed was the fact; Jacques' village no better off than those Lukitt had so recently passed through, negligible amounts of stores set up for winter, Alsace still part of the Confederation of the Rhein and no hard thing for Jacques to confer with the local militia and discover that a murderer was a murderer, no matter he was far from the scene; that goodness would flow from the local overseer's coffers if the goods were worth the price.

And these goods were worth the price, the Electors in nearby Mannheim eager to take up the offer, deliver Lukitt back to where he'd come from, which was none other than Hamburg, the second most powerful city in the whole of Germany, and a city, moreover, that had only the previous year – in 1847 – seen the founding of the HAPLAG: the Hamburg-Amerkanische Paketfahrt-Aktiengesellschaft, guaranteeing maritime trade between Hamburg and the Americas. Mannheim fighting tooth and nail to be a part of it, and this their chance for favour.

Lukitt Bachmann, Saviour of Sansonnet-St-Genès by his serendipitous search for sanctuary, being taken back to the place from which he'd fled. If Jacques had a keen sense of irony it didn't register as he watched the stumbling cart move out of his village from the base of the Lanternes des Mortes into the depths of the night. He'd instead paradoxical feelings of both regret and relief, though neither lasted long, not once he made his way back towards his cottage, pausing briefly at the rough mound of rambling rose he'd planted on the grave of the only life companion he'd ever really valued.

'Hated to do it, my wee monkey boy,' he murmured as he placed a foot amongst its undergrowth, 'but times like this, something's gotta give. Our good luck, old fella, had to be his bad and nowt to be done about it.'

And nowt indeed to be done; Lukitt taken from the village over the river to Mannheim where he wrote his confession full and plain, Lukitt recalling Opapa Augen telling him how every unreasonable act has an underlying logic of its own, even if that logic is flawed. Logic no help to Lukitt, who was sent afterwards in manacles and foot irons from Mannheim back to Hamburg, where Xavier had given him up.

An awful travelling, uncomfortable, as frozen as he'd been in the bell tower; made so much worse when he learned how abuzz everyone apparently was by his capture and upcoming trial, that it had been broadcast far and wide. That Alameth and all the Mingelstrossers would soon know it too - a blow Xavier had tried to save him from by denouncing him in Hamburg, far away from Quedlinburg, which had backfired. A blow that had Lukitt curling up in his cart amongst the foul straw that he himself had made foetid and was the source of its stench.

Several times he tried to throw himself over the edge to destroy himself, each time failing, held fast by his guard. Lukitt wishing Xavier had not given him the chance of escape, only for it to come to this.

51

There's Lawyers, and Then There's Lawyers

Arriving at the courts in Hamburg, Lukitt was met by a lawyer who appeared at least sympathetic, listened to all Lukitt had to say, nodding gently, murmuring softly some legalese about coercion.

'Leave it with me,' he said, gathering up his papers, smiling encouragingly, Lukitt garnering a faint sliver of hope. Nurturing that hope until his day in court when the lawyer took to his stand and - with such casual cruelty it scrubbed Lukitt's mind clear of conscious thought - turned Lukitt's defence on its head, began to read out the deposition Lukitt had made to the Mannheim authorities, emphasising the most culpatory sections, no hint now of coercion, nor the primary reasons that had set him on his course.

'And to top it all off,' Lukitt's lawyer declaimed loudly, staring over his glasses towards his audience – the court house filled to the gunwales with gawkers and tittlers of tat – 'I have here in my hands,' waving a couple of pieces of paper, wax seals blood red against the parchment, 'the sworn statements of both Herr Hans Trudbert and Professor Vannevar – both upstanding and important members of their communities, whom our young defendant has had the temerity to slander - both absolutely insistent that whatever he did, he did on his own. And if we can't believe men like them in these troubled times, then who can we?'

Lukitt's heart clenching at the injustice, gazing up into the gallery, seeing the pale faces of the Mingelstrosser family in a wan line; Alameth soul-shaken and distraught beside them, hands lifted to his cheeks, lips parting as the breath went out of him; Xavier patting Alameth's back in an abject attempt at comfort; Xavier looking down upon Lukitt, closing his eyes, lowering his head, glasses misting over with a sadness he could not quench, knowing all too well where this was going and why, unable to intervene or intercede.

Several times Xavier had approached Lukitt's lawyer before the trial began, putting himself forward to speak for the defendant's character since he'd learned from Alameth the dire circumstances they'd been in that had led to murder one, and from murder one to murders two and three. Xavier going to great lengths to obtain a copy of the Mannheim Confession, the gaps filled in about the how, the where and the why. Lukitt trapped from the start, a hare set off with hounds of the worst order on his tail.

Xavier sick at heart for his misjudgement, and then outraged.

Xavier's arguments for mitigating circumstances denied at every turn, not least by Lukitt's lawyer.

'But this is monstrous!' Xavier had protested at their last meeting

'More monstrous than killing three people entirely unprovoked?' the lawyer countered.

'But that's exactly the point!' Xavier argued. 'They were entirely provoked, but by third parties. You know it as well as I do. You've read the Mannheim Deposition. Lukitt couldn't have been clearer.'

The lawyer raised his eyebrows, peering over his glasses at Xavier.

'And we're to take the word of a self-confessed murderer that this really was the case? That a respected man of commerce like Hans Trudbert truly conspired to get his uncle killed?'

'But of course!' Xavier replied hotly. 'How else to explain the uncle's receipt of the hamper? How could Lukitt possibly have known where it was to be sent? And for what purpose, if not for Trudbert's advancement? And what about Vannevar? He stood to gain richly from his wife's premature death, and I know that man. He'd soon enough strangle his own grandmother than give up his researches. And what on earth would Lukitt have gained by killing Vannevar's wife?'

The lawyer had the grace to fiddle with his glasses and clear his throat.

'I'm sorry,' he said, turning away 'It's out of my hands.'

'Out of your hands?' Xavier was exasperated. 'What do you mean, *out of your hands*?'

He knew Lukitt couldn't be saved from prosecution, but surely something could be said for vindication, mercy and leniency. The entire Mingelstrosser family were of the same opinion and, privately to Xavier and Lukitt's lawyer, Alameth had volunteered to stand up and say what no man should ever have to say about what had been done to him on the boats, which course of action Xavier absolutely forbade. The only point on which Xavier and Lukitt's lawyer agreed, only other people knowing of it being Annely and Anke.

'It would add nothing except more gossip,' the lawyer declared, 'and we can do without any more of that.'

'But we can allude to the bonded service,' Xavier argued, 'that Count Udolpho had them both tied into. And them not alone – thousands of men and boys shackled like slaves to badly paid jobs they can't get of. Surely we can mention that?'

The lawyer shaking his head, quoting what he'd been told to say from those up above.

'The maintenance of social order is of far more importance than the fate of a single itinerant fisherman.'

Beginning to walk away, halted by Xavier grabbing the man's arm, keeping him still.

'But it's not right,' Xavier stated bluntly. 'None of this would have happened if Lukitt and Alameth had been given a fair deal of employment in the first place. And it's not just in Italy. It's all around us. Why the hell do you think the entire country is up in arms? It's because of exploitation exactly like this!'

Xavier swinging the lawyer around, the lawyer shoving Xavier's hand roughly off.

'You may know it, and I may know it!' he shouted. 'But we both also know the entire populace is on the boil, and this trial cannot become the microcosm of the whole! I can't go down because of it.'

Pushing his fingers beneath his glasses, taking a breath.

'They want blood, and example,' he went on, 'them upstairs. I'm only sorry it's me has to deliver it, but I've my own family to think of.'

'But it's going to be a travesty,' Xavier said, the lawyer nodding, the weight of the world on his shoulders because of it. Not a bad man, but coerced, just as Lukitt had been. They irony of the situation not lost on him.

'I know,' he said quietly. 'And don't think I don't regret it.'

Walking away, leaving Xavier dumbstruck behind him, knowing Lukitt was lost.

Two days later Xavier looked down on Lukitt as the trial proceeded, the beleaguered lawyer summing up, doing as he'd been told.

'In short,' he said, 'I think we must conclude that Lukitt Bachmann is a fantasist of the worst order, seeing instruction and conspiracy where there were none, prone by nature to murderous thoughts, acting on them whether anyone else liked it or no; constructing for himself a framework no one else could see. In such circumstances I could ask for clemency due to an imbalance of the mind, but I cannot, for I do not for a moment believe it warranted.'

Sitting down, case closed, small murmur of protest rising from the gallery, specifically from the Mingelstrossers.

'But it's not true!' Lone voice in the wilderness, Alameth leaping to his feet. 'You've got to tell them, Lukitt. You've got to tell them why…'

'Silence in the courtroom!'

Gavel slammed, judge pronouncing.

'Sit down, young man, or I'll have you arrested.'

'But he'd reasons! He was only trying to help…'

Alameth pulled back to his seat by Annely on one side and Xavier on the other.

'There's nothing we can do,' Xavier whispered fiercely, knowing the truth of it as Alameth did not.

Blessed is the man who lays down his life for his friend, Anke had quoted when Xavier first told him the whole of it, Xavier doubting it would have such a beneficent end, Xavier proved right a few moments later.

'The prisoner has admitted his guilt,' so spoke the judge, annoyed at the interruptions, moving swiftly towards the conclusion of the trial whose outcome had been decided before it started. Lukitt seeing the world in dull grey pulses as the judge went on without compunction.

'This prisoner must suffer for his crimes as he has caused others to suffer because of them. This prisoner, Lukitt Bachmann, is to be made an example of in these troubled times. We are reverting therefore to the not so long ago due punishment for multiple murders. He will be hung, drawn and quartered, his remains to be buried outside the sanctity of church grounds.'

'No, oh no!' Alameth's high-pitched voice querimonius from the gallery, shaking off his captors, eyes streaming with tears. 'No! It can't be so!'

But there'd been no other option, no going back; judge and lawyer instructed quite plainly that Lukitt Bachmann be made a scapegoat of the 1848 Revolutions that had wealthy landowners quaking in their boots.

There's uprisings all over the country, they'd been told. *Everything's a tinderbox, and Hamburg must not be the place to light it.*

Put down any insurrections, and hard.

Put them down and stamp them out.

No place for notions flying about that folk from the upper echelons could be murdered willy nilly by upstarts like Lukitt Bachmann - a peasant boy come from nothing and nowhere - and certainly not by him saying he'd been forced into such actions by his betters.

Their purpose served by the general approbation of the crowd, clapping and yelling in gleeful expectation of the spectacle that would be the highlight of their year.

Lukitt's guts retracting into warm coils, trying to hide themselves, keep themselves where they belonged for as long as possible.

Lukitt thinking on the Justice Tree in Quedlinburg and how he'd feared he might be up there one day, swinging from its boughs.

Wishing now it had been so.

Wishing he'd done it himself, spared himself and those he cared for what instead must come.

52

Last Friends, Last Words

'How are you doing?' Alameth asks, surveying Lukitt through the bars of his prison, Lukitt's returning smile a frightful spectacle in a face that has become sallow and thin, prickled with a patchy beard growing from cheek to chin.

Justice in these parts didn't like waiting around, not in the present climate when insurrection and rebellion were a breath away from everyone's lips, and Lukitt's justice would be no different – only two days since the pronouncement of his guilt and only two more before his sentence would be carried out.

'I'm all right,' Lukitt said, winding his fingers about the bars, Alameth reaching out, placing his fingers over Lukitt's.

'Why didn't you tell me?' Alameth asked, tears and Annely his only companions these past two days while he fought to get a visit. 'You didn't have to do any of it. And certainly not for me.'

Lukitt shook his head.

'Of course I did. I got you into it, and I needed to get you out. All my fault...'

Remembering back to that dark alley and Trudbert's words: *I'll make sure you remain a clever little fisherman all your life.*

So not all for Alameth, no matter how many times Lukitt tried to convince himself of the contrary.

'I don't want you to come,' Lukitt said, holding up a hand as Alameth opened his mouth to protest. 'No,' he repeated. 'If there's one last thing you'll do for me then it's this: go back to the Lodge this afternoon. And don't think on it, Alameth. Not on the day, not at the time. Don't think on it. Not ever.'

Alameth close to tears, Lukitt could see it and couldn't stand it; didn't want his last sight of Alameth to be Alameth crying; wanted to depart this world knowing Alameth would go on to have a happy life, work for Xavier, marry Annely, have children, increase the already abundant Mingelstrosser clan.

'Just promise me,' Lukitt whispered.

'I promise,' Alameth got out, closing his eyes.

Interrupted by a heavy-booted guard shouting down the stone corridor.

'Time's up, ladies. Tie up that talking and get yourselves out.'

Alameth putting his hand through the bars, Lukitt taking it.

'It'll be fine,' Lukitt murmured, both knowing it would not, Alameth gripping tightly at Lukitt's hand.

'I'll never forget what you've done for me,' Alameth got out. 'You brought me into my rightful fold and I couldn't have done it without…'

Too much for Alameth, swiping a hand at his eyes.

Lukitt understanding, and glad for it.

The fold the place for Alameth, if never the place for him.

'I'll pray for you,' Alameth whispered, spreading his hand against the bars.

'I know you will,' Lukitt whispered back, hand against Alameth's on the other side. 'And first child called Lukitt?' Lukitt managed. 'If it's a boy?'

'First child Lukitt,' Alameth agreed through his tears, 'whether it's a boy or no.'

Shared smiles then that weren't quite smiles, both envisioning the life of a girl called Lukitt; Lukitt comforted that one day there'd be another Lukitt walking the earth to carry on his name, Alameth always one to keep his promises.

Alameth away then up the cold stone corridor, carted off by the big man in his big boots jangling his keys. Lukitt looking after them as best he could through the bars, seeing another cold stone wall down in the crypts of Goslar and the figures depicted there: real men and women – and that dog – remembered and recorded, inscribed there precisely for the purpose. Remembering too that small figure peeping from the forest, one man at least who'd got out alive, if Henry Von Salza and Josephus could be believed - and why shouldn't they? Every battle, every massacre, having its witnesses and survivors. The Goslar Tapestry proof of that. Lukitt Bachmann may have no hope of surviving his own massacre, but he'd hope at least that he'd not be forgotten, that someday some other miniature Lukitt Habakkuk would be crawling around on all fours calling for his father or his mother, for Alameth and Annely.

Small comfort, but comfort still.

It striking Lukitt only at that moment that he'd never once told Alameth his middle name; remembering too the night before he'd left the farm at Gallapfel to go down to Seiden See, about to be given into the care of Père Ulbert, when Nethanel got out his bible, intention being to read the Book of Habakkuk end to end - only three short chapters – choking through the first few verses, unable to go on:

Oh Lord, but how long shall I cry out to you: Violence!
And yet you will not save me.
Why do you make me see wrongs and look upon trouble?
Witness the destruction and violence that are all around me
And yet the law is slacked,
And justice never done.

Lukitt alone in his cell thinking on those words, on Nethanel trying to speak them, giving up, the bible closed and put back upon its shelf. Neither Nethanel nor Trudl getting to the end of Habakkuk, nor reaching the part where God gives Habakkuk the sleight and speed of a hind, the strength therefore to reach the High Places where he can no longer be touched by either law or violence.

A happy ending for Habakkuk, if not for his namesake.

53

Archimimus Dances

Oh Christ! It's happening so fast. How can it be so fast?

Lukitt taken from his cell into the morning, street packed with onlookers.

Why are they here?

They've come to see me.

Come to see me hang...and the rest.

Body cold, rigid with fear; a beam of ash threaded through Lukitt's bound arms, drumming starting up, solemn and slow. Got to do things the old way, like everyone expects. Got to see the prisoner humiliated. Pity for Lukitt that the old *Rathaus* burned down in the great fire of 1842 and now he's to be dragged up the street from the old warehouses where the prison is to reach the square; little joy in knowing its history that runs through his head: a commentary flowing in tandem with the canalled Alster River on the buildings' other side:

Altstadt Square, centre of the Altstadt district – the old town - settled in the Bronze Age by the Ingaevonians back in 9 BC.

The banging of the drum as it leads them on.

The yells and jeers of the crowds reverberating through the streets, a few spectators skipping ahead, others closing in from behind.

Known in antiquity as Treva, *very important part of the amber trading route.*

Lukitt stumbling along the cobbles, jerking to the rhythm of the leather cord the guard in front pulls at spasmodically as if bringing to heel an unruly dog.

Saxon merchants in the 8th century making Altstadt their base, the beating heart of Hamburg.

Heart beating far faster than the drum that leads the procession. Children running alongside, imitating Lukitt's awkward gait, a collective Archimimus.

Rounding a corner.

First sight of the gibbet set up in the *Rathaus* Square. First sight of the rope dangling from the gallows, its empty eye eagerly anticipating his neck.

Declared a bishop's see in 831...

Lukitt's mind garbling, speeding up the lesson as if it was imperative he get to the end.

And an archibishopric a year later...

Sweat on his skin, panic pulsing in his throat, in the veins on his forehead.

Oh God! I want Ulbert! I need him to bless me, relieve me of my sins, tell me that no matter what I've done I'll...

Tripped over by one of the merry crowd, laughter as he cracks down onto his knees, has trouble getting up with his arms so forced behind him, the leather leash still pulling him on. Ends up face down, broken toothed, stubbled skin of chin scraped away by rough stone.

Angry words.

'Get up! Get yourself up! Ain't gonna be pulling you all the way. Ain't paid enough for that!

More laughter; smell of wet wool in his nose as someone sifts from the crowd, lifts him up roughly by the ash beam, almost pulling his arms from their sockets. But standing again, and still going forward, leaning over at a bad angle, back sore with the pulling.

But what did that matter now?

Trying to keep his focus, keep direction.

Someone else coming at him from the left.

Someone swiping at his face with a cloth.

Someone whispering in his ear:

Won't be long now, lad. Don't show them you're feared.

But feared he was. Right down to the marrow. Dragging his boots. Trying to keep pace. Drumbeats in his ears. Too close now to the gallows. Far too close. Far too close.

'Get him up and strung!' Crowd getting boisterous, eager for the show.

'Sharpen up them knifes!'

Faint refrain of an old childhood song going through him:

Oh where are you going, says Milder to Mulder,

I cannot tell you, says Jack in the can.

We're off to kill the Cutty Wren, says John the Red Rose,

Off to kill the Cutty Wren, cries every, every one.

Pregel's voice in his ears. Pregel's soft sweet voice. Pregel's soft sweet face.

Vision of that first day he'd met Pregel. Of the show-and-tell at school.

That was really brilliant! How'd'you know all that stuff?

Pregel amazed, Lukitt amazed anyone had bothered to tell him so.

I read it all in books.

Everything he'd ever learned, read in books.

Including the beetle.

The Eberswald. The Grafsohn Heddel. Groleshka promising she'd do everything in her power to make sure her Italian Cockerel made good on his promise to reward Lukitt.

That beetle. That promise.

The start of their new life.

And now the end of it.

No more time for thinking; drum no longer single beats but a rolling expectant sound building to inevitable crescendo; crowd positively baying for his blood; gallows no longer far away but right in front of him; leash no longer slack but taut as his guard pulls it in inch by inch and Lukitt goes up the steps; that lapsed circle of rope - no longer a future possibility but a present reality - scraping roughly at Lukitt's throat, at the back of his neck as his head is pushed inside and it begins to tighten, Lukitt's feet lifting as it does so, Lukitt standing on tiptoe, arms still pulled back by the ash beam as he leaves the ground, begins to choke, begins to swing in the breeze, begins his long dying.

Sees his father, his mother, sees Gallapfel, sees Ulbert, sees Pregel, sees Opapa Augen, sees Alameth and Heraldo…

Trudbert's uncle giving him a stern ticking off.

Julida sighing somewhere in the distance.

Old man Kompter crying softly in his ear:

Oh Lord, how long shall I cry unto you: Violence!

Fighting for breath, arm bones snapping as they reflex forward in an attempt to free his neck. Agony. Executioner an old man who hasn't done this for years but knows how it must go, having some pity, quickly jerking the rope upwards in an effort to break the prisoner's neck; not quite managing it, but enough to send Lukitt into an unnavigable darkness where all he sees are the stars of the universe exploding all about him, blood supply cutting off from his brain, last conscious thought of Lukitt Bachmann being to wonder at the magnitude of the universe being revealed to him and regret that he's no more time to...

Body dropped suddenly to the ground, hitting the wood.

Distant noise of tumult, of waters rushing, no awareness that this is people goading his justice on.

Sudden inhalation of breath as the knife goes in just below his ribcage, sudden cold in Lukitt's darkness as the blade slices him stem to stern;

Stars going out in droves, black universe emptying itself and taking him with it.

Steaming guts dragged out by hooks, draped about the gallows...

Lukitt roaring like a storm-wind as he's dispersed into the darkness.

Stray dogs swiftly appearing from adjoining alleys, drawn by the enticing smell of fresh butchery, folk swiftly making way for them as they growl their way towards their feast.

Last shreds of Lukitt fleeing to the High Places with the sleight and speed of Habakkuk's hind, every sinew stretching, almost there... almost there...fingertips on the top of the mountain, bright red dawn beyond its heights...bright red dawn...

Last of Lukitt's guts cut through and chucked to the dogs, kicked off the gallows in slippery grey confusion; sounds of retching at the fraying edges of the crowd as the prisoner's body is laid out upon the boards, axed through at neck, stomach and groin by ex-soldier Falk Wulf who is annoyed at the blood splashing on his trousers, but not overly inconvenienced: has a woman at home to do the clean-up, though God help her if she doesn't boil that blood right out of every inch.

Crowds clapping and hullaballooing as head, torso, and two legs - with their allocated amount of pelvis still attached – are laid out for inspection.

'This is what happens,' yells out Falk Wulf – well rehearsed - holding up his dripping axe for all to see, 'when you disobey the Rule of Law!'

Looking around for the judge, expecting his approbation, seeing the man vomiting, a feeble wave of his hand telling Wulf to go on with the show.

'Get the horses!' Wulf not a man to be put off by anything so mundane as hacking a man into pieces.

Horses brought, hooks attached to three of those pieces of Lukitt that Wulf has so expertly excised the one from the other - though not the head. Something special waiting for that.

'And away!' Wulf shouts, would've slapped those three horses on the rump with his own hand if he'd leave to, but away they went anyway, the crowd laughing and racing after their chosen steed – bets already made on which would reach their destination by the riverside and still have their pieces of prisoner intact at the end.

Only one part of Lukitt Bachmann left in the square – his head rocking gently on its side on the gallows' platform as the old executioner gathers up his rope; and only one part left of the crowd – mostly those who, like the judge, hadn't found the spectacle quite so entertaining as imagined, hiccupping and burping as they leached away into the back streets of Hamburg, shoulders juddering as they pushed past the growling dogs still tearing at the prisoner's guts, fighting for the last scraps, lapping up the blood. Lukitt Bachman a lesson learned, quelling the fires of revolution in Hamburg at least, where insurgence had been dispersed, sporadic, no one at the head.

Falk Wulf having one last duty to perform, and a small expectant audience waiting for him to play his part; Wulf not disappointing, placing the flat of his axe-blade against the top of Lukitt's head – as if about to play croquet – to stop it rolling off the rood as he rammed a metal spike as far into the neck as he could get it before hoisting it triumphantly aloft.

'To the bridge!' he yells, running with his prize, jogging quickly down the street towards the water, acolytes at his heels clapping and whooping, eager to be in at the end, see the murderer's head placed at centre stage, right in the middle of the bridge where all and sundry would have to pass it by, witness its gradual disintegration as they went into the old town and back again; warning that here too they might end up if they didn't toe the line.

The old executioner left behind to wash down his gallows, get it dismantled, kick away the dogs, hoping he wouldn't have to get it all out again, at least not soon. No knowledge that he, Wulf and Lukitt Bachmann had played small walk-on roles in the mish-mash of the 1848 revolutions.

Himself: executioner and studious non-thinker, back home to bed after a tiring day;

Falk Wulf: soldier and sociopath, who gloried in his run to the bridge, blood dripping from the severed neck making his hand slippery, almost missing the allotted holder, almost tipping Lukitt's head into the water as he jammed his spike home;

Lukitt Bachmann: reader of books, who'd tried his best to get out of bad situations and never got to his right end.

A triumvirate of individuals who'd no idea they'd participated in a theatre that would ultimately bring into existence something extraordinary, that because of all the ructions of 1848 and their aftermath a democratic constitution would be agreed on twelve years later that would change the governance of Germany forever.

Acorns and oaks.

And those oaks can survive two millennia, far longer than lime trees.

Xavier would be overjoyed when that time came, when his researches into Goslar became an integral part of that unification, but not right now.

Winter wedding all very formal at Anke's chapel, everyone sick at the backstory that had to happen to bring it about; all quiet on their return to the Lodge…until the Mingelstrosser boys took to their stage and played out their retelling of the old Commedia dell'Arte's routine of Columbine's marriage to Pierrot with so many mishaps and slips nobody could help but laugh.

Even Xavier.

Even Alameth.

Even Annely.

New lives coming from the old.

In Sansonnet-St-Genès Jacques has no idea what barbarities have resulted from his betrayal, knows only that it had to be done; wipes a finger beneath his nose to remove the drip that is threatening to freeze there, takes a swig from his flask as he stands – as he often does – at the grave of his one-eyed monkey.

'See you?' he says, noticing the last leaf of the year has fallen from the rambling rose planted on the grave despite there still being – incongruously – a couple of flower heads. 'Gonna get me that little plot of land by the river, thanks to this,' tapping at his jacket and the coins given him for handing Lukitt over. 'Gonna take you with me. You an' me together, monkey boy. Telled you I'd never let you down.'

And away goes Jacques to toast his old friend's passing - meaning his monkey not Lukitt, to whom he's not given a second thought since All Hallows. Jacques picking up his lamp, going first to rekindle the Lanterne des Mortes because the night is turning foggy and people will need it to find their way home from the fields. Then back to his home, planning what he will plant on his little plot of land, now he's the funds to purchase it. Going to bed a happy man, sleeping soundly the whole night through.

Lukitt's head on the stick on the bridge: dropped jaw clicking gently in the breeze; eye-sockets mere hollows, iced over; skin yellow-cured by the wind; hair frozen to his scalp, uncared for by winter cold.

Still there three months later, when the early floods of 1849 overwhelm the bridge with sudden melt-water, river levels rising several metres in a matter of days, Lukitt's skin lax and in tatters, head easily taken from its pole, bobbing away on the floodwater with all the other detritus, pieces of him scraped away on tree boles and swept-away chicken houses, pig-huts and sheds built too close to the river's edge; slipping away each from the other down canals and tributaries; skull knocked into several pieces when it gets caught in a stramash of old bits of machinery from the paper mill, separating and dispersing, scattering on their way down to the sea.

Exit the last scraps of Lukitt *Ludicrum* Bachmann, his own Archimimus, who'd gone from guise to guise: from child to man, from friend to inspiration to murderer, who'd fulfilled his purpose – if not the one he'd imagined - and been moved on.

Gone but not forgotten.

Not by Xavier, nor by Alameth and Annely, and not by Frau Ingpen who occasionally wondered why her favourite young charges had never returned to the Academy of the Curious as she removed a pin – or put one back – into her strawberry-shaped pincushion, a little frayed now, a little faded, but still of use.

And not by Brother Zebediah - far away in the hills of Voralberg at the Brethren's Paradise on Earth – a very ancient man by now as he lay on his death bed, bad memories roaming, learning lately of the fate of the boy he'd caused to be born in the hills and the terrible end that became because of it.

'I see him,' he whispered, arthritic hands scrabbling at his sheets, disturbing young Brother Markus who was sitting vigil by his side.

'Who do you see?' he asked kindly, assuming a vision of the Lord, here to guide the old Elder onwards.

'That boy,' Zebediah croaked. 'Born outside the circle. I see him. Come to take me away.'

Pointing a crooked finger into the darkness.

'There's no one here but me,' Markus comforted, dabbing the old man's lips with tincture of cloves as Zebediah began to cough and choke; Zebediah trying to sit up, fend away what no one but he could see.

'He's come to fetch me! To condemn me!'

Zebediah so agitated that Markus yells for help, the old man fighting against him, getting halfway off the bed before keeling over onto the floor, tangled in his eiderdown. Markus terrified, trying to lift up his charge.

'It's that boy…it's that boy…'

Zebediah blaming the blameless to the last.

Obadiah coming in, Obadiah and Markus lifting Zebediah onto his bed where Zebediah expires a few minutes later; one more choke, one more gasp, and then gone.

'Any last words of wisdom?' Obadiah asked lightly, seeing how pale Markus was, wanting to make this first experience of death easier on the lad.

Markus shaking his head.

'Nothing,' he murmured. 'Just some gobbledegook about a boy come to fetch him away.'

Obadiah nodding. Obadiah not making the connection.

Exit Archimimus, an empty construct, stage left.

Job done.

Author's Note

This book is dedicated to Michael Lafferty, who loved libraries and books as fervently as I do; a friend who suffered a cerebral haemorrhage on 11th August 2015 and died four days later at the age of forty five without being given the opportunity to open his mind or eyes one last time. The irony of that fact, given this book's subject, would not have been lost on him, as it has not been lost on me.

The Archimimus, for those who don't know the term, was a stalwart of Roman funerary processions who dressed in the clothes of the deceased, imitated his gait and mannerisms, spoke as he – and occasionally she – might have, reminding everyone that their own time, and mine, as it did for Michael, will inevitably come.

The history of Sedlec, Goslar, Leignitz and Hamburg is as presented, except for the fact that – as far as I know – the Goslar Tapestry never existed although, if it did, it would not be far from the truth. 1241 a marker of European history never given its true due, for if Batu had not been forced to return to his homeland to fight his cause for the Mongol Khanate then history – our history - might have gone very differently.

Clio was born in Yorkshire, spent her later childhood in Devon before returning to Yorkshire to go to university. For the last twenty five years she has lived in the Scottish Highlands where she intends to remain. She eschewed the usual route of marriage, mortgage, children, and instead spent her working life in libraries, filling her home with books and sharing that home with dogs. She began writing for personal amusement in the late Nineties, then began entering short story competitions, getting short listed and then winning, which led directly to a publication deal with Headline. Her book, *The Anatomist's Dream*, was nominated for the Man Booker 2015 and long-listed for the Bailey's Prize in 2016. Clio has always been encouraging towards emergent writers, and founded HISSAC (The Highlands and Islands Short Story Association) in 2004 precisely to further that aim, providing feedback on short listed stories and mentoring first time novelists, not a few of whom have gone on to be published themselves. Clio previously published the critically-acclaimed Scottish Mysteries trilogy with Urbane Publications and the historical adventure Legacy of the Lynx.

IF YOU ENJOYED **ARCHIMIMUS**,
TAKE A LOOK AT CLIO'S OTHER TITLES:

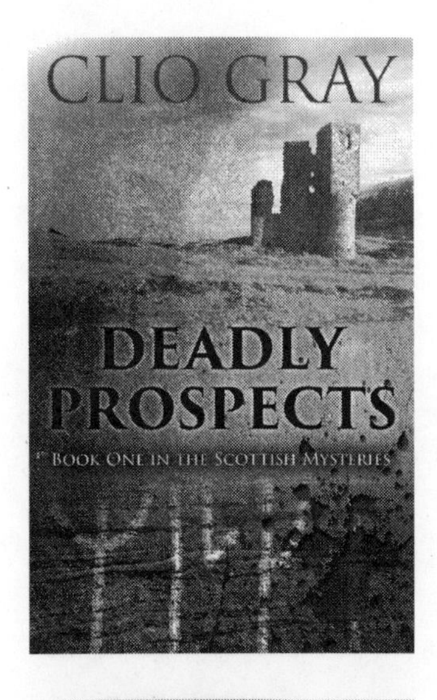

URBANE